The Strangeness
of Beauty

The Strangeness
of Beauty

Lydia Minatoya

W. W. Norton & Company

New York · London

to Emiko and Seiji, with love

First published as a Norton paperback 2001
by arrangement with Simon & Schuster

ISBN 0-393-32140-1

Designed by Jeanette Olender
Manufactured in the United States of America

Library of Congress Cataloging-in-Publication Data
Minatoya, Lydia Y. (Lydia Yuriko), [date]
The strangeness of beauty / Lydia Minatoya.
p.   cm.
Includes bibliographical references.
1. Japan—History—20th century—Fiction. I. Title.
PS3563.I4632S73   1999
813'.54—dc21   98-55250   CIP

W. W. Norton & Company, Inc., 500 Fifth Avenue, New York, N.Y. 10110
www.wwnorton.com

W. W. Norton & Company Ltd., 10 Coptic Street, London WC1A 1PU

2 3 4 5 6 7 8 9 0

note on pronunciation

In Japanese, vowels are pronounced as they are in Italian:

a = *ah* (as in *hurrah*)

e = *eh* (as in *cliché*)

i = *ee* (as in *beet*)

o = *oh* (as in *no*)

u = *oo* (as in *zoo*)

Syllables are evenly spaced and spoken quickly; and if one must choose a syllable to accent, it is best to lightly accent the first.

The major names in this book are

Akira (AH *kee rah*)

Chie (CHEE *eh*)

Etsuko (ET *soo koh*)

Hanae (HAH *nah eh*)

Naomi (NAH *oh mee*)

Masao (MAH *sah oh*)

Tadao (TAH *dah oh*)

The Strangeness
of Beauty

chapter one

It has been said that at any given moment, sixty percent of Japanese are involved in writing a novel. And all of them auto-biographical.

This phenomenon, though not new in form (the autobiographical novel is an ancient art), is certainly new in frenzy. There's even a word for it, *shi-shosetsu*, the "I-story."

Critics have questioned the motivation behind the amateur I-story. Often it seems so futile. Why would so many work so long to create novels meant for their eyes alone? The answer involves social upheaval—in which a sudden infusion of excessive education (the progressive arts and sciences of the last two imperial reigns) has clashed with limits in opportunity, to turn a nation of habitual haiku writers half mad.

The theory is that in Japan, the self-consciousness of modernism has collided with the tradition of reticence—of not burdening others with one's subjective experience—to create a people just roiling with confessional angst.

It's true, I think. There seem to be few people as concerned with being understood as the Japanese.

Unless you consider the Americans.

But I'm delaying. This, of course, is my I-story.

Etsuko Sone
  Seattle, Washington

Hanae's Birth

I can't imagine that Hanae enjoyed being born. To be squeezed through a convulsing corridor is, at best, an experience one would call unsettling. And to hear her mother's breath—for months so rhythmic and reassuring—ripping jaggedly, to feel her heart staggering. No, my niece wouldn't have liked it.

Maybe that's why she grew distant and drowsy, why she drifted toward failure. She had no interest in this thing called life.

But her mother was fierce. She forced her child forward. She tore herself open and Hanae slid into my cold, shaking hands.

Clean, salty scents of blood and birth tickled Hanae's nostrils. She drew breath and sneezed.

"My baby!" cried Naomi.

I glanced at Naomi with reverence and fear. Who was this new creature called Mother? Sweating and savage, she bore no similarity to my little sister.

But Hanae twitched with immediate recognition. Here was the voice that had sung and whispered, that had confided its secret hopes. Here was the voice that had prodded her toward moral goodness, with nightly readings of Buddhist sutras, *A Tale of Two Cities, King Lear*.

Still I failed to give baby to mother, hurriedly bundling Hanae in soft cloth, rushing her to the other side of the room.

"My baby, my baby!"

Hanae seemed to watch Naomi's hands, waving thin and pale. Were these the hands that had calmed her in the womb? That had stroked her when she hiccuped? That when she kicked too hard and lodged a bony heel beneath her mother's rib cage, had smoothed it back into place?

Now those hands clawed the air with maternal hunger, that mouth opened with greedy need.

And Hanae *wanted* to be devoured, to return to the safety of that body. Like a wolf drawn by the moon, she was pulled by her mother's voice.

She filled her lungs and wailed.

The Heavenly Sign

Akira Shinoda was twenty-four years old, a handsome, earnest young dentist and the father of that baby. After the turmoil subsided, after Hanae was holding her little neck steady and sleeping through the night, I approached him. I wanted to talk about the birth. I asked, "What do you remember?"

"A competent midwife, a rapid delivery, the outcome a healthy child."

But I stood there—my arms empty, my body absentmindedly swaying in a manner that would soothe a fretful infant—and Akira felt an obligation. He couldn't brush me aside.

So he put down the dental text he was studying and said what he knew I wanted.

"What do *you* recall?"

Later, at night when the house was quiet, he answered the question I'd forgotten in my relief to share my tale. What he remembered.

It was Sunday, October 23, 1921. Naomi slept until noon. Akira poked through the kitchen like an amateur, singeing a dish towel as he lit the stove.

Naomi laughed when she saw the scorched rice and watery miso soup he'd prepared. A breakfast already grown cold. She pulled at his sleeve until he sank to the bed. She unwound the eyeglass stems from his ears.

Later, brushing her hair by the window, she saw Mount Rainier. Free from its usual cloud cover, the mountain rose close and startling.

"Rainier-san is out."

Akira glanced past her shoulder. Three-story frame tenements scrabbled toward the crest of Jackson Street. A cluster of leaves, dead and dried, bounced along the buckling sidewalk.

Like a facetious Fujiyama, Rainier was floating over Oki's We Never Close Cafe.

Akira frowned. This was Nihonmachi, Seattle's Japantown. A strange, in-between place where, by day, the streets were filled with American-style industry—with shrieking trains snorting in and out of the King Street Station and delivery carts from Uchida's Uncle Sam Laundry or Kato's Straight-To-Your-Home Ice clattering on cobbled streets. Where truant Japanese American boys in knickers and golf caps flipped milk tops and shot marbles. Yet at dusk Nihonmachi became suffused with Japan—with lantern light, the aromas of soy sauce and Japanese soba noodles wafting from upstairs windows, and the restful sight of neighbors heading home from public baths. Laughing softly, the bathers scuffed in split-toed straw sandals and cotton kimonos across improbably wide American-named streets (Main, Jackson, King) or more intimately scaled numbered avenues (Sixth through Twelfth). Still later, as midnight approached the southern edge of Nihonmachi—the only time and place whites came into our part of town—the mood shifted to things faster and darker: secret-door gambling clubs with knifings at blackjack and mahjong tables; hurried transactions of prostitution.

Thinking of these things, Akira knitted his brow. Though Naomi was happy in Nihonmachi, the idea that he'd brought his bride to so shabby a place always made him feel guilty.

"Look at those scurrying outlaws."

Chuckling, Naomi was pursuing the leaves, watching as they evaded a broom being wielded by Kozawa, the barber.

"I know!" She turned to her husband. "Let's go leaf viewing."

Akira looked at his nineteen-year-old wife, beyond the beauty of her tranquil oval face to the hard work of carrying a child. Naomi's legs were swollen. Her blood pressure was high. Her pregnancy hadn't been easy.

"No," he said, "you're too close to your time."

But she smiled at his stern manner.

"Just to the university," she coaxed. "Soon we'll be too busy."

Akira knotted a tie under the starched high collar of his white shirt. (Indeed, back in Japan the word used to denote a progressive young intellectual was hakara, an altered form of the English words "high collar"). He slipped on the vest and jacket to his three-piece gray suit.

Naomi dressed in a dove blue long-skirted suit (to accommodate her pregnancy, the usually fitted jacket fell from a yoke into soft gathers), high black shoes, and a broad-brimmed hat.

As Akira walked sideways beside her—lending his arm and solicitously watching Naomi's every quite confident step—they negotiated the narrow stairway down from their second-floor flat.

They boarded a streetcar on the corner of Main Street and Occidental Avenue. Akira dropped two dimes into the glass box at the top of the stairs, watching as the motorman flipped a lever that made the money disappear, listening to the coins' clinka-clinka noise as he wound the crank that sorted the change.

The streetcar was already half full with Japanese American passengers out for a Sunday excursion. Most rode as if in Japan: in orderly anonymity, nodding whenever someone they knew boarded but not speaking, respecting one another's need for some distance in a too-crowded society.

After a few minutes, Akira felt Naomi nudge his shoulder.

"Listen to that old couple," she whispered.

It didn't take long to find the pair. The couple—perhaps in their late fifties, dressed in worn go-to-city clothes—were bickering loudly in Japanese.

Yet even after locating them, Akira had trouble following Naomi's instruction. A stray thought popped into his mind—the old fellow needed a partial bridge—and he couldn't track their conversation.

"Aren't they charming?"

Wanting to be a good husband, Akira shook himself back to the moment.

"Stay on the trolley, north to Pike Street," the sturdy wife was exclaiming. "Then take Pike east. That's the best way to the public market."

"No, no!" said the husband. He waved his skinny arms in disgust. "Too much traffic. Get off at Yesler; go north on First,

16

along the waterfront. Then, *zoo-to!*"—the husband had made a zippy sound ending briskly with his tongue just behind his incisors—"you're right there!"

"Your way is fast, all right," grumbled the wife, "but passes all the fishing fleets." She folded her weathered hands in her broad lap and gave a triumphant snort. "Your way *stinks!*"

"What's so charming about them?" Akira whispered in complaint to Naomi. "It's stupid, really. We've already passed both Yesler and Pike; it's clear they've no intention of going to market. And besides, look at their clothes. They're farmers. Probably in from Bainbridge Island. I bet they've been going to the public market twice a week for at least fifteen years!"

"And each time having the same argument." Naomi chuckled.

"They should hear themselves," Akira muttered. "So discordant. It's a disgrace."

"No." Naomi's voice turned firm. "It's no disgrace."

She looked at the couple with tenderness.

"*Listen, Akira,*" she said softly, like a mother sharing life's secrets with a child. "In their argument is the melody of marriage."

Akira paused. Now the couple was squabbling over whether or not the husband should put on his sweater.

"That? *Melody?*"

"Yes," said Naomi. She listened awhile and smiled. "It's a blending, not always smooth, of attachment and independence."

"But in public? They sound so foolish!"

"To a couple it's background music, a little scratchy, perhaps, but something they play over and over, like a much loved, well-worn gramophone record."

Akira looked at Naomi with appreciation. Among the

earthbound pioneers of Japantown, this type of insight, along with her beauty and high birth in a samurai family, had earned Naomi a reputation as being a bit too ethereal.

Yet he found her radiantly wise.

He gestured toward the old couple.

"Do you think we'll end up like that?" he teased.

Warm laughter poured from Naomi's lovely throat.

"Oh, Akira! We already are!"

The trolley turned east, passing big houses facing the lake. At Madison Park, Japanese houseboys—old men with glinting eyeglasses—raked long, sloping, shadowy lawns.

The sky was increasingly overcast. Warm light came and went, streaming like sudden sun showers.

By the time they reached the university, Akira could tell that Naomi was tired. Yet when she saw the leaves she seemed to revive.

She crunched her feet through the splendid carpet. Too big to bend over, she made him pick a bouquet of the brightest colors. She arranged them in a fan and studied them like an exceedingly good hand of cards.

The air smelled of chestnuts roasting.

In a gesture of sharing—similar to times when she drew his hand to her kicking belly—Naomi pushed Akira's cheek toward the grassy quadrangle.

"There." She smiled.

Amid Gothic stone buildings, the first few Japanese American college boys—wearing flannel pants and white varsity-style sweaters—were joking in accentless English and kicking a football around.

"That's the future," she promised.

But his eyes were too full with Naomi.

The sky had shifted. Sun slanted through branches, anointing her shoulders and hair.

Silent and satisfied, filled with mysteries and blessings, she was as luminous as a Renaissance painting.

That night, well after midnight, Akira awoke with a start.

Naomi was rigid and shuddering. She clutched at the edge of the bed.

"No worry, we have hours to wait," she said with a nervous laugh.

Akira placed a cool towel on her brow and ran down the street to get me.

He knew I came as fast as I could: thrusting my feet in my shoes, grabbing my coat, not caring that he saw me in my nightdress. Yet when we arrived, the baby already was crowning.

As he paced the parlor, Akira noticed many things. The scarcity of furniture. A tear in the carpet. The endearing way that the pattern of dust around the spines of books on the bookshelf revealed Naomi's haphazard housekeeping.

Near dawn, when the quiet finally came, Akira noticed his relief. He rested his head on the cool windowpane, then drew back—amazed and laughing—to see the delicate lace of frost. It was so unexpected for Seattle in autumn that he thought it was a heavenly sign. A miracle, just like birth.

It *was* a sign, the early frost.

It meant that his young wife had died.

chapter two

NOVEMBER 9, 1927

While sifting through some belongings, I found this manu-script and realized I'm not a highly dedicated novelist. A five-year lapse! The truth is, I write—as do many people, I suspect—only when I'm uneasy, as a way to drag life from the dark clutch of the belly, where it's experienced, up to the mind's sorting light.

And for five years my life has been placid. Yet as I read this, my memory rises. Write, it urges. Master me. Take me to some brighter place.

What I Remember

I remember the blood. The brazen blood turning white towels scarlet and splattering across the floor.

And the cry, "My baby, my baby."

"Hush, Little Sister," I crooned to Naomi. "Your daughter is fine. You'll hold her soon enough."

I grabbed at gauze, at hot and cold packs. I tried elevation and the application of pressure.

Naomi looked suspicious. Her ears pricked toward the corner of the room, where Hanae lay tucked in a fruit basket. Maybe she was recalling the proprietary way I watched mothers and babies, my too avid interest—was the darling child wrapped in the kind of blanket I would buy?

Her eyes glittered.

Like she'd caught me trying to steal something precious.

It was the anger in Naomi's eyes that made me realize she was dying.

"My baby," she demanded.

And finally I knew.

I ran to the fruit basket and picked up the shrieking bundle.

She startled, throwing out her arms, almost jumping out of my hands. But I brought her to Naomi.

Naomi wasn't satisfied. She batted at the swaddling cloth, extracting the naked infant.

She pushed her own clothing away.

Then as the baby sought and found her breast, there was quiet.

Naomi touched the baby's hair, still stiff with blood and the creamy wax of the womb.

"Hello," she whispered, using a form of speech reserved for addressing elders or men, for reverential occasions. "Our initial meeting brings me great honor."

The baby, finding no milk, grumbled in complaint.

Naomi laughed and something bloomed between the two.

That's why, even though it was a lie, I insisted that Naomi had named the child.

Hanae, Blossoming Flower.

I came one night—my hair uncombed, my shoes on the wrong feet—and have stayed ever since.

Hanae was Naomi's parting gift. I could never have any children.

When Hanae was born, I was a twenty-four-year-old widow.

I loved my husband. But his death didn't leave me bitter. Bitterness comes from disappointment, from marrying for position or obligation and finding no friendship therein. I was lucky. I knew how it felt to wake in a soft bed on a cold morning, Tadao's warm hand on my belly.

Tadao was a good husband in that he really didn't know me well.

I'm no enigma; anyone could have told him what type of person I am. Simple and sturdy (sixty-one inches, 109 pounds), with a pleasant face—a little too round to be classically comely—and a slightly too blunt nose. Accommodating and placid. But Tadao just didn't see it.

In Tadao's eyes I was different from the woman I faced in my mirror. Not only prettier but more interesting. Someone with opinions and choices, with a whole inner world well worth knowing. And the truth is, I found this unorthodox juxtaposition—of the concepts of me and more—so refreshing that I was willing to overlook its fundamental inaccuracy.

I met my husband in Kobe, Japan, on a 1915 summer morning filled with small singing finches and the sweet fragrance from huge peony blossoms. A morning so ripe with beauty that my womb seemed to swell and my fingers ached to stroke a baby. As an elevator girl in the exciting new department store Daimaru—which had four stories, a restaurant, an exhibition-and-lecture room, and even a rooftop garden—I was wearing a simple but stylish black kimono with pinpoints of silver and a broad pewter-colored obi, or waist sash. I was standing at a trolley stop near a park on a busy boulevard lined with big European-style buildings. While waiting to board a streetcar, I fumbled and dropped my coin.

A young Japanese man in Western clothes, standing at the end of the line, leapt to my assistance with such alacrity that we smashed foreheads as we began bending down.

"Forgive me!" He rose, shifting in his arms a number of handcrafted kites (an ashen phoenix, its head raised with nobility, is the one I recall), and held out my coin.

I looked at his face. The sun behind him was so bright; I was so dizzy; he was so handsome—with his engaging smile and slightly reckless straightforwardness—that I hardly could breathe.

"My clumsiness," I stammered. "Thank you for your kindness."

Automatically we began to bow.

"My clumsiness!" I heard him declare, as our skulls crashed again in concordance.

When I met my husband I was eighteen. In Japan it is an age called "early spring," when a certain restlessness, like the rising March wind, stirs behaviors meant for breaking away. In addition, in 1915, Japanese society was the perfect reflection of my adolescent turmoil.

The modernizing Meiji emperor had been dead for three years and his son, the Taisho emperor, had just held the great Taisho Industrial Show. Inspired by the opportunity for exhibition, desirous of a departure from the somber and monumental Western-style architecture of the Meiji era, Taisho architects flew to fanciful extremes. New construction (always plentiful in a country where fire is constant, devastating, and beautiful enough to be considered diverting; where firefighters—traditionally accompanied by standard-bearers—are considered acrobatic, aerial heroes) took on a confectionary Venetian look.

Subtlety and suggestion—those mainstays of the silk-and-shadow world of Japanese traditional arts—were rapidly disappearing. At Kobe's Kabuki theater, electrical floodlights had replaced gaslight, enlivening appreciation of costume and color but extinguishing some of the magic. In the nation's pleasure districts—where the new architecture was swallowing block after block of wood and paper and roof tile—"flower" houses of licensed prostitution were gaining ascendancy as "willow" houses of geisha arts declined.

Internationalism carried the day. In girls' upper level, I had studied democracy, Marxism, and existentialism. Universities all overflowed. Within the next three years, Albert Einstein and Margaret Sanger would have wildly successful speaking tours.

Yet amid all this change, though I worked in the city, though I had somewhat shortened my hair (when I was sixteen a call came forth for women to donate their hair to weave a new rope pull for a bell at a sacred Buddhist temple; too timid to make a dramatic sacrifice, I nonetheless wanted to be part of a romantic grand gesture and trimmed my waist-length hair to just-grazing-my-shoulders), I remained a rustic.

Oh, I was worldly enough, in the innocent, eager-to-please way of well-brought-up Japanese girls. I could speak some English—indeed I had been hired to narrate the contents of various floors to affluent American and European female shoppers. I had browsed through German bakeries and peeked into galleries featuring the latest in modern French art.

But I had no personal expectations or desires.

Then one day early in our courtship, Tadao made the following casual observation: "You're cannier than you let show. It grants you a great deal of freedom."

I picked him as my spouse on the spot.

It wasn't because I felt Tadao had discerned my true inner nature—the statement seemed a total misconception—but I had heard the word "freedom," a word I'd never associated with myself. And it awakened a kind of ambition.

This was my ambition: to become a good wife and mother. Plus one improbable extra: I wanted to be what Tadao saw— to find, deep inside, my own wiser self, to locate my own special future.

I thought these were modest ambitions. They didn't seem too yawning or huge. But perhaps wanting what's essential and simple is the most extravagant wish of all.

These days, following trends in imperial family weddings, people get married at beautiful restaurants and scenic shrines; but Tadao and I had a traditional wedding.

One Saturday shortly before dusk, my parents and I stood in our thatch-roofed farmhouse and exchanged ritual sips of sake. It was a ceremony called "three times three." Using a delicate nesting of three lacquered cups—tiny, medium, and slightly larger—my father began with the smallest cup. He raised it to his lips three times, then passed the cup to me. When I had done the same, I passed it to my mother. Moving to a larger cup and beginning with a different person, we repeated the ritual until three sips had been taken from three cups with a different person starting each time.

Like an American bride, I was dressed in white—but for an entirely different reason. In Japan, white represents the absence of life. It is the color worn by the dead. From the point of leaving my parents' house, through the procession to my husband's family house, until the third morning of my marriage, I was considered to be without family. Dressing in burial robes symbolized my vulnerability on this transitional journey.

My poor parents seemed to take this all literally. As we faced one another over our cups, they stared at my white linen kimono and gulped back more tears than wine. Afterward, they seemed to gain heart as they bundled me and my trousseau—a dressing table, a half-dozen kimonos, linens, dinnerware, and housewares—onto two four-handed palanquins. Led by a lantern bearer—an old superstitious ritual meant to prevent me from being eaten by demons as I traversed the netherworld—I made my way to Tadao's family house.

A bridal procession was a sight everyone loved. Along the entire seven-mile route, neighbors rushed outside, bowing. Children crying, "*Oyame-san o mini yukimasho!*" skipped by my side, craning their heads, cataloguing (for detailed reportage at family dinner tables) the value of all my possessions. It has been said that this nuptial parading of family wealth (and the competitiveness inherent in such a practice) is one reason why Japanese household articles—textiles, *tansu* chests, lacquer and pottery dishware—have reached such heights of artistic mastery.

As darkness gathered and my carriers walked on, more people gathered to cheer us. One little girl in a tattered kimono passed me a paper bag filled with fireflies she had collected. "For your journey!" she called, as I bowed my head in thanks. And for the rest of the route, the bag glowed in my hand like a candle.

Torchlights greeted me as I arrived at Tadao's house. As he helped me disembark and led me inside, Tadao's touch was as tender as the warm night. Then, with the entire Sone family to witness, Tadao and I reenacted the *san-san-ku-do* or "three times three" sake-sipping ceremony.

This time nobody cried, though if they had, I would not have noticed. I was deep in Tadao's dark eyes. Three days later, when my husband and I moved into a tiny city house all our own, I shed my white robes. I had found a new life of belonging.

As I'd hoped, marriage to Tadao brought happy implausibility and the kind of disorder from which miracles sometimes grow. Before long, like orphaned children on a grand adventure, we were bound for America.

It was odd. Though my parents had wept at my wedding, they were as expansive as Tadao and I were about our American plans. So expansive that one time—after my mother had made the hour-long journey by foot and streetcar to Kobe, to help me with my packing—I interrupted her endless optimistic chatter.

"Won't you miss me?" I demanded with petulance as we knelt, kimono clad, by my big black lacquer trunk.

Mama smiled. She brushed at a stray wisp of my hair.

"On the evening you married, Etsu-chan," she said, using my baby name, "I lit a lantern and sat at your place at the dinner table. Through the worn tatami-grass floor matting, I thought I could feel a trace of your warmth."

Mama laughed, a small glitter in the corner of her eye. "I wallowed in maudlin reflection, thinking how the next time you sat in this spot you would be only a visitor, and that sort of thing. But when, the next week, you came to see us, I could tell how happy you were. And I so enjoyed hearing what new things you were up to, it seemed foolish to grieve for the past."

Mama folded a crocheted pale pink shawl and placed it carefully within the trunk. Then, to make more room, she leaned over and pressed down on the trunk's contents, applying the full weight of her body.

This, I suddenly realized, was her way of saying she loved me. Stuffing as much solace as possible into my traveling bags. It had been the same at my wedding, when Mama had run around in a frenzy, minutely supervising every detail as my carriers loaded my trousseau onto its palanquin. Papa, too, had been uncharacteristically bossy, so overinstructive: lecturing the carriers on how to balance my palanquin, positioning me at exact center, saying over and over, "Now, you're sure she's secure?"

When the time came to leave for America, both Tadao's and my parents accompanied us down to the pier. They stood at dockside dwarfed by the massive ocean liner (which would be stopping in Yokohama and Honolulu before arriving in Seattle), oblivious to the parade of pinstripes and bowlers, silk dresses and feathered hats as the American first-class passengers boarded. On board, way on high, Tadao and I saw our parents: tiny and distant, waving and bowing, middle aged, unfashionable, and dear. Like all the other Japanese passengers, Tadao and I stood on third-class deck, holding large balls of rolled-up crepe paper tape. As the steam whistle blasted and the loudspeakers blared "Auld Lang Syne," we held fast to our ends, tossing the balls down to our parents. Then, as the great ship pulled out, the balls slowly unfurled, tethering ship to shore, heart to heart, until finally, with multitudinous cries of "Itte irashaii" (Go now, but hurry home to us) and "Itte mairimasu" (I go now, but will hasten home to you), they snapped.

There's a myth about immigrants: that we come on the wings of our dreams. For most the tale is too simple, turning convoluted personal motivations into a kind of cliché.

But for my husband, the myth was literal.

Tadao was a professional kite maker. He was an amateur engineer. All of his life he was enthralled with the science of flying.

One warm spring morning in 1916—a morning when all of Japan awoke to find that cherry trees had burst overnight into intoxicating full bloom—I heard the jingling bell on the mail carrier's bicycle.

"Letter from America, letter from America!"

Wearing everyday indigo cotton kimonos, Tadao and I were seated on the tatami in the living/sleeping room of our pretty little unagi-no-nedoko, "eel's bedroom," a type of wooden city house so named because of its narrowness.

At the sound of the mail carrier, Tadao put down the kite he was finishing—a great silver octopus with eight streaming tentacles. Its eyes were made of translucent rice paper lacquered red that would shine like rubies against the sun.

He padded in tabi, split-toed socks, to the edge of the raised living area, stepped down into the entry vestibule, slipped on street sandals, and slid open the dark wooden door.

As I completed my mending (darning the big toe in one of those white tabi socks), Tadao stood in the entryway reading the letter.

He was facing the open door; sunlight and flower fragrance rained in.

"Who's it from?" I called.

"Junichiro."

I thought of Junichiro, a cheerful man given to bad puns, a

shipwright working in the bustling boat sheds of Seattle's Lake Union.

I hummed as I started to clean.

I liked housework, the craft of caring for objects with gentle attention to the nature and function of each. Like all housewives, I had one cloth for scrubbing the wooden hall and entry and another, softer, cloth for dusting the tatami in the living/sleeping area. Now I took from its special drawer a cloth I used only for artwork in the alcove.

"Etsuko!" cried Tadao.

His voice broke with great emotion.

I jumped to my feet and rushed to the edge of the entry.

"What's wrong? A death?"

My husband still stood with his back toward me. Over his shoulder and out the door, high on a gray roof tile, I saw a spider wrap her lunch in a shroud.

It didn't seem like a very good omen.

"Who is it? What's happened?"

As he turned toward me, Tadao threw the letter, a scrap of light crinkled paper, high into the air.

My panic deepened.

But then I felt his arms: lifting me, whirling me round and round with such exuberance that the small crinkled letter soared upward again as if alive.

"Bill Boeing." Tadao laughed. "Bill Boeing, Bill Boeing."

He said the funny sounds over and over until I too was laughing.

"There's a man in Seattle, name of Bill Boeing, making fabric-and-wood aeroplanes!"

We unearthed some relatives and applied for our immigration papers. Though America had tried to stop the entry of Japanese with the 1907 Gentlemen's Agreement, one provision—allowing continued immigration for family members—had resulted in the sudden identification of innumerable relatives (never difficult in island nations, where everyone seems to some degree related) and the phenomenon of "picture brides."

We practiced our English, Tadao practicing particularly hard. His plan was to break tradition, to defy segregated labor, and to work instead with the sky-gazing, English-speaking men of Boeing's Pacific Aero Products Company.

By summer 1918, we were fluent. We arrived in America fully competent at such phrases as "Please give us a first-class compartment on your fastest train to New York" and "The wing should be made of oak and spruce, fastened with waterproof glue."

Phrases as useless as they were diverse.

For, coming from a Kobe filled with Italian opera, French fashions, and British banks, we had envisioned America as not too distant from home. We weren't thinking geographically, of course, but we'd expected Seattle to have a kind of international dynamism: brimming with libraries and museums, humming with immigrant energy, hopping with social mobility. As we left Seattle's Immigration Building and then the store, located directly at the exit of Immigration, where we traded my kimono for American clothes, we were startled (but not daunted, our enthusiasm still running quite high) to see the eroding hills stubbled with severed tree trunks, the fish offal in the harbor—the mud and guts that were much of Seattle.

And the very next year, when Seattle businessmen formed the Anti-Japanese League, it became clear to me we wouldn't be going anywhere first-class.

In addition, by the time Tadao and I had found a tiny walk-up apartment, Tadao's aeronautical future was over. The world had changed; armistice had been declared.

At least Tadao met his hero, Bill Boeing. They stood together one late afternoon, in an echoing hangar by Seattle's Duwamish River.

"Sorry, fellow," Big Bill said, not unkindly. He carried himself with a sort of rangy dignity. "With the war over, all our aeroplane orders have been canceled."

Tadao looked around. Besides sawdust suspended in weak streams of sunlight, there wasn't much to see.

A small core of Boeing's crack craftsmen were bumbling around, assembling French Provincial bedroom furniture.

Tadao walked over to a bureau. He opened a drawer.

"Strong yet lightweight: oak and spruce."

He examined the drawer at its joining.

"Waterproof glue?"

Big Bill nodded. He gave Tadao a slow, rueful grin.

"Too bad about the timing; you know your aeronautics." He gestured to the furniture with a small laugh of embarrassment. "We call it Chifferette."

Tadao—ever generous and kindhearted—extended his hand, compelled to initiate a ritual of respect that he'd never before attempted.

"Keep your crew, build whatever you can," he said with a smart shake, giving starch to the genius's sagging dream. "And until your fortune shifts skyward again, my congratulations on your fine furniture line."

My husband was philosophical about his career loss.

"Oh well," he said, "I can hardly be disappointed by the end of a war."

Instead of an aeroplane engineer, Tadao became a cook on a fishing boat that trolled off the Alaska shore.

Tadao specialized in weak coffee and large servings of oily, inedible food. His skills were typical of the crew—no one knew how to do his job, each made more money than he could believe.

One bitter night this floating barge of cheerful and incredibly inexperienced sailors hit an ice floe. Water rushed aboard the overloaded vessel and I never again saw my lover and friend.

I dreamed of returning to Japan. The America that with courageous, adaptable Tadao had remained ever promising now felt as treacherous as the cold Arctic Sea. But I had few living attachments there. (Oh stupid youth! When I stood on board the ship—waving to my four bowing parents, crying, "I go now but will hasten home to you!"—how was I to know that, due to the influenza epidemic of 1918, in five months they all would be dead?)

Besides, Naomi was due to arrive in Seattle.

And despite my losses, I was well provided for. My husband had left me a craft. Between voyages, in the intimacy of early marriage, when a couple shares everything, Tadao had taught me to cook.

So it came that I moved from the small apartment of my marriage to the large kitchen of Hotel Samurai Gardens, down by the Seattle docks.

The hotel catered to Japanese immigrants. Japanese country boys, they staggered off boats where they had done little besides vomit for close to two weeks, through Immigration, clothing exchange, and out onto the street.

The first thing they saw was an intimidating marvel—the peaked pinnacle of Smith Tower (tallest building west of the

Mississippi)—their very first glimpse of a skyscraper. The second thing the immigrants saw was a reassuring sign in Japanese:

Rooms to Let
Clean, Cheap, Fireproof

The hotel was prosperous. Its boarders were stunned.

Coming from tiny hamlets where everything and everyone was familiar back for seventeen generations, they were stunned by the sight of enormous red-haired residents, by the smells of sewage and rotting salmon, by the sounds of constant construction and the backfiring of Mr. Ford's automobiles.

They were so stunned they failed to recognize that my cooking was awful.

Month after month, year after year, they mechanically devoured huge quantities of my strange greasy offerings until one day, like a miracle, automatic eating yielded to honest appetite and they found themselves dreaming in English.

And though I never grew to be the woman of audacity and action that my husband had seen—though I remained accepting, obliging—in the kitchen of Hotel Samurai Gardens I found an odd self-expression.

Each dish, if not edible, was at least unforgettable. I made every meal a wonder.

chapter three

FEBRUARY 12, 1928

The Gift

With the death of his wife and the birth of his daughter, Akira Shinoda figured his days of intimacy were over.

A responsible father, he thought, doesn't stand within the family circle. For protective purposes, he hovers *above* it—distant, awkward, mostly useless—like a large and ungainly umbrella.

So he was startled by the gift Naomi left—Hanae—and by how easily he could love her.

At first he thought he'd leave her to me. What did he know of babies? At first he was too numb with the loss of Naomi.

But conscientiousness, his old plodding virtue, saved him. Before the third week was over, the guilty thoughts probably began.

Etsuko has disrupted her life: moving in, managing my household, staying up with my howling child.

He felt an obligation to give me a hand.

One evening as I huddled over the stove, lullabying loudly, bouncing rhythmically, stirring what he felt was some certain culinary atrocity, Akira gestured to the screaming lump that was swaddled to my back.

"Here, let me take her."

I turned and grinned. "I *knew* you couldn't resist her!"

Akira winced. To him, Hanae seemed utterly resistible. He'd offered out of duty, not desire.

I wiped my rough hands on a soft towel and began to unwrap the swaddling clothes.

Akira stared as if, layer by layer, Hanae was shrinking, was growing more vulnerable and less daunting.

"Here you go."

I shifted the baby into Akira's arms.

"Ahhh!" he cried.

Hanae was so light he'd almost dropped her.

Hanae stopped shrieking.

Alarmed by the change in touch, by her sudden insecurity, her mouth opened in a wide O.

"*Kore wa!*" Akira exclaimed. "Look at those healthy gums!"

He gestured with authority.

"See, Etsuko, these little ridges? Beneath them are baby teeth."

I laughed.

"Hanae-san," I said, "meet your Honorable Dentist Father."

With a jolt, Akira remembered this was *his* child. He examined her features more closely.

Hanae fixed him with a frown.

"She's an American child; she doesn't bow." I smiled. "But if you touch her fist with your little finger, I know she will shake your hand."

Vacantly Akira extended his pinkie. He was preoccupied. Hanae felt so soft and loose that he was concerned. What if—

he worried with stupid protectiveness—what if she hadn't developed any bones?

Hanae's hand gripped reflexively.

She regarded his pinkie with interest and began to make small smacking sounds. Akira wiggled his finger, feeling the strength of her little arms, laughing when finally she pulled his finger to her mouth.

And like a kiss from a butterfly, like a blessing from Buddha, her touch traveled straight to his soul.

FEBRUARY 13, 1928

After writing the last section, I realized that I had a narrative dilemma. No doubt Akira is a fine man, a scholarly man, a man who cherishes his daughter. But now I need to present some additional information.

He's a gambler as well as a dentist.

For although Akira is a man of science, a man who filters his world through cognition, there's one area where he never thinks yet always knows.

He's a wizard with a billiard cue.

Akira's game is three-cushion. Its action is elegant—caroming down a six-by-twelve-foot field of felt, calculating what to leave for your opponent, three or four moves ahead—and he has always loved it.

The thing is, with three-cushion, you can't just *sink* the shot. It is played with three balls and no pockets, and the cue ball has to glance off at least three sides of the table plus one other ball before finally striking the third.

Thump, thump, thump, crack, crack.

Fifteen shots and you've won the game.

Akira's start in gambling was modest.

After Naomi's death, he'd joined a billiards club. Unlike pool halls, they are gentlemanly places and he joined just to pass the time.

The first time he made money from three-cushion was in 1924. Someone told him the Japanese/Japanese American international championship would be held in San Francisco. Akira knew the Japanese champion—he'd played him back when they were both intercollegiate contenders in Japan— and he was eager to test his skill.

So he borrowed a tuxedo from Kuramatsu's Fine Photos, where with one popping flash! clumsy boys were transformed into gay blades—one patent-leather-pumped foot resting casually on the seat of a brocade chair, one hand slipped into the pocket of a silk evening jacket—and sent back to awestruck relatives in Japan. Then he talked a freight-train friend into a free ride.

In San Francisco, Akira played game after game, steadily working his way to the top. Between games he nursed long, slim bottles of Dr. Pepper and read dental texts. When Akira finally crushed the Japanese champion, the people from Seattle were ecstatic. For though he seemed like a modest dentist, the word was out. Akira Shinoda had a future. The entire betting population of Seattle's Japantown had wagered on his winning.

That might have been the end of it. Akira won fifty dollars and his friends gave him cuts from their earnings. Impervious to the hostile stares and mutters of "mongrelization" that came from some of the other passengers, he came home by scenic coach train.

Having reached the peak of Japanese/Japanese American

competition, Akira had no place left to go. He longed to play the American and world billiards champ, Willie Hoppe (the "boy wonder" who, in 1906 at the age of eighteen, had won his first world championship with already *ten years* of lesser championships under his belt!), but that was a privilege reserved for players on the white tournament circuit.

Once, however, in 1926, Akira *was* summoned to the Alexis Hotel, where he met the legendary Russian opera basso Fyodor Chaliapin. Chaliapin was a physically enormous man who was not only an operatic powerhouse but also a sculptor, an actor, and a billiards player of very high rank. Yet despite his talents, with his Russian accent and theatrical ways, in America Chaliapin found himself regarded as a bit of a foreign freak. Akira loved Chaliapin, who, having heard of Akira's prowess, had graciously invited Akira to a game of three-cushion. I can well image the scene: the somewhat snobby hotel and the slightly disreputable brotherly players. The huge, passionately disheveled fifty-three-year-old Russian in perfect concordance with the trim, elegantly self-contained twenty-nine-year-old Japanese.

Back in 1924, when Akira won the Japanese/Japanese American international championship, what he was expected to do was retire. For a few months he tried—staying within the Japanese American world, giving lessons here, an occasional demonstration there—but he missed the competition.

So he bought some fancy clothes (and found that he liked them). Then, knowing full well that he would never be allowed to play in white tournaments, that he would be led into white gentlemen's clubs through back doors and kitchens—baited and betted against as a matter of racial pride—Akira started challenging white players.

I've spent considerable time analyzing this situation.

Much as he loves her, Akira can't recreate Hanae's image except for the knowledge that she's a six-year-old, about so high, who wears a sailor suit. Yet he can close his eyes and feel, in every muscle, every move of last night's three-cushion game.

Akira has wondered if he's an evil man and for the most part has decided that he isn't. He sees himself as being one of those ordinary people you hear about, with some aberrant gift—like the ability to tell you the date of every Tuesday back for the past thousand years.

It's not that Hanae is less important, he tells himself, it's just that billiards are his aberrant gift.

And he tells himself that he's putting the gift to good use. Forcing members of exclusive clubs to acknowledge that Japanese can have formidable talents, that he's more than the Dapper Jap.

Yet I have another theory. Dentistry and billiards call for similar skills: a supple wrist, a scientific precision, and something else as well. Both call for professionalism while engaging in acts that are barely removed from violence.

For although billiards is a gentlemen's game, the stakes are money and pride.

To excel in either billiards or dentistry, you have to be comfortable with blood.

chapter four

Critics have complained that the I-story is too narrow. Not only because everything centers on a handful of closely related characters but also because it follows the meandering flow of memory. There's no solid sense of setting or plot.

The setting problem I think I can handle. While Japan is fairly homogeneous and readers are expected to just know the specifics, I live in America—an odd, improvised place where a "shopfront" could mean anything at all—and have the advantage of richer material.

The plot part, however, is a problem. So far my life has failed to provide any clear sense of pacing or premise. It's odd how I fret over these things. How even though I don't expect anyone to ever read my I-story, I still want to make it *good*.

But back to setting. I don't actually live in America. I live in Seattle's version of Japan.

My Observations on Setting

Eighteen lively blocks of upstairs flats and ground-floor restaurants, barbershops, bathhouses, fish and meat markets, laundries, tailors, interpreters, physicians, cigar and candy shops, formed by real estate covenants and employment discrimination—I know this about Japantown: its inhabitants think they are lucky.

Honestly. Even in the face of contradictory evidence.

So that if some misfortune were to befall you—say you were a man who lost a hand in a sawmill accident—you'd turn it into a joke, a good one you could use over and over in front of an unvarying audience.

Lucky it wasn't my you-know-what!

And hearing the familiar laugh, seeing everyone's eyes shine with gladness that your sense of fun had survived, you'd think, *Merciful Buddha! I really am lucky!*

We can't help it. It's second nature, our thinking this way. I suppose that, coming as we do from islands racked by sudden losses from earthquakes, volcanoes, typhoons, from two thousand years of feudal warlords and an inestimable number of autocratic patriarchs—so that a favorite Japanese humorous saying is "Fear fire, flood, and *Father*"—it's a way for the heart to endure.

Yet in this grateful community, Akira has had some trouble.

Take the autumn when Hanae was three and the Seattle Buddhist Church went *matsutake* mushrooming in the lower Cascades.

It was quite an expedition, this annual quest for the elusive matsutake. Into a fine 5 A.M. fall morning would rumble a caravan of open-topped black Model T Fords. Within each car would sit five or six people, ranging in age from infancy to late sixties, wearing their oldest cotton coats—as protection from dirt and gravel—over their finest flapper-era American clothes.

The cars' occupants would be perched on blankets—to cushion the jolting ride, to spread on the ground for a picnic, to camp with in the very likely event of a breakdown—and wedged between at least two huge spare tires. For on the mountain roads of Washington State—either dusty and deeply rutted or muddy and slickly treacherous—balloon tires burst as often as bubbles in a glass of champagne.

Each passenger would carry a huge collecting basket—representative of our overinflated hopes—and an heirloom-quality three-tiered lacquered lunch box artfully filled with individual compartments of sautéed cucumbers, rice balls, pressed fish cakes, and fried chicken *kara age*. (My lunch boxes would contain something more inventive, say, cheddar-cheese-and-mayonnaise sushi.) The lunch boxes would be stacked by courses, tied up with decorative cords, and wrapped in huge silk squares stenciled with each person's family crest. Coming from a land of earthquakes, where insulation equals protection from breakage, the Japanese have made an art of extreme overpackaging.

Yet no matter how jolly the journey, when we arrived in the old-growth forest our mood suddenly changed. As we scattered in our search, thin streams of sun slanted through canopies so high and dense that the light barely brushed the soft forest floor. Among the ancient trees, there was such a sense of sacredness that we all felt subdued and reflective.

Probably for Reverend Mitsui, our spiritual leader, this was the whole point of the excursion. For although the Seattle Buddhist Church always arrived as a clattering caravan, upon disembarking, the beautiful vastness would swallow us completely: separating us, muffling our insignificant voices, enveloping our ridiculously clad bodies. (On the outing when

43

Hanae was three, I—silly twenty-seven-year-old that I was—wore a newly bobbed Dutch-boy hairstyle, a drop-waisted dress, and a pair of strapped high-heel shoes! Since then I have allowed my bangs to grow and now wear my hair in a more flattering, side-parted, chin-length cut. In addition, I no longer wear high heels in the forest.)

And when we gathered for lunch in the late morning, we were invariably a more humble, more reverent group.

On the day of three-year-old Hanae's outing, after lunch, as we sprawled on deep fragrant pine needles, Kenji Kubota's boy—Billy, the smart one who had wanted to be a lawyer—offered ways around finer clauses in the Washington State Alien Land Law of 1921.

"Ah, Kenji-san," cooed Mrs. Ota, an angular widow who had her eye on the widower Kenji, "aren't we lucky we have your Billy to explain these things?"

And though his stomach was stuffed with rice balls and his basket brimmed with rare matsutake mushrooms—destined to be so wonderfully pungent in broth or steamed with bits of chicken in rice—Akira voiced the thought we avoided.

"We'd be luckier not to have these restrictions at all!"

Akira is a good Buddhist but he can't help noticing the material world.

He sees Jackson Street: Yamada's Number One Public Baths, Oki's We Never Close Cafe, Uchida's Uncle Sam Laundry. Despite the proud names, they're sagging frame buildings facing a poorly cobblestoned road. A scientist, he must compare them with the world beyond Japantown: the Neo-Florentine office buildings on Second Avenue, the *Arts Décoratifs* skyscrapers—with marbled lobbies and bronzed elevator doors—that are going up so fast people say Seattle will be the next New York.

Even I can't ignore so much data.

In a place like this, gambling is a kind of men's whooping cough. So I wasn't surprised when Akira took to three-cushion. And like a mother waiting out a child's fever, in the past few years I've watched him go through a kind of progression. *Interest—Entrapment—Obsession*. I sit at home and I label the stages.

There have been some strange symptoms. For a while, Akira was determined to give us high culture. A set of Chippendale chairs, like crazy toadstools, sprang up around our old dining table. Our wooden chopsticks all disappeared, leaving me fumbling with flatware marked *International Sterling*.

"My little girl," Akira would mutter, "will grow up with every advantage."

One warm spring night—startled from my sleep by the jolting explosions of illegal beer brewing in neighborhood basements—I saw Akira sitting in a Chippendale chair. He was smoking in the moonlight.

"Late, *neh?*" I rubbed my eyes. I checked on Hanae, who always slept with me on a narrow daybed in the parlor. At six years old she was a solitary, watchful girl with glossy braids and Naomi's lovely face.

Just looking at her made my heart feel too big for my chest.

When Hanae was born, I'd left the hotel and entered a state of satori. A somnolent, sensory place—soft and shifting as a cloud of insects hovering, barely visible, on a hot summer day.

The feel of Hanae's head in my palm—fragrant, fuzzy, light as an apricot. The warm sharp scent of a freshly wet diaper.

Motherhood seeped through my body, swamping my thoughts, until like some sort of anemone—mindless yet

45

with perfect awareness—I felt love's currents creep over my head. There was nothing to do but go under.

Akira interrupted my thoughts.

"Etsuko," he said softly as he put out his cigarette. "Do you know where I've been?"

Dressed for an evening out—in a silk, custom-tailored, double-breasted, wide-lapeled suit—Akira looked like he belonged in one of those Florentine-style office buildings, in some far finer world than ours.

"Conducting your business, I suppose."

Akira and I had a tacit agreement. We never explicitly mentioned his gambling.

I slipped on a sweater and house slippers and scuffed across the room to the stove. Akira sounded sad; maybe I'd fix him something to eat.

"I've been in a paneled room, on a Persian rug, under the heads of big animals killed on safari."

Akira paused and studied his hands.

"*So desu?*" Not certain how he wanted me to respond, I made mild female listening noises.

Akira walked over to Hanae. He tucked a skinny leg back under the blanket.

"Look how long she's getting!" he exclaimed with awe.

Hanae began grinding her teeth in her sleep.

Forever concerned about the future of his daughter's bite, Akira leaned and massaged Hanae's jaw. He winced as he moved to straighten.

This was the price of his gambling success, the bruised ribs that he tried to hide.

I poured green tea into an English bone-china cup. I placed it on the table.

"Everything all right?"

I heard the tact in my voice, a discretion close to cowardice.

Akira returned to his Chippendale chair. A chair purchased, I suspected, during a period of trying to change us to white.

"I'm fine." He gave a short laugh. "Guess no one likes losing to a trained animal act." He rubbed his hands together. "Mmm, the tea smells good."

I took a breath. Where were the audacity and courage I'd longed to develop? There was Akira—killing himself. And there was I—not presuming to intervene—acting like some grateful governess fearful of being fired for overstepping her role.

"Akira . . . ," I began.

But Hanae rescued him first.

"Papa!" She laughed.

Akira whirled with alarm, like a man responding to sudden gunfire.

"Hear that?" he whispered. He gestured toward his sleeping daughter.

"Wha-at?" I stammered.

"That trust!" He angrily shook his head. "Tonight when she saw me in these clothes, remember what she said?"

With stupid obedience I tried to recall, but Akira interrupted my effort.

"Have a nice time at your dental meeting." He gave a small snort of shame. "Dental meeting," he repeated, his voice low. "She's completely accepted my lies."

"Don't worry, Akira," I said soothingly. "She loves you."

Akira looked at me sharply.

"It's *easy* to win a child's love. The work is being worth it."

47

The Obon Festival

That night, Akira must have made a decision.

In just three months he went from *Disenchantment* to *Disengagement*, until by Obon, Japantown's midsummer festival, he was through with his gambling life.

I was feeling relieved: happily thinking patience pays off, glad that Akira had come to his own cure without needing my intervention.

And Obon, a day when the dead return for public rejoicing, had pleasures of its own. For Obon—with no private rituals, with its roots in ancient wonder of nature rather than in Buddhism—is less a religious observance than a ritualized community party. Without it there's a certain melancholy to mid-July, what with Canadian geese already honking down Puget Sound and a knowledge that shadows—now waiting until 9 P.M.—would soon fall at eight-thirty, then eight, then seven. A big picnic with a bonfire to welcome the spirits, boys playing baseball, girls in summer kimonos, and everyone drinking soda pop and dancing the *tanko bushi* always seemed just what was needed.

As I squeezed my contribution—macaroni and cheese marinated in soy sauce and ginger—among the ordinary platters of chicken teriyaki and sushi *norimaki* crowding the tables outside the Seattle Buddhist Church, the world seemed rich with possibilities.

Perhaps, I allowed myself to think, my culinary boldness signaled some interior potential, some true self I couldn't yet imagine.

That afternoon, even Teddy Tanaka was hopeful. Sober and

silent, a solitary seventh-grade English-language failure, Teddy was a continuing concern to his parents.

One afternoon three years earlier, having heard about our eccentric European decor and Hanae's bright bilingual patter (interested in preparing Hanae for eventual admission to the University of Washington, Akira and I mostly spoke English at home), Teddy's mother had appeared at our door.

"Just let him listen," she'd pleaded, pushing him past me into the parlor, staring longingly at Hanae, who at three and a half could read aloud short sentences from the *Seattle Times*. "Let him absorb the atmosphere of your house. All he needs is the right frame of mind!"

Teddy's mother thought his problem was based on not hearing enough English. Her solution was a scheme wherein Teddy would come each day after school for two hours and just listen (in his mother's mind, Teddy would be doing this listening with all of his might) as Hanae and I went about our daily routines.

To me, it didn't sound like a promising plan; but Mrs. Tanaka seemed desperate, Teddy seemed lonely, and I thought having a younger child around might engage him.

My original assessment was right. After years of this osmotic tutoring—hundreds, perhaps *thousands* of hours—Teddy still hadn't graduated from the new English speakers' classroom at, first, the mostly Japanese American Main Street Elementary and then the larger, predominantly white Bailey Gatzert School.

I wasn't surprised. During our "lessons," Teddy rarely uttered a word. Indeed, for the past year and a half, I'd given up speaking in English and welcomed any response from him, even in Japanese.

Maybe it was the excitement of the day or the freedom of

the outdoors or, more likely, since I considered myself off duty, the freedom from my overly conscientious instructive chatter—but at the Obon picnic Teddy was transformed.

"There's Sayuri Sakimoto," he observed with casual fluency, like a child used to being heard. "She was with me in third grade. Terrible English. Her parents finally sent her off to Japan."

"That's right, Teddy!" I gushed in encouragement. "I heard she was back. And look at her in that kimono; what a poised young lady she's become!"

"I'll be a surprise, too," Teddy said slyly.

He lowered his thirteen-year-old voice in conspiracy. "I'm going to Hollywood: Universal City, maybe, or RKO."

"Why, Teddy," I asked, "what do you mean?"

Teddy's bony shoulders broadened with pride.

"I'm going to be a star."

If for men in Japantown the means of escape was gambling, then for women and children it was the Nippon Kan Theater. Built in 1909 with community funds, the theater was positioned—like a castle or cathedral in a medieval city—at the highest point of Japantown so that at any time, all could see its sturdy permanence. And like a castle or cathedral, the Nippon Kan provided social structure. By presenting a stage for community political debates and judo exhibitions, for actors and musicians from Japan, the Nippon Kan offered women the shelter of our misconception: a belief that we could live in America without losing touch with Japan.

But our children knew better. At Japanese shows and community events, they ran noisily up and down the aisles, heedless of the cultural lessons. Only the Nippon Kan's Hollywood movies engaged them: froze them openmouthed and rapt in their seats. So that every Saturday, as mothers—most of them non–English speakers, unable to follow the admittedly diverting movies—gossiped and reminisced about things in Japan, their toddlers did something quite shocking. They turned into American children.

Hearing Teddy's ambitions, I felt a wave of dismay—not another setting where he'd be crushed!—and couldn't stop myself.

"But, Teddy, motion picture stars have to be *white!*"

Teddy looked at me with affront.

"Not necessarily," he said with dignity. "Just look at Rin Tin Tin."

I could think of no suitable response. As I cast around, floundering for a new conversational topic, I was grateful to spot Akira.

Dressed in a pale single-button suit with slash pockets, laughing and nodding as he made his way through the crowd, Akira had the easy elegance of the Broadway star Fred Astaire.

When he arrived at our side, he asked warmly, "How are you, Teddy?"

"Healthy, Dr. Shinoda!"

Teddy indeed was glowing. Among the boys of Japantown—because of his dashing style, gambling wins, and free dental services—Akira was idolized as a Robin Hood.

"Am I interrupting?"

"Oh no, Dr. Shinoda! Mrs. Sone and I were just talking about Hollywood . . . and Sayuri Sakimoto."

"Hollywood, eh?"

"Yes." Teddy hesitated for only a moment. "I'm going to be a star."

"Wonderful!" Akira grinned. He leaned over and whispered in confidence, "Brush daily to ensure a good smile.

"Actually," Akira continued, looking at me, "I was just talking about little Sayuri."

I heard something in his voice, a deliberate caution.

"Everybody is!" Teddy enthused. "Japan sure gave her something. Came back and went through New Speakers' class, *zoo-to!*" He swung his head as if watching someone fast zipping by.

"Confidence." Akira nodded. "It comes from growing up with your kind."

Fear nibbled my insides.

Was he thinking of Hanae?

I looked at Akira. "Maybe Sayuri got special English tutoring," I suggested with careful casualness.

"Tutoring!" Teddy yelped with skepticism. My tutoring certainly hadn't gotten him far.

I avoided Teddy's incredulous eyes.

"It wouldn't be forever," Akira said to me. "Just a few critical years."

"Sayuri would have grown confident anyway. It wasn't because of Japan."

"But she was a *worm* before," Teddy complained, "so timid and cowering, and now she's a—"

"Butterfly," Akira finished.

He and Teddy shared a look of appreciation for their likemindedness, as if they were falling in love.

In the warm sun, I suddenly shivered.

He's taking my little girl!

Akira turned his dark eyes on me.

"They learn tea, flowers, poetry," he noted with gentleness. "They develop character."

"Hanae *has* character!" I dropped all pretenses that this was a general conversation. "She's smart, she's strong, and she is with her kind. Just look at her watching the kendo exhibition, over there with the other children!"

"Not with them," said Teddy.

And immediately I saw he was right.

Walking Hanae to the festival I'd been excited, hurrying her along, reminding her of the children's games. But now I saw her standing apart.

"She's independent," I declared with an edge of hysteria. "It can be a good thing, independence."

"Not for children," Teddy corrected with wise condescension. He shook his head with the weight of his knowing. "For children it's just no fun."

We stood a long time in silence.

From the corner of my eye I saw Hanae, chin raised in deliberate nonchalance, suck forlornly on the end of her braid.

"Of course you'll go with her," Akira offered.

I felt a small shock of electrical current, a regenerating twinge of hope.

"I've been thinking about this for a while; you could take Hanae to her grandmother."

"Grandmother?" I wondered. "But your mother is dead."

"Not my mother. Naomi's. We could send her to the House of Fuji. To Chie."

Hope mutated into alarm.

"Chie disowned Naomi. She cut her off when you married!"

"We've been in contact. She's willing to take Naomi's child."

"And me?"

Like Naomi, I'd been cast out of the House of Fuji. At birth I'd been given away to the dear people I thought of as my real mama and papa.

Desperate, I changed the topic.

"Why send her so far? Are tea and flowers so important that you're willing to lose your child?"

Akira rubbed his hands over his cheeks, like a man trying to refresh himself with a hot *oshibori* washcloth.

"The cultural lessons are secondary. It's something else that drives me, a *feeling*."

I stared at the ground unconvinced.

Akira tried again.

"Hanae's stubbornness doesn't trouble me but she has an aura of sadness that does."

He spoke slowly, translating his thoughts into words.

"Hanae is a lonely child in a country that cries, 'Yellow peril!' In Japan, maybe she could find a sense of belonging, a connection with her mother and grandmother, a knowing, 'This is who I am,' to take wherever she goes."

I sighed. On the air floated the scents of our Obon picnic— toasted seaweed, roasted sesame seed—nostalgic smells reminding me of home.

I raised my eyes. In the middle of South Main Street, people were forming a broad snaking circle. The dancing was about to begin.

"My parents talked of sending *me* back," Teddy confided. "I was getting beat up when I first started at Bailey Gatzert. But they finally decided going back is mostly for girls."

"Why is that?" I asked quietly.

Teddy shrugged.

"Boys are supposed to be like carp: swim upstream, have it rough. That's why they give us names like Teddy and Tommy: we're supposed to stay in America; we're supposed to get used to this world."

He paused.

"But girls get names like Haruko and Hanako, Springtime and Little Blossom. I guess getting beat is not what you want for a girl."

I listened to the plaintive chords of the Japanese *shamisen* banjo. The dancers stepped and lifted, pretending to shovel, imitating the labor of coal mining. I felt a flash of irritation. Why was so much of our music about making the best of life on a work gang?

"Maybe I'm putting you in a difficult position," Akira said with formal discretion. "You and Chie lack a history of closeness. Perhaps I should make other—"

"No! If Hanae goes, I'm the one who takes her."

Akira bowed in quick capitulation.

On the grandstand, musician Minoru Hata was starting the *kanko odori*, a dance from the region near Ise. The music was slow, stylized; it hadn't varied for generations.

With a certain defeated admiration I thought of tap dancing, jazz, conversational repartee. Like its people, American art demanded immediacy, irreverence, dazzling improvisational verve.

I shook my head. No wonder Americans found Japanese wooden. Eloquent silence, poetic hindsight, conversation crafted with the masked formality of actors performing ancient Noh theater: all these qualities, so artful in crowded Japan (where repartee, with its thrust and parry, could prove to be too prickly a neighbor), seemed ridiculous here.

I and a whole generation of Japanese had come to America giddy with youth and promise, only to find ourselves tongue-tied and shambling. An ocean swelled between us and our children—who gave voice to dreams of being Rin Tin Tin, dreams as incomprehensible as the twittering of birds! No wonder we split our families, sending sons forward into the

55

jazz age to contend with the baffling future, and daughters back to familiar Japan.

I thought along these lines, as the old music played, and I retailored the situation.

Maybe it would be good to go home again. Indeed, maybe it was karma and I was *supposed* to go back, as a prelude to claiming my own special future.

I squinted, picturing life as a kind of unclaimed handbag waiting for me in some distant rail station locker.

"Chie was my mother as well as Naomi's," I finally conceded. "When I was little, she scared me. But now that I'm grown with—if you'll permit me to say—a daughter of my own, part of me is curious. What is she *really* like?"

Akira bowed with gratitude.

"You're a good mother." His voice was low and formal. "A treasured friend."

"You're a good man." I bowed in return. "A worthy father."

It was our way of saying farewell.

Akira removed his round tortoiseshell eyeglasses. Unwinding the pliant gold stems from behind his ears, he breathed on the lenses and polished them against his sleeve.

Now Akira's house would be empty.

He was a handsome man, only thirty years old, but at the moment he looked old. He jerked his head up with sudden confusion.

"Maybe we should discuss this some more . . ."

"Yes," I said.

But both of us knew.

What would come had begun to happen.

chapter five

OCTOBER 19, 1928

Kobe, Japan

I've returned to a Japan poised on the cusp of two seasons. The Taisho emperor, long incapacitated by rumored mental infirmity (a disadvantage of pure family lines), has recently died and has been succeeded by the young Showa emperor, Hirohito. The Japan of my early childhood—where late summer was dedicated to the moon viewed through tall meadow grasses, and early spring to picnics amid blossoming cherries—has become a place where September means little more than the opening of baseball season and April is enlivened only by April Fool's.

Such modernization has come at a cost. Throughout Japan, fine oily soot has been falling. It falls invisibly onto scarlet leaves of maple, into morning bowls of miso, so that housewives—slipping the sleeves of children's kimonos from bamboo laundry poles—pause in momentary puzzlement, turn to the clear skies, and frown.

Besides the housewives and the farmers, whose tea and mulberry bushes are failing, few have noticed the soot. In

Kobe, where summer is yielding to autumn, temperatures have finally dropped below eighty. Western women, in eager display, dangle furs along boulevards lined with international giants: British banks, Dutch trading companies, French hotels—all shouldering for the best harbor view.

For the view is very impressive. Evergreen islets lie scattered, their rocky cliffs white with egrets, their bases skirted by undulating seaweed, their swirling channels populated by a thousand species of saltwater creatures.

Fishing boats fleck the horizon. An ocean liner navigating among them looks ungainly yet oddly impressive, like a dowager dragging her evening skirts through a lily pond.

Worldwide, business is booming. In Kobe the sidewalks, a flood of dark heads with a swirl of light-colored ones, are as electric as morning coffee. Affecting a pale, thin world-weariness, short-haired, kimono-clad (all Japanese women wear only kimonos) *moga*—an abbreviated form of the words *modan garus*, or "modern girls"—dash to cinemas, an entertainment so popular that a best-selling style of eyeglasses is round-rimmed *Roidos*, named after Harold Lloyd. Lingering outside the cinemas, combing their hair straight back off their foreheads and watching the girls, are tight-suited Valentino-like "modern boys."

At the marketplace, uniformed university students mingle with housewives and union activists. They haggle over stalls sagging with dried bonito and imported pomegranates, with pornography, political manifestos (recently, universal male suffrage has been achieved), and any number of books on personal improvement. For in addition to traditional schools of tea and flowers, the country is rife with driving schools, beauty schools, tour guide schools: every manner of education embodying self-enrichment and urban life.

Into every orderly artery of Kobe's commercial life spill a thousand undisciplined veins—a happy helter-skelter of alleyways crammed with tiny, irregularly shaped lots, each erupting with its own vision of promise. Thus a four-stool bar is crammed next to a wedding photography shop, which in turn is lodged between a temple, a typing school, and a brothel.

Yet amid all this chaotic vitality, a foundation of tradition endures. For Japan is a country where piety has long been married to pleasure, as constancy has been wedded to change.

Indeed, even the continual tearing down of buildings and businesses—where today a futon shop stands, tomorrow a cafe milk bar will be—represents continuity. For it embodies the community attitude of *kodomo no tame ni*, "for the sake of our children," in which the sacrifice of older businesses for newer ones has long been embraced as a way to give young architects and entrepreneurs their own day in the sun.

Where the soot originates, in Kobe's sulfurous central city, September's cool is creating relief. There in the tightening tangle of home workshops—where women hunched over sewing machines or wielding soldering irons are forging an industrial revolution—neighbors are heading to their nightly baths.

"*Kore wa!*" the women exclaim, shifting their drowsy babies from one hip to the other. "The air is clearing; the sky looks actually lighter!"

Their high wooden *geta* drag along cobblestoned alleyways. Their small sons ride, each on his father's back, toes braced against the low-slung waist sash of the man's cotton *yukata*, arms wrapped around Papa's neck.

The neighbors reach the bathhouse, pushing aside blue curtains marked with three vertical, wavering red slashes—

the ideogram for steaming hot water. They diverge at two inner doors separating back-to-back bathing areas: one for men and one for women.

In changing rooms, babies are admired, snacks are consumed, excess weight is assessed on scales and publicly lamented. A gay confusion of posters invites patrons to support the military, to order food from nearby noodle shops, to familiarize themselves with the faces of criminals still on the loose.

In both the men's and women's bathing areas, a skylit room adjoins the changing room. Here people scrub and rinse at low, evenly spaced faucets. Then, saturating small towels with ice-cold water and situating them on their heads, they sink sighingly into a huge overflowing hot tub. This is the essence of Japanese neighborhood life, *hadaka no tsukiai*, socializing in the nude.

Later as they scuff home, damp clothed and wet haired, the neighbors—who come from all prefectures in Japan and who represent a full range of professions—will cool themselves with round paper fans. Pausing to observe an impromptu sidewalk musical, magical, or literary performance—for we are a people who love to publicly reveal our privately cultivated talents—they will reminisce about bankrupt farms with voices more cheerful than sorry.

It is autumn, after all, a time for acceptance of loss, and they're glad enough for the break in humidity.

Indeed it's the break in humidity—and an emboldened autumn wind—that have democratized the soot. Wafting it beyond city bounds, redistributing it across all social classes.

Some of the soot flies to a high hill overlooking a small coastal town and falls upon Hanae Shinoda.

Bored with the traditional Japanese game of wrapping scraps of silk around twigs—fashioning crude dolls in make-believe kimonos—six-year-old Hanae Shinoda paces the broad veranda of her grandmother's 330-year-old house.

She considers the house. Crafted by the architects of the Katsura imperial villa, it is a masterwork of calculated simplicity: elegant and austere, surrounded by spare and evocative landscaping tucked into hills of bamboo and cherry.

She scowls at the verdant moss garden.

All this exquisite tranquillity is killing her.

It has happened too quickly. First the confusing, inadequate explanations.

"You'll learn so much from your grandmother's samurai training," said Akira in lame summation. His voice was plaintive, his face stricken. Hanae began to cry. She clung to his arms as if trying to still the delivery of frightening, incomprehensible blows. "What did I do?" she sobbed. "I didn't mean it! I promise I won't do it again!"

Then the botched, all-for-the-best good-byes.

"Throw the crepe paper ball!" I heard myself scream as the steam whistle blasted and Hanae stood frozen on board the ship, the symbolic tethering tape tight in her fist. Yet I failed in my instructions; Hanae hurled the wound-up crepe paper, forgetting to hold on to her side. As Akira caught the ball, Hanae's end fluttered away. "Hurry, take mine, try again!" I cried as the big ship shuddered and Akira rapidly grew smaller and smaller. I stuffed my ball into her hand and aimed her at the shore, but I might as well not have tried. Too savvy to be consoled by the performance of an old farewell ritual,

Hanae was superstitious enough to be undone by the bungling of the same. "Bad luck!" she shrieked in a panic. "I'll never see Papa again!"

Sickening as it was at first, the ten-day Pacific passage provided relief. We made a friend. Hanae played tag with the sea spray and learned to recognize the constellations. Yet upon landing, she was confronted by the certainty that what had been familiar now would be missing. "Where are the seagulls?" Hanae had cried as she stared at the too-motionless dockside sky, baffled by a place so remote from any mainland that few seabirds have ever arrived.

Hanae, however, is resilient. After three weeks, she has found much in Japan that intrigues her. Though nothing in her life as a samurai child.

Hanae sighs. With a pang she thinks of the village far below her, an oasis of coarse vitality. The rice harvest: rippling paddies green as a salamander's belly, beautiful as a thanksgiving prayer, pushing up from unspeakable slime—scented with night soil, oozing with leeches. She pictures herself as an agricultural warrior: scythe glinting and arching, cloven-toed shoes slurping through snake-filled waters.

Or as the chicken dealer riding his bicycle house to house, town to town. Buying up chickens just as fast as he can, stuffing them into large woven baskets four feet across (losing precious time extricating random children who find these baskets perfect for play), balancing three baskets, sixty birds, 250 pounds on his fender and shoulders. So that as he pedals furiously back to Kobe—in time to deliver his birds to the afternoon markets—he looks like the circus strong man.

Or even as the tofu maker: waking two hours past midnight, grinding and boiling, squeezing and molding. His only company the night and his own rhythmic breathing. Break-fasting, then going forth (a good twenty miles a day, his children making the nearer deliveries) to sell from two wooden buckets attached to a pole balanced over his shoulders.

Hanae ponders the tofu man, imagining that this would be a fulfilling life. Wearing a *hachimaki*, a sweatband, round your forehead, the name of your shop proudly emblazoned on your jacket.

Hanae paces even more restlessly. Compared to these homely occupations, the life of an *ojosan*—fine daughter of a samurai family—with its emphasis on the embracing of emptiness, seems so insufferably quiet.

It's not that she is lacking activity or duty. Hanae, of course, has chores.

But they all seem so esoteric.

Take sweeping the garden path with a light bamboo broom: the point isn't just to clear off debris. Designed to develop dedication and spiritual depth, the *real* task is in repeating the activity—morning and dusk, over and over, for *decades*—until she learns to leave light, flowing impressions on the soft surface earth. Until she understands that creating these lines is a kind of ephemeral calligraphy, an expression of the balance between self-expression and self-control. And that—despite the transience of these tasks—each little broom stroke deserves as much concentration, and can provide as much beauty, as the construction of a poem.

But Hanae is lost to Zen lessons. Stillness and the transcendence found within utter humility come hard to an American child.

Snapping out of her reverie, Hanae stamps her foot on the veranda's smooth nightingale floorboards. Floorboards that were constructed with just enough give so that each plank would sing should samurai from enemy camps have attempted even a nighttime, tiptoeing entry.

With as much force and freedom of motion as her sailor suit will allow, she hurls her stick dolls at her grandmother's prizewinning carp.

Hanae's plan is to agitate the placid pool, to see a sudden flash of orange, black, and white like the surfacing of a drowned calico cat. It's a senseless activity: disruptive in intent, ineffective in result. The twigs fall lightly. They float harmlessly on a reflection of sky.

"Hanae!"

Hanae's grandmother, Chie Fuji, appears on the pool's surface. Fifty-nine years old with dark hair—only now beginning to silver—pulled back in an impeccable bun, she is an imposing woman. Sixty inches, one hundred pounds, with a regal, unbending back.

Japan is a country where one's clothing denotes taste, social standing, and age. Bright primary colors are worn by children, and pure vibrant pastels by young unmarried women. Young matrons wear deeper pastels, peaches, and violets; while hana no chu nen, "flowers of middle age," wear pearlized grays, taupes, and blues.

In this strict fashion hierarchy, where increasingly deeper and richer tones are worn by increasingly older women, Chie is the essence of elegance. On this day, she wears a silk kimono the color of cultured black pearls, with a light stenciling of pale autumn grass on its hem and an obi of silver brocade.

Perhaps Chie sees some sadness, some homesickness, in Hanae's petulance, for she bends down and pinches her arm.

"Come," she orders.

Her arthritic fingers grip with the knowing of an animal trainer. Firm and irresistible.

Chie pulls Hanae beneath the huge sweeping eaves. She pulls her through sun-splashed outer hallways, their white-stockinged feet polishing rich wooden floors. She sweeps aside a delicate rice-paper shoji screen, with one violent throw and pulls her across fragrant floor mats of tatami.

With each brisk step her kimono whispers, *shhh*, *shhh*, *shhh*.

She halts so suddenly in front of a tall *kiri tansu*, a wardrobe of sweet-smelling paulownia wood, that Hanae stumbles.

Chie doesn't notice. Far off in another hallway, she sees *me*—recently arrived from America—down on my hands and knees, happily dusting.

"Etsuko!" Chie barks.

I drop my dust rag and scuttle into the room. My blue cotton kimono is covered with a *kappogi*, the sleeved apron housewives wear. It is the kind of simple middle-class farm woman's clothing my mama used to wear, and since returning to Japan, I wear variations in daily proud tribute.

Chie's eyes flicker across my costume with displeasure. The color is too old for me, the fabric and style are too common.

"It is time we introduced the girl to her *heritage*," she declares, thrusting the word from her mouth with euphemistic distaste.

Chie's fingers move. Hanae feels pressure on the back of her neck. Involuntarily she sinks to the floor.

My cheeks lift with pleasure. I tuck my chin-level bob behind my ears.

"We have something special!" I grin.

Chie and I kneel by the wardrobe.

Leaning forward, Chie lifts a pair of iron pulls and a heavy drawer slides open. She sits back on her heels again.

My fingers poke through protective layers of packing.

"Your mother made these," I whisper. "They signify the start of life outside the nursery."

Hanae waits.

The fifteenth of November will be Seven Five Three Day, a holiday when all three-year-olds receive their first haircut, and five-year-old boys stand—facing a lucky direction—on a board designed for the playing of a traditional chess game called *go*.

As a soon-to-be-seven-year-old girl, Hanae expects her first real obi and a kimono printed with some auspicious pattern. A thousand cranes heralding health and good fortune or, for youth and longevity, branches of plum and pine.

As she waits, Hanae is not very eager. She sees clothing as camouflage, as a necessary part of belonging.

However, she does watch the unveiling with interest.

Hanae prides herself on her ability to logically anticipate occurrences. She likes seeing her hunches confirmed.

At last, the wrappings are laid aside.

Hanae stares.

This is what she sees.

Dozens of pieces of underwear. Sets of seven, for the days of the week, in gradually increasing sizes.

Chie catches the disbelief in her eyes.

"There are enough for you to wear from your seventh birthday until you graduate from girls' upper level."

She looks closely at Hanae, her expression unreadable.

"Are these not *extraordinary*?" she inquires.

The underwear is all one-pieced and in the same pattern. Lace-edged camisoles attached to ruffled bloomers. Crisp cotton piqué for summer. Warm woven wool for winter. Each is painstakingly hand embroidered with little pink flowers. Tiny pearl buttons run down the back.

I press one of the remarkable garments to my cheek.

"I brought them from America. Your mother sewed each one during her pregnancy."

My voice rises with rapture.

"Such is the sweetness of motherhood!"

Chie traces a lace-bordered neckline with a slightly arthritic finger.

"So strange and useless," she says, her voice flat with knowing. "Such is the madness of love."

chapter six

FEBRUARY 27, 1930

The Legacy

Naomi must have known that Hanae would be a girl and that she wouldn't be here to raise her. Naomi left a legacy—a token of her love.

It isn't easy to live with Naomi's love. Daily, Hanae finds herself in the cramped darkness of the schoolyard outhouse with minutes ticking by and layers of clothing to remove. In cold Kobe winters, she struggles, removing first peacoat, then sweater, middy blouse, sailor skirt, and finally the accursed underwear. Because the underwear is made of one piece and buttoned down the back, this is the effort required.

"Hurry, Hanae!" her schoolmates demand, dancing outside the outhouse door. "Hurry or we'll tell Sensei, it's *you* who always makes us late!"

"Coming," Hanae snaps, her teeth chattering, her voice muffled in a tangle of clothing. Numb and clumsy and certain that she'll drop some critical garment down the deep and foul-smelling hole.

Hanae's classmates have no idea of her dilemma. They wear

68

no underwear. They're Japanese children simply clad in layers of quilted kimonos. But Hanae is a Japanese *American* child—a child born to a world of climbing and wrangling, transported to a world of kneeling and waiting. Hanae is wearing American clothes.

The outerwear comes from Akira. On each of the two birthdays Hanae has had in Japan, I've lugged a meticulously packed box into the room—a box of identical proportions to one Akira had presented each year when we lived in Seattle.

"I can't wait to see," I've cried.

Hanae marvels at my unwavering ability to anticipate surprise, for both times the box has contained larger sizes of the same custom-tailored sailor suit Akira has been giving her since she can remember.

At first Hanae resented her father's predictability. She thought it betrayed lack of feeling. But this year, I persuaded her. "Your father misses you," I explained. "It's not easy to have the same garment continually remade. Maybe while acknowledging that you need to grow, he wants to preserve you as he has known you."

Hanae is just a child—whose mother died in childbirth, who is separated from her father. She knows nothing about married love.

But each morning as she puts on layer after layer of her parents' providence, she considers the odds against the meeting of two people so obsessed by uniformity in children's clothing. It seems proof that her parents were soul mates.

And day by day as she dresses, Hanae develops a vague but certain knowledge of love. That it's excessive and insensible. That it's inconvenient and imperiling. That it wraps around you. As essential as skin.

After the separation from her father, after more than a year spent in a new land, I ask myself if Hanae seems happy.

The answer is no. She's as alone and standoffish as ever. But then, a change in external scenery can't alter one's internal nature.

Perhaps I'm asking for Hanae to be somebody other than who she is. Someone accommodating and jolly (like me!).

It's a dilemma. I know my bias, my Japanese American predilection to be pathologically cheerful. And yet—when not exercising an unsavory talent for precocious uncharitable humor—Hanae is often so grave. Drawn to awful ponderous poetry about broken bird wings and the bleak futility of life.

Granted, there *are* places for this sort of self-conscious moping. They are called autumn and adolescence. But what's also true—and I'll not apologize—is that I think the purpose of childhood is joy.

I try to inspire her. In spring, as sudden gusts blow, I stand tiptoed and twirling beneath blossom-laden cherry trees.

"*Hanafubuki!* Flower blizzard!" I cry, raising my arms to catch the soft falling sky, the flurry of pink-tinged petals.

"Hanae, come join me!"

A part of her wants to. Hanae loves her undignified auntie. And she's not unmoved by the blossoms—so delicate, yet each with the adaptability and generosity to grant beauty to branches, breezes, and billowing drifts on the ground.

It's childhood she distrusts.

To Hanae, childhood is a dangerous seduction. Behind all those snuggles and secret shared jokes, childhood hides a more sinister face. Mothers die without your permission. Fathers suddenly send you away.

At first she sleeps lightly—a small beloved rock carried from Seattle clutched in her fist—waiting for the clink-clink of her papa's razor against an enamel basin. She learns about time zones and lives in two, always knowing: now he is eating, now he is walking to work.

Weeks pass, then months that turn into a year. In a satin pouch, Hanae hides a well-creased pencil drawing of the flat where we lived in Seattle. Carefully annotated: "Where Papa keeps his cigarettes and hid pennies for me." "Where I sat when I was sick and drank lemon honey tea." The self-admonition "DO NOT FORGET!!!" is underscored on the back.

And though her photograph of Akira has not changed, in the past year and a half Hanae's brow has furrowed. It's been an effort to keep him perfectly clear.

Toward that end, she works on her memory: testing it, perfecting it. She tries to strengthen her mental powers because she figures, in childhood, that's about all the power she'll get.

Yet even that power is flawed.

Hanae remembers a game she used to play with her papa. Hiding beneath the dining table when afternoon shadows grew long. Listening for his hand on the doorknob, for his footsteps as he wandered from parlor to back bedroom. His voice calling, "Where's my girl?"

She remembers staring so hard at the place where she thought his face would appear that lights would start flashing at the back of her brain and the red tablecloth would appear to be green.

For Hanae, childhood is like that. A time of waiting so exaggerated and beyond your control that even your thoughts betray you. Hanae's intention is to leave childhood with as much speed as possible.

My intention is to detain her.

chapter seven

OCTOBER 15, 1932

Thanks to savings from Akira's gambling days, Hanae and I had traveled special third class on the luxury liner from Seattle to Yokohama, then Kobe. What this meant was—though we were segregated from the first- and second-class passengers—we still had a private cabin.

On our first night out, on a pitching, wall-smashing stroll around our strange new surroundings, Hanae became suddenly ill. As I grabbed for a tobacco tin that was rolling by, a large handkerchief materialized from out of the gloom.

The handkerchief was attached to a trim white man, perhaps forty years old, who stood at courtly attention while I held the tin beneath Hanae's chin and patted her back. Then he carried her back to our cabin. And although he vanished as quickly as he had come, we later, of course, became friends.

This man, Viktor, was European, a Munich-born photographer; and when I expressed surprise that a white person was traveling third class, he told me that he was Jewish.

We spent much of the ten days of passage together. In Viktor's company, Hanae found the playfulness she missed in her papa; and I suspect, for Viktor, we filled some sense of missing family as well.

Viktor reminded me of Tadao. Like my husband, Viktor had a gift for turning uncertainty into adventure. The Japanese have a word for such skills. We call it *myo*, or the art of creating "strange beauty."

One clear chilly night, Viktor sneaked Hanae and me up to the first-class deck, where we spied on couples in evening wear, dancing. As we stood outside the warmth and the music, the novelty soon yielded to melancholy. With my bobbed hair, slim sheath, and wool wrapper, it was clear that I was no longer the Japanese woman who had sailed the opposite way across the Pacific. Yet it was just as clear that I'd never be viewed as American.

Viktor read my mood. He led us away toward the dark of the rail, the *swoosh* of the sea, and he showed us the constellations. "There's fair Andromeda, cast out by her mother's folly. There's exiled Perseus, Andromeda's loyal husband." He brought mystery and magic back into the cold night.

Afterward, he waltzed a dazzled Hanae around the starstrewn deck and all the way back to our cabins.

Viktor showed us his photographs then, in chronological order. Great bundled sequences of startling individual images. First a series in Munich: streets, gardens, a synagogue, slyly comical portraits of family occasions. Then slowly the images changed, grew dispersed, disillusioned, disjointed. Gypsies outside of Paris, a woman of indeterminate age and emotion (laughing? weeping?) eating a piece of bread in the rain.

It was disturbing. What was I to make of such pictures? A proud-looking porter at New York's Grand Central Station, a skinny American boy at his family's farm auction—his shoulders bent like an old man. Loss, hope, expectation, exhaustion. The photos seemed a series of disparate moments—beautiful, moving—lacking a coherent story.

Later—with Hanae wrapped in a blanket and snoring, her head resting on my lap—Viktor began to speak of his exile. Of the 1923 Beer Hall Putsch when a man named Adolf Hitler was arrested for trying to overthrow Bavaria's republican government; how during his brief imprisonment Hitler wrote *Mein Kampf*, a frighteningly well received treatise of hate. Shortly afterward, Viktor had printed a series of photographs —portraits of Hitler's friend General Ludendorff—in which the subject emerged looking pink, porcine, and stupid.

"I left then," Viktor said quietly. "I cannot return."

As he picked up a bundle of his hundreds of photographs and began to go through it once more, I came to a realization. The pictures were Viktor's I-story.

Through a kind of time-lapse photography, those images held the threads of his life. Together they wove a tale of detachment and engagement—his camera first looking *at* dispossessed others, then *through the eyes* of assorted kindred souls.

Until finally, with a slow shuffle through a mountain of photographs, Viktor told how he'd regained his life.

OCTOBER 16, 1932

There's a reason for this digression about Viktor; for four years my I-story has been stalled.

What I had wanted was to sail on with my life and my narrative, to give my history not a second thought. One thing I'd always admired in America was the idea—a well-crafted fiction, really—that what has happened in the past simply *pales*, to a pleasingly translucent level of nonexistence, in contrast to what comes with the future.

Yet a novel, even an autobiographical one, must be more than a posting of observations about the present, must be more than the type of cheerful future speculation that proves so useful at a baby shower.

So I see no way around—let me be quite explicit—My History with Chie. And this is the narrative point where it should go. But the truth is that whenever I begin to delve into my relationship with Chie, my writing goes suddenly flat.

Since I entered Chie's house, I've struggled. Generating multiple mutant drafts—too caricatured, too scattered, too whiny—and storing them all in a box. I began to wonder why I was writing this I-story. Why, like the painter of a Japanese scroll (an ancient precursor to the motion picture, whereby a passing horizontal image was scrolled away on one side as the present emerged, fed from a roll on the other), was I inching along, trying to capture experience unfurling?

Perhaps to self-document, to paint myself in the world and say, "I am here." Perhaps to extend myself into the future, hoping to read this back from some later and wiser place. Or perhaps—and I felt uncomfortable as I thought this—I was only killing time. Trying to escape an unsatisfactory present.

I stopped writing.

Then last week, in a moment of karma, as I was clearing away my old manuscripts, I found a photograph Viktor had earlier sent. A photo in an envelope postmarked Yokohama, which had arrived four years ago, after I'd been living with Chie for nearly one month.

"Dearest Etsuko," Viktor had written on the back, "may all of your journeys lead you home."

When I first received the photograph, I had been feeling sorry for myself—living with Chie yet not feeling as if I were her daughter—but reading Viktor's strong script, realizing that he could never return to his Munich, I felt grateful to have traveled back home.

At that time, Chie had surprised me. Though she saw the masculine English writing that clearly was not Akira's, she had respected my privacy. She had delivered the letter to me, tucked among other pieces of mail so that, if I preferred, we could pretend that she never had seen it.

"Your life is your own," she seemed to be saying. "You are under no pressure to have to explain."

In the four years that have followed, I have revised that cheerful initial interpretation. Chie's staying out of my business now seems a matter of disinterest more than one of respect.

Yet the America I called home seems to have brutally changed in my absence. In an attempt to keep Hanae connected, Akira has been sending us issues of the *Seattle Times*. In it, I have been reading about the American financial depression. Nine thousand banks have gone out of business and eighty-six thousand businesses have failed. Hundreds of shoe shiners—women and children included—beg for nonexistent business in the streets of Seattle. Imagining such things and others, like the fate of the Lindbergh baby, make me concerned for America. As if hearing an old friend, with an essentially noble nature despite a propensity to distrust those not of her social class, has been struggling with a serious disease.

Feeling I belong neither here nor there has been dispiriting. Yet rediscovering Viktor's photograph has proven a blessing. For I was the picture's subject. Me on a windy deck—just beginning to straighten, just beginning to smile—glimpsing my first school of flying fish.

I remember that day: the chilling fog, the rolling gray monotony. Then the thin flashes of silver. First two, then four, then none. A long pause, then five or six. Each time so surprising and sudden that for the rest of the trip—though the weather was inhospitable and I never saw the fish again—I was happy to hang over the railing and wait.

What Viktor had caught in his photograph was that very first moment of sighting, a delicious shock so delightful that you could see it turning (already!) into anticipation on my face.

He'd caught it perfectly. And now when I needed it, he'd returned that hope-filled moment to me.

What a transforming thing! I thought.

I sat in Chie's cold house—surrounded by old letters, forgotten photographs, abandoned manuscripts—and considered the example of Viktor's life.

Viktor hadn't wallowed in anger or self-pity; he'd chosen photography instead. By deliberately, repeatedly stepping straight into the eyes of others, Victor had found his way from exile.

Maybe I could too.

OCTOBER 20, 1932

A Snapshot of Chie Fuji

Chie likes having a child in the house again, though Hanae is no ordinary child. Hanae is tight and unyielding. A spring bud stunted by sudden frost.

She is nothing like Naomi. When Naomi was small, Chie

would come across her in play—humming the high, sweet, tuneless tones that little girls sing to themselves.

Hanae never sings. She seldom plays.

Hanae watches. She studies adults, searching for strategies, as if we were grand masters and life a somewhat grim game of go.

She frightens the servants. In the past four years, five have given notice.

Thus a great house, once served by multiple generations of lifetime retainers, now is staffed by a changing parade of fifty-year-old cooks (who leave for the homes of sons and soon-to-be-tormented daughters-in-law) and seventeen-year-old (imminently eloping) maids.

Of course, these changes in staffing can't be explained by oddities in Hanae alone.

"That child is unnatural," the last cook was heard muttering. "Her presence attracts vengeful ghosts."

The cook left, taking two of Chie's best knives, leaving small purifying altars—a pile of salt here, a cup of potato wine there—and the precautionary scent of incense.

Chie and I know about the missing knives because Hanae told us. Eleven years old, Hanae spends her time padding stealthily room to room.

At first Chie tried to soften her.

"Come," she demanded, "sit on my lap. I'll tell you a story."

But they were too alike, too thin and sharp. Their bones pressed against each other in uncomfortable ways.

And it is not in Chie's nature to expose her affections. Although Chie's own mother was open and loving, perhaps restraint is in Chie's samurai blood.

For in ancient samurai training, it was believed that demonstrations of attachment could jeopardize the beloved. In times of war, an involuntary glance, a sudden intake of air would reveal which persons were heirs and thus worthy of assassination. A samurai woman could best serve her children by keeping her distance. Affection made subsequent life-or-death demands for coldhearted playacting—for seeming indifference to the fates of children posing as unknown farm urchins—too hard.

Still, Chie is pleased with her granddaughter. Hanae has a quick mind, an unnerving memory.

And if Hanae applies her cleverness toward useless ends, perhaps that makes her more of a Fuji.

In Which I Recount Fuji History

The Fujis are samurai: warriors belonging to a category of elite shi families that included nobles, members of the imperial court, and priests. An ancient proud people, samurai traced their ancestry back eight hundred years, ranked only one step below nobility, and pledged to serve—unto death—the honor of their family name and that of their liege lord.

By the year 1500 Japan was divided between 250 continually warring regional warlords, each hoping to attain centralized power. During those years of constant civil wars, birth into a samurai family meant a boy might see battle by the age of thirteen. In preparation, a mother whispered war strategies to the child that slept in her womb. As a toddler, a son was taught respect for elders, compassion for women, and cooperation with other boys. By age seven, he spent ten hours a day drilling in mental discipline, moral integrity, archery, lancing, and swordsmanship. He shot arrows into racing rabbits as a means of preparing to kill. Between the ages of thirteen and fifteen, the boy took part in a *genbuku* ceremony, at which he received an adult name, a haircut shaved and styled into a topknot, and a suit of armor. Whether he survived his first year in battle boiled down to two factors: how well he had learned his lessons, and random dumb luck.

During those days, many samurai daughters also trained to do battle. In addition, they studied philosophy, history, and literature—frequently gaining distinction as poets, novelists, or scholars.

Although a samurai daughter's primary duty was to provide her father with military and political alliance through marriage and, following that, to provide her husband with a male heir, in 1180 Tomoe Gozen fought by her husband's side at the battle of Uji. After bravely fighting off enemy forces—to allow her besieged husband time to commit a suicide that was more honorable than conceding defeat—the noble lady's life was spared and she retired to a monastery, where she won praise for her holy life. And there was samurai Hosokawa Jako, who became famous for climbing her castle's highest rooftop, to spy on an enemy encampment, and sketching a detailed map with her lip rouge.

Yet despite their great heritage of courage and honor, samurai have become obsolete. The decline of the samurai began in 1606, when warlord Tokugawa Ieyasu reneged on a deathbed promise. Having sworn to protect the six-year-old heir of his old ally Toyotomi Hideyoshi—who had succeeded in suppressing other warlords and had seized control of Japan—Tokugawa instead killed the boy. Thus began fifteen generations (1606–1869) of the Tokugawa shogunate.

Introducing a policy of "peace at home, isolation from abroad," the Tokugawa shoguns prevented the reemergence of domestic military competitors by developing a threefold strategy. First they banished the emperor and his court to fig-urehead status in Kyoto. Then they demanded that regional lords and their samurai leave their wives and children at the shogun's Edo (Tokyo) court. Finally they forced these lesser lords and samurai to spend half their time alone in their home provinces, and half visiting their families in Edo. They were to alternate every other year.

The shoguns' plan was a shrewd one. The expense involved in maintaining double residences neatly removed any money that could be used for mounting insurrections. More impor-tant, the policy made hostages of family members living lav-ish yet closely surveyed court lives.

As a result, during the two centuries of Tokugawa power, the lives of the samurai changed. Cut off from their lands, they could not farm. Taught to believe in a society where "no man should be too rich or too poor," they were suspicious of trade, in which they were forbidden by law from engag-ing and which they saw as benefiting some and bankrupting others.

Thus samurai families grew accustomed to living on gov-ernment stipends, embracing genteel poverty, and searching for meaning in relative inactivity.

Samurai men trained for war—retaining constant battle readiness in the event of foreign assault—yet largely worked as government functionaries for whom literacy and numer-acy were the most needed skills.

Ever so gradually, the samurai became more the intellectual than the warrior class. Educated by Buddhist priests and Con-fucian scholars to be students of philosophy, poetry, calligra-phy, and tea, samurai turned into literati, as apt to have studied Western physical sciences as Eastern martial arts.

And over time, with so little of real importance to do, a number grew both arrogant and indolent.

Yet the Tokugawa shogunate finally stumbled—after heavy-handed restrictions had antagonized all classes of people, after the fiery cannons of American warships had proven the shogun's swordsmen useless, after 1862, when the court attendance rule was relaxed and wives and children returned to their homes—and many samurai from the southwest regions were quick to employ their battle readiness. Chie's father joined them.

He backed the emperor, and in 1869 two years of political and military confrontation culminated with samurai from the imperial armies marching through Tokugawa territories. This conclusion to the Boshin Civil War ended 263 years of Tokugawa shogun rule.

The victorious samurai went home rejoicing. Chie was born later that year.

However, with the end of the shogunate came the end of the samurai. In the new egalitarianism of a largely one-class society whose motto was "one ruler, ten thousand subjects," there was no need for an elite warrior class.

Losing first their hereditary income, then their right to wear swords, and finally all perquisites of legal status and elevated forms of address, the samurai were systematically declawed.

Still, one thousand years of tradition do not easily vanish. Some samurai were sent to Korea, where Japan welcomed the continuing practice of their intimidating ways. Even at home, where samurai were encouraged to fade into the fabric of democracy, they retained their social status.

Throughout Japan, everyone knows who comes from a great samurai family and who does not.

Yet receiving your community's respect for past glories is not the same as maintaining a personal sense of vitality. Without their swords, many men of Chie's father's generation withered away.

Chie's father was different. An adopted son, he was used to accommodating fate. He became a landowner farmer, selling or renting plots of the vast Fuji estate. Had he had sons, they would have trained at universities—as did other samurai sons—for roles as government cabinet members.

But there *are* no sons.

The House of Fuji is female. Raised in a tradition where women are born to serve fathers, brothers, and husbands—the liege lords of samurai woman—we are living without any men.

Daughters, only daughters. The family curse turned the fine Fuji name into a social embarrassment. For in a class where the honor of one's family name meant so much, who could respect a family incapable of producing a boy?

Matchmaking was impossible. Other great houses offered only their wastrel sons. Prosperous nonsamurai families, affluent landowning farmers, subjected the Fujis to the humiliation of financial investigations and doctors' certificates of health.

Yet the Fuji name of honor endured. Although, for four generations, Fuji men had come only through adoption from close relatives or through marriage, they had distinguished themselves nonetheless. They had a reputation for being fair, even generous, for retaining dignity without ostentation. Some samurai families—known for behaviors dissolute, lazy, unkind—even though bursting with sons, had a harder time with the marriage broker.

And as is customary in high families that lack a male heir, Chie took a *yoshi*. As eldest daughter, she married a second son who—having no obligation to continue his family name—was willing to change his surname to hers.

That man was Kan.

A Meeting with the Go-Between

One April afternoon in 1888, Chie and her parents descended from a red rickshaw in front of one of Kobe's most exclusive teahouses.

It was a boisterous time. In the thirty years since Admiral Perry's warships had blazed their way into Japan—humiliating the shogun with their superiority—Japan had been scrambling to modernize.

Now, the Kobe harbor was crammed with ships of every nation. Members of the rising Japanese merchant class, hot with imitative fever, were rushing about in top hats and carefully trimmed chin whiskers. They stopped their rushing when they saw Chie. As she stepped down from the rickshaw, men paused in admiration.

At nineteen, Chie looked like the essence of fresh refinement. Though her parents were dressed in dignified black silk subtly embossed with the esteemed Fuji crest, Chie's kimono—light blue silk with a pattern of pink peonies and one yellow canary dipping delicately in flight—was worn slightly pulled back to reveal the smooth nape of her neck.

A horse-drawn bus bumped past. Its passengers—three

nouveau riche women, cross and corseted in their endless tiers of bustled skirts—twisted around to stare.

Though she lacked the allure of modesty—the shy step, the tentative glance—though her elegant cheekbones were a little too sharp for her to be considered a great beauty, Chie's face displayed an intelligent alertness that was arresting.

"Where's she going? What's she up to?" Chie heard the women whisper.

The women's curiosity was natural. In those days, like fairies in folklore, samurai women—engrossed with managing a great household, with practicing their skills in the arts—were seldom seen, and then only near dusk.

That fading afternoon, when the air smelled of spring earth and industrial coal, what Chie was up to was this: she was on her way to yet another in a long series of failed arranged-marriage meetings.

Her father, a tender man with graying temples and a stern, soldierly bearing, dismissed the rickshaw. They approached the teahouse gate.

"It's an elegant site," whispered Chie's mother, who at thirty-eight possessed the graceful oval-faced beauty (later inherited by both Naomi and Hanae) and the gentleness that we Japanese view as a classic ideal. "It has a pebbled pathway, an exceptional moss garden."

The meeting place was the choice of the potential groom's family; Chie's mother had begun the evaluation.

"Perhaps they're a tasteful family?"

Chie's father disagreed.

"Look here," he said quietly, "you can see what kind of company they keep."

By the door, next to the restaurant's name, Mikado, in

beautiful Japanese calligraphy, was the same word in neat English letters.

Chie liked the teahouse, the sense of substance in the low, swooping eaves, the sound of the running stream in the inner courtyard, the fragrant scent of cypress wood. Like her parents, she based her judgments on two philosophical and aesthetic principles vital to the samurai life: *wabi* (simple quiet strength) and *sabi* (rustic timeless elegance).

These two seemingly simple ideas, linked with the concepts of *giri* to the world (duty to bring honor to one's nation, employer, family, and associates) and *giri* to one's name (personal integrity), had for thousands of years governed every aspect of samurai conduct. They were the principles of dignity and duty that guided critical decisions such as how to flee invading armies: never endanger one's servants, commit ritual suicide in the event of defeat, adhere to these rules whether woman or man. They also underlay small daily decisions and behaviors as mundane as how to arrange one's body during sleep: men flinging arms and legs boldly outward in the shape of the written character for *dai*, or "greatness"; women curling carefully inward in the modest dignified shape of the character *kinoji*, or "self-control."

Yet even with her rigorous standards, Chie thought her father's judgment slightly harsh. After all, even their family followed habits that appeared to be Western. Chie would be the first, after two generations of girls in the household, who upon marriage would not be expected to blacken her teeth.

Among samurai women, blackened teeth—first arising from the expensive habit of betel nut chewing—was not a traditional custom, for it evidenced a frivolity not in keeping with a warrior woman's nature. Indeed, Fuji women began blackening their teeth only as a means of resisting the dictated Western vanity of white teeth and, after a short time, had relinquished the custom. Chie's mother no longer blackened her teeth. Fashion wars, though viewed by the samurai as a glorious means for making an initial arresting visual statement, when protracted were deemed to be both foolish and futile.

The Fuji family was shown to a private room.

Seated around the low banquet table, looking a little awkward in the fine traditional clothes her family wore with such ease, Chie saw a slender young man and his family.

She slipped into place, eyes modestly averted.

The middle-aged female go-between—an essential moderator of discretion whose job it was to preserve, for both parties, both choice and face—bustled about, engaging the elders in innocuous chatter.

Platter after platter arrived: eight spare exquisite courses reflecting the colors, shapes, and textures of the season. Each was perfectly placed on individual lacquered raised trays, one foot square by one foot high. For in Japan, refined food is more a matter of visual, tactile, and presentational art than one of flavor or filling.

Then, as the elders politely oohed over the arrival of the final course, Chie deliberately did what—to the bafflement of her parents, since the exact reason for a refusal never is given—had made her unacceptable at all other meetings.

She glared boldly across the table. She caught that young man in his stare.

He dropped his eyes and blushed.

Deference!

Chie liked that. The oldest child in a powerful family, she was accustomed to having her way.

"Well, Kan, what do you think?" joked Kan's uncle.

It was a crude remark, placing everyone on the spot.

"Do try these spring fiddlehead fern fronds," twittered the go-between. "They've made the restaurant's reputation."

"You'll be carrying a good family name," the uncle persisted, "but can you live with this woman? She seems a bit haughty to me."

Kan's mother shot her husband a look of pure frozen panic. The comment made Kan's family look common. Its directness, to say nothing of its disrespectful tone, was highly improper.

Kan's father tried to restrain the uncle.

"Maybe you've been too good a judge of this restaurant's sake to be a good judge of character," he said with a feeble laugh.

Chie's father gave his wife a thin-lipped nod. She began to collect her belongings.

"I would be honored if this woman would accept me as husband."

Chie flashed a glance of astonishment across the table.

Kan's face was burning, yet he looked straight at her and his voice was steady.

"I'm only a humble farmer. Maybe I lack refinement. But I'd serve you faithfully."

"Kan-san, you *are* an ardent one," cooed the go-between. She unknowingly had snatched up a napkin and now fanned herself furiously.

"Let's relax and enjoy this meal. Later I'll consult the parties involved and transmit any important understandings." The go-between looked around in a daze. All these unedited declarations, she seemed to be thinking; what can I do to control them?

Chie wondered too. She thought of a go-between's reputation, built on the orchestration of tactful, understated events. Surely, this woman's was ruined.

Chie's father sat stupefied. Usually the greatest drama was mild complaints about the weather.

Chie's mother placed her delicate hands around her small cylindrical teacup. She idly tapped it three times.

Her husband stirred. This was their special code.

"Bumpkins!" Chie's mother was signaling. "Let's get out of here!"

"I would be happy to be your wife."

Chie heard the words and almost looked around to find out who had spoken.

Kan's parents exchanged a look of terror.

They were afraid they'd be stuck with a lunatic daughter-in-law. No sane girl would accept a marriage made in the midst of such chaos.

Tap-tap-tap. Tap-tap-tap. Tap-tap-tap.

Chie's mother's fingers drummed maniacally.

Across the table, Chie saw the big smile she would grow to know so well.

OCTOBER 23, 1932

I think I should pause here. Although my writing is going reasonably well, I'm not doing what I intended. I'm looking *at* Chie rather than through her eyes. That may prove somewhat trickier. It's easier to tell someone's story than to let them have their own voice and—the hardest part in an I-story, by definition a self-centered effort—to give them the floor.

90

Though I suppose I had to start by looking at Chie. Somewhat like Kan, gaping at her across the table. You have to *see* people, I suspect, before you can step into their lives.

Although unlike Kan—brave, forthright, taking all manner of risk with his heart—I have started surreptitiously. I have approached Chie, for years my least cooperative fictive character, as a lawyer approaches a reluctant witness: elliptically, strategically, exploring small points of gradually widening mutual interest.

At this point, however, the writing gets sticky. Because—although the story is known, the stuff of old village gossip—Chie's feelings for me are involved. Yet writing has given me a sly kind of courage. I want to keep approaching this Chie character, to coax from her more of the story.

It's almost a challenge. Somewhat like seeing if I can wheedle confidences from a forbidding third cousin, by whose side I've found myself seated during the course of a long formal meal.

Chie's Children

Chie married Kan; for twenty-nine years they were together.

Chie wishes Kan had been alive when Naomi picked a husband. Maybe he would have reminded her that unseemly matches can work. But he was not, and stubborn audacity, the very quality that gave Chie her husband, cost Chie her sweet Naomi.

Naomi was Chie's youngest, born so beautiful that Chie forgot her fatigue.

"She'll break hearts," predicted the midwife as she tied a ribbon in Naomi's thick black hair.

Chie didn't realize that Naomi would break hers.

Naomi wasn't the first baby to break Chie's heart. Her first-born was a son. There were many congratulatory cries of *Omedeto* at what was perceived to be a miraculous redemption of family honor. But to Chie the child's sex did not matter.

As was customary in their affluent family, after the baby had been admired for a few days and Chie's breasts had begun to flow, she took him to bed for a month.

For four weeks they lived in a milky haze, barely knowing daytime from night. The servants tiptoed in and out bringing fresh diapers and plump glutinous rice cakes sprinkled with toasted soy sugar. Chie and her baby took no visitors. They were too busy falling in love.

At the end of one month, Chie showed him again to Kan.

"What a fat little pig," Kan noted with pride. "He has four folds in his thighs!"

Soon the baby was smiling at them. He was waving and saying "ah goo." He lay on his back, his fisted hands flung over his head in surrender, and turned his head to and fro. "No, no, no," he seemed to be saying as he wore a bald spot on the back of his head.

By the middle of the second month, Chie could feel a bristly little stubble on the back of her baby's skull. One night she cried (a samurai woman's stoic eyes were supposed to never know tears) and worried Kan to distraction until she revealed the cause of her sorrow. The baby's hair was returning. He was growing up. One day, he no longer would need her.

By the end of the second month, life had settled. Kan returned to Chie's bed.

The baby grew dimples in every joint. He chortled when he was tickled. Each afternoon—though samurai women were expected to stay inside the house and their children to be carried only by servants—Chie would tie the baby to her back and find any excuse for walking through town. As a mother she was shameless. She simply had to show off.

In the middle of the third month, Chie awoke from a nap.

It was early evening. The sky was the color of violets.

The rice paper shoji were open, and beside the veranda, by the main wing, where her parents lived, Chie could see the gnarled trunk and tiny starlike leaves of her father's favorite Japanese maple.

The baby lay on his stomach, beside her on the soft futon piling.

Chie turned to nuzzle him. She leaned forward intending to nibble on a fat foot and began to scream instead.

She screamed for three days: tearless, rasping gasps of horror.

Her little baby boy was dead.

On the third day Chie stopped screaming. Her throat was numb. Months passed. With flat detachment, Chie noticed that whenever she saw omochi—those sweet glutinous rice cakes, so white and soft and yielding—her breasts would ache with worthless milk.

Eight months after the baby's death, when the midwife placed Chie's second child in her arms, Chie gave me the blank look of a stranger.

When I was born, Chie turned her face to the wall.

"That's not my baby," she said.

She shuddered at the touch of my lips on her breast, as if leeches sucked upon her body.

Her husband, Kan, worried.

"She wasn't this way with the first child," he said to the midwife.

"It was a difficult labor," the midwife soothed. "Let Chie rest. Soon her natural instincts will return."

Chie rested. She spent days drifting in and out of a shallow sleep, not eating, not speaking. No motherly feelings emerged.

One morning, Kan's voice pierced her lazy mind like the irritating buzz of a mosquito.

"We can't go on feeding the baby this way!"

Chie opened her eyes and saw him pacing the shadowy room.

Her mother, Most Honorable Mrs. Fuji (whose husband was now Most Honorable Mr. Fuji, since Kan and Chie had become the Honorable Mr. and Mrs. Fuji) knelt in a corner, cradling me—the hateful infant.

Chie watched as her mother dipped her elegant white fingers in a pot of water and honey and placed them one by one on my tongue.

"No," sighed Chie's mother, "we can't."

And so on the fourth day, I was given to a farming family whose own child had been stillborn.

Chie continued to rest.

She drifted in and out of nightmares. Often she saw her baby boy, but when she reached to caress him, he shrank and shriveled. He turned hideously into me. My head lolling like a drunkard. My fat sluglike tongue protruding obscenely from between my lips.

Chie forgot time. She lay on her futon, her long hair tangling across the fragrant tatami like the thoughts tangling in her brain.

Once she felt her father brush a strand of hair from her forehead. For a samurai who'd served as lieutenant general in the Boshin Civil War, it was an extraordinary gesture of tenderness. But to Chie his touch felt sticky, as if it were meant to entrap.

"Spiders," she whispered, brushing at its imprint.

Her father's face collapsed. A hollow choking sound escaped from his lips. After that, he came no more.

Yet each night Kan would hold Chie in his arms. Lifting her head, feeding her a thin gruel of tea and rice, he would sing the lullaby she had sung to their son.

"Nenkoro, nen, nen, nen, nen. Sleep, my precious darling."

Each morning Kan would open the sliding screens to the veranda. He would tell her about the day.

"Look, Chie. A mole has burrowed beneath the moss garden. See the ridge top of its little tunnel? The ground is softening. Spring is here."

"Listen, Chie. The cry of cranes. See how they cross the sky? Autumn is coming."

A refined man would never have done it. The sickroom is no place for a lord. A refined man would have left her to the women and servants.

Kan stayed. Word by word, he poured peasant poetry into her addled brain.

Until one evening she found herself singing with him, "Nenkoro, nen, nen, nen, nen. Rest now, little baby," her voice and cheeks slippery with tears.

That night Chie dreamed of her son, fat and chuckling in his next life, a happy bodhisattva. Then as the sun rose, so did Chie. She folded her futon—as if she had slept one night instead of one year—and matter-of-factly put it away.

chapter eight

NOVEMBER 16, 1932

These things happen. People do the best they can. Chie's and my lives separated, that's all. And I've never once regretted the course of my life.

Yet here I am living under her roof.

Anyone with the slightest literary bent would be tempted to see this as a New Beginning. Particularly a diarist. It triggers all those fantasies of years rushing forward to the triumphant entry. *Dearest Diary! Years ago when I began this record, who'd have believed I someday would be embraced as rightful, most beloved heir . . .*

Reunion is an artistically pleasing thought.

But here's the curious, incurable problem: there's a gap between fiction and life. The fact remains. With proximity, opportunity, and even desire—sometimes the spark never happens.

DECEMBER 1, 1932

Again, my I-story has stalled. After two weeks of trying to describe the present relationship between Chie and me, I find that I just cannot do it. If I write from my perspective the story becomes self-pitying and whiny. If I try to write from Chie's, I find I just don't know her perspective. I reread what I've written only to realize I've created a character who is arbitrary and confounding—a Chie whom, instead of having her own point of view, I've manipulated to continue to support mine.

It hardly seems honest. And it's doubly disappointing after I felt I'd gained some perspective on Chie's past.

Yet this may be a time to remember Viktor's lessons: approach your ambivalence *gradually*—it took hundreds of photographs before Viktor accepted his present. In addition—before presuming to present another's perspective—choose a moment or person that you understand.

DECEMBER 10, 1932

Having failed in my attempts to describe my relationship with Chie both from her point of view and mine, I am left with one possible solution. To consider the situation through Hanae's eyes. It just might work. Children see the world simply but fairly. All adults, to some extent, are fools in a child's eyes. And by allowing Hanae her own voice I might gain a richer understanding, not only of my situation but, more important, of my eleven-year-old girl.

How (I Imagine) Hanae Sees Things

Obaa-san, my grandmother, can't stand Auntie Etsuko. It's a dislike that seems related to food.

You see, Auntie loves to cook. A few months ago the cook

left—secreting in her kimono sleeve two knives and three persimmons. Auntie has taken the job.

But Obaa-san thinks cooking is common, a task best left to servants or daughters-in-law. The truth is Japanese kitchens are set below the rest of the house; their floors are made of packed earth. Kitchen workers stand beneath threshold level and wear street shoes.

It's clear that they're not family.

So here's my obaa-san—wearing a slate-colored silk kimono, kneeling on a hand-stenciled cushion, far above the edge of the kitchen—watching Auntie Etsuko sweat.

Or maybe she's watching me. Obaa-san is vigilant about my whereabouts and behavior. I'm in the lower-class kitchen with Auntie. Obaa-san doesn't like it.

"What's that you're humming?" she demands of Auntie.

In the samurai code of discipline, about which I am developing far too much firsthand knowledge, humming is about as acceptable as spitting.

Auntie looks up from the roaring gas range. Nearby is a big pottery hibachi, which can be used only for the cooking of rice—the source of life for Japanese—and which must be fueled solely with items of purity. Only straw can be used to start the fire, and charcoal to keep it burning—to feed a rice hibachi with scrap wood or paper just wouldn't be proper.

Auntie's big eyes are wondering. She didn't even know that she was humming.

"It's a persistent little tune." Obaa-san pauses, then strikes. "One of those lovelorn *enka* I've heard peddlers sing, as they shuffle from door to door."

Auntie doesn't notice.

She isn't like me. I notice everything.

Auntie snatches a skillet off the blazing brazier. She tips her wrist and a brownish mass of scrambled eggs slides atop a mound of snowy white rice.

The combination looks shockingly disrespectful—one doesn't treat white rice lightly—like a Kabuki theater wig for a thunder demon placed on the head of a beautiful bride.

These eggs are why I'm in the kitchen.

I didn't intend to be here, but as I was cutting through the kitchen on my way to the house, I was arrested by Auntie's cooking.

She had taken two eggs from the big camphor-smelling, ice-packed box (the ice brought daily by a man who carries it in a straw harness across his back) that's nestled under the floorboards of a wide step leading up to house level. She was beating the eggs into a dark pool of soy sauce.

"What are you making?" I heard myself ask.

I couldn't help my curiosity. I'm constantly impressed by the distance between Auntie's ambitions and talents.

Now Auntie frowns at the unsightly mass of rice and eggs.

"This isn't the effect I wanted."

She shakes her head and laughs.

"What were you trying to do?"

Auntie leans against the sink, a huge wooden box standing on the packed earth like a table with water pipes for its legs. I can't get used to this Japanese kitchen. In Japan, cooking is an elaborate production with certain food to be eaten only on certain occasions, after being washed and sliced and cooked in one way and no other, then served on particular little plates bearing meaningful patterns.

In this country, eating can never just *happen*. Every part of making and serving food is agonizingly drawn out so that we can appreciate the miracle of finally getting one tiny bite into our mouths.

Auntie, however, seems to enjoy these rituals both in following them and in breaking them.

"Do you remember how in America I always cooked scrambled eggs and catsup, piled high on golden hash browns?" she says now.

I nod. I conceal a little shudder.

"I thought I'd improvise. Have scrambled eggs and soy sauce on top of a mountain of rice."

Auntie makes a face of exaggerated rue, clowning for my benefit. She bends over and whispers in my ear.

"I'd even hoped to give my masterpiece a title."

She pauses tantalizingly. When I was little, we used to play with the naming of dishes.

"What?"

I go along, although I've outgrown the game.

"Spring Snow Melting on Top of Mount Fuji."

In spite of myself, I laugh.

Obaa-san scowls. She doesn't like our intimacy. Or maybe she doesn't like the lightness with which Auntie is taking the Fuji family name.

"Hanae, come here," she demands. "Come now or you'll smell like scorched oil."

DECEMBER 14, 1932

Love drew me to the House of Fuji. An accommodating kind of love—for Hanae, for Naomi and Akira, for my dream of becoming someone special.

But it was curiosity that drew me to Chie. I didn't love her. Until I was ten years old, I didn't even know she was my mother.

My Introduction to Chie Fuji

In 1907, on the day I turned ten, the woman I called Mama knelt behind me on worn tatami. Unlike wealthy families, who replaced their mats when the green fragrance faded—almost like replacing wilted floral arrangements—most people had fresh mats made in December and placed in the house for the new year.

On that birthday morning, Mama was dressing me in a new pink, green, and azure flower-and-river-patterned rayon kimono.

"Etsuko! Stand still!" she snapped with uncharacteristic irritability. "You'll want to look good for your great opportunity."

Her callused fingers snagged on the smooth surface of my broad chartreuse-colored obi. They fumbled with the elaborate knot of the obi's back bow.

I contorted in my attempt to see the bow from over my shoulder, like a kitten trying to pounce on its tail.

Like all other country children, even fairly prosperous ones, I was accustomed to wearing clothing that was patched, worn, turned inside out, patched, and worn again. Usually I would get new clothes only at New Year or for the summer Obon.

"Opportunity? What? Where?"

Mama ignored my questions. She grabbed a wooden fine-toothed comb and grimly tried to flatten my cowlick.

"Ow, why so hard? You're hurting me!"

I twisted out of her grasp. I looked up at her with confusion.

Mama turned away. She hid her face.

"Disobedient child, unruly ragamuffin, we'll be well rid of you!"

I blinked back tears. Mama's ill temper had spoiled the excitement of my new clothes.

Why is she so cross? I fretted. Has she forgotten I'm the birthday girl?

"*Ikimasho*. Let's get going."

Mama grabbed my wrist. She pulled me toward the door.

As always, I paused at the threshold for one last breath of the sweet smells that came from our steep sedge-thatched roof. Bunches of medicinal plants were hung upside down from the eaves: green gentian (said to be most effective if picked on the Day of the Ox during the last eighteen days of the summer) as a peptic, cranesbill as an antidiarrheal, lizard's tail for swelling and boils. I loved the aromas of the drying herbs. They reminded me of happy times. On full-moon summer nights when work was done, Mama and Papa—straw baskets on their backs—would lead me up twisty mountain paths to gather herbs in moon-shadowed cryptomeria forests.

"Dawdling dreamer," grumbled Mama as she watched me go through my deep inhalation ritual. But her voice sounded considerably less angry.

Outside, the day was still new. Nekko the cat, our neighbor's mean mouser, picked her way home, pausing every few steps in delicate distaste to shake drops of dew from her paws.

As we came face-to-face, Nekko stopped to eye me.

I too was walking strangely, scuffing down our pebbled pathway in my new split-toed *zori* sandals.

"Hurry, Etsuko."

I picked up the pace of my shuffle. I turned toward our high bamboo fence. By the gate I saw an astonishing sight.

A rickshaw driver waited. Dressed in short trousers, a headband for concentration, and an indigo jacket with his company crest on the back, he stood smartly, as if at attention. The rickshaw had a folding awning like those I later would see on American baby carriages. Two long poles lay along its sides. At twilight, rickshaw drivers would hang lanterns along these poles, where they'd swing festively—like fireflies—as the drivers trundled along.

"Get in," said my mother. She gestured vaguely toward my split-toed socks. "We want your tabi to stay snowy white."

"Oh Mama, a rickshaw ride! Is this the opportunity you were planning? What a wonderful birthday surprise!"

Mama reached out and, in an automatic gesture, smoothed my cowlick. Her touch was gentle.

"Is this the opportunity?" she wondered, her voice subdued. "No, but perhaps it is the beginning of many others."

We climbed in. I was excited. In my town, rickshaws were used mostly by doctors on house visits or by affluent wives. As we jostled along I leaned well forward, past the edge of the awning, hoping my friends would see.

It was a ride both thrilling and lulling: the sound of the driver's breathing, the muffled rhythm of his running feet on the dusty road. We rode past large thatched-roofed farmhouses with their small, private rice paddies, past rounded groves of mulberry and tea. In the early morning, from my high and speeding perch, the landscape looked larger, familiar routes seemed suddenly exotic.

Nature seemed to find us exotic. At the sound of our approach, invisible treetop birds would stop singing. Then as we traveled beyond their territories, they would start twittering once again. I hugged myself with pleasure; I pretended the birds were gossiping about my pretty clothes.

As we reached the village, houses shrank and clustered. Their gray-tiled roofs glistened with morning dew. The village, of around three thousand people, was built on what had once been Fuji land. Until a hundred years or so earlier, peasants had paid a portion of their rice harvests as rent to the House of Fuji; in turn, the House of Fuji had paid rice to the regional warlord, who then had paid rice to the shogun as tribute. Yet during the two-hundred-year Tokugawa reign, the Fujis had been forced to slowly sell this land, and when the Meiji emperor ended samurai stipends, Chie's father sold the land on which two neighboring villages stand.

On my tenth-birthday morning our village consisted, as it does now, of three packed-dirt streets, parallel to a small river, and a tangle of innumerable back alleys. The rickshaw man carried us through the central street of the town. On either side stood two-story shop buildings made of wood that was darkened with age. I counted the businesses as our driver ran by: barrel maker, general store, public baths, tofu maker, police station, rice merchant, doctor. In the early light, shopkeepers were removing night shutters. Behind the shutters stood latticework sliding doors. Within an hour, I knew, the lattice doors too would be opened and the whole business section would be one long promenade.

As we reached the outskirts of town we passed the elementary school attended by children from four villages, and the market where farmers and fishermen brought their wares. I saw silvery baskets of fish, some still slapping their tails, and piled bunches of early carrots pointing like accusatory fingers. Though the fishermen were too busy to pay heed to a rickshaw, the farm women smiled and nodded at me.

We rode on, passing the mosquito coil factory, where chrysanthemum flowers were ground into repellent incense. At 7 A.M., the workers had yet to arrive, but over the hedge wall I saw the ground gleaming golden with pollen.

104

The driver slowed. He began the long ascent into the Fuji-owned hills.

It was planting season. Along terraced paddies, lines of women—in cone-shaped hats, their work kimonos tucked and twisted above their knees, their sleeves tied back with colorful ribbons—bent to the beat of a drum. As the drummer tossed his tasseled sticks skyward, as a Shinto priest chanted prayers for sun and rain, the women plunged their arms into water and mud, securing each stem of green rice.

We turned a curve in the hill. The rickshaw entered a bamboo grove, shady and cool like a tunnel.

Saaa, saaa, sighed the wind through the leaves.

"Almost there," called the rickshaw man.

"Where are we going?" I thought to ask my mama. "Are we visiting Most Honorable Mrs. Fuji?"

Most Honorable Mrs. Fuji was a frequent guest at our house, but because of class differences, we'd never been to her home.

"Visit?"

Mama seemed distant, as if I had wakened her from a spell. "Yes, and perhaps you can stay awhile."

"Stay? You mean, go daily? Is this the opportunity? Will I receive training as a maid?"

Mama opened her mouth. She began to speak but fumbled with her words. She closed her mouth and sighed.

The gateposts of the high tile-roofed gate to the Fuji estate were made of ancient timbers. The family crest was stenciled high on the wooden double doors. Joining the gate was a thick clay wall that rimmed the circumference of the family property.

On my birthday, the big gate stood open. We were met by a

105

woman servant who, wordlessly, led us across endless grounds.

We passed azalea, moss, and rock gardens. We wound through a tsukiyama-style strolling garden (arranged to evoke nature in miniature with hills, ponds, forests, and streams), where men with the intensity of physicians pruned imperfections—invisible to the untrained eye—from exquisitely sculpted Chinese black pine.

We reached the main house.

The servant gestured and we climbed on the broad veranda. Its fine floorboards were as smooth as those in a high Kyoto temple. I looked down and saw the reflection of my face.

In single file, we followed the servant along a singing L-shaped verandah. We passed an interior courtyard where cream-colored sand was raked into fanlike patterns of swirling waves.

Had I been a more strictly reared child, I would have seen nothing of gardens or house. More mature and self-restrained, Mama politely kept her eyes trained on the heels of the servant's white tabi, but—being last in line, with no one to see and scold me—I swiveled my head and gawked.

We were led to a serene, spacious room. A branch of quince was arranged with narcissus and artfully placed in the alcove.

The journey to and through the house was calming and slightly hypnotic. Like guests at a tea ceremony, my mother and I were free to talk. But as if at a tea ceremony—that soothingly orchestrated, unvarying ritual—in this eloquent setting, we felt more freedom in our freedom from words.

The servant knelt before us. To indicate an invitation to use the silken floor cushions, she placed the fingertips of both hands on the sweet-smelling tatami and lowered her forehead to the floor. Then, so as not to rudely turn her back on us, with her head still touching the ground, she pushed herself backward out of the room.

Mother stirred from her trance.

"Sit here," she whispered. "No, not like that. This way, on your heels."

She tugged and straightened until I was arranged to her satisfaction.

"Is Most Honorable Mrs. Fuji going to interview me for a maid's position?"

"You're no servant, Etsuko. You are the Fuji granddaughter, the eldest-surviving heir to this great house. When you were born your mother was too ill to care for you. Today you may reclaim your rightful place."

The room returned to silence. I stared at my mother. Had I heard correctly?

"Silly Mama, is this a birthday joke?"

"I am not your mother, Etsuko."

Her remoteness frightened me.

"Don't tease," I said, my chin and voice beginning to tremble. "Of course you're my mother!"

But Mama wouldn't meet my eyes.

A rice paper screen slid open. Most Honorable Mrs. Fuji and her daughter, Chie, stepped inside.

I caught the light sweet scent of face powder as they sank to the floor.

"Good morning, Etsuko-chan." Most Honorable Mrs. Fuji's voice was warm; she knew me well. "We'd like you to come home."

I turned in panic to Mama. She sat impassively. Like a boulder on her tiny heels.

I swiveled back to gape at Most Honorable Mrs. Fuji. She was smiling in a natural way.

"I dare say it's a shock to you, child, but there will be great advantages. You'll be well educated. In time you'll marry a yoshi and carry forth the family name."

"Mama!" I struggled to control my tears. "Mama, take me home!"

My mother's voice came high and strained.

"Of course you'll still see us, Etsuko-chan. The Fujis are the finest people. You should be proud to return to your kind."

I wheeled around, searching wildly for an ally, and caught sight of Chie.

She yawned and looked away.

My blood ran cold.

There was no tenderness in Chie's expression. She yawned, as if my pain and panic bored her, but there was no casualness in her body. She was like a cat stalking a squirrel: rigid with attention.

"No!" I cried, deliberately disobedient for the first time in my life.

I turned to my beloved mama, flattening myself on the floor with obsequiousness, burying my face in the folds of her mothball-scented best kimono.

"Let me be a maid in training," I pleaded, "but please don't abandon me here."

From the corner of my eye I saw Chie studying me like a butcher appraising a calf.

Mama turned to the others.

"My humblest apologies for my inadequacies in raising your child. This is my fault. I'm so attached that I failed to prepare Etsuko for this day. Let her come home with me. We'll discuss it."

"I won't discuss it! If you make me come back, I'll die!"

"Foolish child," Mama scolded. "You're overly dramatic. Don't be so rude."

"Let her go." Chie's voice was cold and flat. "She'll do better beyond my grasp."

We walked home, our socks growing dusty from the road. There was no one we sought to impress.

"Obstinate child, you have relinquished a rare opportunity." All the way home, Mama scolded.

But her words held no pelting power. Her voice rained, warm and relieved, into the open curve of my ear.

That night Mama broiled a sea bream—a fish eaten only at weddings or other celebratory occasions. Papa gave me the biggest piece.

Yet as I fell asleep, tucked between my parents' warm bodies, I felt a small pang of hurt.

That woman, supposedly my mother, had needed only to glance at me before deciding I wasn't worth keeping.

chapter nine

JANUARY 8, 1933

I'm growing bored with my I-story. All reminiscence, no action. Critics say that's the trouble with I-stories. Action. There never seems to be any.

This wasn't always a problem. For a long time (over nine hundred years if you consider *The Pillow Book*—written by a courtesan—to be the first I-story) having no action was fine. I-stories weren't tales of purposefulness so much as scrapbooks: journal entries, lists, unfinished fragments of poems and plays. Filled with witty meditations and chronicles of literary and erotic effort (*The Pillow Book*, a satire, was intended to savor with equal and ample attention "the delights of literature and flesh"), these novels were something like portrait paintings. Depictions of moment and mood.

And in these early I-stories—each so idiosyncratic and richly rewarding—action was rarely portrayed. Action, instead, was something *experienced*—as a delicious aesthetic and sensory tickling—inside the reader's head.

Then came the Americans: warships, westerns, and now Steamboat Willie. Such a rapid, dazzling progression! I know about Steamboat Willie because once a month, on the pretext of going shopping, I take the trolley to the movies in Kobe. It's different than in Seattle. Here a *benshi*—a modest yet loud-voiced man—stands beneath the screen, taking both female and male parts, translating American dialogue into Japanese rhyming stanzas.

Ah, the Americans. Here are a people who seize opportunities, poke cows, invent a large cartoon mouse who can talk.

Needless to say, the I-story has started to sound a bit dull.

Or perhaps I-stories don't sound dull so much as *look* dull. After you've seen a few motion pictures, you start visualizing every tale you encounter. Then what used to feel exciting—imagining the turmoil in someone's soul—starts looking like a few characters, kneeling in isolation on tatami, thinking about their lives.

Since this is my I-story, my hands are tied. I can't suddenly become the sort of person who runs around *doing* things. Neither can most Japanese. Our strengths are receptivity and the appreciation of human and physical nature. But this gives me an idea. Nature. Naomi loved nature. Now here is something that moves me to write.

My Sister, Naomi

Naomi and I were opposites. She, complicated and pretty. I, simple and plain. Yet there was no competition between us. We knew with simplicity can come beauty. We knew with complexity can come pain.

We knew we were sisters. From our first fleeting exchange, a glance met and held across a crowded play yard on Naomi's first day of school.

"Onee-san!" Naomi called to me. She used a name of household respect.

"Onee-san, Elder Sister," she called again as she darted to my side. "Isn't it funny? You have my father's face!"

I was eleven years old. I looked at her and saw in her six-year-old, little-girl prettiness a foreshadowing of elegant beauty. I saw our obaa-san, Most Honorable Mrs. Fuji.

"Younger Sister," I replied.

My parents encouraged our friendship.

"Buddha wishes it," Mama sighed.

For the next five years, Naomi and I flitted from her garden to my house. Back and forth endlessly, our kimono sleeves billowing full in the breeze like butterflies playing tag in a meadow.

Yet I was careful never to go beyond her garden, never to go into her house.

Then one day, by accident, I did. It was a hot summer afternoon and our cotton kimonos stuck to our backs. Naomi ran into her kitchen, meaning to fetch us long cool drinks of barley tea, and—chasing her footsteps, closing in for a tag—I dashed right in after.

Chie was there, hidden in the earthy shadows like a bat inside a cave. She startled as we came. But I saw that she had been watching us. I saw her hungry face, her pinched mouth. It was as if she'd been caught eating something dark and bitter.

When I was seventeen, I left Naomi behind. I graduated from girls' upper level and became an elevator girl in a Kobe department store. The store, Daimaru, was a branch of a modern Osaka shopping dynasty. It was a four-storied emporium designed to appeal to wealthy foreign patrons and their imitators. Instead of having shop boys rushing to and from upstairs

112

storerooms bringing merchandise to lay before shoeless customers seated on tatami, patrons retained their shoes and strolled freely through attractive displays staffed by appealing (and, whenever possible, bilingual) shop girls.

Daimaru's job selection process was not easy. Besides school transcripts and recommendations from teachers, the store required letters from applicants' village registrars. In the letters would be a listing of all births, deaths, and marriages (and information about the circumstances surrounding these events) in an applicant's family line. Only girls with generations of unimpeachable family conduct could apply.

In addition, there was a final series of individual interviews to assess our personableness. Later, during new-employee training sessions, Daimaru would reveal that they hired only the top ten percent in appearance. Thus flattery served to instill gratitude and loyalty.

As a graduate of girls' upper level, I'd been exposed to an advanced liberal arts curriculum and English language studies. I therefore was considered worldly. And though I did not possess the slender elegance of Naomi, I had a round-faced sweet-temperedness that people considered comely. At the time, with my young girl's vanity, I thought I'd been hired on my personal merits. But from an adult perspective I now realize that if my academics or appearance had been judged somewhat lacking—it seems overly generous to consider my looks as upper ten percent—my connection with the Fuji name undoubtedly would have pushed me over the top.

I began my job in 1915, two years into what would later be called the Great Taisho Democracy; it was an interesting time. In the southwestern region of the island of Honshu, in which Kobe is located, it was a time of ascendancy. For centuries known mostly for its glorious past, for its imperial courts at

Nara and Kyoto, southwestern Honshu had recently become known for its present. For Osaka—that great spreading megatropolis built on mercantilism and manufacture—belching with power and money.

Suddenly, the balance of influence was reversed. Tokyo, the site of the new imperial court, became the traditionalist, and Osaka (and to a lesser extent Kobe) was the trendsetter—perhaps not of culture and taste but certainly of commerce and pleasure.

My relationship with Naomi also reversed. Suddenly I was the complicated one. Brimming with exciting—though not particularly practicable—ideas from Voltaire and Rousseau. Moving with comfort and competence through an urban professional life. Even at home in the countryside, I was changing. Stirring with new sensations, feeling a quickening restlessness in the sultry summer nights.

At twelve Naomi was still, simply, a child.

She missed me.

One evening I disembarked from the streetcar at the suburban boundary of Kobe, ready to begin my walk to the rural outskirts where we lived. I stepped down all chic in my Daimaru elevator girl black silk kimono, worn with the store's tasteful yet modern pin. The pin was a small cream-colored enamel circle in which was painted one bold black character. *Dai*, or greatness: its arms and legs flung wide with assertion.

Naomi was waiting.

"Onee-san, good evening," she said with unaccustomed formality.

She hesitated.

"You look so grown-up in your uniform: so important, so . . . busy."

She trailed off shyly.

I saw her there in the twilight, her summer linen kimono a little short on her growing body, its hem and her tabi covered with dew.

I felt protective.

In our village we'd been peers, Naomi's higher social standing compensating for my greater age. But here on the edge of the city, amid the trolleys and motorcars, I belonged. Naomi was a vulnerable outsider.

"Little Sister," I said with warmth, "you've come to meet me!"

Naomi nodded. She looked at her damp dusty toes.

"Maybe I shouldn't have."

"You've brought your butterfly net and a cricket cage."

Naomi nodded again. "Forgive me, it was a poor idea."

She looked back across the meadows, toward the village, as if wishing herself home.

In my mind's eye I saw her only a few minutes earlier, crossing those flowering fields, full of confidence and sweetness, insect-collecting paraphernalia in her arms.

I looked at the sky.

"It will be clear tonight, warm with the moon nearly full."

Naomi said nothing.

"It will be a fine night for fireflies."

She looked up, hope in her eyes.

"I thought I could walk you home. Maybe we could collect together?"

So we did. For one evening, she lured me—as in tribute to her memory, I try to lure Hanae—back to the magic of childhood.

Frogs croaked in the marshes, filling their throats with the loamy scents of July. We ran across darkening fields, chasing small blue points of phosphorescence, my white split-toed socks growing green with grass stain.

I didn't care.

All that mattered was the velvet of the sky, the softness of the ground, the flickering of fireflies, and the sound of Naomi laughing.

Throughout my girlhood I rarely thought of Chie. Indeed, whenever I felt a twinge of curiosity about her, I quickly pushed it out of my mind. Any other action struck me as disloyal—as well as somewhat imperiling.

To me, Chie was a strange, spooky figure: a woman who had spent a year in madness, who had rejected me at birth and at my tenth birthday, who—a week after my tenth birthday—had written me a dense incoherent letter that had made my father's hands shake with fear.

When I grew up, married, and moved to America, I was busy with adult life. I never thought of Chie at all.

Then Naomi came. Arriving in Seattle—disowned, seasick, and skinny—marriage papers clutched in her hand. With Akira's friend Harry Hasegawa, I stood behind Naomi at the Seattle Buddhist Church on the afternoon of her formal wedding.

Naomi wrote Chie every day. Long, apologetic, explanatory letters. Short, casual, gossipy notes. But no matter the tone or topic, Chie never wrote back.

"Why bother?" I asked one day when, just for a second, I saw Naomi's sweet face sag with disappointment and fatigue.

Wilting from the heat and humidity issuing from Uchida's Uncle Sam Laundry, which was located next door, we stood scanning our letters at the seemingly modest but soon-to-be-bankrupt Okamura Company, a business providing mailing, banking, and mortgage services.

"Stop writing. Let her feel your absence. Why reward her, each day, for her silence?"

Naomi smiled slightly and shook her head. "That would be cruel. You don't understand our mother."

The word "our" startled me. I didn't consider Chie my mother.

"What's there to understand? She's unloving; she cut you off."

I heard the hostility in my voice and wondered. Was my anger all for Naomi's pain? Did I mind that, twice, Chie had refused me?

Then one day the wedding mirror arrived: long and graceful, attached to a low dressing table made of hand-finished Japanese chestnut.

The smooth surface was near perfection, enriched by a gnarl here, a knot there, evidence that the tree had suffered and prevailed. It was the perfect gift for a young bride, providing the lesson that beauty is enhanced by time.

"Oh," I said when Naomi unpacked it.

Clean-smelling pine shavings and slightly mildewed newspaper wadding, the scents of Japan, lay scattered across Naomi's whitewashed American floor.

Whitewash, I thought with sudden irritation. Maybe it had something to do with their history—a people arrived to remake their past—but Americans seemed unable to leave nature alone.

Abruptly, after years of living amid the patterns and paints of American interiors, I found myself missing my Japanese home.

"From the American missionary women who taught you, a part of your old world to take into your new." Naomi was reading the gift card's typewritten English. "Please do not write to acknowledge this."

She frowned. "How odd."

Then she laughed. "But look at the quality. I had no idea those spinsters knew anything about Japanese marriage rituals, let alone had exquisite taste!"

She paused. "You look funny. Is anything the matter?"

"No, no. I'm just, uhmm, surprised."

"So am I! Those cagey old women. How thoughtful. After all their talk of Protestantism and self-denial! I wonder how they found my address. And not wanting to be thanked; it just goes to show that you never really know some people!"

I let Naomi prattle. It gave me a chance to think.

The truth was, at the time of my wedding, I had received a similar mirror.

"From the people at the department store," the card had read. "Something to take into your new life from those who cared about you in the old. Please do not contact us with unnecessary and burdensome acknowledgment."

"Nonsense," my mama had said when she saw the card. "Look at the craftsmanship, the detail. This wasn't purchased through the donations of a group of shop girls."

Her eyes narrowed in contemplation, then sprang open.

"I know! It's from your obaa-san, Most Honorable Mrs. Fuji. After all, the wedding mirror is usually from the bride's family."

But then, an official gift arrived from Most Honorable Mrs. Fuji: a half dozen silken kimonos.

Years later, after my husband died, whenever I needed cheering I would wear those kimonos. I would stand in the steaming kitchen at Hotel Samurai Gardens, slopping greasy hash browns onto barely washed plates, clad in claret-colored shimmering silk. With every stare of total disbelief I received, I was reminded of my grandmother's affection.

At the time of my marriage, Mama finally conceded that maybe the mirror *was* from my salesgirl friends. Maybe one of them had a connection with a cabinetmaker. It seemed like the kind of present a group of young women would buy: inappropriate, romantic, beautiful, but totally impractical.

I didn't give it too much thought and when I sailed for America, I left the mirror behind.

I never mentioned the matter to Naomi. Since Most Honorable Mrs. Fuji had died (like my parents, Most Honorable Mrs. Fuji and her husband had died in the 1918 influenza attack), the mirrors couldn't have come from her. Besides, there was some variation between Naomi's wedding mirror and mine. Perhaps they had not really come from the same cabinetmaker.

I reasoned like this. I worked hard to convince myself that the mirrors had not come from Chie, that the whole thing was coincidence. Then Naomi learned she was pregnant, and in the excitement of the next months, I forgot all about the mirrors.

When Akira sent the telegram saying Naomi had died, Chie didn't respond. She didn't even ask about the health of Hanae, her only grandchild.

My anger simmered. On the first anniversary of Naomi's death, it rolled into a boil.

On that first anniversary I marched into the bedroom that Naomi had shared with Akira, the bedroom where she had died.

The wedding mirror sat neglected on top of a tall chest of drawers. At some point in that past year, Akira must have bumped it, for it hung on its hinges at an awkward angle. The glassy surface that once had shown Naomi's lovely face now reflected a cracked corner of the ceiling.

"It serves you right, you old hypocrite," I muttered as I dragged a Japanese lacquered trunk over to the American chest of drawers.

"It serves you right for coming, like a Trojan horse, offering gleaming best wishes. Now you're abandoned. Now you're neglected. How does it feel? You give once-in-a-lifetime fancy gifts so freely but won't give your daily presence!"

I climbed on the trunk and wrestled with the weight of the mirror. My intention was to drag it from its perch, to throw it out of the house.

"Glad you're rescuing that mirror."

Akira startled me with his cheerful voice.

I turned wildly, my heart pounding.

He didn't notice.

"Here, let me help."

Akira took the mirror in his arms and tenderly eased it to the floor.

"It's a beauty, isn't it?" he commented. "Naomi really loved it."

He shook his head. "She didn't like housework but she used to polish it with an odd gentle diligence, sort of like scrubbing a child."

"Did she know who sent it?"

Akira seemed surprised. "The missionary women who taught her English. I thought you knew that."

He knelt by the mirror, adjusting the tilt of its glass.

"Naomi couldn't get over the surprise of it," he said. "She mentioned it all the time."

My throat tightened.

"Saying what?"

"Oh, you know, remarks."

"What kind of remarks?"

Akira heard my sharpness. He looked confused.

"I don't know, comments."

He saw my face and tried harder.

"Comments about the ladies' kindness. 'Can you believe they sent me this,' and that sort of thing."

Akira was watching me with wounded wariness, like a puppy that had been scolded unfairly.

I took pity on him.

I climbed down from the trunk, my anger spent. Maybe Naomi had known, maybe not. What did it matter?

Akira sensed my exhaustion.

"It's a wonderful birthday idea!" he said, shifting the topic with a heartiness I knew he hoped was contagious. "Giving this mirror to Hanae."

Hanae's birthday! For a moment I'd forgotten that it was an anniversary of joy as well as pain. In my breast, I felt a wave of melodramatic magnanimity. Today would be a day of forgiveness, not blame.

"Yes!" I cried, startling poor Akira with my abrupt capitulation to his dogged good humor. "Yes, it will be a gift for Hanae. But not today. Later, so that I can explain."

I returned to Japan. Though I was nervous about entering the House of Fuji, I also was hopeful. I brought Hanae. I brought my good luck talismans: framed pictures of Mama, Papa,

Tadao, and Naomi; the six wedding kimonos from Most Honorable Mrs. Fuji; an old sweater that Tadao used to wear. I brought all the odd underwear that Naomi had sewn, and something else. I brought Naomi's mirror.

I didn't pack it. It didn't come in a carton, wrapped in old newspapers, traveling baggage class. I carried it in my arms—tall and fragile like a beautiful invalid—up the gangplank, into our special third-class stateroom, all the way across the Pacific. I carried it off the boat, onto the pier, and set it at Chie's feet.

She was dressed in a pearl gray kimono, as simple as a perfect line of prose.

Ships sounded, stevedores shouted, foreigners rushed into one another's arms.

Over the years, I had grown quite sentimental about the wedding mirrors. Traditionally a mirror is a gift of severance, given by the bride's family as an act of farewell.

But given by Chie to her abandoned and disowned daughters, the mirrors were gifts of reclaiming. They said loudly that we were her own.

"Here is your family restored at last!" I cried unsteadily as I put down the mirror, overcome by the glittering water, by the sensation that the pier was rolling beneath my feet.

I meant it to be a reunion.

If she gives some little sign, I told myself, then we can start again.

But it was a mistake in timing.

Chie sniffed the sea air with distaste.

She gestured toward the mirror with dismissal.

"Take this with the other baggage," she said to her waiting servant.

Worse yet, she barely gave me a glance.

Chie's eyes were busy devouring Hanae, noting how she resembled Naomi, and for one horrifying moment I was filled with jealous hatred.

I stood—choked with disappointment and shame—in a linen drop-waisted sheath and a cloche hat that in America had made me feel smart. From the looks I was attracting (at that time not even slightly scandalous modern girls were wearing Western clothes), I might as well have been wearing a bath towel and a lopsided bowl.

The mirror rested between me and Chie. Gleaming glass rose from a base of satiny wood.

Elegant and serene, it belonged in the House of Fuji.

Not I.

chapter ten

When I lived in Seattle, I sometimes wondered what made us Japanese so foreign. It wasn't just physical things—skin, eyes, food—that separated us from other Americans. (Though those were things that repelled them.) It was something less visible, more essential. I never fully figured it out.

Yet now that I've returned to Japan—which, after an absence, feels, itself, slightly foreign—I think I've identified what Americans found so annoying. *Kata.* A word meaning "way-of-doing," or "process," a word roughly translated as "form."

In Japan there is a kata for every behavior: *kangae kata,* "way of thinking," *yomi kata,* "way of reading," *kaki kata,* "way of writing," *tabe kata,* "way of eating." Beyond that, there are sub-kata for every discreet category: separate ways of thinking about family, work, and so forth; varied ways for reading novels, poetry, newspapers, and the like.

There's a specific way of counting large flat objects that is different from the way of counting small round objects; a correct way of folding a kimono for storage that differs depending on whether the kimono belongs to adult or child. It's the same for hundreds and hundreds of situations: one commonly utilized, ritualized form.

It is kata, I suspect, that makes Americans (a people as obsessed with individuality as we are by uniformity) see the Japanese as insufferably, inhumanly *same*.

Yet to the Japanese, kata represents an illuminating philosophical principle rather than an inflexible conduct code.

In traditional Zen Buddhism, kata was the means of expressing and maintaining *wa*—essential universal harmony. It was a means of insuring that humility would win over arrogance: demanding that pride be subsumed by the small modest steps involved with the perfecting of any attitude or skill.

Kata requires a lifetime of training, the goals of which are an appreciation of the universe in each waking moment, a dedication to beauty and goodness in any endeavor, and a relinquishing of personal vanity so that the pupil becomes one with his training.

Hence the painter becomes the tool of his paintbrush; the potter feels the soul of his clay.

Through the ages, Zen Buddhism slowly reduced the principles of kata—as a French chef reduces a sauce—until every skill contributing to community living was distilled to its basic elements.

No part of life was ignored. Even the humblest activity (like sweeping the garden path with a bamboo broom) became a ritualized series of gestures—each imbued with the pleasure of serving the universe.

Of course, no philosophy—especially one as time consuming as Zen—gains broad adherence unless it is useful in everyday life.

Zen's emphasis on humility and restraint (particularly on the part of warriors) was warmly supported by the general populace during the centuries when a samurai was expected to behead, on sight, any person performing acts he judged as disruptive of order. The frequency of such killings, however, was held in check by a shrewd parallel expectation: after such a beheading, the samurai was obligated to kill himself.

As a result, knowing exactly what behaviors and thoughts might be viewed as offensive to order—or more specifically, knowing exactly what acts in what sequential patterning could be publicly displayed and not be judged as offensive to order—were critical skills for everyone's survival.

Why am I holding forth in such a didactic manner? The answer is embarrassing to admit.

I'm afraid of Chie.

You see, there is simply no kata for how to behave in the house of your estranged samurai mother. Particularly if you're farming class. And though in my cooking and mothering I pride myself on not being bound to meaningless form, without it I'm paralyzed.

Initially, even though Chie ignored my opening speech about the wedding mirror representing restoration of family, I was optimistic.

As I listened to Chie for cues about what kind of kata I was expected to display—she was the hostess, after all, and I was the guest, or maybe merely the nanny—I noticed that she employed neither the form of language used by superior to address an inferior nor the form used to address a nonintimate.

I thought it gave me an inside role.

But then, neither did Chie use the form of language—casual, spontaneous, affectionate—employed among family members.

It was confusing yet oddly refreshing. Chie used the same language, the same manner with everyone, regardless of closeness or class.

To me she seemed downright democratic—treating everyone the same by being not particularly courteous to any. While lacking volubility (Americans do love to go on!), Chie's style reminded me of Western forthrightness.

How strange, I marveled, to find an oasis of Americanism in the midst of a samurai house.

Yet if I first took Chie's abruptness as Americanism—as an omen that I'd soon feel at home—it could only have been my Americanism, a misguided Yankee optimism, that prompted such a gross misperception

Misguided optimism, as well, that led me to write those early sections from Chie's perspective. A wild hope that, by imagining her point of view, I might gain some common ground from which we could proceed.

But writing about Chie has provided only a false sense of knowing. Having created a Chie who is essentially accessible to me, impatient and self-certain but bearing no particular malice and owning a sudden surprisingly, wry sort of wit, I keep expecting to encounter this woman.

It doesn't help that in many ways Chie is quite close to that character. With each piece of dry humor she utters, each confident (and unnervingly accurate) proclamation, I keep seeing my intuitions confirmed. So I am continually stunned to find I don't know her. And that (and how ungrateful, after all my work to make her character sympathetic!) she seems disinterested in knowing me.

Possibly, I'm being unfair. I *have* noticed that once we determine what sort of person somebody is, we often absorb no further information.

Take my husband and me. As soon as Tadao decided I was clever, he saw evidence of it constantly. Even in matters of aeronautics, where I had no understanding at all, Tadao would attribute my displays of downright obtuseness to fine and deliberate irony.

There was an odd collateral effect. With Tadao, I *did* tend to be clever. Astonishing wit winged right off my tongue. Piquant observations popped straight out of thin air. So of course Tadao remained innocent of the fact that, in most other company, I was really quite ordinary.

What this might mean is that, though I can write about a more humane Chie, in real life I may begrudge her any traits beyond wry, blunt, opaque, and rejecting.

Chie may, in fact, be someone totally different! I pause and try to picture her. Hesitant? Vulnerable? Needing of others' acceptance?

But wry, blunt, opaque, and rejecting seem true.

A Trip to the Market

Two weeks after I arrived in Japan, Chie came to me in the moss garden.

For me it had been a tumultuous two weeks. Foremost, I was relieved that Chie seemed to accept me as Hanae's mother. Hanae and I were given a shared room. I planned Hanae's days. Even in front of Chie, we continued to talk in our old blend of Japanese and English.

Additionally, I was free to spend my time as I wanted. There was no trying to retrain me as samurai.

Perhaps Chie knew that it couldn't be done. As far as I know, there are no formal methods of teaching membership in social class. It's absorbed through daily family example. Beginning in the Meiji era, with its emphasis on a one-class society, many middle-class families began taking lessons in samurai kata—*kendo*, the way of the sword; *ikebana*, the way of the flower; *cha no yu*, the way of tea (I myself was sent for tea and poetry lessons)—but not one of us would ever be mistaken for samurai.

When we arrived in Japan, I initially busied myself showing Hanae all the things that I'd loved in my childhood. Each day, she and I would go walking through town, where I'd renew relationships with farmers, shopkeepers, and artisans. In Japan many traditional professions are inherited and I was amused to see that the class cutups with whom I'd gone to elementary school now were running their family businesses. As I introduced people to Hanae, as she politely bowed as I had instructed, these sober citizens were—in my mind's eye—still ear-waggling, eye-crossing fourth-graders.

I took Hanae on several trips to Kobe and once to nearby Osaka. In these glittering international cities, we received a kind of first-class service that, as a nonwhite in America, Hanae never had known. Yet of all the sightseeing we did, Hanae most liked seeing the stream where Naomi and I had searched for tadpoles, the cafe where Naomi and Akira had met. Things connected to her parents.

Chie never accompanied us. At the dinner table, she asked no questions about where we had gone or what we had done. I felt freedom in Chie's absence but it did make me miss my own mother. Had she been alive, my mama would have been there for every step: pushing us forward to her friends in proud display, smiling with me over Hanae's head with approval at every clever comment our little girl said. And though I explained to Hanae that her grandmother's distance was due to samurai kata—when Chie was a girl, samurai females were rarely allowed beyond estate walls—I didn't really believe it. Had Chie's mother, Most Honorable Mrs. Fuji, been alive—a venerable samurai if ever there was one—I knew that *she* would have come.

Midway through the second week, I began to run out of things to do. I was used to working hard, having a role—as student, daughter, worker, wife. Hanae would soon be starting school; how would I spend the blank days?

What did Chie do, I wondered, besides dressing beautifully, reading, and putting small cups of water and morsels of food on her family shrine?

Traditionally, samurai women wrote novels (noblewomen wrote novels and had love affairs). My I-story, therefore, seemed the perfect vehicle for transporting me into my new life.

In addition, I wanted to function as a housewife. It's an honorable profession to clean, cook, and shop. But Chie had maids, and in those days she had a cook. The only thing left to me was shopping.

And so, after all this indifference from Chie, I was surprised when she walked over to me in the moss garden.

"When are you going to market?"

It was closer to a demand than a question.

"Er. Day after tomorrow, I believe."

Chie turned on her heel.

"I'll be going, as well," she decreed.

During the day and a half between that moment and going to market, I pondered Chie's motivations. In my head, realism wrestled with hope.

Had Chie wanted to establish a relationship, wouldn't she have accompanied Hanae and me on our sightseeing? Maybe Chie was merely exercising a kind of quality appraisal, evaluating whether I was competent at shopping.

Market day dawned hot and restless. A typhoon was predicted to be heading our way. As shopkeepers eyed the strength of their shutters and housewives assessed the stock of their pantries, Chie summoned Ishigawa's taxi.

The jolly, balding driver—a village man familiar with all the gossip—beamed when he saw us together.

"Mother and daughter off to morning market. What a tender tradition!" he sighed.

By the time we arrived at the market, Mr. Ishigawa had stopped smiling. Fretful lines of concern creased his broad amiable face. In his rearview mirror, his eyes went back and forth from me in a cotton kimono to Chie all splendid in silk. Our cool silent ride had crushed all his cheerful reunion expectations.

Yet despite the plunges in barometric pressure and Mr. Ishigawa's mood, I still harbored some hope. As an aristocrat it was highly probable that Chie had never before been to the public market. She might intend reconciliation, I thought.

Clearly, the market was made for mothers and married daughters. Beneath the makeshift awnings, they were everywhere we turned. Laughing and whispering, discussing the freshness of the eggplant, the sweetness of the carrot, they strolled together arm in arm.

I studied those mothers and daughters. How effortlessly

they bantered! I tracked them as they moved among the stalls, from vegetables to fruits, from fruits to flowers. I eavesdropped, hoping to pick up conversational cues, fondling produce I had no intention of buying.

The mothers imparted wisdom in a casual way.

"The skin of the tangerine should feel thin and have fine pores like a beautiful woman."

"Poppies are better than camellia for the bridal bower. Poppies shed their petals one by one in a suggestive manner but the camellia bloom drops off all at once, in a disturbing act, like the victim of a beheading."

The daughters laughed and shared their small secrets.

"See this parsnip? How thick and shapeless? My husband has a mistress whose legs look no better."

Their conversations heartened me. There was nothing exceptional about them. The bond those mothers and daughters shared was concrete, day-to-day, specific.

Maybe I can do that, I thought.

Nervous yet deliberate, I paused at a fish display. I took a deep breath and wished that I hadn't.

The air hung heavy with fermenting fruit. Too sweet, too close, like the breath of an alcoholic.

Somewhere one of the fishes had gone bad.

"Look at the beautiful display!" I choked, sounding too breathless, too gushing.

I swept my arm to indicate the rows of glistening iridescence and, in so doing, accidentally brushed against Chie's hand.

She gasped and gagged. She recoiled as if touched by a leper.

"This is ridiculous," she snarled, wiping her hand against her brocade obi. "Let's find Ishigawa and go home!"

It's been about a week since I wrote about that last part, and in reading it back, I wonder. Maybe the biggest problem with the I-story is its terrible self-absorption. Take mine, for example. Have I even mentioned that there's a war brewing in China?

War bothers me, of course. As do flood, famine, disease. And in comparison, surely the concern of having an emotionally distant mother has absolutely no significance at all.

Yet the big issues seem too big, too completely out of control. Even if I could understand all the historic, economic, and psychological factors behind war, what possible good would it do?

So here's what I find myself contemplating. My family, my history.

Me.

My childhood was happy. Unlike Chie, Mama and Papa weren't from an ancient samurai line, but they were prosperous nonetheless. They were silk farmers benefited by Japan's plunge into international commerce, by the approach of the jazz age, by an era when around the world a new class of wealthy merchants clamored for cummerbunds and cravats, for dressing gowns and evening gowns, for hats and hosiery— for anything made of silk.

The silkworms lived in our attic loft, under the eaves of the high thatched roof. Season following season. There were tens of thousands of them, an ocean of bright green caterpillars, heads rearing like little sea horses, jaws moving in small sharp bites, bodies inching through tray after tray of minced mulberry leaves.

Naomi thought they were cute. She stroked their snowy

cocoons with reverent fingertips. She watched, enchanted, as they lay their eggs like minuscule mustard seeds, in perfectly symmetrical rows.

Of course she would find the worms charming. Naomi didn't have to sleep beneath them. I did. And in the strange inhuman roar of their endless eating, I heard something sinister. Something that, as a child, I couldn't name.

I can name it now. Now that I see Shanghai, carved and served to the West. Now that I see Manchuria, devoured by Japan and blithely renamed Manchukuo. It was greed I heard in the worms' moving mouths, the greed that arms many militias.

Now that I'm grown and can see the cruel satisfaction of conquering armies, I think maybe Naomi was right to admire the worms. They exercised restraint.

I never saw them cannibalize one another.

chapter eleven

MARCH 4, 1933

I read in the newspaper that scientists have installed a glass wall in a cow's stomach. The headline was *New! Visible Cow!*

There was an accompanying photograph. A cow stood happily munching while a group of men peered excitedly through a porthole into her inner workings.

It made me laugh: it was so silly. Our eager longing to know. A cow digests, it's a private act, we don't need to stand and see it.

But I can understand the impulse. There was a time, between her ages of one and three, when I could see straight into Hanae's brain. The portal was speech, her new use of words, and she narrated every thought. I miss that. I miss those days when I could look into Hanae's mind. When it was easy to be what she needed.

MARCH 12, 1933

See into Hanae's head? What an odd, voyeuristic desire! That's another problem with I-stories. Their authors spend too much time indoors, alone. It seems to me writers need something that gets them out in the world. Some type of *real* occupation.

I have a related story. When I was nine, my family and I spent a week at a seaside hot-springs resort. Our little hotel, nestled east in the hills, was of course made of paper and wood.

After midnight, on what was to be our last night, a mild earthquake tremor overturned a candle being used by a widowed father. Owner of a bicycle repair shop in the village of Itami, hard pressed to find time for a family vacation, he'd fallen asleep as he worked on his books.

I'll never forget this man's screaming as they struggled to drag him from the smoke and the fire.

He was so hysterical, it took us a while to understand.

Then comprehension came.

"MY THREE-YEAR-OLD SON IS IN THERE!"

And suddenly, fifteen dazed and sundry adults flew up—drawn together in strength and will—like a magnificent phoenix bird.

Women—with neither a shared word nor a false thought to modesty—ran down to a stream and then back again, tearing their soaking clothes from their backs as they came. Men—heroes armed with hissing kimonos—wrapped their faces and heads with the women's wet sashes and beat their way back into the flames.

Time stopped. The men disappeared.

Then came the cry.

"HE'S HERE!"

Later, as half-naked women treated mildly burned men, the toddler—who prior to the fire had wandered off in search of an outhouse with the sleepy obedience of a recently toilet-trained child—fell asleep in his father's arms. And as I looked around, I saw everyone laughing.

Of course, life can't be filled with such moments. We'd have to be stupid in order to wish it. Those rare times—when clocks stop, bodies blend, and boundaries all disappear—are meant to be conserved. Like passion at the end of a long, happy marriage, they are meant to sing both of life and of death.

Yet there are other moments, every day. Brimming with just as much beauty.

Though you have to be out in life to catch them.

Farmers find them in the rhythms of the seasons, in their bonds with the earth and the rain. Tadao felt them in the wind and the sky.

And parents? Ah, we're the luckiest ones. All the pain of childhood, all the boredom, all the magic. We live with it all the time.

Cow Gazing: A Glimpse into Hanae's Life

One day as she joins the flow of children into the school yard—the only custom-tailored sailor suit in a flood of homespun ikat kimonos—stringy, skinny, yet gravely pretty eleven-year-old Hanae catches sight of a white organdy pinafore.

With impure motives, a desire to be replaced as school scapegoat by someone in more ridiculous attire, she sneaks forward for a closer look.

"Shinoda, Hanae!"

She hears the bark of Headmaster Kido, the scrunch of his crepe-soled shoes on the gravel.

She straightens immediately.

"Sorry, sir! I forgot!"

Hanae trots back to the school yard gate. By the gate is a little shrine with a picture of the moat of the imperial palace. She offers it a little bow.

For Hanae, bowing to a picture of a moat is no great capitulation. It's something students are supposed to do whenever they pass the shrine, and in these days of creeping militarism (such acts were unheard of during my school years), Hanae does it unthinkingly. To her, it seems a polite but nonessential act, like hiding your teeth with your hand when you smile.

Once, however, Hanae was startled. While trying to retrieve a badminton birdie, a fourth-grader fell headfirst from a tree. As the teachers rushed her unconscious body toward Ishigawa's hastily summoned taxi, Hanae was surprised to see that they bothered to pause at the shrine. They stopped dead in their tracks and pushed the girl's lolling head down in a bow.

Now, Headmaster Kido ascends a small podium in the school's front yard. He stands there, slightly fat, prematurely balding.

"Children, decorum!"

The headmaster is part of a new phenomenon, one of the first generations of farm boys to take advantage of educational access and win a place at a prestigious, nationally funded college.

For a young man who has achieved so much, the headmaster is remarkably sour. Perhaps he is disappointed with having gone so far, only to find himself returned to a provincial elementary school.

"Decorum!" he repeats.

Hanae and her seventy-eight schoolmates start to snicker. Behind his back, the headmaster is known as Old Decorum.

He clears his throat.

"Know this, our subjects! Our imperial ancestors founded this empire on broad and eternal bases, on deeply planted virtues . . ,"

With half a mind, Hanae listens to the headmaster's recitation of the Imperial Rescript on Education.

"Be loyal toward parents, affectionate toward friends, kind toward those in need."

She stares at the headmaster's shoes.

Something about them disturbs her. Buttery black leather with thick crepe soles, his shoes are too beautiful—tailored for the vanity of a handsome man.

The speech ends. Hanae enters the frame building, exchanges her street shoes for slippers, and finds her fifth-grade classroom. It is designed to resemble a Western school; rows of desks face a blackboard, above which hangs a British-manufactured wall clock replete with Westminster chimes.

Yet this is most definitely not a Western school. The windows shine, the floorboards gleam, the kitchen is antiseptic—the source of all this sanitation being the children. There are no school janitors in Japan. After each of the many recesses—Japanese elementary schools have longer hours and shorter vacations than American schools but also more frequent periods of play—squealing students race through corridors like inverted Vs pushing floor-scrubbing cloths in their hands.

The point is not for the school to save money, but for the child to learn teamwork, self-discipline, and a certain Zen transcendence of social class. For after a childhood of merry menial labor, in adulthood it becomes difficult to disdain people performing such tasks.

Hanae, however, has proven impervious to such hopes of happy socialization. Hanae hates her Japanese school.

I suppose I should have seen it coming. Accustomed to the direct, matter-of-fact nature of American schools—where twenty-six alphabetic characters are arranged into clear and precise types of words, where sentences march forthrightly through linearly sequenced paragraphs—here Hanae contends with a written tradition that is extraordinarily rich and devilishly confounding.

Take the alphabet. By sixth grade Hanae must learn to read and write over one thousand characters (and in the upper grades, thousands more), some being Chinese ideograms, some representing Japanese phonetic sounds. Additionally, there are an infinite number of writing styles to be mastered: all those infernal rules of kata or form. The language of men, the language of women, the language between equals, the languages of subordinate to superior and vice versa, the language of newspapers, the language of poetry, the languages of traditional and modern prose.

In America, Hanae heard only simple, conversational, familial Japanese. *Do your homework. Quiet down. Be sure to use the bathroom before we leave.* She had no idea of the complexities the language had in store.

Though it isn't the complexity that defeats her. It's the obliqueness, a notion the Japanese call *yugen*. Hidden in every act of communication (indeed, in every act of life) should be a more profound, underlying meaning. Thus in Japan, a statement, a paragraph, an I-story can never proceed directly (like an American walkway leading straight to a front door). Instead, communication must pause and meander (like the pathway in a Japanese strolling garden), offering unexpected, seemingly unrelated, yet ultimately universal perspectives. In Japan words are meant to beckon, not inform.

Now, Hanae takes a seat in her classroom.

The white organdy pinafore comes in, looks around, and—to Hanae's horror—*deliberately* takes the seat next to hers.

"Don't sit there," Hanae hisses. "I have impetigo. You can catch it."

It's no accident that, in her haste to discourage, Hanae thinks first of a contagious disease. Hanae thinks conspicuousness is a contagion. Her classmates have just begun to ignore her oddities in dress and she doesn't want to be reinfected.

The pinafore rustles and smiles engagingly from beneath pageboy and bangs. "I'm Mari Miyata. You must be Hanae Shinoda."

Hanae tries to ignore this. Her brain searches for some curt, distancing remark.

"I recognized you immediately," continues Mari, "by your clothes." She grins, sharing a little joke of understatement. "You're famous in this town."

Hanae makes no comment.

"You're American," says Mari, providing information as if preparing to introduce Hanae to herself. "Your father sent you here."

Mari's tenacity is annoying, yet Hanae finds herself listening. Mari makes her sound like someone interesting, someone worth knowing. She speaks with enthusiasm, oblivious to the abandonment, the exile, the shame Hanae finds in her situation.

"I'm American too," Mari confides. "I was born in San Pedro, California. Father died when I was little. Mama keeps

141

house and translates for Miss Langley, an American lady; we all just arrived in Japan. Miss Langley teaches at the foreigners' school in Kobe and she's going to open an after-school *juku* for Japanese students right here in town."

She pauses with a little gasp and looks up with cheerful expectation.

Against her will, Hanae is beginning to find Mari's verbosity disarming. In five years, no one else has spoken to her with so many sequential sentences.

As she wonders what to do, she notices her classmates.

They're staring at the pinafore. Kimiko Takahashi, daughter of an up-and-coming import-export man, points at Mari and snickers.

Kimiko is Hanae's nemesis. Two years earlier, Hanae had invited her home after school.

I'd clapped my hands when Hanae said that Kimiko would be visiting—an act that made Hanae shudder. My enthusiasm was painful to see. I wanted, too much, for her to have friends.

Hanae remembers the day before Kimiko's visit, when I'd crafted dozens of colorful paper origami in the shapes of cheerful animals. By nightfall pink cranes hung from every high rafter; red frogs hopped across all the smooth floors. In the kitchen I'd laid out individual snack trays, and on each, an origami penguin stood stiff with anticipation.

Hanae knew my hopes were inflated. As we readied for bed she tried to forewarn.

"Kimiko's not all that playful."

I was too excited to hear.

"Maybe when Kimiko comes we can have a treasure hunt," I mused.

Hanae was lying on her futon. I was sitting on mine by her side.

She watched as I rhythmically kneaded her forearm, gently squeezing with distracted affection.

"You'll like treasure hunts, Ha-chan," I said, using her baby name. "Your mama and I used to play them."

I went on and on—about treasure hunts and tea parties and Naomi—until Hanae lost the heart to dissuade. Until she fell asleep and dreamed she was playing with her mother: a young girl who looked just like her.

The next day Hanae approached Kimiko.

"Are you still coming over?"

Oval faced and pretty, Kimiko looked around the school yard, trying to make certain no one would see her talking to Hanae.

"All right, but you leave first. I'll meet you."

Hanae walked home alone—wondering what insanity had prompted her to invite such a girl—and waited under the massive timbers of the high samurai gate.

When Kimiko arrived, Hanae led her past moss, rock, and water gardens.

Iridescent dragonflies hovered over enormous pink and white lotus blossoms; wisteria wept from their vines.

"This compound is so grand," Kimiko sighed. "It's everything they say."

She ran her tongue across her lips, as if looking at something delicious.

The gesture made Hanae startle. She thought of me, eagerly waiting with some culinary failure.

She winced. Maybe she could divert the disaster.

"My auntie has planned a snack, but if you like the grounds, I can show you them instead."

Kimiko's mind had been elsewhere.

"This land is so valuable—given by the regional lord to one of his favorite vassals. No one could come close to buying it today!"

Hanae heard the awe, as if Kimiko was reciting some sacred text. She saw Kimiko's face light with indecent rapture.

As they entered the elegant old house, Hanae brought Kimiko straight to Chie—a prompt introduction is the samurai way.

Chie was sitting at a low table in the reception room, her back to the art in the alcove, her eyes facing the door. Historically, this was a samurai's position of defensive welcome: granting guests an opportunity to enjoy a work of great art while retaining, for the host, a view of the entry. In this way the guests' soldiers could not creep, in unnoticed attack, through the door.

Hanae watched her grandmother study her nine-year-old guest—who in correct kata should have been admiring the scroll in the alcove. Instead, Kimiko was appraising Chie's kimono.

"Nishijin silk," Kimiko whispered as she eyed the subtle shell and wave pattern on Chie's dove gray kimono, "smoother than a baby's skin."

I bustled into the room, my face flushed with welcome, my movements awkward as I hurried to remove my soy-sauce-splattered apron.

Kimiko's hauteur returned.

"This must be Etsuko," Kimiko said, "raised outside of the House of Fuji."

Hanae flinched. Kimiko spoke as if she were an archaeologist excavating a royal tomb, assessing skeletons, establishing their rank and dismissing some as inconsequential.

I was undaunted. "Why not play stone, paper, scissors?" I smiled. "I'll be in the kitchen fixing a treat."

"The kitchen?" Kimiko had mouthed in silent astonishment. "Your aunt works in the kitchen?"

Hanae had meant to say something. An idea had flashed across her brain.

I should flatten Kimiko with the sheer authority of my voice. If someone was insulting Mama's auntie, she would've let them have it. Not in a mean way but angry and effective.

But Hanae did not speak. And in that moment, she found a cause for self-loathing.

Now Hanae hates the memory of her disappointment. How it rose like a rock, blocking her throat, cutting off her angry, effective words. She hates the memory of her vulnerability and her longing.

As horrid as Kimiko was, Hanae thinks, *I still wanted her to like me.*

"Hanae, are you all right?"

Two years after that visit, Hanae is startled to find Mari Miyata peering anxiously into her face.

"You look a little absent."

Hanae blinks a few times, clearing her mind.

Mari leans closer. "Maybe you should ask for a drink of water."

"WELL, MARI." In her determination to, this time, state her affiliation with the scorned, Hanae's voice comes so loud that Mari jumps.

Across the room, Kimiko Takahashi turns and stares.

"IT LOOKS LIKE WE'RE GOING TO BE FRIENDS."

Sweetened Black Beans

When Mari comes to visit, I go all out. I poach two eggs in a thick soup of sweetened black beans.

"Come and get it!" I gaily call. As if part of a coronation procession, I walk slowly. On a raised lacquer tray I balance two brimming bowls: one filmy yolk staring from each, like an enormous occluded eye.

With each step, the bloated yolks bobble grotesquely.

"*Itadakimasu*. Thank you for the food I'm receiving." In a normal voice, Mari says the standard polite phrase. She has yet to notice the contents of the bowls.

Then her eyes open wide.

"My . . . what a . . . surprise!"

Hanae holds her breath. She watches as I radiate pleasure.

"It isn't quite what I expected," I confess, "but I've given it a title nonetheless."

"What, Auntie?"

Hanae speaks from loyalty, not curiosity. She leans close, ready to shield me from any callous response.

She closes her eyes.

"Radiant Sun Bursting Through Dark Clouds of Misfortune."

Hanae hears Mari's delighted laughter and opens her eyes.

"Oh, Hanae," Mari wheezes, "how lucky to have such an auntie!"

chapter twelve

MARCH 28, 1933

I've been thinking about women writers: Lady Murasaki with her Prince Genji, Mary Shelley with her Frankenstein. I wonder if they found women's lives dull. It's quite possible their lives were dull. Privileged women, after all, frequently found themselves living as shut-ins.

Small wonder their imaginations so often turned gothic.

And I ask myself if being a woman has hampered my story. It has certainly influenced the kind of tale I can tell. Being a mother—where one's actions are reactive, contingent, inexorably linked to another being's; where one's universe is dazzling but small—makes it impossible to cast myself in anything remotely resembling the heroic model.

Yet in current literary fashion, if not heroic, your main character runs the risk of looking insipid. It makes an unpromising I-story: following a character who is seen as insipid through a world that is perceived as small.

This idea creates a question that bothers me. Must I write myself out of my plot? Hoping there's enough in my life to sustain a reader's skeptical interest, I start a list of actions I initiate in a typical day:

1. anticipate needs of Etsuko, Chie, neighbors, and servants
2. read moods of (see above)
3. cook and perform light housework
4. shop, take walks, think, write

I trail off in a rush of dismay.

I hardly ever speak!

This, I realize, makes for very thin dialogue. And even less "onstage" drama.

Please don't misunderstand me. I'm not saying motherhood lacks meaning. There's great dignity in the smallness of motherhood; we're essential in our contingency. And though we may not follow the Western model of the epic hero, we mothers *can* find a metaphor for our lives.

The metaphor is in the *kuroko*, the Kabuki theater stage assistant. You've heard of Kabuki—with its wildly theatrical actors, its gorgeous costumes, and spectacular scale. The kuroko are assistants who help the actors move through their elaborate dramas. Meant to provide unobtrusive assistance with props and costumes, kuroko try to remain in the wings. They huddle in half-kneeling posture, wearing black bags over their heads and bodies—the better to recede into both actors' and audience's preconscious mind.

Scurrying to arrange the trailing hems of heavy brocade kimonos, like an American mother repeatedly straightening her daughter's wedding train, the kuroko's role is to support the *real* players of life's dramas.

My Life as a Kuroko: An Overheard Scene Between Hanae and Mari

It's late morning.

In the room Hanae and I share for sleeping, March light slants through a crescent-shaped window. On a low table, tea steeps in a sixteenth-century Satsuma pot. A spider traverses a wall.

Hanae and Mari sprawl on the tatami. In recognition of Japan's withdrawal from the League of Nations, the girls' afternoon school lessons have been canceled.

"Don't you ever put your bedding away?" Mari gestures toward a scattering of cotton futon and buoyant silk quilting that is patterned with flower prints to match Hanae's name.

In keeping with samurai expectations about bedding, Hanae has many quilts. In summer, she uses a lightweight blue-and-white fawn-spot tie-dyed quilt patterned with iris, ocean waves, and fishing nets. In September, this is exchanged for an autumn quilt: a repeat-pattern silk of maple leaves and asters. During the winter, Hanae snuggles beneath white and purple patterns of snowflakes and early plum. And in spring, she switches to the quilt Mari is currently viewing: a stencil-dyed silk featuring sprays of multicolored blossoms against a background of cream and pink.

Hanae's quilts do not represent meaningless luxury. On the contrary—light and puffy, slippery and whispery, their astonishing loveliness is intended to teach. By sleeping with them in an artful room that in winter is drafty and icy and in summer is sultry and hot, Hanae is supposed to learn that life provides beauty and repose—even while demanding adaptation to conditions of severity.

The luxurious quilts and the austere room are part of

Hanae's samurai legacy. A paradoxical legacy due to conflicting court philosophies. For in Heian court life, which began in 794 and was similar to the spirit of Athens, there was a tradition of beauty, poetry, spirituality—an exquisite refinement in everyday life; and in Kamakuran court life, which began in 1185 and was similar to the spirit of Sparta, there was a demand for personal sacrifice and emotional austerity. It was the Kamakuran court that developed the code that coupled prohibition against shedding the blood of opponents of unequal strength or rank with a willingness to "receive arrows in your brow but never your back."

A samurai philosophy emerged from the blending of those two historical periods: beauty can be found within hardship; treachery can be disguised within pride. For as indicated in the samurai motto "Face nature and self—and learn," samurai were supposed to be vigilant against self-delusion. They were supposed to find—in the bounty and cruelty that occur out in nature—lessons about goodness and evil within.

Yet in a modern world, it is difficult to absorb wisdom through the soft whisperings of one's beautiful bedding. And despite the eloquently indirect lessons found in every aspect of her grandmother's elegant and austere house, Hanae has little affinity for a tradition that stresses awareness, self-correction, and—as the path to all that is worthy—*patience*.

Now, Hanae looks at her scattered quilts with nonchalance. "Auntie or Makiko, our new maid, will get it."

Mari shakes her head. "That's not nice," she says mildly. "Leaving work for others."

Hanae shrugs, displaying an attitude that has endeared her to none of our maids. Makiko—a dreamy seventeen-year-old, in hopeless love with the tofu maker's indifferent son—is the latest in a long line.

"Here, I'll help you," says Mari.

She stands and struggles with Hanae's thick futon, trying to fold it. She thinks of something and smiles.

"Remember," she quotes playfully from the Imperial Rescript on Education. "Bear yourself in modesty and moderation, extend your benevolence to all, advance public good, promote common interest . . ."

Hanae watches Mari's exertions without rising from her spot on the floor.

"What did you think of the assembly this morning?" she interrupts.

Mari stops working. "I don't know," she muses. "They say withdrawal from the League is a suitable protest, that Japan shouldn't be censured for promoting peace and prosperity in Manchukuo, but—"

"Must you always be so profound?" Hanae says with annoyance. "I was only asking what you thought of Old Decorum's unveiling. The white gloves, the striped pants and tails. I know it's done this way all over Japan, but isn't it a little *too* much?"

Hanae squares her shoulders and extends her chest in imitation of the headmaster.

"Children, decorum," she intones. "Bow flat on the floor as I pull this golden cord and slowly unveil a portrait of our Imperial Majesty.

"Please, children, do not glance at his divine form," she continues. "Do not raise your heads until you hear the drapery closing again."

Hanae pauses, her voice growing crafty. "Actually, I've observed his divine form quite closely. He's nowhere as handsome as his grandfather the Meiji emperor."

"Hanae! Don't say things like that! If anyone heard!"

151

Mari is silent for a moment.

"Well, I suppose you could always say that he was hanging right there, in the front of the room, and you just looked up a second too soon."

Hanae lifts her chin in defiance.

"It's no accident. I've studied him. Minutely. Whenever we have these kinds of assemblies." Her face takes on a look of cunning. "And you know, at some point or other, I've caught just about every other student sneaking a peek."

Mari begins to giggle.

"Including you, Miyata-san, Mari!"

Mari laughs aloud. Hanae looks faintly pleased.

Hanae stands. Together she and Mari fold Hanae's futon and quilt and try to stuff them inside the oshi-ire—a closet hidden behind a sliding paper panel decorated with an ink wash of grazing deer.

As soon as they remove their hands, however, the slippery silk quilt—like a living creature—begins a languid unfolding.

"Quick, slide the door shut," says Mari. "It's too luxurious, it won't lie flat."

They struggle with the door, with the relentless silken oozing. When finally successful, they fall on the floor with exhaustion.

After a moment, Mari speaks.

"Is that your mother?"

She points to a picture I've propped among ones of my parents and Tadao, as a makeshift shrine, on Naomi's wedding mirror.

"Yes."

Hanae studies the photograph. In it, eighteen-year-old Naomi Shinoda is seated on the edge of a brocade chair in an American photographer's studio. She's wearing a loosely belted, softly gathered tea-length dress with a rectangular "armistice" neckline.

"She's pretty," says Mari. "You look like her, you know."

Hanae goes over to the mirror and examines her mother, noting the angle of her chin, the position of her mouth.

She arranges her features in a similar pose. She frowns, dissatisfied with the effect.

"Here, like this," says Mari, who has followed Hanae to the mirror.

She pulls Hanae's braided hair backward and up, achieving the look of a softly knotted chignon. "Yes, that's it."

Hanae does something unusual. She smiles.

She leans a little closer to the mirror.

"Wait, hold still!" cries Mari as the glossy braids shift and slip from her hands. "I can't keep it this way. Do you have any hairpins?"

Hanae reaches down, opens a drawer on the mirror's base, and rummages for a hairpin. She finds a stack of old letters.

The Letters

September 1919

Dearest Elder Sister Etsuko,

How fortunate you are to live in the land of opportunity. In my literary discussion group, Western Masterpieces in Translation, we've been examining the American Constitution. What an interesting document!

I am enjoying the Western Masterpieces group. Initially, I was suspicious. After all, world literature and Western philosophies were topics we'd covered in girls' upper level.

"Why should I go?" I demanded of Mother.

"To stimulate your mind."

"Not for one more accomplishment to list on my dossier for marriage?"

Mother almost smiled.

"Perhaps that too."

I was living a life of exquisite uselessness. My tutors—in poetry, tea, and flowers—came and went like elegant court physicians, in crested *haori* jackets and rustling *hakama* trousers. It was mostly as an excuse to get out of the house that I joined Western Masterpieces in Translation.

But Etsuko-san, it is thrilling! We sit in the European cafes of Kobe growing dizzy on coffee and ideas. Spurred by my Masterpieces group, I have started English language lessons with some missionary women. I have not told Mother but my hope is, one day, to visit you in Seattle.

With love, your sister,

Naomi

November 1919

Dearest Elder Sister,

I've met a man.

One afternoon in my Western Masterpieces group, Toshiro Tanaka was blustering.

"Emma Bovary, Anna Karenina, these heroines are intended as lessons. A woman may have passions, but in the end, she should conform to social expectation."

He sat smugly in his black university uniform, like a policeman giving a presentation at grade school.

"Nonsense!" I cried with melodrama. "The tragedy is

not the expansiveness in a woman's dreams but the re-strictiveness in society's soul!"

Toshiro looked cross.

"My dear Miss Fuji," he said, "I can imagine how, as a woman, you may identify with these foolish, ill-fated characters. However, I am a literature major at Osaka University; if I'm not mistaken, you are not? And as such, I believe I am in a better position to know about an author's intention."

He looked at the group with self-certainty.

"It's a concept called determinism. No matter how we struggle, the environment determines our fate. And in this world . . ."

He looked directly at me.

"A *defiant* woman is a *dead* woman."

"Hardy was a determinist, not Flaubert!" I retorted. I must admit, I meant to show off. "And since when does your university training supersede all other opinion? I thought the purpose of education was to open minds, not seal prejudices!"

We went back and forth.

He arguing for the sport, I for something uncertain yet precious.

Although several other women were in the group, no one spoke up for me, and by the time we disbanded, I was impatient and angry.

"Excuse me, Miss Fuji."

What a nuisance! It was the man I thought of as the Quiet One.

"I agreed with what you said today, Miss Fuji."

He shuffled his feet. He took a deep breath and started speaking as if reading from a card.

155

"In fact, over the past weeks I've been thinking, why do we always study the lives of women through the minds of men? And I've located some other authors."

He finished in a rush and thrust forward two translations.

"Virginia Woolf and Colette?"

"I'd be honored if you would read these."

His voice was calmer now, earnest, and involved in its message.

"They're very different women from very different backgrounds, but it seems to me they tell us quite clearly that a woman's life must be her own."

I looked at him with amusement. "Well, Mr. . . ."

"Shinoda. Akira Shinoda."

He seemed to be addressing his shoes.

"You appear quite articulate, Mr. Shinoda. Why didn't you help me out back there? Say a word or two to Mr. Tanaka?"

Akira Shinoda looked up in surprise. He looked straight in my eyes—giving me a jolt of confusion as I realized how handsome he was—and smiled.

"You don't need any assistance, Miss Fuji."

With love,

Naomi

February 1920

Dearest Etsuko-san,

Akira and I want to marry. Mother is opposed.

Last night Akira came to ask permission and she, who listened willingly to ideas of women's suffrage, was shocked that I'd selected my own husband.

I tried to reason.

"Self-determination, unalienable rights," she ranted. "Who put these ideas in your head?"

"You did! You're the one who encouraged my education."

But Mother was stubborn.

"Foolish girl. Reading about America doesn't change the fact that you live in Japan. Western ideas are fine to quote but you must live by Japanese standards."

"And what would Japanese standards say?"

"Obligation is more important than freedom."

"They're wrong!" I cried. "Give me liberty or give me death!"

Mother looked at me with amusement, as if I was a naughty child. "Perhaps it's my fault," she said, giving me hope. But she simply was setting the stage for a witty rejoinder.

"Do not teach your children to speak," she quoted, "unless prepared to hear them argue."

With determination, your sister,

Naomi

Hanae's Reaction

Hanae is concentrating so hard that her eyeballs dry out from not blinking.

"Should we be reading these?" Mari whispers.

"Of course. They're from my mother. I have a right to know."

Flushed and flustered, daring and slightly guilty, Hanae and Mari read to the end of the letters.

"Your mother was such a fighter, so beautiful and so

strong." Mari's voice is envious. "You're lucky, Ha-chan. I wish I had such a mother."

"Don't be stupid, Mari. You mother, at least, is alive. And she's raised you by herself, taken you back and forth across continents, taught you English . . ."

Mari brightens.

"You're right," she says with pride. "Mama is like your Aunt Etsuko. Gentle yet strong."

Hanae looks surprised and annoyed. She's never thought of me as strong.

"But back to these letters," says Mari. She gestures to the stack with excitement. "They're so romantic!"

"They are not!" Hanae shouts.

Mari's sudden shallowness makes Hanae angry.

Hanae likes to think that Mari needs her, that Hanae's suspicious nature is the gravity that keeps Mari glued to the ground. But in truth it is Hanae who is dependent. Mari has a gift; she accepts herself and the world as she sees them. She has little need for pretension or myth. And although Hanae is a competitive girl, one who hates to admit disadvantage, she likes Mari's clear-sightedness. It makes the fact of Mari's friendship, of her finding Hanae likable, more valuable and astounding.

They rarely argue. A casual observer would say that Hanae has all the power in the relationship. She's the difficult one. But Mari isn't acquiescent. She has a gentle firmness that keeps Hanae under control, a restraint Hanae finds reassuring and maddening.

"My parents were never involved in anything as soft-headed as romance!" Hanae piously snorts.

Mari waits with patience.

"My parents were *fiercely devoted to their convictions*." Hanae

158

emphasizes every word. "My mother was a scholar. You saw how she was always reading those masterpieces. Before I was born, she read to me every night."

To her horror, Hanae hears her voice tremble and break. To cover it up, she speaks faster. "My mother wasn't just some pretty, silly girl. She was smart. She could memorize anything. She knew things nobody else knew. Things way ahead of her time, like the importance of the American Constitution and the advantages of Western underwear."

Mari looks at her with an infuriating kind of sympathy but Hanae cannot stop herself.

"My mother was a true samurai. She would have given her life for the things that she loved. Without a moment's hesitation. And she loved me, maybe even more than she loved my father. 'Cause she chose me over him. She died so that I could be born."

She pauses, panting. Her breath comes in short, shuddering sobs.

"It's all right to cry, Ha-chan."

"I'm not crying!"

Hanae takes a deep breath and exhales with great dignity. "I'm overexercised, that's all."

Mari tactfully busies herself, opening other drawers on the mirror's vanity.

"Hanae, look!" she calls. "Here's another letter!"

Naomi's Letter

August 1920
My Dearest Elder Sister,

Akira has sailed for America. Our arrangements are secret but later I plan to join him.

As the time approaches, I realize I will miss Mother. Sometimes I cry and when she sees my puffy eyes—believing I have given him up—she thinks I am mourning Akira.

"Shi kata ga nai; there is nothing that can be done." Her voice is curt, yet, considerate of my lovelorn heart, she's more gentle than she's ever been.

"Come," she demands, trying to distract me. "Practice your English conversation."

Appreciative of her attempts at peacemaking, I go along.

"How good it is to see you again," I say, offering my handshake.

Mother gingerly extends her wrist.

Imagining that I'm in Seattle greeting you and Akira, I grow animated.

"How kind of you to come to meet me. How glad I am to be here!"

I pump her hand. I hug her, smacking a loud kiss on her cheek.

"Naomi!"

Mother is aghast. For a woman raised in her era, kissing is an unfathomable Western barbarism, like letting a dog lick your face.

"That's what they do in America, Mama!"

I laugh. At the sound, Mother's face floods with maternal relief; and I am sickened by my deception.

When I leave she will feel betrayed.

And an odd thing has happened. The closer I come to seizing my American future, the more I cherish my Japanese past. I've put away my opera gramophone disks;

I listen to Japanese flute and okoto. I've stopped going to coffeehouses; I practice the tea ceremony instead.

Last night I dreamed I was composing ancient court poetry. I woke and wrote down my poem:

Hardened in dispute over marriage, the old parents
    hear the news.
A baby!
Plum-blossom confetti spins over the thawing pond.

With love and hope,
Naomi

MARCH 31, 1933

I know more of this story, more than Hanae knows. Naomi told me, back in Seattle, during our daily post office walks.

Why did she tell me this? I wonder. Was it to help me understand "our" mother? Probably not. I have noticed that when people tell their own stories, often it has less to do with wanting to communicate an idea to another than with clarifying an emotion for themselves. Or when the subject of the story is beloved and missing, as a way to make them here and alive.

I think that was Naomi's reason. Happy as she was with Akira and the possibilities of life in America, she missed her mother. Talking about Chie brought her into Naomi's daily routine.

I could understand that. I missed my mother. From Japan I'd brought recipes for dishes we'd eaten every night and that had bored me to tears in my childhood. Mama had written them

out for me in her very own hand. I used those recipes repeatedly, even though I soon knew them by heart. Particularly after she died. After the telegram came, saying both Mama and
Papa had died of influenza—*influenza*, some small sneeze usually so harmless in a land where bathing is sacred and people
rarely touch hands—I used her recipe cards every night. The
simple reason being that when I read them, I heard Mama's
voice in gentle instruction. And when I ate the food, it was as
if I was still at her table.

Perhaps this is why I try to know Chie. Having lost Mama
and Papa—and Tadao too—having let them slip from my life
without notice, in a moment when my back had been turned,
perhaps I've learned that time can be short. Or maybe it's em-
pathy I've learned. An understanding of how simply, with no
premeditation or malice, one could let all her loves slip away.

The Marriage Proposal

Chie disowned Naomi. Why? Most likely, Chie couldn't tell
you. Now it must seem the most stupid of things.

Akira came directly, breaking all tradition. Was that it? Had
he followed form—had he asked his mother to speak to his
father to approach a go-between—would Chie have been
more receptive?

He came on a winter's eve. He pounded on the door while
a cold rain beat on the shuttered veranda, so at first Chie
thought him only the wind. The maid knew better. Chie heard
her soft scuttling footsteps, the creak of the door. Then the
maid brought a calling card to the drawing room, for Chie.

Chie was reluctant to go to her guest; perhaps she was feeling too cozy. She and Naomi were reading at a low table set atop a charcoal brazier. A thick quilt spread over the sides of the table so their legs were tucked inside with the heat.

"Who is it at this hour, in this weather?" Chie questioned as she picked the name card off the maid's lacquer tray.

"Shinoda, Akira. Kobe Dental College," she read.

Naomi recognized the name. Chie heard a soft intake of air.

"I think you should go," said Naomi.

Akira was waiting in the entry. He was in his early twenties, slim and serious, wearing the black military-style uniform of a student. As he bowed—his hands hanging straight down, a black cap in one, a yellow oil-paper umbrella in the other— Chie glanced beyond him. In the glistening surface of the courtyard's rain-drenched paving stones, she saw his reflection like a dark double.

"Madame," said Akira, "forgive my disruption, but I come with a matter of urgency."

His voice was soft, refined. He straightened and stole a deferential peek at her face.

In the dim light his eyes shone with sincerity. Chie felt herself starting to like him.

"Come inside, get out of this nasty night. Surely your business can wait for a moment or two."

"I don't want to trouble you. Normally I would approach you more properly but I've received word of a position. I've an opportunity to go to America, as dentist for Seattle's Japanese community."

"Congratulations," Chie said with amusement. "That *is* an opportunity, I'm sure. But how am I involved?"

Even noting Naomi's breathless reaction to the name card, Chie had no idea. Akira's message, delivered like a formal speech, filled her with maternal amusement. You know how children speak so earnestly, so hurriedly, so endearingly about things that have no importance in an adult's mind? That's how she viewed him, as a child.

It was how she viewed Naomi. Even though Naomi was eighteen and training endlessly in the arts needed to make a good marriage, Chie had made no effort to find her a husband.

Akira blushed.

"Depending on your response, I may stay in Japan. I've come to ask for Naomi's hand."

Suddenly Chie felt the dampness of the night.

"Does Naomi know anything of your . . . ambitions?"

"We have an understanding. Please don't judge my candidacy by the unseemliness of this proposal. I ask directly because the use of a go-between takes much time. Either method comes down to the same thing: a matter of parental approval. If you give your consent, I become Naomi's yoshi. We'll live in the House of Fuji. Without your consent, I must go to America, to secure a new home for my bride."

Eager to make his point, he'd been looking her full in the face. Abruptly, his voice turned gentle. "I see I've startled you. My humble apologies. I'll take no more of your evening. My address is on my card. If you don't wish to contact me, I'll reapproach you in two week's time. Until then, good night."

He bowed and left. Taking her ease, with effortless grace, like a cat making off with a fish.

"Mother?" Chie heard Naomi's low voice and turned from the door. "He has asked you?"

The sight of Naomi's clear eyes, her dark brows gave Chie strength. Maybe his hopes were preposterous.

"Where did you meet such a fellow? Imagine! He thinks he

can marry the Fuji heir and take her to America all in the snap of his fingers!'"

Chie waited for Naomi's ripe laughter.

Naomi was silent. She stood a full half minute looking straight into Chie's eyes. Finally, she spoke. "I met him at my literary meeting."

Naomi turned to go back into the house, then stopped.

"Mother."

"Yes?"

"I mean to have him."

After a few days, Chie came around. She tried to be flexible. She hired a private investigator.

"If the report on Akira is good," Chie told Naomi, "I'll accept him as your yoshi."

Naomi was elated. She deliberately displayed a formality she thought would be pleasing. "Thank you," she said, bowing low to her mother, "for acknowledging the seriousness of my intentions."

When the maid brought the report, Naomi recognized the investigator's red signature seal.

"May I be present as you read it?"

They sat in a patch of weak winter sun, overlooking the azalea-and-sand garden.

Chie hesitated. She glanced at the garden. White sand was raked in the pattern of swirling waves. Planted close together in one undulating line, the azaleas were pruned for winter into the soft rounded shape of a sea serpent.

She looked in the eyes of her daughter, so full of excitement and trust, and she wanted to be gracious.

"Yes," she incautiously replied.

As she scanned the report, Chie felt hopeful. Good grades,

solid references. Competition-level skill in something called three-cushion billiards. The second son of an established Osaka family.

But what was this? He'd missed being the first son by only eight minutes?

Chie frowned. She glanced up in surprise. "Akira is a twin?"

Naomi flushed. She raised her chin in defense.

"Such a small thing can hardly be a problem."

Chie looked down, confused. She couldn't let Naomi wander, defenseless, into an ill-conceived marriage.

She read further. "An identical twin."

"Surely you don't believe those old superstitions!"

"We must take everything into consideration."

"That identical twins are a public shame? That they're evidence of their parents' lascivious nature? How can you consider such nonsense!"

"Even nonsense, if believed by others, can cause serious social damage." Chie heard her voice rising.

Naomi began to panic. Her eyes grew wild and wide. "Akira is a fine man. If being a twin is a concern that would stop this marriage, then no one will ever meet your approval."

For the first time in her life, Naomi shouted.

"Give me your answer! Say yes, Mother! Say yes!"

Suddenly Chie was scared. Her throat closed. She couldn't breathe.

Marriage is a matter of gravity. How could Chie consent unless she was positive, absolutely certain, that she could see the full course of Naomi's marital life stretching forward without any shadows?

"Now, Mother! Say yes!"

"No!" Chie cried. "I'm not ready!"

Had Chie thought the matter over for a day or two, would her answer have changed?

Probably not. Although she didn't believe the superstition about twins, she did have a sense of foreboding.

Most old families treated identical twins unequally: the firstborn as the recognized child, the second-born as an unworthy impostor.

In Chie's experience, second-born twins grew to be responsible and upstanding but with a sense of goodness that could be almost obsessive. Sometimes she detected something unhealthy about their achievements, as if they were motivated by an internal hunger.

Additionally, the investigator's report revealed an ominous secret.

The House of Shinoda was in debt. Akira's older brother was a debaucher with astonishing bills at teahouses and gambling dens. Like Akira, he was a handsome boy, but he'd been raised as a pampered darling. It was rumored that an apprentice geisha, in the Osaka willow district, had recently aborted his child.

"No!" Chie had cried when Naomi pushed. "No marriage! Akira is a twin, obligated to pay his older brother's debts. The House of Shinoda scrambles to cover multiple shames. You won't be sacrificed to recover their honor!"

"Instead I'll be sacrificed to maintain yours?"

Like Chie, Naomi was shouting.

Maybe Chie had indulged Naomi. Always, she had allowed Naomi to speak her mind. Perhaps—seeing so many girls trapped within their gilded cages of appearances and tradition—Chie had enjoyed the span of Naomi's wings, the arc of her ambitions.

Naomi often had argued, telling Chie about freedom and individual rights, challenging her with notions gleaned from Western Masterpieces in Translation. Chie had liked the play of ideas, pretending to be unpersuaded just to see the clever ways her daughter could move her mind. Always, she'd enjoyed Naomi's pleasure: her lively voice, her flushed complexion.

But now Naomi faced Chie with voice shaking, skin ashen. The difference frightened Chie and in her fear she forgot her strategy.

"He's a man with debts, you're a girl with money," Chie said coldly. "Don't flatter yourself that he loves you."

Naomi recoiled, as if she had been struck. When she spoke her voice was chilling and quiet.

"Let's talk about this sensibly. Cruelty is unbecoming."

"Silence! I'm your mother!"

"I must speak. I will marry Akira. You can't stop me."

"Silence!"

"Would you have silence between us?"

"I will not have a disobedient child!"

"I know it's hard to see me as grown." Naomi's voice softened, grew wistful, almost sad.

"Since Father's death you've clung to my girlhood. I'll be your child forever, but you must allow me to be other things as well. I don't mean to abandon you. If you give your approval, Akira can be my yoshi. He and I would be like you and Father, living here in the Fuji compound."

At the mention of Kan, Chie felt the ache of loss like the throb of a poorly mended bone. She'd been a widow for only three years.

She fought her sorrow with anger.

"Akira as yoshi? Don't make me laugh. Akira is nothing but

a castoff from a dissolute family. How dare you compare him with your father!"

"Be careful how you speak," Naomi cautioned. Her voice turned cool. "I cannot allow you to use Akira for the displacement of your frustrations."

Chie's chest grew tight. Who can tolerate a condescending child? Her heart shriveled and hardened, growing opaque and impenetrable like ice around a blue flame of rage.

"I cannot allow your displacement," Chie mocked in a prissy tone. Her voice dropped, menacingly. "My how lofty you've become." She sneered. "Now you are Herr Sigmund Freud? Be careful how I speak? Listen to me, Miss Western Masterpieces in Translation, be careful how *you* speak. Never mention this matter again!"

"Why must we be like this?" Naomi began to cry. "Why can't you just share my joy?"

Her tears gave Chie an advantage.

"You are mentioning it," she crooned.

Chie heard the cruelty in her voice, the dark tip of sadism. She left it unchecked. This was the moment to break Naomi's will.

"Please, Mother, let's not do this."

"Speak again and I'll disown you!"

The sun had slipped sideways. Shadows of the bare branches of bordering trees stretched across Naomi's cheek, like marks from the clawing of nails.

Naomi stopped crying. She lowered her head with defeated exhaustion.

"As you wish," she finally replied.

chapter thirteen

OCTOBER 10, 1933

I've noticed there is less and less I in this I-story. I've become hardly present at all. "Where *are* you?" a reader might ask, for they certainly would have recognized as self-protective blather my talk of Kabuki theater kuroko and the notion that mothers must be inactive.

The answer is somewhat embarrassing, given my dreams of growing forthright and bold. I've been hiding in housework.

The question is one that Chie might ask. It seems she forever is circling me, staring down, frowning with appraisal.

Consider this morning.

There I was diligently—if mindlessly—scraping food wrappings, separating tinfoil from its waxed paper backing, when Chie came to the kitchen's high threshold.

Sixty-four years old, impeccably dressed in a midnight blue silk kimono with persimmon-colored obi, she towered two feet above, distant and critical. "What are you doing?" she demanded. Light glared off her elegant cheekbones, off her classically formed Fuji nose.

"Separating foil from paper!" My voice emerged gratingly chirpy.

Internally I winced. In Chie's presence I tend to act cheerful and dull witted. Like an anxious job applicant on an interview that is going badly.

"And what do you propose to do with it?"

Perhaps to reassure myself, I smoothed my simple azure cotton kimono over my still-slender hips—at thirty-six I was vain about the fact that I weighed no more than when I first met Tadao.

"I, uhm, I don't know. A citizens' committee came to the house saying tinfoil needs to be salvaged."

"I see," Chie continued. "So you'll hoard it for months, supplement it with foil found in gutters, and turn it over to the authorities when you have a clump the size of a quail's egg?"

"Something like that." I made myself smile.

Chie snorted with derision. "Why? So your name can appear in the evening paper as a housewife helping to build Japan's army?"

"It's for Hanae," I explained, hating my note of pleading.

"Tinfoil?"

"The collection of it." I forced some dignity into my voice. "All the mothers are doing it. Hanae will look bad if ours is the only house not participating."

"An expanding illegal war and you're concerned about looking bad?"

Chie's voice, all superior ethical reason, drifted down like recrimination from a god.

"She's just a little girl." I sulked. "What's wrong with wanting her to have friends?"

Chie cast me a glance of disgust. "Are you stupid? She has

Mari. Those other friends—the ones you plan to purchase with tinfoil—aren't worth their price."

My voice came out with the clipped enunciation of the injured. "I don't think trying to be a good mother is stupid."

Chie looked at me with exasperation.

"What's this good mother thing?" she said with annoyance. "Did I say anything about wanting you to stop being a good mother?"

She sank shockingly down to her knees on the bare floorboards. She leaned over and looked straight in my eyes.

"Tell me," she invited in a voice stripped of its harshness, "what would you like Hanae to learn from your example?"

Her gentleness caught me off guard. I couldn't remember Chie ever seeking my opinion.

"I don't know," I stammered. "Patience, I suppose, devotion, kindness . . ."

Chie appeared to be listening.

I grew bolder. "An eye for beauty, a sense of humor . . ."

With mounting enthusiasm I trotted out for display my sizable collection of maternal ambitions.

"Integrity?" Chie inquired encouragingly. "Commitment? Valor?"

"Oh yes!" I was almost rhapsodic.

"Then stop saving tinfoil."

Abruptly Chie stood.

"You have big dreams, Etsuko," she said from aloft. "Why be so blandly compliant?"

OCTOBER 10, 1933

It's late at night and I'm still thinking about the tinfoil.

It seems whenever I'm in Chie's presence, I feel myself

disappear. She stands there—the House of Fuji, Keeper of Morality, Mother of Us All—and my concerns seem silly and small.

Still, the longer I live with Chie, the more like her I wish I could be. I am a woman who edits her opinion, who avoids confrontation. Chie is a woman who *acts*.

And there's the way she speaks: dismissive yet somehow demanding. Almost as if, like my husband, Tadao, she sees in me something more.

It's very confusing.

I'm never certain if I'm being under- or *over*estimated.

Chie Fuji: Daughter of the Samurai

Chie wasn't always against the army. The House of Fuji is samurai. Hers was a military family for twenty-two generations. Then, when Chie turned ten, the samurai disappeared. One imperial edict, and a thousand years of tradition vanished.

On the evening they read the horseback-delivered edict, Chie's parents leapt from the dinner table. They hurried to the bonsai garden. Their departure, though neither angry nor anxious, was sudden and odd. Chie felt unsettled. Her baby sister, Kazuko, a fat and cheerful fourteen-month-old infant, began to whimper, then cry.

"Shh," crooned Machi, Chie's seven-year-old sister.

Machi struggled to lift the baby from the tatami and held her in her lap. "Tell me, where is baby's nose?"

"Nose," echoed little Kazuko. She patted her own nose and chortled.

"What does it all mean?" Machi whispered to Chie.

Now that her parents had left the room, Machi shifted her

weight to a more comfortable position: sideways, off her knees and her heels.

Momentarily unbalanced, the baby seized one of Machi's pigtails for stability. She began to chew on its end.

"She's getting a new tooth!" exclaimed Machi, forgetting the uncertainty of her family's future in her delight over her baby sister's progress.

"Shh," Chie hissed.

Chie dipped her forefinger in a hot cup of tea, rose from the table, and tiptoed to the rice paper shoji.

"What are you doing?" asked Machi.

Chie pressed her moistened fingertip into the shoji paper. It melted like cotton candy.

"Making a peephole."

Chie peered through. Standing about twelve feet away, her beautiful twenty-nine-year-old mother snipped at the wisteria arbor; her thirty-five-year-old father wound copper wire around the limbs of a tiny cypress.

Their movements were calm and measured. Only the incongruity of the act with the hour—the growing darkness, the certain swarming of mosquitoes—indicated that something was wrong.

"What's happening?" whispered Machi.

"Mother is gathering ikebana material. Father is training bonsai."

"Calm the body and the mind will follow," said Machi, quoting one of their mother's many maxims.

Machi's insight into the motivation for their parents' behavior irritated Chie. Machi was the younger sister. She had no place being wiser than Chie.

Their father spoke.

"They've offered me a lump-sum settlement. Four hundred years of family honor for a lump-sum compensation."

Chie's father had been a warrior: a lieutenant general at age twenty-four. With two swords—a long one for battle, a short one for ritual suicide in the event of failure in battle—he had fought the shogun's army in the Imperial Restoration War. During one close battle he had sent word to Chie's mother— at eighteen, pregnant with a child she later miscarried—that should he be captured, she was to place the servants into other households. Then before hiding herself in a peasant family, she was—with her own hands—to set fire to their three-hundred-year-old family house.

Now, Chie's mother said nothing. Snip, snip went her shears. Her role was to listen in the dark.

"This has been coming," said Chie's father. "I can't pretend surprise. Samurai have always provided a check, limiting imperial power. Small wonder, now that we've helped him regain power, Emperor Meiji wants to be rid of us. To draft farm boys, instead. They're more malleable as soldiers."

Her father laughed: a mirthless bark.

"But the training they've planned! No philosophy, no history, just tactics and drills. How will they learn the courage of restraint? What will happen to reason and honor?"

He sighed. "Others are saying they'll take the money and become shopkeepers. Shopkeepers! The class we've scorned for producing nothing, for making profit from the work of others."

Chie's mother spoke with graceful indirection. "How lovely it is in the garden tonight. How soothing the smell of the earth."

Her husband chuckled. "So you think we should be landowner farmers, eh?" He paused. "Yes. I'd thought so myself. Farming is honest work."

Both continued with their own task, silently, side by side.

"I am a man of middle years."

There was an intimacy in her father's voice that Chie had never heard.

"As yoshi, my duty was to smoothly carry you and this line. You have been the best of wives. Yet now, you too must start over."

He dropped to his knees and Chie flinched with surprise—a man never bowed lower than a woman. He pressed his face flat in the dirt before her.

"Forgive me."

"*Stop!*" Heedless of her silken kimono, Chie's mother threw herself on the ground, grabbing her husband by the shoulder, yanking him upright. "*Never* apologize for our life together!"

The heat of their ardor was shocking. Chie reeled away, falling back from the screen, realizing she was witnessing something she wanted, something only adults can know.

That's when she began to understand all the village gossip. That her parents' love was erotic. The scandal had less to do with the fact that her parents had only girls than with the fact that Chie's father—himself adopted from a cousin family to carry on the Fuji name—had refused to take a mistress. He valued his wife over his duty to produce a male heir.

Maybe that's why Chie finds my passivity so galling. What she saw that night taught her a lesson. A legacy she expects me to share.

Pay the price.

But always choose passion.

176

chapter fourteen

Why, I've been asking myself, does the I-story persist? With all its problems of plot and pacing and action, with its limitations in settings and characters, with its disquieting tinge of narcissism—why does everyone in Japan want to write one?

And I think I've developed an answer. The I-story is life.

Of course I don't mean it's actual life. It's not as if people in Japan are omniscient or that we go around speaking in multiple voices—but we *do* live our lives through our fictions.

I once heard an American say, "Poker is life." I asked my husband what this could possibly mean. Tadao's interpretation was that, in America, certain skills were useful to own. Evaluating competitors, taking chances, engaging in a certain amount of strategic playacting. This particular game of cards honed them all.

Poker, my husband explained, was a way Americans practiced for life, went through life, escaped from life.

Perhaps for many Japanese, autobiographical fiction writing is life. We are a people expected to complement, to harmonize, to anticipate one another's needs. All without a single spoken clue.

Here's an example. Two six-year-olds—let me call them Hiro and Toshi—meet in school. They become friends and visit each other's house. Their mothers always give them a snack. One day Toshi stops by Hiro's house. Hiro's mother welcomes him and the two boys play. After the customary interval, Hiro's mother brings in a tray. On it is a platter of beautifully arranged sliced peaches. The mother smiles as she sets down the food. But the guest, Toshi, feels a surge of discomfort. Isn't June a little early for peaches? He takes one bite, makes his excuses, and rushes away.

And the reason is that he's in training to be a writer. Observing detail, understanding irony, interpreting motivation. Hiro knows that acts are symbolic. The hard sour fruit offered too soon in its season carries a message. He has made an error in the timing of his visit. He has inconvenienced the family.

This is the Japanese way. Cogitating on inner meaning. Revealing ourselves and perceiving others through carefully crafted scenes.

Writing our endless I-stories.

NOVEMBER 19, 1933

I wasn't always so careful, so one-step-removed from life. I married Tadao, didn't I? I met a man who loved the wind and we sailed off across the sea.

There's a joke about Seattle. That living there is like loving a beautiful woman who always seems to be suffering from a cold. You know there is something special, you catch glimpses of dazzling vivacity, but mostly there's her dull, muffled affect, her constant confounded drizzle.

Tadao and I arrived on one of Seattle's healthier days: a

clear blue July morning when we awoke to find ourselves turning south from the Strait of Juan de Fuca. Overnight the flat gray sea that had been our perpetual backdrop had been whisked away—as if by an irritable set director who found it unsuitable for the dramatic theme of Arrival in the New World—and replaced by a vision of rounded evergreen islets rising from fertile clear waters.

America, I found, looked reassuringly like any scene along Japan's Inland Sea. With one delectable difference. As if representative of our vaulting immigrant dreams, beyond the soft hills—on the horizons both east and west—rose magnificent snowcapped mountains.

Tadao and I looked at each other and laughed. He hugged me right there in public. And as we released each other, a beautiful black-and-white whale leapt playfully out of the water.

Tadao and I soon learned that the land we'd first sighted was, in fact, Canada. But these little details didn't deter us. The euphoria carried us through the repugnant sights and smells of canneries along Elliott Bay, the confusing hostility of Immigration, with its rough searches and cagey questions, the fun and funny unfamiliarity with my own body as I tried to walk in my newly purchased American dress and high heels; and when—at last—we tumbled out onto the street, it didn't surprise us to be met by a young Buddhist priest.

Who better to welcome us to a new, blessed state?

That young priest, Reverend Mitsui, himself a recent immigrant and pastor of Seattle Buddhist Church, gave us a booklet that he had painstakingly authored. Written in both Japanese *and* English (perhaps to begin our process of acculturation) and entitled THIS IS AMERICA!, it was a kind of taxonomy.

179

Japanese education, impressed by the science of Darwinism, tends to produce graduates who are besotted by systems of classification. From memory, I can reproduce part of its premise.

Japanese Culture	American Culture
Focus on the group	Focus on the individual
Emphasis on duties and obligation	Emphasis on rights and freedom
Cooperation, harmony, restraint	Competition, drive, spontaneity
Patience and receptivity valued	Action and activity valued
Success comes from self-discipline	Success comes from seizing opportunity

There was more. Tips about postal rates and money exchange. A calendar of church-sponsored events and excursions: a Fourth of July picnic, a late-July Obon festival, an August moon-viewing/haiku-writing trip to the Oregon shore.

I recognized the effort our young spiritual leader had put into producing THIS IS AMERICA! and I took it as an enlightenment guide. An eightfold path to Americanization.

The fact that, in English, the title was completely capitalized seemed an underscoring of its importance, an empathic endorsement from above. If I could think more for myself; if I could be more active, competitive, and driving; if I could leap into life's stream and seize opportunities (I pictured myself here as a sort of samurai angler), I'd have all the skills needed to pass the American test.

Then Tadao died.

Almost as if drowning with him, I became dreamy and diffuse. Disengaged from actual life.

I began looking for portents and omens. I read through

THIS IS AMERICA! and suddenly the capitalization seemed cautionary, meant more in warning—as in *THESE ARE POISONOUS WOODLAND FUNGI!*—than in exultation.

About that time I began thumbing through catalogues from Sears Roebuck and Montgomery Ward. They required less energy than actual reading. Like the priest's taxonomy, which I began to see was probably written in response to a crisis of his own, the catalogues imposed a soothing order. They provided a neat narrative about acquiring meaning in life.

That was the key word. Acquire. From underwear to outdoor wear to housewares. From houses to farm and garden equipment. Everything in life—from next to your skin out to the fence between you and your neighbor—could be conveniently and confidentially mailed.

I liked that. It seemed an affirmation for the isolated, interior kind of life that I was leading.

It was a dangerous way of living as well. One where caution could harden to cynicism and disappointment decay into despair. You have to be careful with self-retreat, I'm convinced. It can become a form of self-violence.

Necessity saved me. The bracing prospect of poverty drove me to Hotel Samurai Gardens, back to the world of people and work.

Please don't misinterpret me. I'm not saying dreaminess is a bad quality.

In fact it's considered a beloved national trait. A sprinkling of dreaminess and a dash of perception are believed to be the recipe for haiku.

But haiku—and here's the beauty of the form—forces you to be structured and brief. Two lines of dreaminess followed by the jolt of awakening. The awakening wrapped in mystery and surprise.

My problem is I can get lost in diffusion, and that I do it deliberately. Hiding among ambiguities, wading through complexities, lost in an admiring fog.

That isn't haiku; it's sleepwalking.

And therein lies the purpose of human connections. They're jarring.

They demand you pay attention to life.

That's why I'm glad Hanae has found Mari. We all need to be rescued sometimes, from the recesses of our too clever minds.

And there's something I like in Mari's mentor, Miss Langley.

Misplaced, unedited, undaunted: she reminds me of Tadao. Someone to pull Hanae into immediate, uncertain life.

chapter fifteen

DECEMBER 23, 1933

Hanae Assesses Miss Langley

Hanae's first impression of Miss Evelyn Langley—employer of Mari's mother—was of a long face bending close to her ear.

"HA-NAH-AY! SO-NICE-TO-MEET-YOU!" it shrieked in excruciating well-enunciated English. "WOULD-YOU-LIKE-TO-COME-TO-MY-AFTER-SCHOOL-JUKU?"

In the beginning Miss Langley spoke to everyone that way. As if she thought she were speaking Japanese.

Hanae thought her a fool.

"What kind of language teacher," she stated with her preadolescent acid perception, "thinks *volume* substitutes for *vocabulary?*"

And what kind of student would enroll?

Hanae, for one. But to her mind, only out of loyalty and disgust.

Initially Mari was the lone pupil, and being the daughter of Miss Langley's employee, Mari's tuition was waived. How exactly, Hanae wondered, is this woman going to meet her payroll?

But it turned out Miss Langley wasn't just shouting in English. She was taking language lessons from Mari's mother and also shouting in elementary Japanese.

This led to a phenomenon that Hanae finds amazing.

Practically all the village has taken to Miss Langley. People find her willingness to be pupil—to cheerfully engage in humiliating displays of public awkwardness—to be an endearing demonstration of character.

It's an old Japanese principle: Honor those with the courage to learn.

A result of this odd admiration being five fidgeting boys who sit every weekday at five with Mari and Hanae in Goro's General Store.

It's hardly an impressive schoolhouse, a general store rented during dinner hour each day. Like all the narrow, two-story, dark wooden buildings in this village, the store looks just as it did at the close of the nineteenth century. At the front are shutters, closed only at night, and behind them latticework sliding doors.

Inside, the store is designed and operated like general stores all over Japan. A central earthen path, about ten feet wide, runs back to the family quarters. On the left side of this earthen walkway is an upper shop: a broad platform about three feet high, bare but for tatami flooring. The upper shop is where fabrics, abacuses, flower vases, and better household items can be brought for display. To the right of the earthen path is the lower shop: a similarly barren tatami platform from which wooden wash tubs, bamboo laundry poles, and similar mundane objects are sold. Because of the lesser nature of its wares, this platform is one foot lower than the upper shop.

Following general-store kata, shoeless customers kneel on the matting and describe their desires, as the shopkeeper scurries (trying to keep his head lower than the customers') to and from an upstairs storeroom accessible from rear family quarters.

Yet each weekday at dusk, when Miss Langley uses Goro's as a classroom, all the general-store form disappears. Standing at the back of the earthen floor area, Miss Langley writes on a portable chalkboard while her seven pupils crowd the tatami of the upper shop. A democratic woman, Miss Langley would rather cram her students together than to seat some in the lower shop.

Crowding is also more comfortable in winter in the unheated shop. An American, Miss Langley sees little value in the notion that willingness to transcend physical discomfort is a prerequisite for learning. Her attitude conflicts with ancient samurai training, which demanded that a child's longest lessons take place—with a straight back, on a hard floor, in an unheated room—on the coldest day of the winter. And as more and more resources are being diverted to military expenses in China, this traditional attitude is returning. The cozy, cheerful classrooms of my youth are colder now; broken playground equipment goes unrepaired.

Sitting in Goro's General Store, wearing her mother's woolen underwear and father's sailor suit and heavy pea jacket, Hanae doesn't notice the cold. Though her breath hangs visibly and her classmates huddle, the only element of the environment to attract her attention is the annoying unassertiveness of the room.

Hanae hates the architectural principles of Japan. Accustomed to American construction, in which every room shouts its true function—bedroom, laundry room, music room—Hanae finds traditional Japanese architecture impossibly passive. Spread a futon and a reception room becomes a bedroom. Depending on whether a low table is used to support a book or to serve a meal, a space becomes either a study or dining room.

In their determination to preserve flexibility and serve receptivity, Japanese rooms are like Japanese language, in which subject and predicate often fall at the end of a long string of qualifying phrases. Thus a person, place, or thing and its action can always be changed as the sentence moves along, depending on the listener's reactions. For example, "This hot summer evening, beautiful fireflies are" can be shifted to "This hot summer evening, annoying mosquitoes are," should the speaker detect a swatting, not-in-the-mood-to-appreciate-nature attitude in the listener.

To American-born Hanae, this all seems intolerably wishy-washy.

I can understand her contempt. Like a cat's arching and puffing and hissing, cynicism often arises when we face something that makes us feel small. Indeed, often the very thing that first triggered our attraction later comes to repel us. So that Americans—first drawn by Japan's emphasis on beauty and harmony, by its appreciation of paradox in everyday life— soon find the country less mysteriously beckoning than deliberately obfuscating.

I know the feeling. Lured to America by its reputation for encouraging self-definition, I was intimidated by the sheer scope of its self-assertion.

Objects were more assertive than I.

In America, lights glared, teakettles shrieked, silverware not only clattered but also *dictated* my action. "Use me for *salad*," demanded one style of fork; "use me for *dessert*," ordered a practically identical other.

To me, it seemed a perversion of nature. In Japan, rooms, objects, and language had waited—flexible and ambiguous— to take up any function I required.

Similarly, Americans—usually so comfortable with freedom and choice—often feel irritatingly inadequate when faced with Japanese belongings and rooms. They seem *too* adaptable, *too* open to the user's imagination. So that any attempt to assign objects a singular function makes Americans suddenly feel as if they're failing some sneaky creativity test.

On this particular day, as Hanae sits in Goro's store, she is bored. Miss Langley's instruction is more earnest than lively. Additionally, because Hanae is already fluent in English, there is little for her to do.

Except to examine Miss Langley. Tall, gangling, thirtyish, she strikes Hanae as a clumsy woman—always blundering into places she doesn't belong—who is mostly a magnet for lint.

Hanae has to be careful around Mari, though.

Once Hanae called Miss Langley "Miss Gangly" and Mari gave her a look similar to what you'd give a puppy who has proved to be poorly trained.

But it didn't deter Hanae, who figures her job, in their friendship, is to keep Mari from cloying.

Not that Hanae has anything against humility or sweetness. In others, Hanae finds humility appropriate and sweetness nice. It's *anxiety* she finds annoying; and Miss Langley seems anxious to please.

Take this moment, for example. Gingerly, as if fearful of being bitten, Miss Langley is distributing cookies.

"FIG-NEW-TONS," she explains.

Hanae rolls her eyes.

"How patronizing," she hisses at Mari.

"She knows the boys are hungry," whispers Mari. "She's trying to be kind."

Hanae is skeptical. *If Miss Langley understood hunger,* she thinks to herself, *she'd feed the boys nourishing food.* Hanae shakes her head. At best Miss Langley seems awfully inept.

As Hanae studies her, Miss Langley begins blushing in splotches. "My brother sends them," she blurts.

The children look at her without comprehension.

"The cookies," she explains with awkwardness. "Our family's from Newton, Massachusetts, and he started it as a joke. As a way to help my homesickness."

The five boys, strangely swollen in well-patched layers of winter kimonos, blink blankly at her revelation.

"NEW-TONE," they politely parrot.

But Hanae understands homesickness; she startles like an accidental voyeur.

Suddenly she pictures Miss Langley: hunched like a fugitive in the dark, overhandling a cookie, taking too long with each bite. She's trying to extract, from some small grainy sweetness, a comfort she'll never replace.

SHREE!

A siren screams from the local police box.

Hanae snaps from her reverie.

"*Omedeto!*" shout the boys, jumping to their feet, knocking one another over in a scramble to leap from upper store directly into split-toed sandals and crowd to the front door.

"*Omedeto!*" Congratulations!

Across the narrow road, customers of the public bath—half naked, pink, and steaming—peer out from their doorway.

"What sex?" the bathers call.

"A boy!" shouts wiry, beaming, middle-aged Goro, bursting with the accompanying blare of a radio from family quarters in the rear of the store. "A baby crown prince is born!"

The Children's Parade

Suddenly the snow comes. Fat flakes swirling sideways through the darkening sky, blanketing thatched roofs, temple tiles, mountains deep with bamboo and pine.

And soon after, the minstrels. Streaming from the entertainment districts of every Japanese city, fanning across the snowy countryside with the sirens and the tolling bells. Dressed like ancient court musicians, sending skyward the sounds of *shamisen* and *shakuhachi*.

After nine years of marriage and four disappointing daughters, the imperial line is secured for the 125th generation.

Miss Langley's students hear them. In the deepening dusk, they watch the town's children tumble from their doors, following the lutes and bamboo pipes, forming a long line, lugging the sleeping babies and reluctant livestock they're supposed to be minding at home.

Miss Langley, too, is watching. Animation lights her face. She laughs aloud.

"The musicians are magic pipers; the children enchanted mice!"

She surprises her students.

"Let's join them!"

Let's. The students look at one another in slow astonishment. Their bashful teacher intends to join a parade?

Miss Langley pulls floppy rubber boots over her sturdy shoes. The jolly procession has transformed her.

"Come on!" she hoots to her gaping class. "Come on or I'm gonna beat you!"

Then they're out the door, trailing and singing. "A baby! A baby!" Over and over. Their wonder warming the winter night.

Hanae hobbles behind. Despite her mother's woolen underwear, she's cold. She looks at Miss Langley—her face flushed with joyful immediacy, the only nonminstrel adult in this children's procession—and feels a kind of hatred.

"What's she doing?" Hanae mutters to Mari. "She looks stupid; people will laugh. Can't she tell she doesn't belong?"

"Be generous," Mari says mildly. "You just hate her because she reminds you of us."

The children weave through the village, past barren rice paddies whose harvest has long since been consumed as food, wine, rope, candy, paper, paste, walls, flooring, and even— when burned—black pottery glaze.

A long wavering line, the procession turns upward following the forest path.

At one point it pauses. Candles are distributed and lit. Neighbor to neighbor, like a necklace being strung through the night.

At hilltop it stops at a simple wood shrine. Candles flicker in silence.

Below stretches the sea: a dark curve edged with the lights of a town.

Thump.

Snow slides from a drooping pine.

Miss Langley turns to her students. "Thank you," she whispers. "Thank you for letting me join in such beauty."

Snowflakes fall on her eyelashes.

Mari smiles at Miss Langley. "Now you're a part of Japan."

Their words rise in vaporous wisps.

Standing beside her teacher, Hanae stares. Miss Langley actually looks pretty.

Hanae feels a shiver of loneliness; maybe it's she who doesn't belong.

The musicians begin to chant.

> May the baby prince come into his reign in an era of
>   enlightenment and peace.

Their voices echo once and are absorbed in the snowy stillness.

Miss Langley takes Hanae's hand.

DECEMBER 30, 1933

Recently I discovered my first gray hair. At thirty-six, I was caught unprepared; I suddenly recalled all my young girl dreams. I had wanted to fall rapturously in love *and* to find my own special self. Was it true that I would never know another lover? That I'd never display any particular distinction?

In addition, though I knew Hanae—at twelve, caught between defiance and insecurity—needed an ally, I was unable to serve in that function.

If the task of early adolescence is to break bonds with Mother, then what comfort can the object of your ambivalence give?

Whenever I tried to cast Hanae a look of affection or sympathy (for she was so obviously miserable, as well as annoying, in her isolation), whenever I tried to catch just a glimpse of her beloved face, she would squirm with extreme discomfort.

"What are you looking at?" she would demand with suspicion.

Hanae Gains an Ally

After the birth of the baby crown prince, Hanae began to like Miss Langley.

Suddenly less a teacher than a generous playmate, Miss Langley took them on field trips to the foreigners' market and treated them to tiny wax soda-pop-shaped bottles filled with colored sugar water. Bottles that, when empty, Hiro Saba comically would thrust under his upper lip, like fangs, and into his ears.

One Sunday Miss Langley took the class to the harbor, where a San Francisco freighter was docked. After a brief, yet to the children embarrassingly unladylike, dock-to-deck shouted encounter, Miss Langley wrangled an invitation to come on board and tour.

Two good-natured middle-aged seamen led the way, one of whose English was delivered with such an unintelligible slur that skinny, earnest Kenji Moritomi whispered to Miss Langley: did she think he'd once suffered a stroke?

Miss Langley laughed when she heard Kenji's question. "Mr. Reynolds," she called, "my students are curious about your regional accent!"

The big, balding, yet still crimson-haired man grinned and gargled a word that clearly started with G but rapidly decayed into a series of small lapping sounds. A word Miss Langley later translated, while pointing out its location in a big book of maps, as the city name Galveston.

And though she still thought Miss Langley wore dumpy dresses, after a couple of these novel adventures Hanae found herself admiring her teacher's remarkably loud, honking laugh.

It seemed the class had developed esprit de corps.

Then—shortly before the new year, when women were scrubbing their houses, and men were settling their business obligations, and even the youngest child was deciding what to carry forward or leave behind in the coming year—Hanae found herself waiting in Goro's store.

It was fifteen minutes after the hour and Kenji Moritomi had yet to appear.

"That's odd," worried Miss Langley. "Kenji is always on time."

Hanae stifled a snicker.

Kenji wasn't just punctual. A model of responsibility, he was something of a teacher's pet.

Miss Langley opened the door. She leaned this way and that, bending so far that her dress rode up, revealing her slip at midcalf.

"There he is!"

Her voice rose and blew down the street.

"Don't run, Kenji. You might fall!"

But Kenji kept right on running.

He tore into the building, forcing Miss Langley far back in the room.

"Kenji, what is it?!"

Kenji's face was purple; his mouth opened and closed like a dying fish.

He hurled his books to the floor.

"What's wrong?" repeated Miss Langley. She reached toward him with concern.

Kenji pulled away. Tears of shame and rage welled in his eyes.

"Foreigner!" he screamed. "Subversive!"

He turned and ran out the door.

After a few stunned moments, the students tried to make it all right.

"Kenji doesn't mean it," they told Miss Langley. "His parents don't either. His father is postmaster, a government servant. Maybe he's getting pressured at work."

But two days later Tomo Yamaguchi didn't come.

And the day after, Hiro Saba.

DECEMBER 31, 1933

I blame the boys' withdrawal from Miss Langley's juku on the Tokyo earthquake of 1923. Not entirely or directly, of course, but to me it seems a significant factor.

Perhaps, though, I should first explain my ideas about medieval cities.

I have read that medieval cities, both West and East, were built at the foot of some aristocratic symbol. Located high above some not particularly provident place, a castle or cathedral (or later, a university) would provide the organization and force—the *fear*—required to keep commoners cultivating food and supplies.

Look at London and Paris and Tokyo.

Yet modern cities are different. Formed around some natural feature—the desert oasis, the accessible harbor—its sacred ground is the market. And with this secularization often came democratization, as residents—from distant places, with disparate histories, talents, and beliefs—converged, traded, and communicated, not ruler-to-subject but face-to-face.

These modern cities created a sense of vitality *and* a great deal of social change. Consider New York, with its melting-pot ethos, or Osaka, with its merchant-king families, its elite courtesans, actors, and restaurateurs. In a country where merchants had historically been relegated to the lowest class and where actors and courtesans—grouped with itinerants, butchers, and grave diggers as "unclassified" people—had fared even more poorly, Osaka turned class upside down.

What's more, a great many medieval cities now have turned modern (such as London and Paris and Tokyo), bursting forth from their feudal molds, flash flooding outward along riverbanks, railway beds, and telephone lines to create systems of commerce and information exchange.

It makes traditionalists very uneasy.

And so, when an earthquake leveled the old city of Tokyo, all were anxious to see what would rise in its place. It took seven years, filled with aesthetic argument and architectural bidding, until in 1930 the emperor opened a Festival Celebrating the Completion of Tokyo's Restoration.

Restoration it was not. Although total restorations with their strangely ghostlike constructions—familiar but sterile: too clean, too structurally improved, yet spiritually withered—are not always what one would desire. And in the case of old Tokyo—hundreds of square miles of wood and paper, where fire could consume tens of thousands of buildings in only a few hours—restoration would have been impossible anyway.

Yet this new Tokyo shocked traditional people. Tokyo—unveiled, promoted, photographed, and displayed to the nation—looked nothing like its old self, or at least like the old Tokyo of sentimental memory.

The new Tokyo was a jumble of architectural styles: Edwardian, Venetian, Beaux Arts, Bauhaus, and even some Old Tokyo. All molded in pale concrete.

I liked the newsreels I saw of the new city.

Unlike Kyoto, Tokyo has never been a city of architectural distinction or visual beauty. And for the past fifty years, its struggles to modernize have been thwarted by lack of space. Now, at least, roads are broader, bridges more plentiful. Only five bridges had spanned the Sumida River at the time of the great quake: all with wooden roadbeds that burned before the eyes of the fleeing citizenry and contributed to more deaths from drowning than from the earthquake itself.

A subway roars under this new city.

And against this shining albeit undistinguished new backdrop, all the changes that have been occurring—incrementally, almost invisibly—now stand out sudden and stark. Vending machines multiply in the halls outside government offices. "Stick girls"—female gigolos who go up to men and adhere to their arms like a walking stick—stalk at noon on Tokyo's grand boulevard, the Ginza.

Compounding the insult, hedonistic young Osaka has sent an arrow into the heart of old Tokyo by erecting, near the western terminal points of the Osaka-to-Tokyo railway, huge Osaka-style department stores.

These department stores are nothing new to the people of Kobe. Living close to Osaka and having a sizable international population, we've adapted many of Osaka's worldly ways. Indeed, as a young woman, I had worked at such a department store. It was an exciting place, where customers retained their shoes and—instead of kneeling on tatami while a shopkeeper slipped back and forth to a storeroom to retrieve familiar goods—roamed freely through glittering displays, where every counter held never before imagined but now keenly desired items.

These department stores understand human nature. Despite a long tradition of hiring only shop boys in dry goods stores, young shop girls are the rule. Like the new traditions of female bus conductors and gas pump girls, department store girls have been instituted both to appeal to men and to make public settings feel more familiar to women.

Starting late last year, by store regulations, these department store girls wear Western dresses (the stores have given the girls an extra clothing allowance). More important, they are required to wear Western underwear. The reason being that, during the end-of-year shopping season, Christmas tree lights started a fire in an eight-story department store. Thirteen shop girls—not wearing Western underwear—died when modesty forced them to hold their kimonos together with one hand, leaving each with only one hand to descend tricky rope ladders.

The fire triggered massive lingerie sales. It was a public safety cause that the newspapers leeringly championed. Mothers flocked to department stores to buy underpants for themselves and their daughters. One survey showed that within months, every girl zipping down the sliding boards at Tokyo's Ueno Park was wearing Western underwear.

Additionally, once an underwear-seeking mother had stepped into a big department store—with its galleries, gardens, restaurants, lecture halls, and at several sites even a rooftop zoo—she became a regular customer.

Indeed, the stores are so alluring that the traditional word for wife, *okusan*, or "honorable person remaining within the house," has become a misnomer.

Suddenly even wives from the finest old families find it essential to do their own shopping. And if some are squeamish about mixing with common people, little services—free delivery, door-to-door bus service—provide a soothing touch.

These department stores have triggered social revolution. Once women had experienced a tiring day of shopping and had refreshed themselves in the department store dining room—once they had traversed the traditional line, which held that, for ladies, spending the day in public and eating away from home were improper—then women were seen everywhere.

Now women are meeting for lunch in restaurants where it is permissible not only to retain one's shoes but even to eat wearing one's topcoat and *hat*.

These little etiquette slips have led to breaches far greater.

One wealthy middle-aged society wife, whose husband pays the rent and bills of a popular Tokyo courtesan, has become infamous for openly taking (for it is the "openly," not the "taking," that has caused the scandal) a talented young Kabuki actor as her lover.

Yet all this might have gone on—even in traditional

Tokyo—just as merrily as it had during the Taisho Democracy had it not been for one other result of the 1923 great Tokyo earthquake.

Widespread financial panic.

What had begun as a reasonable national response to a natural disaster—limited debt moratorium—was extended, and extended until in 1927 the finance minister committed an act of greedy stupidity. To improve the standing of another bank —in which he held interests—he announced that the Watanabe Bank would be bankrupt in just a few hours. The panic that ensued was phenomenal, ruining not only the Watanabe (and the bank the minister had sought to strengthen) but bank after bank all over the land.

In the subsequent six years, thousands of businessmen have committed suicide. Farmers—already suffering from the loss of the silk market due to the American financial depression and now dependent on the rice trade—have been destroyed by two years of harsh weather and competition from Japan's forays into colonialism: Korea and Taiwan.

The repercussions have been tragic. As a response to crushing family debts, loyal farm sons have emigrated to Brazil and Peru, where they quickly die from tropical fevers. Their deaths leave no children at home, for their sisters have been sold to houses of prostitution.

In the face of such reversals of fortune, Japan has become marked by a kind of frenzied hedonistic despair. Where not long ago people flocked to cafes and milk bars to read literary works and discuss topics like women's emancipation, now there is a new focus at cafes and cabarets.

Eroguro nansensu. From the English "erotic, grotesque nonsense."

So that whenever you go to the city, handbills and posters assault you. *See the* (seminude, if the poster's illustration is to be believed) *Woman Who Smokes Through Her Navel!*

Of course, fewer men are drawn by the grotesque than by the erotic; and cities are filled with dingy clubs where, for the price of a drink, loosely clad hostesses will sit at your table, leaning against you as they light your cigarette, engaging in conversations of double entendre. For men of more limited means, there are tea shops where conventionally attired pretty young waitresses will, after bringing your order, sit silently under your gaze, blushing with modest anguish.

When people can't recognize their present and are scared to imagine their future, a kind of nihilist fever takes hold. It has infected even the children. Not long ago two university student lovers, facing parental disapproval, committed suicide at a picturesque mountainside site. Their story was made into a popular song and a movie entitled *Love Consummated in Heaven.* Soon after, a young girl threw herself into a volcano. Now dramatic death—twenty young couples on the same mountain, almost a *thousand* (four fifths of them boys) in the same volcano—has become an adolescent trend.

Whatever happened to the sweet youth fashions of just a few years ago, like mastering the Philippine Islands invention, the yo-yo?

In such an atmosphere—where a sensational press, prevented from reporting anything substantial by the Peace Preservation Law of 1925, makes it seem that even the most cherished child is heir only to death in some horrible manner—parts of society seem to have gone mad.

Young army officers, the sons of impoverished farmers, enraged over the inequities of capitalism (city people have suffered significantly less from the depression), crusade against internationalism and democracy. Frequently they murder the men they feel have failed them. Indeed, last year, during a highly publicized visit by Charlie Chaplin, the army assassinated the prime minister. He was the third prime minister to be assassinated since 1919. On the afternoon of the murder, Charlie Chaplin had been scheduled to visit the famous sumo wrestling stables with the prime minister's son, who, of course, canceled. Perhaps seeing the assassination as too commonplace to warrant great inconvenience, Mr. Chaplin went anyway.

Mr. Chaplin's nonchalance was mirrored by the Japanese public, which increasingly believes the country could benefit from a strong military hand. As newsreel audiences watch the imperial army march triumphantly across the Chinese plain, as they hear explanations of how broader territories will lead to new markets, more and more boys have begun to wonder, *Why not join a glorious war?*

chapter sixteen

FEBRUARY 2, 1934

New Year's Morning

On January 1, I woke early and performed the first ritual for the first day in a new year. I went to the courtyard and took a long sip of ice-cold springwater.

So pure and simple, it was a tradition I loved: a reminder of what is essential.

By the time I'd finished preparing the day's auspicious foods—*ozoni* soup, sweet beans, extra-long noodles for extra-long life—Hanae was up and dressed. Long and slender at twelve years old, she prowled around the kitchen stealing loud, slurping samples.

"Not bad."

She looked outside, at the darkening sky. "Freezing rain. Think it'll start while we're at the shrine?" She returned to her perusal of the kitchen. "What's this?"

She pointed to a slightly charred broiled fish arranged rippled-fashion on a skewer.

I was pleased.

"Luck for your upper level entrance exams. See the way I've arranged the grated cabbage? Like swirling eddies? Doesn't it look like it's leaping upstream!"

"Oh, Auntie." Hanae shook her head with pitying condescension.

Suddenly, like a great Kabuki actor in an astonishing costume, Chie appeared at the threshold.

"Well?"

She turned slowly to exhibit her kimono.

"It's beautiful!" Hanae gasped.

Against a purple hem of heavy silk damask, chrysanthemum and winter paulownia were artfully rendered.

"It's sunset, isn't it?" Hanae observed. "Those angled strokes of gold on the petals."

I glanced at Hanae with surprise, as pleased with her aesthetic astuteness as I was stunned by Chie's aesthetic audacity.

Chrysanthemum and paulownia are the imperial flowers.

Hanae studied the fabric.

"Isn't that real gold foil?"

"It isn't tinfoil."

Chie shot me a significant stare.

Who could miss it? The kimono was an editorial against hoarding metal.

"Does it have a name?" Hanae inquired. "A kimono this beautiful should have a name."

"Dying Sun. I had it commissioned."

"You mean like Rising Sun?" breathed Hanae. "To signify Japan?"

She laughed aloud. She clapped her hands.

"Oh, Obaa-san, how exquisitely wicked!"

I felt a flash of jealousy.

Forgotten in the kitchen was my artistic statement.

I looked at the fish.

Meant as a symbol of triumph, its skin had begun to shrivel and sweat. Like an old man coming down with a cold.

Dressed like three totally unrelated people—Chie in her aristocratic antiwar costume, me in my staunchly ordinary indigo kimono yet fashionably modern chin-length (for this occasion, marcelled) hair, Hanae in her foreign-made pea jacket and sailor suit—we joined our neighbors on the hillside path up to the shrine.

New Year is a time of celebration more than reverence. After dedicating December to house cleaning and the final payment of bills, everyone is glad to start over. My papa used to laughingly tell stories of how, red with embarrassment about the brazenness of his bill-collecting task, he would approach the homes of silk weavers to whom he'd extended credit—only to see them slipping out the back door. So that the entire month of December—as everyone in town scurried to and fro, seeking and avoiding payments—he rarely saw any of our neighbors. When New Year's Day with its absolution of debts finally came, folks who'd been hiding from him came sauntering out, shouting, "Congratulations on the New Year!" and bowing with sheepish relief. Papa was so glad to see them again, he couldn't help grinning and shouting his "Congratulations!" right back.

As they had when I was a girl, vendors lined the path to the shrine. From tiny portable booths with striped red-and-white awnings, they sold food, toys, and lucky amulets.

Young fathers in their best clothes—their anxious wives hovering with a blanket tuck here, a chin dab there—proudly toted autumn-born babies.

Chie bought Hanae some bright paper streamers.

"*Omedeto*. Congratulations on the New Year!"

Approaching was another odd-looking trio: Miss Langley in strange rubber galoshes and a mended coat with a collar of world-weary weasel, Mari in a pristine princess-style American coat, Mari's mother in festive kimono.

We split off in pairs. While Chie and Mari's mother paused to adjust each other's obis, Miss Langley and I strolled on together.

Watching Hanae and Mari as they ran farther up the path, I reminisced.

"This is one of my favorite holidays." Even in my careful English, my words brimmed with sentiment. "Reaffirming relationships, recommitting to dreams . . ."

Miss Langley interrupted with a little sidelong look. A blend of curiosity and surprise.

"I think it's rather sad."

Now I was surprised.

"Every New Year's, I'm told," she continued, "everyone looks slightly more shabby."

Shabby? Miss Langley cared about shabby? I glanced at her clothes. Once they were top quality.

I imagined her upper-middle-class family. Despairing over the fate of their Mount Holyoke–educated daughter, sending tasteful outfits—doomed to disrepair and ill matching by their oblivious recipient—from one Christian outpost to another.

"Don't you agree?" prodded Miss Langley.

I shook myself back to the moment. I examined the New Year's celebrants.

Our village farmers, as suppliers for the city's tables, were doing financially better than many. Yet at the vendor stalls,

I saw skinny children eyeing food more wistfully than toys.

"It's this depression." I clicked my tongue sadly. "There's hunger all over the world."

"It's not just the depression." Miss Langley studied me with an odd intensity and began rummaging through her coat. "Japan's spending her money preparing for war."

She pulled a scrap of paper out of her left pocket.

"I saw this ad. I was going to go but it seems my plans will be changing."

Quickly she tucked the scrap into my kimono sleeve.

"Here, you go for me."

"What is it?" I scrambled through my sleeve, past tissues and coin purse, searching for the paper.

"Women meeting to oppose the army."

"Forgive me"—I searched more frantically—"but I'm really not the suitable . . ."

"Happy New Year, ladies!"

Walking downhill, returning from the shrine, was Mr. Kido, Hanae's headmaster. With him—heads swiveling in sudden panic, eyes darting furtively in search of escape—were Postmaster and Mrs. Moritomi.

We paused in the path together.

"Miss Langley," began the postman, blushing furiously, bowing in a beseeching way, "our son, your school . . ."

"No need," murmured Miss Langley. She reached for their hands, tugging upward as if to right them from their cringing posture.

The Moritomis would not budge. Bobbing brokenly, mumbling apologies: in their penitence they seemed stricken by sudden osteoporosis.

Miss Langley bent to join them. "Don't worry," she whispered. "I understand. Give my love to little Kenji."

The postmaster's wife made a choking noise. Her bobbing accelerated sharply.

Miss Langley straightened. Slightly embarrassed by the scene she'd created, she glanced cheerily at the gathering sky.

"Well, I need to be finding my group!"

Mr. and Mrs. Moritomi unfolded slightly. Crumpled and damp, they huddled like a pair of wadded-up hankies as Miss Langley turned and sprinted ostrichlike back down the path.

We watched her go. A woman who was awkward, sincere, and appealing.

"So hopeful and hapless," murmured Headmaster Kido with a rueful shake of his head. "Like a farm boy at university."

Then, as Miss Langley rejoined Chie and Mari's mother, the headmaster startled and stiffened. He stared hard at Chie's kimono.

Abruptly he turned back to me.

"Mrs. Sone," he said in an officious voice. "We're certainly pleased to see *you* looking so well."

We all knew what the headmaster meant. Unlike Chie and Miss Langley, my clothing looked utterly conventional. *Perhaps, the comment meant to inquire, your attire is a statement of deliberate disassociation?*

I wanted to refute his compliment. Not to do so would be a betrayal.

But there were Postmaster and Mrs. Moritomi—feeling disloyal about withdrawing their son from the juku—looking pained to the point of tears.

Who was I to flaunt a greater morality? Wouldn't it have

sounded tactless and self-serving? And wouldn't it have been hypocritical? The headmaster—in part—had it right. I *did* dress with an awareness of my simplicity, of how it distinguished me from Chie's grandeur.

People swirled past us on the path to the shrine. I stood frozen.

And so it happened, as I continued my internal debate—there, on the first day of a new year, when each act is so richly portentous—the moment to speak slipped away.

Taking my silence as agreement, Headmaster Kido softened.

"I know it's hard to oppose them," he said gently. "Miss Langley, Mrs. Fuji: there's something compelling about those who stand out."

He smiled with a kind of sad knowledge.

"When I was at university there was this boy, a scholarship student like me. Wore his bad haircut and country accent as if they were a rich boy's hand-tailored clothes. It targeted him for greater taunting—his oblivion. But he kept on, by himself, winning more and more academic honors."

Headmaster Kido sighed. He looked down at his soft leather shoes.

"His dignity made me feel petty. My going along, my concern about fitting in. Then just before graduation—when I was secretly rooting for him to go out into the world and show us all—he hanged himself. Just like that. No note. Alone in his room."

The headmaster looked at us searchingly.

"I swore I'd learn something from it; a life can't go like that, all in vain."

He laughed a little harshly.

"Remember that childhood maxim? 'The nail that sticks

out gets pounded down.' Let me tell you, I learned that it's true."

"Poor pitiful boy," murmured Mrs. Moritomi.

"Poor *dangerous* boy."

The headmaster snapped to sudden attention.

"The children think I'm rigid but it's my job to protect them. I *refuse* to let some maverick, no matter how appealing, seduce them toward self-destruction."

"So we were right to take Kenji out of the juku?" Mrs. Moritomi asked faintly.

"Absolutely."

Headmaster Kido wheeled to face me.

"And the girl Mari, who plays with Hanae? I think it's a bad idea."

My mouth opened to defend Mari, but still moved by the headmaster's story, I couldn't seem to make words come out.

"She's too strange: that pinafore, her mother a maid, her connections with the foreigner Langley."

"Excuse us, we must be going," Postmaster Moritomi interrupted.

Unwilling to be party to the slander of a child, he and his wife honorably exited the scene.

I tried to follow.

"I too should—"

Headmaster Kido held up one hand and continued.

"Associating with Mari will mark Hanae as a sympathizer, as some kind of kooky internationalist."

Finally I found my voice.

"We *are* international—Hanae is American; her father lives there—and it's an *asset* not a probl—"

But my passivity had placed me in deep collusion.

"Yes, of course," the headmaster interrupted without hearing. "Hanae faces some difficulties. Her father an expatriate; her grandmother—well, we all know Chie Fuji. Still, Hanae comes from one of the oldest and finest families. People expect *some* eccentricity."

He grew more emphatic.

"Help me with Hanae; she's loyal to foolish ideals. You're a sensible, responsible woman. Mari is a lost case, an outsider—"

"TRAITOR!"

Recognizing the voice, I snapped my head up in horror. Hanae and Mari had been skipping ahead of us along the path, but at some point Hanae must have turned back. Now she pushed past me in her flight away from the shrine.

Had she witnessed my whole gutless performance?

"Hanae!"

I stumbled after her, hampered by my narrow kimono.

"Let me explain!"

Clouds roiled, sleet started. My words were hopelessly lost.

How was I to know that a few hesitations could compromise me so completely?

New Year's Afternoon

Hanae ran—through freezing rain, past doorways decorated with New Year braids of rice straw, across ditches rank with rotting leaves—all the long way home. Her heart pounded. Her festive streamers grew soggy. Soon they began to dissolve.

When she reached our entry, her frozen fingers fumbled with the heavy wood doors.

"*Tadaima!*" she shrieked. "*Tadaima*, I'm home!"

The door was opened by our maid, Makiko, who since finding her love poems disturbed and immediately suspecting Hanae, had been feeling markedly hostile.

"Stop pounding," Makiko grumbled. "It's not my fault the door was bolted, you weren't expected until—"

Her voice changed. "*Arrah!* So wet?"

Hanae pushed past. She struggled with her shoes. Rushing to our room, she grabbed a book of martial essays and began a harsh, chanting recitation.

She was still chanting when, later, Chie and I arrived home in the town's only taxi.

In a display of tact, Chie went to her sleeping quarters to water the spirits in her family shrine. Concerned, shamefaced, and nervous, I was left to approach Hanae's and my room.

"Hanae?" I called through the closed sliding door. Not knowing what I was going to say about my failure to defend Mari and the things I believed in, I was slightly afraid to enter.

Hanae increased her volume.

"GALLOPING PURE AS THE EMPEROR'S WHITE HORSE, MAY OUR NATIONAL AMBITIONS PROCEED."

"Hanae, I'm sorry! Please let me explain!"

"What's to explain?" Hanae's voice was bitter. "I've been betrayed; they're leaving!"

"Leaving?" I slid the door open a crack.

"Mari! Her mother!"

I slipped my body inside.

Hanae was sitting slumped on the floor.

"Anything else?" My voice was cautious.

I lowered myself to a seated position and tried to look into Hanae's eyes.

"Miss Langley," said Hanae. Refusing to meet my glance, she continued to stare at the floor.

"Miss Langley what?"

"She's leaving."

"Oh."

Hanae shot me a sharp look of impatience. Her annoyance overrode her grief. Where was the warm hug, the soothing murmur? She expected more competent consolation.

"Hanae," I started again, "did you hear anything upsetting at the shrine? When your headmaster and I were talking?"

"I just told you!"

Hanae had never seen me so infuriatingly obtuse.

"Mari said she's leaving Japan!"

At that moment, in a distant part of the house, Chie paused in her lighting of incense.

"Hanae is quieter now," she told Kan.

She snorted with authority.

"Too much pride, that girl. Did you hear all that silly chanting?"

She poured a thimbleful of water into a thin porcelain cup, wiping a drop from the black lacquer butsudan shrine with her kimono sleeve.

Her voice softened.

"Remember, Kan, when Naomi was little? How sometimes—to postpone some unpleasant knowledge—she'd stuff her fingers in her ears and taunt, 'I can't hear'?"

Next to a framed wisp of infant's hair, Chie propped an edible toy: a sweet potato, curved and resembling a horse, with radish legs secured by toothpicks.

"Here you go, Baby," she murmured.

She turned again to her husband's picture.

"It must be bad news," Chie sighed. "Hanae sounds like that."

Makiko showed Mari to the reception area, then knocked outside the room where Hanae sat stewing and I—like a felon who has just learned his crime has gone undetected—sat in a daze of guilt and relief.

"Mari's here."

"Too bad for her. I'm *not*!"

"*Hanae!*" I jolted from my self-absorbed state.

Hanae shrugged with insolence, then wished that she hadn't.

I began dragging her toward the door with a startling new forcefulness and a grip just as painful as Chie's.

"Go out and acknowledge your friend!"

"So what do *you* want?" Hanae demanded as she entered the reception room.

Seated at a low table in the guest's position—facing the art in the alcove—Mari turned and rose halfway.

"Oh, Hanae, don't be like that."

"Like what?"

Hanae crossed the nubby tatami with all the dignity her fine genes and strict training could muster.

She settled with her back to the alcove, facing not only her guest but also the entry. This was the traditional seat of power, from which attempted coups could be thwarted.

"I know you're upset—," Mari began. Hanae cut her off.

"So Miss Langley is fleeing to America," she said crisply. "Fine. She never did belong."

Her voice turned cold and sarcastic.

"But you and your mother must accompany her? Miss Langley is *so* ill fitting that she has need for an interpreter in her own country?"

For once Mari actually grew angry.

"Stop it! Who do you think you are? So self-dramatizing and injured. What did you think you were doing, running away like that? Can't you see? Our leaving has nothing to do with you!"

"Injured?" Hanae sputtered. "I'm *disgusted*, not wounded!" She floundered, trying to find something disgusting in Mari's behavior about which she could expound.

Mari watched Hanae's performance. After a while she sighed. "Oh, Ha-chan, I know. I'll miss you too."

Hanae glared at Mari. Her eyes began to smart.

Thirteen years old, she thought with exasperation, and *still* in that ridiculous pinafore.

Eavesdropping from a nearby room, sitting at a low table set with a New Year arrangement of pine and orange branches, toying with our tempura and tofu, Chie and I were left hanging.

Finally Mari spoke.

"You're right. Miss Langley doesn't belong. She did for a while, she made her own place, but now people are scared and won't let her."

"But why do you have to go? You're Japanese. Everyone will think you're foreign and funny."

"I'm American," Mari said firmly. "Just like you." She shook her head.

"I'm sorry, Hanae. I don't *want* to leave. But in America, I have a future. Here, well, you know, we just don't fit. It's *here* that we're foreign and funny."

After Mari left and Hanae went to bed, Chie grew quiet and cold.

"Maybe Mari's mother is smart."

She spoke slowly, as if testing my reaction.

"Maybe we should send Hanae back to her father."

The idea made me panic.

"Hanae leave! That's too extreme!"

If Hanae left, I knew I could not accompany her. She was too old to need a nursemaid and it would have looked strange for me to return to the home of a man who was not a blood relative.

"Extreme? What's happening at the juku, then? When children betray their teacher?"

I said nothing.

"And her regular school. Do you know what homework she's given?" Chie's voice was exaggerated and harsh. "Effusive letters of gratitude to be copied in her best brush strokes and sent off to anonymous soldiers. Strange strident marching music to practice on her flute."

"In upper level they'll teach things of depth," I stammered. "Chinese court poetry, Italian Renaissance thought."

"Ha!" snorted Chie. "For how long?"

"Maybe it's not so bad," I said with desperation. "Jingoistic teaching happens in every country. Even in America. Children always see through it."

Chie looked at me closely.

"Rumor has it you've been collecting the publications of various peace organizations."

Involuntarily I startled. Chie's knowledge of what I thought were my well-concealed private affairs was staggering. A random thought flashed through my mind. So this is where Hanae had inherited her chilling investigative streak.

"How is it you're now *defending* jingoism?" Chie spoke with knowing patience, like a teacher coaxing a pupil.

In a whisper I relinquished my secret. "I'm afraid of losing her."

"Ah," Chie commented dryly, "mother love."

For a long time we were silent. Then Chie laughed, a cynical barking sound.

"Don't worry, we'll keep her. We'll give her an international education. I've developed some plans." She rubbed her hands in anticipation. "Besides, I hear on the radio that Mr. Babe Ruth is traveling through Japan. Everywhere he goes he's met by thousands of people!"

I stared at her with incomprehension.

"Baseball, movies, fashion," she listed in glee. "The Ministry of Defense can't get rid of *all* Western influence!" She became serious. "These things may save us."

"Baseball, movies, fashion?"

Chie gave a sharp nod. "Of course, there's greed and ambition. There are those who would push us toward war. But people resist. Generally, people don't want glory. They want small gentle pleasures like baseball."

"Baseball?"

Chie leaned close.

"Have you ever *observed* a baseball game?" she whispered in a conspiratorial tone. "It's like being at a Japanese tea ceremony."

She swept her arm across the horizon as if painting a lavish picture.

"There you are, sitting on a hard surface, in a position of discomfort, participating in a slow-moving ritual." She checked to see if I was following. "Little happens. Your mind wanders. Gradually, you notice the small moments that make life rich. The sun's heat, the ball's arc."

"The sky's beauty, when glimpsed through a moon-shaped window!" I exclaimed, remembering the moment in my girlhood tea ceremony classes, when I first grasped the meaning of Zen.

"Exactly, and it's this love of small things, by most people everywhere, that just might keep us from war."

Suddenly, Chie looked tired. "War is large and loud. It disrespects the taste of tea."

The hour was late. Before us on a tray rested a snack I had brought from the kitchen: dried persimmons, roasted chestnuts, and a plate of omochi—glutinous rice cakes sprinkled with toasted soy sugar.

The aromas rose. These were winter foods, suggestive of loss and regret.

Chie picked up a plump rice cake. She cradled the cake in the palm of her hand, feeling its round yielding weight, its soft pale skin.

She lifted it to her nose, inhaling its sweet dusty fragrance. Then carefully, as if handling a newborn baby, she laid it back down.

"War is jealous of ordinary beauty," she said quietly. "It seeks to destroy out of spite. For all its size and fury, war has no enduring power."

She nodded in thought.

"The most powerful things are small: the taste on our tongues of our favorite childhood foods, the rub of skin against skin."

She paused.

"The quick moment," she murmured to herself, "between unfamiliarity and claiming, when you breathe your new baby's scent."

"Ah," I said softly, finally understanding the train of her conversation, seeing her on a human scale for the very first time. "Mother love."

The Gay Divorcee

On January 7—as people made a new round of resolutions in anticipation of lunar New Year—Chie telephoned Toshiro Ishigawa.

Owner of the village's only car, he is proprietor of Peerless Taxi.

When the maid announced Mr. Ishigawa, Chie couldn't conceal her impatience. As the jovial driver appeared in the doorway, she rushed straight to his side.

"This one! Can we make it? Is there time?"

She jabbed at a newspaper listing she was shaking under his nose.

I was hanging over Chie's arm, also eager, but I remembered the etiquette of the holiday season.

"Won't you have tea, some refreshments?" I distractedly inquired.

"No, no, I mustn't," the plump man demurred.

He settled himself at the table.

Much later, burping gently, chattering constantly, oblivious to the random backfirings of his ancient bouncing vehicle, Mr. Ishigawa drove us to the entertainment district of Kobe.

His monopoly on the taxi trade has made him insensitive to standards of smooth, silent service.

"Here we are, quite the place!" he beamed as we wheezed to a stop in front of a glittering Moorish palace. "Le Cinéma Grand Oriental!"

I was no stranger to the entertainment district, but Chie and Hanae had never been there before. I looked around, trying to see things with a newcomer's eyes. Radiating out from several glamorous movie palaces—a German castle, an Egyptian temple, a replica of the Eiffel Tower—lay a warren of tiny noodle shops, tattoo parlors, and pinball halls. Though the buildings were old, their roofs, traditionally clay or gray colored, gleamed with modern new tiling in bright artificial-looking variations of blue or pink. Indeed, perhaps because of the color of flesh, the new euphemism for things related to the evening trade is *pinku*.

At night, I knew the entertainment district would fill with customers of cabarets, casinos, and brothels. Yet despite the somewhat tawdry nature of its wares, during matinee hours the district seemed doggedly wholesome.

Modern boys with tight pants and slicked-back hair stole shy peeks at groups of modern girls—clustered for safety—wearing pert Western dresses and permanent waves. While waiting for a midday showing of a popular samurai movie, nine-year-old boys crowded a comic-book store. Mothers and fathers queued with their children outside theaters showing the latest in sentimental family drama—a characteristically weepy form of Japanese moviemaking featuring plots such as polio-stricken child reunites her absorbed-by-materialism but still-in-love-with-each-other parents. To enhance the tragic atmosphere of these family dramas, theaters burn real incense during the movies' numerous funeral scenes.

Near the ticket booth of Le Cinéma Grand Oriental, a dozen members of the Women's Patriotic League—dressed in worn brown farmer's pants to signify willingness to forgo luxury in support of Japan's higher needs—were picketing against foreign diversions.

I looked to see how Hanae was reacting to all this, but she seemed completely absorbed by the billboard. High above the movie theater spun a magical man and woman, laughing figures one-story high.

"The Gay Divorcee," read Mr. Ishigawa. He twisted in his seat to squint at us, as if trying to discern some masked malevolence, some subterranean support for domestic discord. "Now, what kind of movie is that?"

Hanae suddenly grinned. She didn't need an answer; from the billboard, she could tell.

This was a movie about immediacy, about joy. There wouldn't be a single drifting autumn leaf or billowing cherry blossom in sight. For once, she was not going to be instructed about the fleeting bittersweet quality of life!

As we entered the theater, it became clear that the Women's Patriotic League had much work to do.

Every seat was taken.

Additionally, a number of viewers were highly familiar with the script: they shouted the subtitles, exhorting and advising the affable Mr. Astaire in his pursuit of the skeptical Miss Rogers.

I liked the raucous nature of the crowd. It reminded me of the days before subtitles for foreign films, only a few years ago, when a benshi would stand below the screen, loudly narrating all dialogue. Above the sound of creaking seats and clanking floor fans, above the voices of Garbo and Cagney, would roar one indefatigable orator, usually an ancient be-spectacled man who'd been doing this sort of thing—indeed, in traditional alternating syllables of five and seven—since before the advent of talkies. To me the benshi—an offshoot of the ancient profession of Japanese stage theater narrators—had seemed both unwaveringly faithful and astonishingly inventive: the embodiment of the old Meiji-era slogan "Japanese spirit joined to Western technology."

"They're behaving as if at a Kabuki play," I explained in Hanae's right ear. "Listen, they're complimenting him on his imaginative dance."

"A divorcée is a woman who has left her husband's house," Chie lectured in her other ear. "An American woman can do as she pleases: travel, receive direct proposals of marriage, go to nightclubs. She need not feel any shame."

"You're missing the point of the movie," Hanae complained. "And this is *comedy*, not Kabuki."

Hanae found our lessons annoying. She barely could follow the plot. But she *did* notice a curious synchronization in our behavior.

Right-ear, Japanese culture. Left-ear, American choice. One, two, we worked her over like a team of cross-cultural boxers, softening up an opponent.

chapter seventeen

MARCH 7, 1934

I've always found Japanese novels slightly annoying. Rambling hodgepodge, they often juxtapose snippets of poetry, snatches of dialogue, descriptions of outings and meals. And although critics have described these novels as "moments of disconnected beauty," I have to ask myself, Is this Art? Is this pleasingly deceptive contrivance?

In my opinion, it is not. To me, the Japanese novel is too much like the living of life. You have to work for your wisdom, panning an endless stream of banalities for the tiniest flickers of truth.

Maybe that's why I prefer Western fiction. It seems so tidy and cunning. Like a well-hurled javelin, the story soars upward through its introduction of characters and situation, hits a life-transforming crisis at its zenith, and descends—frequently with perfect symmetry—toward the resolution.

Everything moves with such elegance toward one preestablished premise! It stands in sharp contradiction to the shape of my life. It was part of what drew me to America. The hope that, like Western fiction, I too could be crafted and molded.

And though my life has remained largely formless—a series of accommodations to random occurrences—I *have* learned something from Western art.

It's *character* that propels the plot.

An Attempt to Develop My Character

Women opposing military aggression. Come join in discussion.

For almost two months, the same personal advertisement kept appearing in the English-language edition of the *Kobe News*. It's curious how topics so strictly censored in formal Japanese publications breeze by as if nonexistent when crudely distributed or published in any foreign language. Thus a disgruntled private citizen can hand out lists of all his political grievances and be ignored as a crackpot. International newspapers can provide piercing analyses about Japanese governmental actions and it is assumed their audience will be too small (and already predisposed to such heretical thoughts) for its publication to matter. To me it seems a government attitude both arrogant and naive, although highly convenient for the public. For example, during the wildly controversial publication trial of *Lady Chatterley's Lover*, this "banned" novel was easily available and eagerly purchased in foreign language editions at every corner bookstall in Japan.

One by one I cut out these antiwar advertisements, lining them up until there were seven pieces of paper, all matching a scrap pulled from the sleeve of my New Year's kimono.

Finally I looked at a trolley map.

With some degree of self-consciousness—to exercise opposition was new to me—I went to the address provided, a little after the time indicated. My plan was to blend inconspicuously into the group, to listen, and then to decide if I would participate.

As I climbed down from the streetcar, I found myself in a formerly European neighborhood.

It was a lovely district with views across the straits and the harbor. In the bird market near the trolley stop, songbirds—canaries and finches—sang *piyo chee chee*, preening in tiered cages of narrow bent bamboo. Soup birds—assorted chickens—nodded nervously in their crates, quaking under the calculating eyes of cook maids.

Kobe is full of such neighborhoods—town estates staggered in the foothills of mountains. Once they were stocked with two-story stone houses, suitable for the better neighborhoods of Amsterdam or London but precarious on the shifting soils of earthquake-prone Japan. Yet increasingly, in an era when world markets fall as easily as brick residences, these neighborhoods are becoming Japanese.

I followed the road to the number listed in the advertisement. Stepping through a bamboo gate, I encountered a turn-of-the-century Japanese villa. Four fireplace chimneys jutting from the traditional Japanese tiled roof announced that at least part of the house was built Western style.

As I rounded an ornamental grouping of early-blooming camellia, I spotted a plum-colored Packard. The household crest of a Japanese viscount was embossed on its door.

My heart lurched, my breathing stopped; it was as if I'd walked into an electric wall. I'd no idea I would be presuming to associate with women of such elevated stature!

I tried to flee undetected. I crept across crunching gravel, taking pains not to awaken the car's uniformed driver.

I was almost to the gate when a voice called from the villa's entry.

"Are you here for the meeting?"

I froze like a guilty poacher.

"Please, Honored Guest," pleaded the voice.

With great reluctance I turned.

The speaker was a bi-jin, a beautiful, well-bred woman. In her thirties, long and slender with perfect posture, she moved with the lyrical sideways sweep of those trained in classical Japanese dance.

In my breast, curiosity battled with trepidation.

Ours is a society that compensates shrinking income and growing age with certain freedoms. Thus a woman who is poor or over fifty can act on her interests and use language that is blunt, even bawdy.

But the mistress of a great house must be retiring. Any act of assertion, such as answering the door instead of sending a maid, would be putting herself scandalously forward.

The woman waved.

"This way, kochira, kochira."

She scooped her hand in disarming informality, like a mother beckoning children to cookies.

I shook my head with appreciation. Here was a woman— elegant in high heels and bias-cut crepe—who came to her front stoop and called!

"Er, thank you." I started forward.

"I am Kawai, Fumiko," said my hostess.

"Sone, Etsuko," I replied.

Mrs. Kawai led me through a handsome salon decorated with Japanese and European antiques. It had a seventeenth-century six-panel screen painting of scenes from *The Tale of Genji* and what I recognized as Louis XIV chairs.

I know something about Western furnishings, the periods

and the pieces. Before we sailed for America, Tadao and I thought we should learn everything we could about the West: etiquette, architecture, language, literature. In order to prepare for our new lives, we spent many pleasurable hours in the reference room of Osaka University.

We made one mistake, however. As we scanned the library's card catalog, we paused at the topic *Civilization, Western* and became so engaged by it and its cross-references—*See also Europe: Art, History, and Society*—that we never realized the existence of an entirely different category. *West: American Frontier.*

I was amusedly recalling my shock at having left a Kobe filled with French cafes, German bakeries, and Italian opera only to find myself in *West: American Frontier* when Mrs. Kawai and I entered a small adjoining study.

On a French Empire–style settee slouched a Japanese woman in her mid-thirties. She wore pleated silk trousers and a cropped bob with a splay of bangs. Casual, modern, and ironically self-aware, she looked like Claudette Colbert.

"Hi," said the woman without rising. "I'm Aya Ito."

She lifted her lovely wrist in a sort of greeting.

Suddenly I remembered the limousine with the seal of nobility. The *Viscountess* Ito, I realized.

I bowed deeply.

"Mrs. Etsuko Sone," I squeaked.

Acutely aware that I was clutching a cloth shopping bag from which protruded an oversized daikon radish, profoundly grateful that I had not purchased the scratching chicken I'd been contemplating at the bird market, I backed into one of two chairs facing the settee.

Mrs. Kawai sank elegantly into the other.

"Well," she said. "Well."

It appeared that we were the antiwar group.

Mrs. Kawai lifted a tray from a small side table.

"Petits fours?" she inquired.

Out of nervous politeness, I picked up one of the small frosted cubes. I took a distracted bite.

Kore wa!

Fully focused, I peered at its construction. By arranging layers of sweetened bean paste, maybe I could create some sort of home adaptation.

"Let's get to the point," interrupted Viscountess Ito. She leaned forward, crossing her long legs at the knees.

Instantly, I knew she had lived abroad.

"Well," Mrs. Kawai repeated with a slight stammer. "I, uhm, placed the advertisement in different foreign language papers so that women opposed to military aggression might gather."

Her train of thought suddenly veered. "Actually, this is the first week anyone came!"

"There were the holidays." Viscountess Ito shrugged.

"Of course." Mrs. Kawai blushed. "Well, I was thinking we could discuss this new army and then possibly . . ."

She floundered and I felt a surge of affection.

It couldn't be easy for a lady—strictly trained in upper-class kata, in exact procedures for tea, for flowers, for every facet of life—to know how to conduct a protest meeting.

"The army!" scoffed the viscountess. "They're drunk on colonial power!" Her voice lowered dramatically. "They've have had a taste of it, you know. Sitting around the treaty table at Versailles. Watching borders get passed about like so many after-dinner cigars."

She reached into the pocket of her trousers and took out a cigarette.

"The viscountess smokes!"

I breathed in shock, not realizing that I'd spoken aloud.

It was my first encounter with either a noblewoman or a lady smoker. Somehow, I never thought I'd see them combined.

"The viscountess prefers to be called Mrs. Ito," murmured our hostess, and then as if to explain the smoking, "Mrs. Ito and I were just getting acquainted. She's a student of Marxism. She's a writer and used to live in Paris."

A published, Parisian, Marxist, smoking viscountess!

I was shaking my head with the pleasure of so much novelty when Mrs. Ito regained the floor.

"The army!" she repeated. "From houseboys to big boys in one giddy rush, now they'll do anything to keep up with the West!"

She inhaled sharply and blew an angry stream of smoke from her perfect nostrils.

"This depression is a big part of the problem," Mrs. Kawai said with reflection.

"Exactly!" declared Mrs. Ito. "And when the economic future looks bleak, what's more inspiring to an ignorant electorate than a grandiose call to war?"

Mrs. Ito's question—her whole style of speech—was so dramatic and declarative I couldn't think of any response.

"It's not that people are stupid," Mrs. Kawai mused, "but information is censored and democracy is new to Japan."

She paused to ponder.

"So, what can we do?" she inquired.

Minutes passed.

A Swiss-crafted clock ticked from the mantel.

"*Yaki-imo!* Steaming *yaki-imo!*"

Through the open French windows came the song of a

peddler pushing a hibachi in a hand truck, advertising his fresh sweet potatoes.

Inside, the silence continued. We sat and we stared at one another.

Mrs. Kawai began to look pained.

"I have an idea."

My voice erupted as if from an impertinent stranger. I almost slapped my hand over my mouth.

Mrs. Ito turned toward me with interest, as if she saw nothing unusual in having a dowdy, thirty-seven-year-old housewife as peer.

"Yes?" she demanded.

chapter eighteen

OCTOBER 11, 1934

I've been thinking about how the concluding third line of haiku always has to contain a surprise. A twist in perspective or mood, something that sets you off balance, that causes you to gasp. A reaction found both in heartbreak and joy.

The conclusion I've reached is that surprise—or mystery, or anticipation, or whatever you wish to call it—is the basis of life. Beyond compelling us to read to the third line in a poem, it's what makes us leave our beds, fall in love, listen to jokes, speculate endlessly about the weather.

Surprise—or rather, its relative rarity—is what children find so agonizing about childhood. Even I, a placid, undemanding child, used to have moments of soul-freezing terror that I would grow up and *nothing would change*. A fear that, for a period that would feel like infinity, I'd be mincing mulberry leaves for the silkworms, eating steamed tofu and spinach for dinner, and staring at the same tear in the shoji. And as the only child, it was quite plausible that I'd marry a yoshi and that this—with the exception of the shoji tear, which I was determined to mend—would indeed be my fate.

No wonder children sulk and have tantrums and start arguments over who said what first! It's their bid for some vigor and variation.

Perhaps, therefore, the dictating of thought and behavior, the demand for public solidarity, the reduction of choice and surprise are among the earlier sorrows that start as a country creeps toward war. The diminution of mystery for its children. The editing of a poem.

Life After Miss Langley

Before she sailed for America, Miss Langley came to call. Her long legs jammed under her body, she sat with Chie, Hanae, and me at the low table in the reception room.

"Our humblest greetings, Miss Langley," I said. "You honor us with this unexpected visit." Though I spoke in English, I used proper Japanese hostess kata. I pushed a package forward across the table. "Please accept, as a token of our delight, this inferior gift of little value."

From the wrappings, Hanae recognized the package as one I had received from the bathhouse owner's wife during the recent New Year's gift exchange. Inside was a bright pink dachshund, crocheted in the shape of a tube, intended for slipping around the receiver of a telephone.

Miss Langley knew the ritual.

"You are too kind. My apologies for burdening you with my visit."

She placed the box, unopened, behind her back. Later she would go home to unwrap and rewrap the gift, carefully cataloguing its contents, before storing it with others destined to be given away.

Hanae shook her head with amazement and pity.

231

For village women, this process of accumulating and redistributing omiyage, "gifts from here to take there," is tortuous and time-consuming. The crocheted dachshund, for example, presented the double difficulties of being highly memorable and suitable only for people prosperous enough for a phone.

Yet for us the process of exchange also is thrilling. Fraught, as it is, with the ever-present danger of accidentally giving a gift back to its original donor.

"Forgive me for taking your time," said Miss Langley. "I just came to say good-bye."

Good-bye.

So this was it. Suddenly Hanae shivered.

Miss Langley looked at her, awkward with the weight of farewell.

"You're a bright girl, Hanae, with real promise. It's been an honor"—she gave a quick quirky smile—"and a challenge to have known you."

Hanae shrugged. If it was such an honor, said her gesture, why was Miss Langley leaving?

"I know you'll place first on your entrance exams," Miss Langley continued. She peered in Hanae's face seeking some kind of recognition.

Hanae examined the moon on her right thumbnail.

"I won't forget you, Hanae, and I've brought you something to remind you of our juku."

She thrust forward a stack of old textbooks.

"Look," I gushed, trying to prod Hanae toward enthusiasm. "Western reference books!"

Hanae gave them a skeptical eye.

"Naomi studied books like these," Chie interjected in Japanese. "Once she went to a rummage sale at the Foreigners' School in Kobe. Her passion was European literature: Romantic poets, Shakespeare, Dickens, Flaubert."

Miss Langley, whose attempts to learn Japanese had barely progressed beyond standard niceties, listened to Chie with a bright eager face.

At the names Shaku-spe-ru, Di-ke-nu, and Fro-ber-u, she emitted her odd, honking laugh.

"I think I understood that!" she cried with delight. "I'm finally mastering my Japanese!"

As the irony hit her, Miss Langley's cheerful face suddenly crumbled.

Hanae panicked. She reached out and grabbed for the books.

As their fingers brushed, Miss Langley quickly looked down.

Hanae silently studied her teacher.

Ernest and awkward with an inimitable loony laugh.

Something stung in the tip of Hanae's nose. She blinked and looked away.

That afternoon, Hanae was interrupted as she sprawled on tatami, reading the textbooks.

"You're wanted at the storehouse."

It was Makiko, whose yearning for the tofu maker's son— Hanae had discovered—had led her to an attempt to cast magic: hiding love poems and incense near the icebox where he made his deliveries.

"The storehouse? Why there?" In Japan, storehouses are no mere sheds. Handsome buildings made of thick white stucco to resist fire, with swooping tiled roofs, they are famous for housing family myths and malevolent monsters.

"Who knows?" grumbled Makiko. "Maybe to lock you in?"

The idea seemed to enliven her. She grinned with cheerful malice.

As Hanae stepped from the veranda, the earth smelled fertile and damp. February had been warm. Birds tugged on Chie's thawing garden. They flew up to the budding trees carrying patches of moss like small brownish-green toupees.

Hanae reached the storehouse.

Her back to the entry, Chie was peering through the thick double doors. Over Chie's shoulder Hanae saw the clutter, familiar from annual airing rituals, of heirlooms: scrolls, vases, swords, cabinets, even an ancient suit of lacquered armor.

Lately the density of objects—a volume that first had struck both Hanae and me as overwhelming—seemed less.

"Have you found the final one?" Chie was demanding.

I was invisible but my voice emerged triumphant.

"No. No. Oh yes, here it is!"

Hanae gave a discreet cough.

"Ah, Hanae." Chie turned sharply.

To Hanae's astonishment Chie was wearing an apron. Less surprising, it was immaculate.

"Look what we've found!" I chirped, emerging from behind a six-fold screen painting of mountains, executed in the Zen scattered-ink style.

I struggled forward—dust and spiderwebs clinging to my apron, my kimono hem catching on the hilt of a sword—and dropped a stack of books on the floor.

"Excuse me." I laughed. I reached behind my back to untie the strings of my apron.

Hanae straightened with sudden attention.

Perhaps I should explain. The Japanese feel it's rude to work

234

while socializing. In pausing to say good morning, a carpenter will put down his hammer, an accountant will remove his eyeglasses.

With Hanae, I usually ignore this social nicety. In fact most of our conversations take place in the kitchen. By removing my apron, I had signaled this was no ordinary occasion.

Chie gestured to the scattered books.

"These were your mother's."

Never one to perform the polite rituals she expected of others, Chie reached into her apron pocket and put on a pair of eyeglasses.

She bent down and peered at gold lettering on spines of burgundy leather.

Hanae followed and read aloud.

"Western Masterpieces in Translation."

It took Hanae three weeks to absorb all the facts in Miss Langley's textbooks. They were a mere hors d'oeuvre. She began on the masterpieces.

Initially she read to memorize, mindlessly skimming pages, swallowing dozens of chapters and millions of brush strokes, like a whale sifting an ocean through its baleen.

Gradually, however, she found herself growing engaged—pausing to reread a pleasantly metered line or to ponder a provocative idea.

Hanae missed Mari: her humor, her insight, the back-and-forth of a friendship. In a way, the books filled Mari's absence, provided a similar solace.

The books also helped with Hanae's school entrance exams. Despite the recent inclusion of martial poetry and other nationalistic topics, the tests still focus on broad general knowledge.

For many students, the exams for entry into upper-level school are a fearsome event. During elementary school, the prevailing educational philosophy is to avoid comparisons lest the more advanced students grow complacent and the less advanced ones grow discouraged. Children in primary grades are accustomed to attending small friendly neighborhood schools and to receiving good grades for cooperative conduct and for academic self-improvement, no matter what the actual performance. Therefore a competitive national test, naming specific scores and place rankings, provides students with a first-time opportunity for acute public humiliation.

Hanae was undaunted. While her grades have always reflected the fact that she is not the most tractable of children, she rarely makes an error in any academic assignment. With her prodigious memory and even stronger personal will, Hanae fully expected to place first in the Kobe region.

To Hanae's chagrin, on the exams she placed second in our region. Her old nemesis, Kimiko Takahashi, placed first. Hanae has harbored a grudge against Kimiko since Kimiko's disastrous visit to our house, three years ago. And although Hanae says she dislikes Kimiko for her snobbery, I suspect one reason for Hanae's continuing animosity is the fact that Kimiko has always performed better than Hanae in school.

Yet when Hanae started girls' upper level, she hardly cared about her ranking. In school, they discussed existential philosophy; they considered issues in economics and approaches to art. For the first time Hanae found that information was insufficient. She had to think to keep up.

Soon she was thinking all the time. She penetrated the mysteries of the periodic table, watching elements as they linked and shifted—sharing an electron here, forming an ion there

—and converged into intricate beauty. In mathematics she perceived patterns that reminded her of music.

And to complete her happiness—as well as Akira's, for he had dressed his daughter with an eye toward her acceptance into a prestigious high school—at girls' upper level sailor suits were required attire!

Of course it didn't last.

One morning in Hanae's fourth month she walked into the school yard and saw that the standard-sized flag had, overnight, grown enormous.

A familiar voice crackled across the public address system.

"Young ladies. Allow me to introduce myself; I'll be your new headmaster. Young ladies? Please, *decorum!*"

Headmaster Kido had been transferred and promoted.

Almost immediately the other girls' sailor suits started shrinking. Their big boxy collars metamorphosed, first into small shawl collars, then into open round necklines with a touch of navy blue trim. Skirts narrowed from pleats to flares, and finally to utilitarian culottes.

Old Decorum was a pious patriot.

As war expanded, life contracted. The curriculum diminished, reducing the consumption of ideas as surely as the redesigned uniforms reduced the consumption of fabric. Until the magic disappeared and each day was spent on topics of general hygiene, home economics, and the practice of military drill.

chapter nineteen

JANUARY 10, 1936

Aside from my last entry about Hanae's schooling, it's been almost two years since I worked on this story. In truth, I felt too righteous and busy. You see, I thought I'd found my purpose in life.

In a way, it was like the period of Hanae's infancy, when—in the joyous bustle of heating milk and washing diapers and laughing with Akira about some escapade I'd had trying to feed Hanae her peas—I felt truly engaged in life's essence.

Yet this time it was *me* I was raising, and in addition I was saving the world.

But I am being too coy. And simultaneously too bitter. Is it possible, I wonder as I write this, to be *honestly* both bitter and coy? Is it a situation that actually occurs in nature? Or am I putting on an affectation?

It's odd how you begin to doubt everything when you discover that self-deception has been the underpinning of your life.

Perhaps I should take a deep breath and continue with my I-story.

The Dissident Ladies

For two years Mrs. Ito, Mrs. Kawai, and I have published a newsletter and functioned as a dissident ladies' group.

"Not *ladies!*" the Viscountess Ito protests. "Anti-imperialist revolutionaries!"

But her label never seems to catch on.

I like Mrs. Ito's contradictions; she writes antiwar essays (she had published her work in a major intellectual journal until her editor, under the Peace Preservation Act, was sent to prison) *and* romantic short fiction. In fact, the idea of Marxist Mrs. Ito writing romance so intrigued me that I tracked down an early collection. A number of the stories explored a woman's reactions to marital infidelity, her exhilarating yet ultimately ungratifying escape into unworkable love affairs, and her final coming of age through involvement with some socialist cause.

That Mrs. Ito's stories (*I-stories,* I suspected) were deliberately shocking hardly surprised me; but they did make me wonder how her husband, the viscount, reacted to all of this.

One day I asked her.

It was late afternoon and she and I sat in the small, decidedly proletarian studio she keeps for her writing. The furnishings were scant: a low wooden table, three floor cushions, a futon folded in a corner. Six worn tatami—their straw graying, their seams unraveling—covered the warping floor.

The first time I'd gone to her room in its humble neighborhood of butchers, geta shoe repairers, and *taiko* drum makers—outcasts relegated to a separate society because of their handling of slaughter and skins—I'd thought it an odd place for a privileged and somewhat brittle woman like Mrs. Ito.

Yet in those noisy streets, amid clanging bicycle bells and the clatter of clogs on cobblestone, Mrs. Ito relaxed. She slowed her restless stride, stopping to smile and ask, "How's business?"

The residents truly liked her. Grinning, they would pause— in the hacking of bones and hammering of soles—to select an answer along the Japanese continuum of modesty.

"Business is terrible." "Business is bad." "Business is barely so-so."

And after several visits to Mrs. Ito's writing studio, each time hearing her laughter mingling with her neighbors', I came to view Mrs. Ito and her apartment as complementary. Like a meeting of yin and yang.

Mrs. Ito laughed when she heard my question.

"What does the viscount think of my writing?"

She stroked the ring on her left hand, which in Japan is seen in only the most modern of marriages.

"Dear Shigeo." Her voice turned tender. "We've grown up together, you know. Weathered changes. Once our exchange was equal: the marriage protecting him in his choice of affections, the title protecting me in my choice of politics."

She looked straight at me.

"Now I've asked him to divorce me."

"But why?"

"The marriage has grown unfair. Several times he's put himself at risk, exhausting his connections, just to keep me from going to jail."

"And will he divorce?"

Mrs. Ito smiled. "That's why ours is a love story. My husband refuses."

Suddenly she laughed. "But *you're* wondering about my *adulterous* stories!"

I blushed. "No really, I . . ."

"It's fine. Everybody does."

Mrs. Ito set aside a pile of *Women's Words,* volume II, number 2: the newsletters we were bundling for distribution. She lit a cigarette and, with the casual self-assurance of a man, stretched her trousered legs out under the table.

"I'm from the old aristocracy," she said, "based on bloodlines. My husband is from the new aristocracy that Emperor Meiji established to reward industrial contribution. Marriages between the two—blending old blood and new power—are common; and when my husband and I fell in love our families were very happy."

She laughed again.

"Neither my husband nor I were considered good marriage material. He's an artist; I'm a writer. Not exactly the types to promote tradition and financial stability. After our controversial Western-style wedding—when our parents were heaving sighs of relief and hoping marriage would calm us—the first thing we did was run away to Paris."

"That's where you became a Marxist? Studying at the Sorbonne?"

"Not at first. At first my husband and I were too busy: working hard, going out, arguing big ideas."

She smiled in memory. "It was the twenties. Everyone was in Paris. We ate late dinners with Josephine Baker. We went to Antibes with Piet Mondrian, to the baths at Evian with Fernan Léger."

She took a long draw from her cigarette and very slowly exhaled.

"Paris was the perfect environment for my husband. Being brilliant, beautiful, and titled, he was in demand at all the soirees. More important, his painting was transformed. In Japan, Shigeo had been creating Impressionist-style canvases of women and gardens, translating back ideas that painters like Monet had adapted from woodblock prints from Japan. In Paris everything changed. Shigeo started painting *ideas* more than objects. His brush strokes—elegant, formal, well schooled—suddenly swelled with inspiration and passion; they unwound before my eyes."

Mrs. Ito leaned forward with startling suddenness. She ground out her half-smoked cigarette.

Her voice was quiet. "And so did our marriage."

"Pardon me?"

"It unwound."

She looked toward a small sooty window.

Outside the geta shop, a tiny hunched-over woman was attempting to tie a struggling toddler to her back with a long fabric sash.

Mrs. Ito's mood shifted. She started to smile. "There's old Mrs. Yamada with her granddaughter's baby Aiko."

Toting a huge crocheted shopping bag, the baby wriggled to the ground, snatched the sash, and began stuffing it into the bag.

"Look, Granny's giving up." Mrs. Ito laughed. "She's going to let little Aiko-chan walk." Mrs. Ito shook her head. "Old Yamada knows better than to challenge a two-year-old's independence!"

Chuckling, we resumed our bundling. Sensing some rawness, I let the topic of her marriage slip discreetly away.

We worked silently for quite a long time.

"Don't fight nature," Mrs. Ito murmured.

I assumed she was still thinking of toddlers.

She finished knotting one bundle, rose on her knees, and leaned forward to bite off some string.

"In Japan, my husband and I seemed soul mates," she stated, looking across the table, catching my eyes with her earnestness. "We were the only two specimens of our type. In Paris, my husband found his art and learned that he didn't desire me."

"You needn't tell me," I said quickly.

"Am I too frank?"

"No, no. But you don't *have* to tell me about your marriage. I didn't mean to force you into unintended disclosures."

Mrs. Ito laughed with genuine affection.

"Dear innocent! *Unintended* disclosures? I spent three years publishing little else besides retellings of this story!"

She pushed a hand through her silky bobbed hair and returned to her narration.

"When my husband fell in love I was devastated. I was young and perhaps it was less the fact of his infidelity than the nature of it that tormented me. Had Shigeo's affair been casual, I may have felt less betrayed. Ours had been a love based on loyalty, on a sense of 'similar' more than on fire. What made me most lonely was the feeling that my best friend had grown up and left me in childhood, had found some kind of relationship I couldn't yet even imagine. For in Armand, Shigeo had found his true partner."

Mrs. Ito shook her head.

"I fancied myself a freethinker but I was a hypocrite. Had my husband taken a mistress or even a second wife, it would have broadcast the affluence of our house, would have strengthened my social standing. But my husband's choice, to keep me the only woman he loved, shamed me."

Mrs. Ito studied me to see if I was understanding her meaning, then nodded to herself.

Probably she'd decided that I looked neither confused nor appalled. To see a woman smoking a cigarette can startle me, but I know love is a tangled and tortuous thing; little about love can surprise me.

She shrugged and gave a small smile of rue.

"In time, my fog of envy lifted. Shigeo and Armand showered me with brotherly concern and took care that I not feel excluded. Since my marriage had always been a somewhat asexual thing, they'd taken nothing essential away. In time, like Shigeo, I saw what a lively, kind, clever man Armand was. And I saw how happy they made each other."

The peace on Mrs. Ito's face deepened as she studied the ring on her hand.

"Love, honor, cherish," she said quietly. "In ways that count, Shigeo and I have never strayed from our marriage vows."

We sat a while in silence.

"Did you ever find that kind of love you'd never imagined?" I gently inquired.

Mrs. Ito tapped an unlit cigarette on the table.

"When Shigeo first met Armand, I waited in suspended animation for the affair to be over. Then, after a few months, I began taking lovers of my own."

She shook her head. "It was a ridiculous, meaningless frenzy: a way to prove to myself I was worldly. After a while, I gave up on romance altogether. Then much later, when our domestic life had calmed and I'd become friends with Shigeo and Armand, I met Henri."

Mrs. Ito stared at her cigarette.

"He died, you know," she said with quiet bewilderment. "He'd grown up in the French-speaking section of Switzerland and never lost his love of the mountains. Whenever he could, he joined expeditions, and one day—helping another climber on an icy crevasse—he just slipped off the side."

Her eyes filled, but she flicked her tears away with an impatient jerk of her head. "It's the one thing I've never been able to turn into a story."

I did not reply.

Mrs. Ito studied hands. Then, almost in shyness, she looked up with a little half smile.

"Henri and I started in a strange way," she confided. "I was tired of being myself: a child, still unsure and searching. I looked around and asked, Who do I want to be next?"

She shook her head with wonderment.

"Next. It was that conscious, like an actress selecting a role. Words like 'wise,' 'robust,' and 'joyful' entered my mind. Shortly thereafter I met a Marxist writer who seemed to be all those things." She laughed aloud. "Though he turned out to be Henri, at first I was attracted to him not because I wanted to be his lover, but to be some kind of *understudy*."

"I had a love like that," I said slowly, "though at the end, rather than at the beginning."

I paused in memory. "When Tadao died, I took up his occupation. I think, in order not to miss him, I wanted to *become* him."

We sat for a while in silence.

"And have you?" said Mrs. Ito.

"Pardon?"

"Have you become your husband?"

"Oh no!"

Thinking of Tadao, I felt a familiar swell of affection and sadness.

"Why not? What was he like?"

"Oh, nothing like me." I paused. "Fun, he was fun. And kind. And brave enough to risk being foolhardy." I gave a little laugh of embarrassment. "He thought I was really something."

"Then you *are* just like him. Probably you always were."

Mrs. Ito gave me a comradely kick under the table.

"An astute, decent fellow? Not afraid of acting on what he believed?" She smiled, a mischievous smirk. "Sounds a little like that Chie person too."

"Oh no, Tadao was nothing like Chie."

Mrs. Ito started grinning. "No, huh? And neither are you?"

I stopped to think. "Well, Tadao and Chie did share a certain unencumbered quality. A sort of be-who-you-are, come what may."

"And you don't?"

"Oh no, I'm disgustingly timid."

Mrs. Ito looked suddenly angry. "Come on, Etsuko-san! Don't pretend that you're less than you are!"

I cringed under her abrupt disapproval.

"You go to America, you raise a child, you return to face an imperious mother." She shook her finger. "You're the one who suggested we form an anti-imperialist publishing cell!"

"A dissident ladies' newsletter."

My correction came automatically. I was preoccupied. There was something in that long lilting litany that disturbed me.

Mrs. Ito laughed. She thought I was being playful.

"All right, have it your way, dissident ladies, but—*taihen da!*"

She shook her head teasingly.

"These are the acts of a timid woman?"

In a flash it came together and I was swamped. Overcome by my central dilemma.

Nothing in that long sterling list was my own! How could I take pleasure in having claimed my own special future, when my life—*my entire life*—had been somebody else's idea?

"No," I said. "You have it wrong. America was Tadao's dream. Hanae is Naomi's child. Coming back to Japan was Akira's decision."

Mrs. Ito heard something in my voice. She stretched her hand toward my arm.

I flinched away. "This group? I'm here through a departing friend's urging. And what's my contribution? You write the essays; Mrs. Kawai does the interviews."

A short laugh escaped from my throat.

"I crank the mimeo machine!"

Mrs. Ito looked stricken. She began some desperate monologue about complementary effort and universal ownership.

From beneath the flow of her words, a memory surfaced. It was Chie.

For her safety, I'd kept my peace activities secret from Hanae. But I told Chie about my involvement. Proud and eager as an elementary-school child, I'd brought Chie the first copy of our pacifist newsletter.

"How does it look?" I begged.

Chie put on her glasses and perused the front page. "Good writing."

My heart swelled with pride but Chie hadn't finished.

"Poor mimeographing," she said.

Back in her studio, Mrs. Ito was still talking.

I felt exhausted by her energy.

"Everyone grabs on to you," she lectured. "For encouragement, for nourishment, for the knowledge that you'll pull them along. You don't even notice. You just keep sailing upward: serene, buoyant, unburdened. Merciful Buddha! You talk like you're extra ballast! Can't you see? The reason we all push our dreams on to you? You're the *balloon!*"

The idea was so absurd, I almost laughed.

Mrs. Ito, the fiction writer.

chapter twenty

FEBRUARY 7, 1936

After my big realization at Mrs. Ito's, I decided to forge my own separate life.

I taught Mrs. Kawai how to crank the bulky mimeograph that stands on her William IV table. I cooked preserved foods in tremendous quantities—everything dried, marinated, pickled, or salted. I purchased a sewing machine and transformed all my housewife's kimonos into simple Western-style dresses. I was aiming for lightness and mobility—and freedom from guilt—when I made my break in the night.

I found escape would not be so easy.

Mrs. Kawai kept phoning in panic. The mimeograph is jamming! The drum is rejecting the ink!

Chie would stare at her dinner plate—whereupon might rest a pickled plum, two salted radishes, a dried sardine—and would comment, "Is this what we have to eat?"

Hanae was the worst. She began trailing alongside me, critically expounding—"Modern dresses? Out of old kimono cloth?"—on the glaring strangeness of my new wardrobe. Independent for years, she suddenly started pestering me to trim her bangs or to locate some misplaced object.

For every bind that I loosened, five more were flung across me like filaments in a spider's web.

One afternoon as I knelt before Hanae—pinning the hem of one of the skirts I seemed to be continually letting down; ruminating about my life of encumbering tasks, all of no lasting importance—I snapped.

"Stay *still!*"

"I can't! I'm trying, honest, but I just can't!"

I looked up from my work.

Hanae jerked away, fourteen years old, chin raised, blinking in misery and confusion.

I took a breath. Of course she couldn't stay still. Standing stable, while your children move beyond you, is the *parent's* job.

Hanae would be grown in a moment.

There was no point in racing her to the door.

OCTOBER 29, 1936

I decided to stay put until Hanae was grown. Like a baby-sitter hired to straighten magazines and file her nails just in case her charges (actually more competent than she) might need her, I returned to my commitments.

But in an ethereal way.

To escape my purposelessness, I evacuated my body and hovered a few feet above my head: observing life with shallow, jolly dispassion. Up there—floating and diving, not really of this world—I felt like a fetus eavesdropping on a gastrointestinal tract. Blissfully exempt from corporeal matters taking place with such vulgarity nearby.

So when I was told that the Special Higher Police had

raided Mrs. Kawai's—searching for the mailing list she'd carefully memorized—I listened serenely.

"Does it matter?" I blithely said.

Mrs. Ito startled as if she'd been slapped.

"What's wrong with you?" she demanded. "They smashed the mimeograph, they *urinated* on the pieces! Can't you muster some kind of reaction?"

As Mrs. Ito searched my face for some emotional response, her expressive eyes sharp with angry concern, I *did* feel mildly annoyed.

Wasn't it she who'd extolled my buoyancy, my likeness to a hot air balloon?

And on another occasion, as Chie lectured me about my lapse in attention—"Hanae needs a mother, and where are you? Who's this grinning dimwit that's taken your place?"—I again was undaunted. I simply let my buoyancy soar.

Hanae would be fine. All her life she'd been rushing to be gone.

One October morning as I stirred sugar into sesame oil and soy sauce, Hanae flopped on the half wall that separated high house from kitchen.

"I can't stand it!"

She had just turned fifteen and even through my enveloping fog, I noticed that she'd become remarkably pretty.

I stood below her at the stove: tipping the pan, swirling my marinade, watching the fluids merge and separate, slip and slide.

"What's wrong?" I vacantly said.

"I'm bored."

"Well, here's something," I said with a beatific smile. "I'm making a little treat."

I stirred my concoction with a large pair of chopsticks, feeling the gritty texture of sugar crystals—more mindful of them than of Hanae.

"See? I'm marinating these German sausages I found in the foreigners' market."

Hanae didn't respond.

"It'll be a kind of teriyaki, like the hot dogs teriyaki I used to make when we lived in Seattle."

Hanae swung her legs, kicking the half wall. Her white anklets moved back and forth in aimless alternation, like a pair of ambivalent doves.

"I hate my clothes."

"Nonsense," I crooned. "Your papa sends them with all his love."

Hanae looked sullen. "Mari's been gone for over two years."

"Ah, so that's it." I smiled enticingly. "I have something you can do. Come down and help me name my dish. Sausages Steeped in Splendor? Occident Meets Orient?"

"Occident Meets *Accident*!"

Hanae's voice shook with futile anger. She didn't even pretend to smile.

I put down my pan. Inside me a maternal alarm began sounding. I started to wake from my cheerful swoon.

I was familiar with loss. For three years following the death of my husband, I'd slept every night wearing his sweater.

"Sometimes friends leave," I said with gentleness. "It's lonely at first but you'll get used to it."

Hanae leapt from the threshold down into the kitchen. A long graceful girl, already half a head taller than I, she leaned close to my face and sneered.

"Get *used* to it! Dullness, nothingness, you think I want to get used to it? To find it an *acceptable?* You think I'm just a little girl pouting because her playmate's gone?"

"Of course not," I said weakly, startled by her fury. "I know you better than that."

Hanae almost spat.

"You know NOTHING about me," she shouted. "It's not just Mari. I've lost everything I've ever valued. Father, Mari, even school! There's not a single thing left that I love!"

I heard the platitudes pour from my mouth. "That's enough! You have a roof over your head, food on the table . . ."

Her words wounded.

"Do you think you're the only person who's ever been unhappy? And over what? That you're fifteen with your hormones racing!"

In horror I heard myself taunt, almost brag.

"I've known unhappiness. I've seen my loved ones *die!*"

I pulled myself back. Merciful Buddha, what was I doing?

We stood there, stunned strangers, panting at each other.

"Hanae, honey," I finally said. My voice was soft. "I know sometimes things hurt awfully, but if you can't change them, you must accept them. That's what I have done."

Hanae snorted with contempt.

"YOU? Do you think I want to end up like YOU?"

Maybe it *was* hormonal. Or, more likely, a way to regain my attention. Almost immediately, Hanae returned to more normal behavior.

Still, I was disturbed.

A girl looks around to find inspiration, to see who she'll be when she's grown. Hanae looked and found only two choices: Chie or me. A tyrant or a buffoon.

I'd neglected Hanae by setting no stirring example. I'd shown her devotion: ironing nightly all those knife pleats in her skirt. I'd shown her sacrifice: eating the fish's tail, the fruit's bruised parts. I'd even shown her escapism: doddering in cheerful oblivion.

But integrity, dignity, valor?

Still, I was uncertain how to fix it. I spent the next two days wondering what I should do. Should I seize her for a long intimate talk? Should I change myself out of the blue?

Then on the evening of the second day, Chie spoke up at dinner.

"I know her father has final authority in these matters, but to my mind, Hanae's *garments*"—Chie's voice rang with disdain—"have become a trifle tiresome."

I winced. Had Chie overheard our kitchen brawl?

I stole a glance at Hanae. For the first time, she was looking as if Chie might have something interesting to say.

"I have a proposal," Chie continued. "Let's mount an expedition. We'll put on our finest kimonos, take the train beyond Kyoto, and view the autumn leaves at Arashiyama."

Chie's cultivated accent, her rich and regal voice did not merely propose. They *proclaimed*.

"But I have no kimono," said Hanae. She sounded intrigued.

"Besides," I intruded, "the authorities frown on extravagant dressing. It's a display of inappropriate gaiety in this time of martial endeavor." I heard the whine of a spoilsport in my voice. Why was I parroting this propaganda?

Chie ignored me. "Naomi left closets full of kimonos. You can have your pick."

Hanae clapped her hands. She rose to her knees and practically panted with anticipation.

254

I was annoyed. Hanae—an adolescent who usually displayed only irritation, suspicion, or ennui—suddenly looked like a lapdog prancing for treats. Chie, already my superior in self-assurance and candor, was now proving she could meet Hanae's needs better than I.

Overlooked and outshined, I sank into a sulk.

"Mama's clothes?" Hanae's voice, breathless with eagerness, broke through my self-pitying preoccupation. "You'll show me Mama's clothes? You'll let me touch them?"

My antipathy wavered. For once, Hanae's eyes sparkled with hope.

I studied Hanae the way, when she was an infant, I used to memorize the round curve of her cheek, the small scoop that marked the bridge of her nose. Through an accident of genetics, Hanae had been burdened with the astonishing beauty of Naomi and the off-putting hauteur of Chie. It was an intimidating combination, one that—when blended with intelligence, outspokenness, and skepticism—had made her a lonely child.

"Come," Chie said to Hanae. "Let's look through your mother's kimonos. If you'd like, I can help you to try one on."

She paused, as if picturing Hanae in Naomi's clothes.

I did the same. It was like conjuring up the ghost of young Naomi.

Chie made a sound. She blinked and massaged her throat. It was a fascinating gesture, barely perceptible. A stranger would have thought she'd missed in swallowing a small bite of perch and was discreetly dislodging its bones. But I knew at once.

Chie was crying.

Inside, I felt a small grudging shift. It seemed that we all missed Naomi.

Hanae looked up at Chie.

"Yes, please," she whispered, her voice ardent. "I'd like that."

I looked from Hanae to Chie and back again. I felt myself sigh.

Perhaps, I said to myself, perhaps I can bear to share her.

chapter twenty-one

NOVEMBER 14, 1936

The Leaf-Viewing Expedition

Hanae chose a silk kimono the color of burgundy wine. Plumed grass, representing fall harvest, waved along its hem. Azure fans played across her sunflower yellow silk obi, their half-open shapes symbolizing growing good fortune.

"Humph," Chie said when Hanae was dressed. "A sophisticated selection. Dramatic, yet not in competition with the vibrant leaves."

We set out for Arashiyama on a Sunday. Chie wore a violet-gray silk, the color of autumn rain, and an obi shot with threads of real silver.

For the occasion, from the trunk of treasures I had brought from America, I exhumed a champagne-colored silk kimono with a faint stenciling of ripe persimmons.

"That pattern becomes you," Hanae exclaimed, unable to conceal her surprise. "With your short dark hair, you look modern and distinctive. And your obi is the same inky blue as the underwing of a bird!"

"Are you saying I resemble an old crow?" I joked, but everyone knew I was pleased.

Chie summoned Ishigawa's taxi.

"Fancy!" He clapped his hands in applause when he saw us.

We slid across his backseat, the slippery fabric of our clothes making a zipping noise, like fingers pinched and pulled along one string of a Japanese harp.

We arrived at the Kobe train station. Built in the early 1900s, when every architect was influenced by the dazzling 1900 World's Fair in Paris, the train station's roof was a high-arching lacework of glass and steel. Adjoining the station were two huge glass-roofed department stores (resembling Printemps and Galeries Lafayette of Paris), each of which was a subsidiary of a different private railway line. Coursing all around—with competitive weaving, speeding, horn-tooting self-importance—were busy networks of buses owned by the same private railways, municipal buses, and private taxis.

Although it was only 10 A.M. on a Sunday morning, outside the station the streets and sidewalks were jammed. Women selling horoscopes, children selling flowers, and old men selling snacks of sweet potatoes and chestnuts wheeled their pushcarts wherever the population looked most dense. Buddhist monks with black robes and brass begging bowls, uniformed university students, and street musicians playing ancient Japanese lutes wove their way through the crowds.

Though nowhere in observable proximity, the Special Higher Police—a recent manifestation of lifestyle-and-thought control—constituted a felt presence. Only a few months ago the street musicians would have been billing themselves by names such as Maru Shiba Rie or Beigu Kasubei—for Maurice Chevalier and Bing Crosby—and would

258

have been performing zany comedy while singing popular Western songs.

As we hurried under a huge brass clock into the vast train station, light fell from high glass ceiling panes, floating cloud shadows across marble floors. Against those floors, the shhh-shhh shuffling sound of our split-toed sandals joined the crisp clicking rhythm of high heels.

Affluent couples in chic Western clothing dashed by, toting French bakery cakes in silk carrying scarves. Free for a day from factory work, young women in cotton kimonos traveled home to visit their mamas, a festive fish wrapped in newspaper emerging from each girl's crocheted string bag. Milling through the crowd, peering discreetly into trash bins, napping lightly while seated on benches were members of an increasingly large portion of the population. Ragpickers, vagrants, and beggars.

All the while, beyond the grand concourse at multiple gates, long snorting trains—like modern industrial dragons—pulsed with smoky impatience, ready to steam off in every direction.

We found our car, a turn-of-the-century Arashiyama excursion coach hooked to a chain of sleek new cars that would terminate in the ancient yet rapidly modernizing city of Kyoto.

"Ah!" I exclaimed when I entered the coach and saw the red velvet upholstery, the first-class wood-paneled compartment with fixtures of gleaming brass. "I'd forgotten these old excursion cars. The trains I rode in America looked nothing like this!"

My comment surprised Chie.

Chie dislikes trains—"such shrieking, chugging, clanging." To her sensibilities the interior of the old first-class coach was tasteless and gaudy. However—since locomotives are a Western invention—she had always assumed the selection of scarlet and brass to be intentional, honoring a certain loudness that seems central to American culture.

I began to reminisce. "Once in America my husband and I took a trip to Yakima, east across the Cascade Mountains. We had a friend who worked for the railroad and he sent us a pass."

I looked around and repeated myself. "Our coach looked nothing like this!"

"It was less ornate?"

The idea seemed to fill Chie with indignation. If American travelers don't have to put up with such bordello excesses, I could feel her mind huffing, why on earth should I?

I didn't try to conceal my amusement. "Third-class hard seats, littered floors. Yes, it was less ornate."

My comment was not the most kind; it made Chie look foolish. But surprisingly she seemed glad.

Usually *she* was the tactless one, an imperious dowager whose barbs left me stewing in silence. Teasing suggested familiarity.

In a gush of sulfur and smoke, the diesel carried us from the Kobe commercial district.

Our car was barely occupied. A few seats away sat a university student, his shaggy head deep in a mathematics text, and a bit farther a young couple in simple Western clothes who, from the way they leaned into each other, appeared to be newly wed. Near the end of the car sat a three-year-old boy and his mother.

"*Shu shu tu tu*," sang the child. He rolled his mother's abacus along the tracks of the sliding window, pretending he was a train.

We traveled for one hour northeast, passing the ancient wooden temples on the outskirts of Kyoto, exquisite in their unpainted austerity. The train rocked and snorted. The boy's head swung wildly once, twice, then came to rest on his mother's arm.

"Nenkoro, nen, nen, nen, nen," she crooned as the abacus slipped from his hand.

At Kyoto station, more sightseers boarded as our car coupled with a different engine. The train jolted forward and twenty minutes later we entered the deep, forested Arashiyama hills.

Steam hissed, metal squeaked.

Next to a rippling river, by the deserted platform of a two-track (one coming, one going) wooden station, the locomotive wheezed to a stop.

With much production, we disembarked.

Chie led the way. Hampered by her narrow hem, she paused at the doorway of the coach and studied the treacherous metal steps. A raised pattern of tiny diamonds was embossed in the slippery plating.

"Need help?" Hanae's clear voice rang across the quiet platform.

Chie glanced over her shoulder and saw Hanae peering around the door frame.

She wasn't the only one who saw.

Suddenly hands came from nowhere—the conductor, the ticket taker, the just-disembarked university student, even a Shinto priest in a high black hat—all reaching toward Chie, helping her disembark.

Chie found her footing on the rough platform planks and turned to see Hanae at the top of the stairs: her delicate foot in its brocade zori tentatively reaching down.

Long and lovely in Naomi's kimono, yet slightly awkward in her knock-kneed stance, Hanae was surrounded by men with uplifted faces. And when Hanae took the deep downward step, when her kimono hem parted to reveal her smooth straight legs, Chie saw a carnal glint in every man's eye.

Things had changed since I last viewed Arashiyama's autumn maples. For centuries women had come—like an exhibition of late summer's beauty—wearing their finest kimonos, crowding along the long wooden footbridge, peering into the wide tranquil water, blushing with pleasure as their men waxed poetic.

> Elusive beauty, your reflection fills my heart.
> Yet try to seize you and instead,
> Emptiness like tears in my hand.

Over and over, I had come to Arashiyama. First with my mama and papa, and later with my husband, Tadao. Each time family members had competed to create the most poignant verse, knowing that they spoke of the beauty, not only of blazing hillsides and falling, floating leaves, but also of family. For it was a portrait of family, precious and fleeting, that was caught in the river's reflection.

That day with Hanae and Chie, I stood watching the dark water and saw in the swirl of leaves and pedestrians that we were one of the few groups to be all in kimonos.

I listened for the familiar sounds of autumn but instead of poetry I heard distracted chatter: school reports, lunch plans, promotions sought and lost.

I was disappointed.

I had hoped—there, where the spirit of family is so strong, aided by the indirection of poetry—we could tell one another our feelings.

"Mama, Papa, Auntie, come see!"

Not far from us a boy, perhaps six years old, in a middy blouse and navy blue shorts, was dropping a bundle of leaves off the upstream side of the bridge. Quickly he raced to the downstream side to see his flotilla glide past.

"Clever lad!" cried his father, as his mother and aunt rushed to see.

Click, click went his mother's two-toned high-heeled pumps on the planks of the ancient bridge.

Together we watched as the boy, his hands filled with leaves, ran from one side of the bridge to the other.

After a while, the father took a cigarette from the pocket of his double-breasted suit. The scent of tobacco rose on the cool autumn air.

The mother turned to her sister.

"Three generations in kimonos," she murmured. The net of her jaunty little hat nodded in our direction. "There's a sight you hardly see anymore."

Annoyed by the directness of her scrutiny, Chie glared at the woman's reflection. But the river bent and blurred her reproach.

"Timeless," whispered the sister. "Three distinct types of beauty: late autumn, early spring, and high summer."

Mollified, Chie examined our image in the water. She, spare and elegant; Hanae, pliant and pretty; and I, calm and blooming, stood still and striking amid a blur of Western-clad bodies.

We looked like a family.

In my mind I began to formulate a poem.

The boy had a similar idea.

"Fall down, fiery leaves," he chirped in an endearing way.

Chie smiled, perhaps glad that some traditions endured.

The father caught sight of her expression.

"Recite the rest of the poem for the honorable ladies."

"Your beauty is like the splendor of falling bombs," the boy proudly chanted.

Chie's smile froze.

"Advance, imperial glory!"

We ate at a cafe. French wrought-iron bistro tables stood in slanting pools of light, facing windows open to the broad river Oi. The menu was Japanese.

"That little boy on the bridge was quite bright," Hanae remarked to Chie, as if speaking to her equal. Naomi's kimono seemed to make her feel more adult.

"*Otonashiku shinasai*," Chie said irritably. "Don't initiate conversation, follow it."

But she was unable to resist Hanae's lure.

"He wasn't bright. Whatever makes you say he was bright?"

"He *was* bright, brilliant even. For such a small child, his memory was excellent!"

"Foolish girl, don't confuse recall with wisdom," barked Chie. "The boy was a puppet, mouthing ugly words with no comprehension!"

Hanae's enthusiasm died. She sat in sullen silence.

More and more, I could tell, Chie regretted having proposed this whole expedition.

I tried to ease the strain. "Summer has ended but the river is still ablaze." I gestured toward the reflection from the flaming hills.

"Still?" asked Hanae. She reached with her chopsticks to pluck a small piece of sweet potato tempura from a shallow bamboo basket.

Chie examined her form. Soon Hanae would be marriageable. In Japan, the course of a girl's future could hinge on her table manners.

Hanae lifted the sweet potato by a tiny portion of one corner. She dipped it delicately into a porcelain cup of soy-ginger broth and raised it to mouth level. She cocked her head ever so slightly, like a sparrow sipping water, and placed it between her full lips, behind her even teeth, onto her supple pink tongue.

It was a completely unconscious performance yet it made Chie angry.

"Stop eating like that!" she snapped.

Hanae and I startled.

Hanae was eating exactly as Chie had coached her, a way that all innocent girls from good families thought of as simply good manners.

I wondered about Chie's reaction. Perhaps she remembered the train station, the glint of lechery like a knife hidden behind courtly manners. Before too long, a series of utterly unworthy men would be watching Hanae eat. Sitting at the go-between's table, studying Hanae's technique, gauging from it the strength of other appetites.

I shook my head. Such a waste. The men would take no time to appreciate Hanae's more formidable talents. Her razor-sharp memory, her unyielding nature. The way she can swallow the white heat of anger, shaping a grievance this way and that in the pit of her belly—like a master glassblower— until it emerges as a finely crafted grudge.

Men would offer marriage but with no sense of Hanae's

value. They would do so because she eats with the voluptuous refinement of a geisha.

We fell again into silence.

After a while I redirected the conversation.

"When I was small," I said, trying to return to the topics of leaves and rivers, "on summer evenings, people would gather on the terrace of this and other cafes." My voice was slow and lazy, like the river. "They came to watch trained cormorant fishing."

I looked out the window, past the stretch of the Arashiyama bridge, allowing myself to slip back through time.

"One man would stoke a brushfire that danced and snapped inside a wire cage dangling above the prow. Another man would pole. Leading the boat would be a half dozen cormorants, tugging on separate leashes, spanning the water like the edge of an open fan."

I paused and nibbled at a fried tofu cake. I frowned.

The tofu cakes were crisp, light, without a trace of oil. They were nothing like my own.

"Don't these cakes seem a little insipid?" I inquired.

"Go on with the story," Hanae urged, again displaying a tendency to want to steer social intercourse. "Why the cormorants, why the fire?"

Her tone amused me. Even in her shimmering kimono, Hanae's domineering nature was hard to conceal. Maybe she'd do better at marriage than I'd thought. She clearly wasn't meant for a fainthearted man.

"The cormorants' duty was to capture fish that came to watch the fire," I explained. "Every so often, the birds would climb aboard and allow the oarsmen to caress their long slender throats. They'd spit their catch into woven baskets."

I gestured toward the broad river. "On hot summer nights a dozen such boats would rake the river, moving from downstream to up. They were like stars blazing across a dark sky."

The autumn sun streamed through the cafe's open windows, warming where we sat. A small breeze sent dried leaves scurrying along the cobbled street.

Chie sighed.

The aroma of green tea rose rich and bitter.

An old discontentment awoke.

"Were you there, on the cafe terraces, watching the boats?" Chie's voice came sharp and sudden.

"No," I said, not understanding, still lulled by my memory. "I didn't want to be with the revelers. I wanted to be part of the night."

I laughed a little, remembering.

"We came every summer, starting when I was nine or ten. We'd watch from the dark by the edge of the banks. Papa would buy me a bag of assorted fireworks. Mama would cover her ears—"

"I was there too," Chie interrupted. "I was there with Naomi and Kan."

I looked up and caught her watching me: an unsettling, close, hungry stare.

Hanae turned to Chie. "My mother was here?" she asked eagerly. "Here on this terrace? Like us?"

"No, we rode the barges." Chie was distracted and dismissive.

Hanae flinched; I rushed to deflect and explain.

"Tourists drifted among the fishing boats, on narrow barges strung with candlelit paper lanterns. Concessionaires floated past selling sake and beautifully boxed dinners."

267

I paused and glanced at Chie.

"You must have come when Naomi was very small, before I knew her."

I thought a moment.

"Maybe it's best that way," I said. "If we'd been playmates, Naomi and I would have tried to coordinate our outings. We'd have missed the magic of the evening, spending all our time searching for each other."

Chie answered slowly, as if revealing a truth to herself.

"As I missed the magic of motherhood, always searching for babies I'd lost."

I glanced at her with a kind of shy caution. *Babies,* she'd said. Was it true? Had she grieved for me as well as my brother?

Hanae in turn was looking at me.

"You seem different today, Auntie." She shook her head. "I don't know, maybe it's just that kimono."

I took my eyes off Chie. I fingered the lustrous cloth of my sleeve.

"This kimono was a wedding present from Most Honorable Mrs. Fuji, your great-obaa-san." I told Hanae. "I haven't worn it in many years, but now I remember, whenever I did, I somehow felt more confident and calm."

"I know how that is! In Mama's clothes, I feel . . ." Hanae groped for a word, the concept of serenity so alien. "Better."

She trailed off lamely and blushed, made suddenly shy by her disclosure.

"You remind me of Naomi when she was your age," Chie said.

Hanae's head jerked upward with sudden eagerness. She looked so pleased and surprised; it was for her such a rare reaction to something said by her grandmother that Chie looked less gratified than pained.

Chie turned to me. She took a deep breath.

"And you remind me of your father, Kan. Patient, generous, wise."

I looked at her with alarm, fearful of some sudden and profound weakening in the arteries of her head or heart.

Never before had she strung so many nice words together.

My scrutiny seemed to make her uncomfortable.

"Both peasants, mind you, not brisk and purposeful like the Fujis."

She stopped and took another deep breath, almost as if inhaling the aroma of Kan's pipe tobacco—a packet of which she still keeps under her pillow.

"You have the same walk," she mused, perhaps talking to Kan as much as to me. "You have a tendency to meander, lost in thought: your hands behind your back, your shoulders rounded, your neck stretched forward."

"You know how I walk?" I stammered. I'd thought that she'd never really *seen* me.

"Of course!" she snapped. "You walk like a turtle!"

We blinked at each other.

She cleared her throat.

"An *intelligent* turtle," she reluctantly amended, "whose curiosity outreaches its stride."

I felt confused. I studied her closely.

Finally, I smiled.

chapter twenty-two

NOVEMBER 23, 1936

How I Imagine Chie Would See It

I'd been planning that trip to Arashiyama ever since I read Etsuko's I-story. Invasion of privacy? Nonsense! This is Japan, the land of propinquity; there's no such thing as a secret—only discretion. Besides, it was my duty to intervene. Etsuko was falling apart. She was drifting away in an impenetrable fog of inconceivably stupid good cheer, as if she'd become Ophelia.

Which brings me to another topic: her writing. Etsuko is reasonably accurate in depiction of incident and even intent (if I grant her a generous amount of artistic freedom), but she's limited in characterization. Take Hanae as an example. Etsuko makes her seem too savvy, too old. Especially in that early scene, when Hanae gets insight into love from thinking about her clothes. Preposterous! A child of ten?

To be kind—and I am not unkind despite what one might think from Etsuko's story—I imagine Etsuko honestly believes that Hanae (precocious, I'll admit) is the way she describes. Mothers often are overawed by their children: dazzled and a little scared by how fast and how far they are growing.

Speaking of mothers, I have some complaints about the mother character (namely me). Such a narrow woman. No wonder she's so sour. One gets the impression that all she ever does is change her clothes! Does Etsuko reveal where the family finds the money to live in such splendor? Does she describe the mother's skills at managing their properties, at trading international stocks and bonds? I am not a provincial woman. Even when Kan was alive, it was I—the Fuji heir—who handled matters of law and finance.

But again, let me be generous. Etsuko cannot help her perspective. It is difficult to see one's mother as human.

I am reminded of one of Naomi's Western masterpieces. As I recall, in *Pride and Prejudice* the mother suffers a similar fate. Poor Mrs. Bennet, she's made to appear quite the fool. But not to me; I think she's the character who is most real. (It is little wonder readers prefer the proud and passionate Mr. Darcy; he's a fiction if ever I saw one.) Certainly, Mrs. Bennet is rattled about marriage. All those daughters and no dowries; she's trying to keep them alive! And isn't this just the way mothers talk to their children? "Stand up straight." "Smile, Jane." "This family is fraying my nerves!"

It seems to me that *true* maternal affection is communicated through rebuke and instruction.

NOVEMBER 24, 1936

Would Chie really see it this way? Who knows? I am, after all, writing a fiction. But then again, perhaps too much is made of the distance between fiction and fact. Tadao imagined I was witty and by so believing made it come true.

So perhaps imagination constructs reality as much as the opposite way around. After all, things that happen in real life (as opposed to in your imagination) don't actually *happen* in real life, do they? They're perceived and interpreted inside your mind.

My thinking on this is admittedly muddy. But as there is magic in everyday plainness (the softness of moss on an old rocky wall), might not there be truth in what is imagined?

And recently I've been remembering THIS IS AMERICA!—Reverend Mitsui's humble yet ambitious taxonomic tract. Most likely, those neat little columns (restraint/spontaneity, receptivity/activity) weren't intended as endorsement or warning at all. Carrying no intimations of conflict—of good or bad, better or worse—perhaps they were complementary examples instead. Like yin and yang, East and West, fiction and fact.

chapter twenty-three

MARCH 20, 1938

For a while I thought I had reached the end of my I-story, with a muted rapprochement achieved between Chie and me. It wasn't very smooth; we still functioned like a pair of eccentric old maids forced into collaboration for the sake of a child. But there was a cautious complement in our relationship—a balancing of opposite forces—that smacked of mutual liking.

Sometimes I saw us as a pair of vaudevillian partners: one older and irascible—the critic and strategist, the destroyer of ill-founded illusion—one younger, effusive, and burbling.

"Stop that cheerful yammering, that ceaseless blathering," Chie frequently barked.

And though I knew I'd never be loved like Naomi, I also knew—behind Chie's grousing—that both of us saw my value.

With Hanae, my relationship also was changing. At seventeen, she had little need for my nurturing. If I reached to straighten her collar or to brush back a wisp of her hair, Hanae would twist as if being scratched by the scrambling paws of an annoying, overeager dog.

Yet in deprivation there are sudden grace notes, like the sweet hallucinations that come to a sleep-starved man. As Hanae allowed me less and less access to caretaking, she herself began to display moments of tenderness.

One evening as she readied for bed and I offered a small cup of water to the spirits of my mama, papa, Tadao, and Naomi—their photographs propped on Naomi's wedding mirror—Hanae caught me frowning at a wiry gray hair.

She came over and sank down by my side.

"Here, let me," she offered. Then, reaching over, Hanae plucked the offending intruder right out of my scalp.

Since then, on several occasions, always at her initiation, Hanae conducts a gray hair inquisition. Hers is a brilliant strategy of offering comfort and saving face. For as we sit facing the mirror, her warm hands lightly ruffling my hair, we can look at each other—indirectly. Both gladdened by the contact, each providing the other with solace for the discomforts of growing in age.

And if now and then she yanks just a little too harshly, isn't it a fine way to redirect the natural hostilities of an adolescent toward her mother?

So it is I've begun to recognize that just as I am, I still have something to offer. With the relief of homecoming, I've reeled my soul back into my body and returned to my simple life. With an odd kind of confidence, I've even suggested home economics as a new direction for the dissident ladies.

Perhaps I should explain. The February 26 Incident of 1936, a wide-scale plan for the assassination of statesmen and senior officers, was also the date that our mimeograph was destroyed. During the incident, fourteen hundred soldiers led by a cadre of fanatical young officers stormed and seized Tokyo's police headquarters, the War Ministry and General Staff Headquarters, and the new Diet building. Their goal was to kill everyone who had impeded their cause of "imperial glory." The extremists and their followers retained control for three days, relinquishing power only after saner army officials secured the support of the emperor and forced their surrender.

Although the February 26 Incident was followed by genuine efforts to reestablish discipline within the army, by a brief reflourishing of representative government opposed to military aggression, and by economic relief as employment rates rose and the years of depression lifted—it was too late to stop the push for war. The spirit of nationalism had risen too high. Fearing that General Chiang Kai-shek's 1937 alliance with his longtime communist adversaries was intended to drive Japanese citizens from the north China territory of Manchukuo, even ordinary Japanese wanted his Nanking-based government restrained.

In this atmosphere, repression in the name of national unity returned. Government censors banned the importation of foreign newspapers. Overwhelmed by the voices for military escalation, Mrs. Kawai lapsed into listless discouragement and Mrs. Ito flew into high agitation. I, at that time, was just beginning to rouse from my swoony state of mirth. For all of 1936, I'd been sleepwalking as political chaos swirled around me.

With no overseas newspapers to provide information and no mimeograph to disperse it, with the three of us divided by distractions, the ladies' group lapsed.

Then last summer, on a hot July 1937 afternoon, a Japanese battalion searching for the source of some gunfire demanded access to a walled city in China. When refused, Japan declared full formal war.

War wasn't the will of the people. Prime Minister Konoye made a mild protestation—it was an extreme reaction to a minor incident—but by that time the government was largely controlled by the military and he was overruled.

At home—having recovered my interest first in Hanae, then in housework, then in life—I had an idea. I telephoned the dissident ladies. Under a not entirely feigned interest in child care, food, and fashion, we began collecting international women's magazines.

This was our plan. In these ladies' magazines (still not banned because of their perceived triviality), buried beneath tips for curing colic and getting along with your mother-in-law, were facts about current events. Whenever we uncovered some piece of censored news—through seemingly im-promptu gatherings and apparently accidental meetings, in our innocuous, babbling way—we distributed the information.

The women we contacted were helpful; they eagerly passed news along. Of course we were still under surveillance. But as long as we appeared to be a gossipy group of harmless hot-headed women, the authorities mostly left us alone. They'd forgotten that babbling water can wear away stone.

So it was—through the everyday chatter of women, through the passing of small bits of intelligence at dress fittings and moon viewings, at the fishmonger's and the greengrocer's—we were attempting to stop the war.

We had high hopes for our subterfuge.

Then came Nanking.

Hanae Gets a New Teacher

One March morning, in her second-to-last year at girls' upper level, Hanae went to school and found that a war hero had been hired. Lieutenant Matsunaga was in his early twenties and was missing his right foot. He was a veteran of the capture of Nanking. And although General Chiang Kai-shek had retreated to regroup, all of Japan thought the fall of his capital city had broken the general's will. With just a little continued pressure, it was believed, the war soon would be over and won.

From the first moments of his teaching appointment, Lieutenant Matsunaga began changing the format of military drill. The girls stopped practicing bamboo bayonet thrusts and wall scaling. Instead they rolled bandages and learned how to carry stretchers with gentleness and speed.

Each day as they practiced in the school yard—tenderly wrapping a volunteer victim in a soft blanket and rushing, with no jarring movements, toward imaginary medic wagons—Headmaster Kido came to his window. He always looked a little distraught.

Hanae's hunch was that he was disappointed in the mildness of the activities but unwilling to criticize a wounded war hero.

It also seemed to Hanae that, unlike her headmaster, her classmates *loved* the war hero. They imagined him both sensitive and brave. Soon they appeared to be thinking of little else, arranging opportunities where the lieutenant could overhear their declarations of ardor.

"The young officers who attempted that coup d'état weren't deranged!" exclaimed Reiko Watanabe (a girl who, Hanae reported, is famous for the fact that she carries lipstick in her schoolbag). "Calling for the execution of all senior statesmen may have been extreme, but their basic belief was sound social control."

Hanae found Reiko and the other girls stupid but she did not condemn them. Since the curriculum shrank there was little to occupy their minds. In Hanae's opinion, the girls' crushes on military drill instructor Matsunaga seemed as good an activity as any.

Though not for Hanae, who retreated to her solitary ways. Having nothing of substance about which to think, she practiced her memorization. Soon she knew everything about first aid—accidents, airway obstruction, appendicitis, bleeding, blisters, broken bones, all the way through to tick bites, unconsciousness, wrist injuries, and yeast rash.

Hanae also practiced her needlework, making *sen'ninbari*—thousand-stitch waistbands—to send away to soldiers. The needlework soothed her. She liked the idea that the pure-hearted efforts of women could protect a soldier from harm. As she worked, offering stitches on other girls' waistbands, collecting one thousand random stitches for her own, Hanae thought of her pregnant mother embroidering all those dozens of pieces of underwear.

But regardless of her zeal, Hanae earned no praise in school. Her theory was that the disapproval had something to do with her uniform. While the other girls' had shrunk a long time ago, hers—still sent from her father in Seattle—had retained a big boxy collar and a full swing of razor-sharp pleats.

One morning during assembly, Hanae heard her name.

"Shinoda, Hanae. Please come to the podium."

She started forward, somewhat excited, thinking her mnemonic feats finally would be rewarded.

"Young ladies, please note," proclaimed the headmaster, "how Hanae dresses her hair."

Hair? Was he losing his mind? Hanae twisted to give him a stare.

"Notice, please, the long simple braid, a seeming concession to modesty. A commendable coiffure, albeit a bit odd for someone so lavishly dressed in this time of national austerity."

She flushed. Now she understood. She was being punished for her clothes.

"Yet if you look closely, you will notice that this simple braid is not what it seems. At its end, you will note not a plain piece of elastic but a *brass* barrette, a *contemptible* waste of metal!"

The headmaster's preoccupation with metal was no idiosyncratic aberration. In the five years since Chie first chided me for salvaging tinfoil, metal conservation had become a symbol of national will. Indeed, just this year the government canceled what had been a great focus of patriotic pride: the commitment that Tokyo host the 1940 Olympic Games. The reason given for the cancellation was that steel needed for munitions should not be squandered on stadiums.

As Headmaster Kido finished his speech, Hanae's classmates stood stiff and silent. No one seemed to know what to do.

The headmaster waited.

Nervous giggles began to erupt from the tension, rattling like sporadic gunfire. Slowly the giggles amplified, catching here and there, sweeping the room, until Hanae stood under a full volley of derisive laughter.

"Step down."

The headmaster gave a nod to release her.

Hanae walked from the podium a changed person. She resolved to be nobody's fool. As she passed, no one dared to look at her but she saw a number of girls quietly reaching up, removing barrettes from their hair.

Later that morning, Lieutenant Matsunaga canceled girls' drill. Balancing on his crutches, he clapped his hands and declared an early recess.

"Use the time to consider these words," stormed the usually silent hero: "It will take more than barrettes to claim righteousness in this war."

Hanae had no time to consider his words. Kimiko Takahashi began to pursue her. She maneuvered toward Hanae through the thick of the lunchroom. She called out Hanae's name in the hall. Throughout the day, Hanae avoided Kimiko through quick maneuvering and several hasty retreats to the outhouse.

Yet Kimiko proved tenacious. As they rode the streetcar home, Hanae evaded her only by choosing a seat between a window and a large, loudly snoring man.

When they disembarked at the streetcar's terminus and began the dusty walk toward the village, Kimiko pounced.

"Want a chocolate bar?"

What an obvious setup, thought Hanae. "I think not."

She immersed herself in the scenery.

Spring had come early this year. Pollywogs grew legs in the marshes. The meadows, in summer a favorite site for catching fireflies, were blue with forget-me-nots.

"Come on," Kimiko insisted. "Chocolate is good and hard to get. Don't deprive yourself out of pride."

"I am not prideful," Hanae stated with dignity. "I am prudent about my nutrition."

Kimiko laughed. "I used to dislike you," she remarked. "The way you talk, so careful and haughty. But now I like it. It's a way of remaining unbowed."

Kimiko's words were intriguing. Again she held out the chocolate bar.

Hanae slowed her pace and took it.

In her effort to lose Kimiko, Hanae had been hurrying. Because she was tall and a good athlete, it was usually a successful tack. But with Kimiko it was different. Kimiko's strong legs matched Hanae's stride. With a jab of competitiveness, Hanae recalled that the previous year on field day, Kimiko had won all the jumping events.

Kimiko interrupted Hanae's thoughts.

"I didn't think it was fair," she said, "the way the headmaster attacked you."

Out of the corner of her eye, Hanae gave Kimiko a skeptical once-over.

Kimiko was frowning. Her dark brows knit with recollection.

Hanae experienced another competitive pang. Even frowning, Kimiko was remarkably pretty.

Feeling Hanae's stare, Kimiko turned with a little half smile.

"Thank you for the candy," Hanae said stiffly. "It was kind of you to share."

To avoid obligation, she'd decided to show gratitude for the chocolate.

"You're welcome. My father imports plenty." Kimiko paused. Her voice took on an edge somewhere between humor and anger. "It's one benefit of being the daughter of an outcast."

"Outcast?" Hanae was surprised by the word. "Your father's rich; everyone's envious!"

Kimiko grew serious. "My father is an international trader. He's interested in the rest of the world. These days that fact, added to the envy you speak of, makes him the target of suspicion."

She thought awhile.

"I guess that's what made me so mad at the headmaster. It's obvious he was picking on you because your auntie is questioning this war."

"Auntie?"

Kimiko looked annoyed.

"Come on, Hanae, everyone knows she belongs to a dissident women's group."

"Dissident? They clip recipes from *ladies'* magazines!"

Hanae considered the magazines: their tips on how to keep a marriage fresh, on identifying various forms of blight that attack American gardens, on new uses for old silk stockings. Hanae had read them as closely as a fortune-teller reads tea leaves, because the magazines came from her father.

It's not as if Akira neglected her. He sent sailor suits and cans of a questionable new food called Spam. But his letters were full of sentences like "I hope your health is good" or "I trust you are enjoying your studies." Hanae had found little to help imagine his world.

The magazines helped. They provided settings, props, and conflicts that she used to make her father come alive. Mentally, she placed him in the blighted gardens, frowning at the root rot. With the assistance of American women's magazines, Hanae had invented a whole life for her father. Rich with the solace of timesaving meals and the drama of vexing stains.

Kimiko interrupted Hanae's daydreaming.

"Maybe your auntie clips recipes, but it's part of a deliberate strategy, a way to keep information alive."

Changing the world through cooking. Hanae shook her head. The scheme seemed so harebrained she knew it had to be mine.

Kimiko gave Hanae a sideways look. "You know, my parents really admire her. And your grandmother too—the way she stopped collecting rents on her property when the depression began, and began selling her heirlooms instead."

Hanae stood in shocked silence. To her (as it was to me when she told me) this was sudden news.

Then, exercising her resolve to be nobody's fool, Hanae sniffed. "One would never guess it from *your* behavior," she said coldly. "As I recall, when you came to our house, you treated my aunt very badly."

Kimiko blushed.

"I was jealous," she explained. "I was popular but worried because, deep down inside, I was bookish. Then you came to town. Unapologetic about who you are. You seemed so smart, so unapproachable, so above the taunting you got for your clothes." She shook her head. "I thought your confidence came from old money. Your family is samurai. Mine is merchant. You know the prejudices about merchants: ruthless, moneygrubbing. I hated who we were; I wanted to be upper class."

She stopped and looked Hanae full in the face. "I'm sorry I was impolite. I was stupid. If it's any consolation, my rudeness was nothing compared to the contempt I showed to my father."

Hanae looked down and studied her shoes. She was shamed by Kimiko's candor. Hanae had been one of those people who look down on the merchant class.

Hanae searched for some conciliatory words.

"You're not stupid," she finally said. "By the way, congratulations on placing first in the high school entrance exams."

"Placing first doesn't mean I'm not stupid," Kimiko replied with an embarrassed shrug. "Placing first just takes mindless memorization."

Hanae winced. She'd worked hard to be proven second best at a skill Kimiko didn't even value.

Kimiko noticed. She grew flustered. "I sound arrogant, don't I? I'm sorry. I should have just said thanks."

"Not arrogant. Smart. Seeing the meaning behind things. Like the way you knew about Grandmother's heirlooms and the real purpose of Aunt Etsuko's ladies' group."

"That isn't smart," said Kimiko. "That's common knowledge."

Hanae sighed. She didn't even have common knowledge.

Kimiko read her thoughts.

"Don't worry, Hanae, you *are* smart. Before school got so boring, I saw how you performed. You have a good mind. You understand English. You've read an amazing number of Western authors."

Kimiko paused. Her voice grew soft and sad.

"I really was looking forward to high school, the exposure to different ideas. Now they've taken all that away."

She shook her head.

"You're lucky Hanae, to have read so widely. My father, the successful importer, tried to get me a translation of Tolstoy but it was seized at the dock and impounded."

Hanae's head jerked upward.

She had read seven volumes of Western Masterpieces in Translation and the books weighed heavy on her soul. Five thousand pages and no one with whom to share them. Hanae felt like a musician who'd inherited a trunk of orchestral sheet music only to find all her accompanists gone.

She decided to accept Kimiko's truce.

"You're interested in translations?" she said enticingly.

Kimiko nodded.

"Stick with me," Hanae mysteriously punned. "We'll translate our war into peace."

What I Later Learned About Masao Matsunaga's Enlistment

At the time he enlisted, Lieutenant Masao Matsunaga—Hanae's new military drill instructor—was a university student. He could have received a deferment.

Masao's father was neither proud nor angry when he learned about the enlistment. He sat stiff and silent at the low dinner table, as if the flap-flapping of kimono sleeves on their distant scarecrow was suddenly all-important to hear.

"It can be undone," he muttered. "It was a rash act but I know it can be undone."

"I don't want it undone!" Masao couldn't suppress his annoyance. He'd come home with his big announcement, and this was the reaction he received?

"Mother!" Masao demanded with irritation. "Convince him!"

Mrs. Matsunaga looked blankly from her son to her husband. A dish of cold *somen* noodles that she'd been clearing lay forgotten in her lap.

Thirty or forty seconds ticked by.

A cicada cried jiiiii in the hall.

Masao's mother pressed a handkerchief to her brow.

"Tuberculosis!" Mr. Matsunaga seized the word as if encountering, by chance, a beloved long-lost childhood friend.

He eyed his youngest son with shrewdness.

"You're thin. Good, good. And pale. Now if you hunched a bit and held a handkerchief to your lips . . ."

"I wouldn't feign illness!"

Mr. Matsunaga ignored this. Deep in contemplation, he tapped his chopsticks across his palm.

"Remember the symptoms, just before the induction ceremony, when they ask if you have any last-minute doubts. Night sweats, breathlessness, weight loss. Mama, can we do anything to speed up that weight loss?"

Masao's mother, her eyes wide as a child's, snapped to sudden efficiency.

"Starting one week before, no more meals," she commanded with maternal authority. "For mild dehydration, I'll feed him only fermented tofu cakes spiced with red chili peppers."

"Will that do the trick?" wondered Masao's father. Although it was he who had asked the question, he now seemed awed that Mama—the family healer, the maker of hot rice-flour poultices—seemed so conversant with the induction of illness.

"Yes. It will give Masao-kun a weak and feverish look."

The use of his name, his *baby* name, brought Masao back to the matter of manly enlistment.

"This isn't honorable!" he interrupted with rage.

His parents turned and stared.

At the edge of the veranda Masao heard a fly, entangled in mosquito netting, buzz and bumble with impotent fury.

After the capture of Nanking life sped up to a frenzy. Initially, whispered rumors about "excessive force," which we Japanese assumed referred to mistreatment of civilians, made citizens uneasy. With memories of the February 26, 1936, Incident not that distant, the rumors were all too believable. If Japanese soldiers could murder cabinet officers and attempt to assassinate their own military commanders, all for the crime of being insufficiently zealous, who could tell what they would do to Chinese? But protestation was dampened by fear. For if you were perceived as seditious, who could say what the army might do to you?

Additionally, international disapproval only strengthened national resolve. Presented with an image of heroic Japan protecting Asia from encircling ABCD—American, British, Chinese, Dutch—powers (the alphabetically nonsequential French in Indochina were omitted from the slogan), citizens began shouting "Banzai!"

Then, as politicians made speeches extending well beyond listeners' attention, as small business owners started selling miniature flags, as everyone began calculating how best to exploit public mood for personal gain, democracy disappeared.

I shouldn't have felt so surprised. After all, democracy and parliamentary procedure are foreign concepts not fully comprehended by most of the public. Despite two generations of access to an astonishingly progressive educational system, few people have more than a fifth-grade education. Ancient ideas like clan loyalty and unquestioning obedience are much easier to understand.

And so, children have started citizen drives. Fresh troops,

boys in stiff uniforms with eager proud faces, are in transport everywhere. For a while, the Ministry of Education increased its efforts to erase Western words from Japanese vocabulary, but I was pleased to see Chie's prophesy—that small, simple pleasures might save us—has seemed to come true. When ordered to replace, with Japanese phrases, baseball terms like "strike," "ball," "run," and "out" (the ministry was not foolish enough to try to eliminate baseball itself), games froze with self-conscious confusion as players stumbled to recall the new words. A demand to eliminate the practice of calling one's parents Mama and Papa was similarly quickly abandoned.

Movies proved less resilient. The American films to which Chie and I had been exposing Hanae no longer are imported. For the most part, Japanese film companies now are releasing movies like *The Human Bombs*, portraying the valor of soldiers who sacrifice themselves for comrades in war.

The mighty Toho Studios of Osaka even stopped producing samurai feature films. These movies had presented stories of solitary seventeenth-century ronin samurai—a samurai with no bond to a liege lord—who would stride into town, unify villagers in their struggle against some nefarious bandit warlord, then stride away in somewhat lonely nobility. In these movies, the samurai always left behind a populace graced by a deeper understanding of courage and integrity, and a beautiful widow forever grateful and wistful for the example of manhood he'd provided for her fatherless boy.

The demise of the samurai movies made me think of Tatsuo Tanida. A cinematographer for Toho Studios, three years earlier he had come several times to our antiwar group. Tall, thin, and middle aged—with the quiet, focused demeanor of an engineer—Mr. Tanida was not at all the movie magnate, wearing a French beret and shouting directions through a megaphone, that I had expected.

Mr. Tanida was very patient when Mrs. Ito and I (with our ever-present narrative ambitions) shamelessly peppered him with questions about cinematic storytelling. With loving detail, he explained the use of "the pan," "the tilt," and "the crane" for establishing mood and motivation. He described how the shots of "master," "two or three," "over the shoulder," and "close-up" can be coordinated to intensify a dramatic scene. As I listened I realized that Mr. Tanida's films, like Mr. Tanida himself, were more than they initially seemed. Besides providing children with sizzling swordplay and adults with inspiring romance, Mr. Tanida's samurai movies had served the sly purpose of advocating ideas of individual conscience and social resistance.

Mr. Tanida came only two or three times to our meetings. Foreseeing the rise of propaganda movies, he left the studios to take a job as a newsreel photographer. Though he was apprehensive about the effects his new job might have on his wife, his six-year-old son, and his politically cautious mother, Mr. Tanida's intention was to provide the public with an alternate point of view.

As a result, whenever I went to the movies, I found myself examining the newsreels. Sitting in the dark, I'd search for clues that the footage of munitions factory openings and paper conservation drives might be Mr. Tanida's. I was looking for his keen observation and subversive storytelling, for his signature lighting style.

About one year ago, between assignments, Mr. Tanida dropped in at Mrs. Kawai's. He briefed us with information he'd picked up from foreign correspondents and told us he finally was being sent overseas to cover the war. Four months later when Mr. Tanida returned from China, he began giving public lectures. I was alarmed when I read in the newspapers that he'd been arrested for his outspokenness, but recently I'd read that he'd been released.

With all this activity swirling around me, I too became caught in the frenzy. Although the cause I championed was antiwar, I became as seduced by the romance of personal heroism as any seventeen-year-old infantry soldier.

As the last few faculty members fled the foreigners' school, I went to their rummage sale. I made my purchase, a mimeograph machine to replace Mrs. Kawai's, with an elevated sense of historical self-importance.

Therefore I was filled with indignant impatience when, one Sunday, Mrs. Ito suggested we gather at the viscount's Mount Rokko retreat. To travel one hour out of the city, in this period of urgency, seemed a waste of my time.

Mount Rokko

One Sunday afternoon in the foothills of a faraway forest I paced along a small wooden platform. Wearing a bias-cut dress that was made (curiously, an onlooker might say) out of ikat-patterned kimono cloth (deep blue with small white squares) and a too-thin-for-the-mountains jacket of midnight blue linen, I stamped my high heels against the chill. With only grandiose and irritable thoughts to amuse me, I waited for the Mount Rokko cable tram.

By the edge of the woods stood a doe—bracing her fore-hooves along the trunk of a dogwood, stretching her neck toward her dinner. She froze with sudden attention. With a lurch, a bounce, a whir of coiled cables, a tiny yellow capsule arrived.

I boarded with one other passenger.

The capsule swung out, skimming an evergreen forest. Beneath us, panicked rabbits crisscrossed the melting snow—crazily, with only instinctive strategy—fleeing from our shadow.

My pulse pounded in my ears.

Much of my annoyance at having to make the trip was based on the fact I found heights alarming.

Our angle deepened. The forest fell away. On the rim of the universe, an increasing blue arc was the edge of the Inland Sea.

I inched forward in my seat. Manufactured in Switzerland with taller passengers in mind, the cable car left my legs dangling. I found my footing but the thin vibrating floor made me feel slightly queasy. I tried focusing on the forest but the drop left me dizzy. In desperation, I tried inhaling while counting to ten.

Cypress mingled with sulfur fumes curling up from hidden hot springs.

I exhaled and found I felt better.

"Are you coming for the baths?"

The other passenger, a pleasant-featured man in his early forties, was smiling at me.

"Would you like a . . ." He rummaged through a rucksack neatly covered with badges from Buddhist mountain pilgrimages. Finally he pulled out a banana.

291

He frowned. "No, no, too bruised. That won't do." Once again he dived into his sack.

"Thank you, but I don't need anything. It's only a twelve-minute ride." I took another deep breath. Only nine more minutes, I thought, if I'm lucky.

"No trouble at all." Deep in his rucksack, the man's voice was muffled.

The capsule shook slightly on its slender cable. I shifted my focus to the steady horizon.

I had almost forgotten the man when . . .

"Raisins!"

He held out a tiny bag, large enough for only an individual serving, grinning as if he'd reeled in a two-hundred-pound tuna.

How could I help but like him?

"Thank you. Oh no! I couldn't take them all. Please let's share, Mr. . . ."

"Hashimoto, Yoshi's the name."

"Sone. Etsuko Sone."

Mr. Hashimoto leaned over and shook all the raisins into my palm.

I gave him a look of reproach.

"I thought we were going to share."

"I saved some for myself," he assured me.

He leaned back, popping into his mouth with gusto what was certainly the only remaining raisin.

"Don't you love it here!" he exulted, gesturing grandly toward the sea and the mountains. "I'm never certain if it's the hot springs, the air, or the view that's the curative factor!"

I laughed, my fear of heights eclipsed by his good humor.

The tram climbed through cloudless blue space. Below us, hawks swooped and glided.

"In America they say hawks are a symbol of war," I noted without thinking.

Mr. Hashimoto flushed. "Mrs. Sone," he said sternly, "in this beautiful place, I pray, speak of peace, not of war."

Later as I stood in a cool curve of stone, steel, and glass cantilevered on the side of the mountain, I thought of Mr. Hashimoto.

I *had* come to Mount Rokko for peace. Peace from ego as well as from war.

I looked around the Itos' retreat: elegant, simple, and soothing. Sisal rugs, a twentieth-century bow to tatami, were positioned on hardwood flooring. Furniture—angled cushions of leather supported by tubular steel—was arranged as if sculpture.

The only ornamentation was on the southwest side, where from floor-length windows the forest dropped into the sea.

Mrs. Kawai joined me by the windows.

"There are the trams," she pointed.

In middistance, small yellow spots provided movement and industry to the landscape, like bees pollinating a garden.

Mrs. Ito strode restlessly back and forth.

"I've invited a special guest," she explained.

She looked around with distraction. "Tea, coffee. I forgot the beverages!"

As she hurried into a kitchen partially concealed by a wall of frosted glass bricks, I heard her thrashing around with remarkable—for a noblewoman—familiarity, opening cabinets, slamming drawers.

Above her noise came a rap at the front door.

"Somebody's here," I called.

"Can you get it?"

I moved across the room, paused, and opened the door.

Only inches away was the face of Hanae's military drill instructor.

"Lieutenant Matsunaga!" I gasped.

My mind clouded with panic. Perhaps he was conducting a raid!

Mrs. Ito appeared with coffee beans in her hands.

"Lieutenant Matsunaga," she echoed, "thank you for joining us."

chapter twenty-four

Lieutenant Matsunaga Joins the Peace Group

Mrs. Ito barely let her guest settle.

"You say you're a pacifist. So, why join the army?"

Lieutenant Matsunaga stirred his coffee. With delicacy, he placed his spoon at the side of his saucer.

"At first I was disinterested. As an undergraduate I was going through a period of posturing: critical of authority, safe in the knowledge that ultimately my classmates and I would lead lives of position and status. I'd heard rumors about military induction: the brutal discipline, the deliberate breaking of will. Why should I risk it? I said to myself. I already have a soft path to glory."

"What changed you?" Mrs. Ito demanded.

"What indeed?" said the war hero. "I grew idealistic. I decided to save the world."

The lieutenant started to laugh. Loud mirthless choking echoed through the Itos' retreat. We sat politely but his laughter didn't stop. It went on until I worried for him, until I wondered if I should get up, go over, and shake him.

The lieutenant was suddenly serious.

"There was so much poverty, you see. In the villages around my parents' house, fuel was short, supplies were low; people were actually starving."

He looked at us searchingly.

"At the university, life was easy. My friends and I engaged in debate. They saw war as immoral. Not just because it's fought for reasons of evil but also because, so often, it's fought for no reason at all. No hatred, no fear, but as a kind of gentlemen's sport."

"A sport?" Mrs. Ito recoiled.

"Yes, like rugby. A gathering of men bearing no particular malice, willing to inflict and risk pain, even death, for the exhilaration of the game."

He glanced at his beautiful long hands.

"Some even believed that the League of Nations is a perversion: setting rules of sportsmanship. They said that by its very existence, the League provides an ennobled legitimacy to war."

We sat stiff and silent.

"I shock you? Good. Cynicism is dangerous; it excuses inaction. At the university I saw too much cynicism, but where else was I to turn? To our government? The railway scandal, the Matsushima red-light-district scandal: our democratic body oozed corruption like an advanced syphilitic sore."

Lieutenant Matsunaga shrugged.

"Maybe it would have been different if in thirty-one, that nationwide strike by professors and students against expansionism had won. But by the time I got to college, the dissenters had been fired or jailed. I looked around and thought the hope for economic equality rested with a new brand of military officer—young and idealistic like me."

"So you believed in Ishihara and Itagaki," said Mrs. Kawai. Her voice was flat and bitter. "Architects of the state of Manchukuo."

The lieutenant lifted his lips. It hardly could be called a smile.

"I thought cynicism was dangerous. Far worse is overcertainty. But certainty is what attracted me to Ishihara and Itagaki. I was an adolescent, awkward and unsure. How nice to be convinced of a cause."

"But colonialism?" I protested. "How could you choose colonialism as your cause?"

"I didn't see Manchukuo as a colony. I thought it was being groomed for autonomy, to become a place where all nations could live side by side."

The lieutenant sneered at his naiveté.

"Manchukuo a colony? No indeed. Manchukuo was to be a *utopia.*"

"Utopia? Born in bloodshed?" Mrs. Kawai's face was purple. I was startled by her vehemence. A calm, focused woman, Mrs. Kawai had never displayed anger before.

"They called it *gekokujo*," she sneered. "The samurai idea of violating the chain of command. But in the samurai tradition you study your motives; you recognize that what you are quick to call principles may in truth be self-deception. Manufacturing an incident, overrunning a sovereign nation, this isn't gekokujo!"

The lieutenant became slightly defensive.

"The plan for Manchukuo still seemed so reasonable," he too quickly explained. "After a brief occupation, a strong free economy was supposed to keep it democratic and running. But factions formed. Some feared that without continuing military control, the Soviet Union would advance and topple not only Manchukuo, but one after another Asian country . . ."

"So they must kill any senior officer who disagrees? Communism is so frightening a concept, they must resort to *patricide?*"

Mrs. Kawai shuddered; her voice rising with her rage. "Idealistic young officers with differing philosophies?" she spat. "*DOGS!* That's what I call them!"

The Story of Fumiko Kawai

So, she told us. Admiral Sato, marked as traitor by those junior officers, was Mrs. Kawai's uncle. She had grown up in his house.

Fumiko was three and a half when she and her mother arrived at the Sato mansion. Her father had died of cancer—changed by a stomachache from a laughing man to a small urn of ashes in the time between cherry and iris viewing.

Fumiko remembered the move, her mother's face—oddly flat like the small rubber ball Fumiko once had deliberately sat on—as they left the house where they'd lived all of her life. She remembered her mother packing black lacquer trunks and bundles of silk carrying scarves into a waiting rickshaw, then lifting Fumiko to the top of the pile.

"Mama!" Fumiko had cried from her perch, scared of all the strangeness.

Her mother had smiled. Some of the volume returned to her cheeks.

"Look at you," she'd cooed, climbing beside Fumiko and

nuzzling her hair. "Special as an *umeboshi* plum sitting high on a mound of rice."

The air smelled of jasmine flowers. A bowing maid snuffled into her sleeve.

"*Sa neh*," her mother said softly. "Shall we go now to Uncle's?"

Twenty years older than her mother, Admiral Sato had acted more like a doting grandfather than an uncle. Each evening after dinner, with Fumiko's mother and auntie smiling and bowing their good-byes at the front door, the admiral had taken Fumiko for a walk. He had carried her on one shoulder like a prize parrot, swiveling to show her the passing sights, chuckling at the clever things she whispered nonstop in his ear.

If she'd been a very good girl—turning neither limp and elusive nor stiff and resistant when led to her little porcelain chamber pot—her uncle would take Fumiko to the teahouses in the entertainment district, where fish turned prettily in their tanks and geisha ducked modestly, musical instruments in hand, through fragrant shadowy halls.

One week after Fumiko's sixth birthday, on such an excursion, they'd met a man. A friend of Admiral Sato, this man was toting an infant boy.

Fumiko hung back sulking. Her uncle was a busy man who, except on these walks, she forever had to share.

But her uncle pressed forward with eagerness.

"Ah," he'd cried with exquisite appreciation. "How old?"

"Eight months."

"*So desu*," the admiral exulted, sighing like a connoisseur, reaching out to pat a plump dimpled knee. "They're adorable when they're little."

299

"Fumiko is a lovely child too," said the man with naked in-sincerity. His eyes, swimming with infatuation, never left his own baby boy.

Fumiko felt her uncle's glance. In her pretty clothes, she dangled dejectedly off the length of his arm, like a kite that had been left by the wind.

"Not like your little one," Admiral Sato pronounced, giving Fumiko's limp arm a shake. "At Fumiko's age, they're nothing but a nuisance."

Part of her knew that he'd spoken from modesty, from the su-perstition that if praised too loudly she might be stolen by covetous spirits. But the next night when her uncle called her for their walk, Fumiko refused.

When he pulled from behind his back an orange papier-mâché tiger whose neck swiveled on a hidden spring, Fu-miko turned her head away.

He only uses you, she told herself. You're just a doll to de-light the geisha.

Reminded of her father's abandonment, she was angry for having trusted her uncle.

Deprived of her company, Admiral Sato gave up his evening walk. Fumiko was pleased to find that visiting geisha had not been his purpose. But still, she did not forgive him.

After a week or two, her uncle no longer pressed her. It was, after all, time for Fumiko to leave babyhood behind: to go to school, to learn independence and obligation. Before long, she rushed to play with girlfriends after dinner.

And so the years passed.

At Fumiko's wedding, she was surprised to see her uncle's eyes wet with tears. She was moved, but he was an admiral, it was a public occasion, and she showed him no extra attention.

She did, however, visit his house regularly. Whenever she traveled to Tokyo, her mother and auntie would fuss and feed her. Her uncle would pause to say his hello.

"Please extend my sincere best wishes to your husband" is the way he would greet her.

Two years ago on a snowy night that later would be famous for the February 26 Incident, Mrs. Kawai, her mother, and her auntie cajoled Admiral Sato into going with them to the Noh theater. Shortly after their return, someone pounded (as, indeed, they were pounding all over the city) three times on the door.

"Who could it be in this cold?" laughed Mrs. Kawai's mother, still filled with gaiety from their outing.

The pounding resumed, growing thunderous like multiple blows. The gladness left her mother's eyes.

"ADMIRAL SATO, WE DEMAND AN AUDIENCE!"

"Let me," said Mrs. Kawai's uncle, pulling back the maid who was heading to answer.

"Stay here. Make no sound." He shoved the maid and the rest of the women into the small room next to his study.

Huddled together in the dark, they heard the rumble of the storm door sliding open in the entry.

"Good evening," the admiral said.

"WE HAVE ORDERS TO KILL YOU!" The voice was so young that it actually cracked with its message.

"It's cold; it's snowing. Please come in from the night and discuss this."

The soldiers must have been confused by the old admiral's dignity. Mrs. Kawai heard clattering and shuffling as they swarmed into the entry. She heard hopping as they politely struggled out of their shoes.

"There must be a reason I've been chosen to die," her uncle told his visitors. "Please, I'd like to be told."

His voice came from the study. Mrs. Kawai made a peephole in the rice paper wall.

Two dozen teenaged soldiers were crammed together, shifting uneasily. They were looking at one another.

"I suppose you've not been informed," sighed her eighty-year-old uncle. "*Shikataganai*. Alas, it cannot be helped."

He rose and stood at attention.

"*No!*" screamed Mrs. Kawai's auntie.

She ran in as three men opened fire.

The Troupe of Monkeys

We sat frozen in silence in Mrs. Ito's modern house.

"Do you know how strange honor can get?" sighed Mrs. Kawai.

She covered her arms as if cold.

"As Auntie crouched by my uncle, her kimono soaked with his blood, as the maid huddled sobbing in the hall, the captain in charge approached. He ordered his men to salute and with a terrible clatter they knelt by my uncle and presented arms."

Mrs. Kawai's mouth twisted.

"Then the captain turned to my auntie. He gave a small shrug of regret. 'I'm sorry about this; I've long admired your husband. But his point of view differed from ours.'"

No one moved.

"And your uncle?" I gently probed.

"He recovered. He's a strong old tiger."

After a while the lieutenant lifted his body from the low couch and with his crutches hop-swung his way to the window.

He examined the beautiful view.

"I grew up in mountains like these," he said mildly. "When I was a boy, once a day, a troupe of monkeys used to cut through our yard on their way to the river. My older brother was disinterested but my sister and I liked to watch them."

Monkeys? I was somewhat startled.

"Among the monkeys a benevolent old male, with silver in his fur, served as leader," the lieutenant continued. "The females cooperated in watching the babies. The adolescent males wrestled and made mischievous signs of disrespect, such as throwing feces, behind the old leader's back."

The lieutenant faced the window but his voice came to us quiet and sure.

"In the winter, food was scarce yet they shared what little they had." Lieutenant Matsunaga sighed. "My sister and I loved the monkeys. We gave them names and personalities. Then we did a stupid thing. Without my father's knowing, for he had told us repeatedly to leave the monkeys alone, we began to feed them."

He turned and looked at us with a kind of bafflement.

"Do you know? Our good intentions ruined the lives of those monkeys. Mothers ran off to gorge and hoard, neglecting their tiny babies."

He shook his head.

"One day my sister saw an adolescent male kill, and actually begin to eat, one of the abandoned babies. She ran screaming to my father."

The lieutenant lapsed into a silence so long that I began to worry about where his thoughts were taking him. His intensity saddened me. I was accustomed to young men whistling popular songs.

"And your father?" Mrs. Ito softly intruded.

Lieutenant Matsunaga looked up as if surprised to see us.

"My father said the monkeys are our cousins. That we share the same nature. 'Civilization is a thin veneer,' he said. 'Try to avoid the same fate.'"

chapter twenty-five

JULY 18, 1938

What I heard at Mrs. Ito's retreat so disturbed me I was paralyzed. For the first time, war seemed not only a displeasing social concept but something terrifying and ugly, right here.

At subsequent meetings, even after our membership grew and we got more involved in printing peace pamphlets, I still had an edgy, disheartening feeling. (One new member was Kimiko Takahashi, who when I expressed alarm that a child was joining a political group, calmly replied, "I'm almost eighteen and my parents are aware of my choice.")

Nothing I could do would ever be enough.

The feeling stemmed from Masao Matsunaga. Whenever I tried to engage him, to encourage and draw him out, his responses were terse and distracted. Before I could think of a subsequent sentence, he was deep in his own thoughts again.

What's more, I suspected his thoughts were all morbid.

It pained me. With each conversation between us that died, I came closer to knowing: in part, Masao himself was dead.

I raged at the thought. I grew determined to save him. I thought if I could just resuscitate this one lovely boy, then my whole dream of peace might seem less obscenely absurd.

When I saw in the newspaper that my old friend Tatsuo Tanida, the antiwar cinematographer, would be lecturing at the Daimaru department store, I hoped that it might help my cause.

The Department Store Lecture

"*Irasshaimase!* Welcome to Daimaru!"

Four pretty salesgirls in high heels and white gloves bowed as Masao Matsunaga and I came through the revolving door.

The salesgirls flushed. From beneath their eyelashes, they measured Masao: his tautness suggesting containment of fury, the sorrow behind his fine eyes.

The salesgirls sighed. Even without his crutches, they seemed to be thinking, it would be clear that this was a hero.

I stole a glance at Masao. Oblivious to the girls' admiration, he was off in his private war.

"I used to work here," I said, trying to draw him back to the present.

Masao startled with involuntary sociability.

"Is that so?"

He choked on these three simple words.

"Yes, twenty years ago."

I looked around, trying to spin normal conversation from mahogany display cases, walnut wood paneling, high ceilings with chandeliers. "It's basically unchanged. There's handbags and hosiery, men's wear and sporting goods, and on the next floor—"

"What floor is our lecture?" Masao interrupted.

"Fourth and final floor: toys, books, restaurant, and exhibition hall."

It came automatically, the singsong chant. I'd been the girl who called the floors as the elevatorman worked the hinged metal door.

We moved through the store. Still reminiscing, I pointed to a glass-windowed balcony. "Up on the mezzanine, that's where the accountants work."

Wearing special eyeshades, the accountants bent over their books.

"They're all women!" I noted with surprise.

"Women are everywhere," said Masao. "To your left, see the woman in black trousers? She's carrying a case for a—"

"Piccolo."

"Three years ago, she'd never played outside her family parlor. Now she's probably in some martial band. And there, the woman buying sporting equipment."

He counted to himself with bitterness. "Fourteen, fifteen, sixteen table tennis balls. She must be director of athletics at some secondary school for girls.

"Look around," he said harshly. "There are fewer men every day."

"Maybe that's not a bad thing," I replied with some tension, tired of having my brightness ignored. "Women have talents. Maybe when the war ends and the men come back, we'll still be able to use them."

Masao looked skeptical.

"What?" I heard danger in my voice. "You don't think we should?"

Startling both of us, I yanked Masao behind an archery display.

"I used to work here," I hissed. "I spoke Japanese and English and was *invaluable*. In America, I worked hard as any man. Do you know, when I came back to Japan, for seven years I hardly left the house. And why not? Because it wasn't *seemly*. All those women slaving in home factories is all right, but to publicly play a piccolo? Oh no, that wouldn't be seemly!"

Masao was blinking with slow awakening, like a sleep-walker who'd been doused with water.

"And Hanae." I was babbling but I couldn't seem to stop myself.

"She's a smart girl, strong, wanting to be somebody fine, willing to suffer to become it. Do you know what kind of chances she has?"

Masao gulped the air I was snatching.

I plunged on.

"Or Kimiko! Oh yes, I suspect that you've noticed her. If you'd let yourself do something so *human*, you might even fall in love. But no, Mr. Too Busy With Your Own Private Pain, you've no idea who she really is!"

Masao at last came to life.

"Mrs. Sone!" he cried. "Please, I meant no disrespect! Forgive me if I gave the wrong impression! I meant no slander against women; I only meant I was afraid the men would not return!"

I felt a rush of relief. For once Masao sounded completely normal, like any decent young man distraught over offending an elder.

Suddenly I recognized what had triggered my anger: the issue wasn't women but war. What had happened on that front in China? What turns a sweet boy so bitter?

"No harm, no harm," I heard myself crooning. Like a mother whose child's fever has broken.

We stood together in silence, gathering our breath, our far-flung emotions and thoughts.

Masao moved to face me. "Please forgive my miserable self-centeredness," he said with formality. "I dwell too much on my anger."

He executed the bow of the properly raised. "Thank you for your firm intervention."

"Intervention?" I blushed with self-consciousness. "Wasn't it more like a tantrum?"

By the time Masao and I reached the skylit lecture hall, something had shifted in our relationship.

Like a mother who goes haywire trying to pack her delicate boy's bags for college, then sees him blink, straighten, press a cup of hot tea in her hand, and begin packing for himself, I was less concerned about Masao's mental health.

And he was more solicitous of me.

"You'll like Mr. Tanida," I told Masao as he guided me around a sea of set-up folding chairs. "He's a newsreel cinematographer who has been just about everywhere. He used to give us information to put in our newsletter."

I settled into front row center.

"Let's sit here," I said. "It's empty, and besides, I haven't seen Mr. Tanida in a long time. I'd like to catch his eye."

"Has he been to China?"

I glanced at Masao. Bent over, arranging his crutches on the floor beside him, he hid his face.

"Yes," I said. "His assignment was to document the Pen Squadron—you know, those writers sent to glorify our boys —but his intention was to confront complacency by depicting the horrors of war."

"And did he find them?"

Masao's voice had grown clipped and sardonic.

"Pardon me?"

"Did he find the horrors of war?"

309

"Yes."

For a long pause I was silent. "But when he did, he put down his camera."

"Wasn't that what he went for, his moment of glory?" Masao insultingly drawled.

I gave him a look of motherly warning. "You mustn't mock."

Masao flushed but seemed to unwind.

I took a breath, making my voice gentle.

"The images Mr. Tanida developed were terrible. So much so that they were titillating. He put down his camera because he knew: he'd become a pornographer."

The crowd stirred.

A woman with a white sash took the platform and began a florid introduction.

Masao looked around. "There aren't many people, maybe only sixty, and they're mostly Women's Patriotic Leaguers," he whispered with concern. "Are you sure you know what you're doing?"

I patted his arm.

"This is a public lecture about the war. Naturally it's going to attract the Patriotic League. Mr. Tanida can't be openly critical of the government, but he's very clever. Listen. I'm sure we'll learn something."

The woman ended her introduction.

"And now, Mr. Tanida!"

I smiled in anticipation.

Nothing happened.

The woman furtively communicated with someone off-stage to her right.

"Mr. Tanida," she hissed.

An emaciated tubercular-looking man limped with painful resolution out to the podium.

"What gives?" muttered Masao. "He looks awful!"

As the audience broke into hesitant applause and the woman escaped from the stage, I joined the clapping.

I smiled and beat my palms together until the pain finally made me stop.

That man used to be Mr. Tanida.

The speaker stared proudly and unseeingly at his audience.

After a long silence, as the woman from the Patriotic League began stage-whispering from the wings, he spoke.

"Ladies and gentlemen," Mr. Tanida said with quiet resignation, "tonight I will be . . ." He paused and seemed to weaken. "That is to say . . ."

He stopped speaking. The muscles in his jaw clenched and unclenched.

The audience began an uneasy murmuring.

Mr. Tanida took a deep breath of determination and drew himself together. Yet as he leaned forward to speak, his lips trembled as if he was going to cry.

So did mine.

"What's wrong with him?" hissed Masao.

Mr. Tanida was staring at his notes.

I focused on my words, trying to control my voice.

"He was arrested for violating publication laws and held for six months. This is his first public lecture."

Masao blinked rapidly. "I'm so sorry, Mrs. Sone. I hadn't realized he'd been in prison."

Masao's voice was gentle, as if I'd grown suddenly old. He took my arm. "Let's go home now."

I sat stiff and still.

Masao tried again.

"Mrs. Sone, didn't you know? If a prisoner is released, it means he's recanted. This lecture wasn't his idea; it's a public humiliation, probably part of his punishment."

"In Shanghai," announced Mr. Tanida, "in a beautiful public park, there's a sign put up by the British."

"I'm fine," I whispered to Masao. "Let's stay. I want to give him support."

"Four words," said Mr. Tanida. *"No Dogs or Chinamen."*

His voice turned self-mocking.

"Now, that's not very nice."

Mr. Tanida continued, his voice harsh with contempt. He told us that the British are imperialists. He said the Greater East Asia Co-Prosperity Development Sphere, headed by the Japanese, would treat the Chinese with greater compassion.

"I'm leaving!" Masao snapped with anger. He grabbed his crutches and started to stand.

Yet I recognized Mr. Tanida's tone as self-loathing.

I shivered. With what horrors had his jailers threatened his family?

"Look at me," I whispered.

I was sending Mr. Tanida a telepathic message, or maybe I was saying a prayer.

"Please look at me. I know you'll survive this, still thoughtful and whole. Please give me some sort of a sign."

Masao startled at my words. Looking from me to Mr. Tanida with sudden pity, he sighed and sat back down.

We stayed through the lecture. Through the uncomfortable rustlings of the audience, through the sounds of people rising from their folding chairs and making their way to the door. We stayed until it was only Masao, Mr. Tanida, and I—face-to-face in the darkening room.

"Mr. Tanida. It's me, Etsuko Sone," I croaked.

Mr. Tanida looked at me without recognition. He turned and walked away.

AUGUST 8, 1938

The Saying of Sutras

When Mr. Tanida turned his dead eyes on me, I was lost. Life was merciless.

Now—three weeks later—as my trolley slows for Mrs. Kawai's station, I look out my lowered window. The Inland Sea floats on the horizon, green-forested islets rising like plush pincushions. At the bird market, canaries lift their heads: filling their throats with the scents of sunshine and pollen, singing as if they are free.

"Honorable Wife! Please!" As metal squeaks against metal and the trolley bumps to a stop, a frantic face looms at the base of my window.

A woman in mended work clothes—an abalone diver judging from her sunburned skin, the startling suppleness of her middle-aged body—is hopping up and down.

She holds up a sen'ninbari, a broad waistband, intended for some family member, that will be rendered bulletproof by the gathering of stitches from one thousand women. She pantomimes sewing and points to the trolley door.

"Meet me there?"

I nod in assent. This woman is resourceful, gathering her commitments in advance.

I go to the door of the trolley and see what I have expected: half a dozen women, all waving their sen'ninbari.

~

Three weeks earlier as I left Mr. Tanida's lecture, the same thing had happened. As Masao pulled me from my chair, pushed me into the elevator, maneuvered me through Daimaru's revolving bronze-and-glass door, a dozen women descended.

They circled hungrily, clutching their worthless waistbands.

"Get back," I warned.

In the crush of their bodies, the flush of their faces, I thought I saw Mr. Tanida's jailers.

"One stitch," crooned a fisherman's fat little wife. "One stitch and you're on your way."

She hooked her fingers into my flesh. She pushed forward her sen'ninbari—thin cheap fabric stinking of sardines.

I felt a wave of nausea. I thought again of Mr. Tanida: his wasted body, the horror of his blank eyes.

I longed to do something hateful and cruel.

"You want my help?" I cooed.

I grasped the cloth and leaned forward. "What would you do if I ripped it?" I whispered, fondling the waistband in a sinister way. "Eh? What then?"

"Mrs. Sone!"

Masao's cry confused me.

The woman grabbed her waistband and scrambled away.

"Mrs. Sone." Masao's voice was kind. "Let's go home. You're distraught."

"I'm distraught?" I shrieked, gesturing toward the women. "They're deranged! Look at them, everywhere, like lice."

"Now, Mrs. Sone," Masao cajoled, "half of them are just schoolgirls."

"Not the schoolgirls!" I interrupted.

I shuddered and lowered my voice.

"It's the *women*," I hissed. "Their *frenzy*. Do they really believe one thousand stitches are going to make a piece of cloth *bullet-proof?*"

"Yes," said Masao.

His simple certainty made me helpless and mad.

"Well then, they're stupid!" I snapped. "One *million* stitches won't save a single soul. They're stupid and cowlike and—"

"Mothers," Masao said gently. "Mothers, grandmothers, wives."

That stopped me.

"What can they do?" Masao asked quietly. "Their men have been drafted. Would they have them desert and be executed as traitors? Of course not. Would they join our peace group? It's too late, their men have been called."

He shook his head. "Of course they believe in their waistbands. It's really all they can do."

He gave a sad little laugh. "It's just human nature, their passion. In a strange way it's almost admirable."

"Admirable? But the act is so *useless!*"

"It's a matter of faith."

"Oh." My voice flattened. His answer disappointed me. "What kind of fool puts their faith in propaganda?"

"Faith in *mysteries*, not propaganda."

Masao looked at me with a kind of shy eagerness.

"Like parents," he said, "chanting sutras by the bedside of their failing child. Performing over and over with utter devotion some benign but meaningless act."

His voice grew more animated. He peered into my face to see if I was following.

"It's not *about* the sutras; parents know words aren't some kind of medicine."

"What, then?"

Masao paused. "I don't know. That some merciful force will recognize the extreme insensibility of their desire?"

He flushed and suddenly deflated. "Maybe it's crazy," he muttered.

"Kind Wife!" Approaching was a bent old woman. Far from her farm, her faded sun hat stood out like a baby's pink bonnet.

I stared at Masao.

"You're talking about our peace pamphlets, aren't you?" I whispered.

"Kind Wife!" The woman held out her sen'ninbari.

I took her needle and made a stitch.

"Is it too late?" I asked Masao as we watched her hurry toward another woman. "Will a million peace pamphlets not save a single soul?"

Masao didn't answer.

chapter twenty-six

SEPTEMBER 7, 1938

One Tuesday afternoon, I took a train to Osaka to visit Mr. Tanida. In keeping with Japanese kata, I brought a gift. In the foreign language bookstalls of Kobe I'd found a pre-import-ban book on the Hollywood directors Frank Capra, Howard Hawks, and Rowland V. Lee. Chie, Hanae, and I had enjoyed their films It *Happened One Night,* Twentieth *Century,* and The *Count of Monte Cristo*; and though I knew Mr. Tanida could not read English, I wanted to give him this book.

When my taxi dropped me in an old residential section, at the tile-roofed gate of Mr. Tanida's modest family house, his wife answered the door. Dressed in a simple housewife's ki-mono, she invited me in, accepted my gift with appropriate protestations, and served me tea from a handsome wood-fired pot. Her young son was still at school; and though she took my book to him, Mr. Tanida refused to come forward from the recesses of the house.

I was not offended by Mr. Tanida's refusal. Through discus-sions with Masao I had come to realize that not seeing me was a way of protecting me from association with a man under certain police surveillance.

When I stood to go, Mrs. Tanida checked one last time to see if her husband would acknowledge my leaving. She came back alone but with a parcel and note in her hands.

In the note, Mr. Tanida requested that I not visit again. The parcel contained a wonderful gift, one that told me that he'd do just fine. Mr. Tanida had given me a copy of the haiku master Basho's life journey poems.

Mr. Tanida once told me that movies are made by cutting and splicing. He wasn't just talking about film editing, the celluloid grafting of scenes, but also about the way cinema gains resiliency from other art forms.

As Mr. Tanida explained it: film takes from music the ideas of visual and narrative rhythm, from painting the balancing of tones and shades, and from dance the flow of movement and meaning. Add to these theater's use of dialogue, costume, and setting, and you get an art based on inspired adaptation.

What Mr. Tanida strove for, more than artfulness or entertainment in his films, was a quality he called spontaneity. The ability to provide the audience with an ongoing experience of freshness, with a collective gasp of recognition and surprise.

No wonder his movies reminded me of haiku.

chapter twenty-seven

SEPTEMBER 23, 1938

Before I started this novel, I thought that writing began with some idea in your head: a story, a memory, something with a beginning, a middle, an end. Writing about Hanae's birth seemed to confirm this. A child is in the womb; a child is in the birth canal; a child is delivered, howling, into this world.

Very soon, however, I found that my I-story had become as slippery as that newborn baby and that I was writing not to set the stage for telling what was just about to happen, but to try to understand what had just passed.

That's probably not true of real writers. I have no idea, now, how they do it—how they spin tales of more than a page or two. But I do think it explains the popularity of the amateur I-story. The point isn't so much to advance the action as to try and discern where you are.

Something has happened, the meaning of which I can't comprehend.

I've tried to write about it, but my thoughts are too much of a tangle. I tried the trick, learned from my old friend Viktor, of trying to step straight into Hanae's or Chie's own voice and eyes. Yet that technique works best when you're trying to understand someone else's perspective. In this case, it's my own behavior that I cannot decipher.

I once asked Mr. Tanida what he liked most about the experience of filmmaking. This was his reply: *You can't show an audience anything that you have not already seen.*

What Mr. Tanida was talking about was insight. A filmmaker develops insight by screening multiple rushes, by repeatedly reshooting and reviewing what an audience eventually will see. Vision happens only through a slow, uncertain process—during which the filmmaker uncovers the meaning of a scene.

Although audiences enjoy the final smooth showing, it was the process that brought Mr. Tanida his pleasure. With each multiple take, he could see just a little bit more.

And so, just as I once learned from Viktor's photography, lately I've been trying to view life with a cinematographer's eye. To look for patterns and rhythms—if not with a camera's perspective, then at least with a playwright's—with the benefit of some directorial distance.

OCTOBER 4, 1938

The Lost Children: A Brief Autobiographical Scene

SEPTEMBER 1938, RECEPTION ROOM, THE FUJI MANSION.
A spare elegant room is side lit with afternoon sun. Through the rear shoji, a dwarf Japanese maple with scarlet leaves can be seen in the garden. Sipping tea, I am sitting at a low table. I open a bulky letter and we see, on the return address, the words "Seattle, USA." I smile and begin to page through the contents. As I read, AKIRA's voice-over begins.

320

AKIRA

His voice is controlled and efficient.

Dearest Etsuko, I trust you are well. Enclosed, please find your
and Hanae's monthly allowance.

*I chuckle. Akira's letters are so predictable and formal. I shuffle
quickly to the next page.*

AKIRA

His voice becomes thoughtful and urgent.

I am, dearest friend, deeply troubled by this business with
China. I feel it imperative that Hanae come back home . . .

*I look disturbed. I am unwilling to consider this prospect. I quickly
turn to the next page and a thick packet of folded paper falls out. I relax somewhat. I recognize this as Akira's monthly missive to Hanae,
an earnest and somewhat boring compendium of admonishments
(keep up your studies, obey your auntie and grandmother), hopes
(that you are well, that you are enjoying a fine, clear autumn), and
observations about Seattle's weather (a continuum from rainy to occasional partial sun). I unfold the packet and smooth out its pages.
The writing is dense and packed.*

AKIRA

*His voice is much changed: warm, ardent, tender. Though he reads
only three poems we are led to understand there are dozens, written
every season, over the past ten years.*

Poems for My Daughter

Autumn 1928
Colorful streamers bleed

in the wake of your ship.
Grieving, the geese fly away.

Winter 1929
Ice groans in rivers yet I am a happy man.
Tonight, I found a small pink sock in your room.

I slowly leaf through multiple pages. I am visibly moved.

AKIRA

Summer Memory, 1934
How sweet that melon was!
One lucky seed clung to your chin.

From offstage we hear a heavy door slide open. I startle at the sound.

HANAE

Tadaima, I'm home!
Her voice is cheerful and natural.
I look guilty and slightly panicked. I grab the letter and the packet of poems and try to stuff them into the bosom of my dress. They are too thick. I look around with rising anxiety. Finding no hiding place, finally, I sit on them. All this time HANAE can be heard talking with the maid and clattering in the entry.
A long, graceful girl, almost seventeen, HANAE rapidly enters in a pleated sailor suit. Just home from school, she is breathless and smiling.

HANAE

Makiko says we got a letter from Papa?

ME

Not this time.

> I am somewhat flustered from my letter-hiding exertions but I speak
> with genuine puzzlement; I don't understand what I'm doing. I pick
> up the envelope, empty except for Akira's payment, and look at it with
> confusion.

This time only money.

LATE THAT NIGHT, KITCHEN, THE FUJI MANSION

> The kitchen looks shadowy and forbidding. In a kimono-style cotton
> sleeping robe, I huddle furtively by one small electric light. I am
> rereading Akira's poems. Suddenly seized by an unexpected memory, I
> look up both alarmed and enlightened.

DISSOLVE INTO MY MEMORY

MEMORY, OUTSIDE MY CHILDHOOD FARMHOUSE, ONE WEEK
AFTER MY TENTH BIRTHDAY

> A rustic thatched-roofed farmhouse is surrounded by freshly planted
> rice paddies and rounded mulberry bushes. A little girl plays in the
> front garden.

ME

> A skinny little girl in a farm child's colorful but fading cotton ki-
> mono, I am humming and tending snow peas.

Hmm hmm.

POSTMAN

> Rides up on a bicycle.

Package for you, Etsuko-chan!

> His voice is affectionate; he knows everyone in the village.

ME

For me!

My voice is excited.

This is a first!

POSTMAN

He gives a little wink.

It looks like it's something special!

He rides away with a wave.

I tear into the wrappings. Inside is a stick of some fancy unfamiliar candy that I quickly squirrel away in my kimono sleeve. My parents disapprove of candy and I'm afraid that they will take it.

In addition, there are multiple pages of a densely written letter.

I start through the letter, turning pages scribbled front and back. As I read my face changes from eager to confused to alarmed.

CHIE provides a voice-over.

CHIE

Reading the closing.

I am forever . . .

She pauses.

Your mother, Chie Fuji.

At the sound of the name, I jerk with confusion and terror.

ME

PAPA!

Holding the letter by one edge, as if it might burn me, I run into the house.

SEVERAL HOURS LATER, INSIDE MY CHILDHOOD FARMHOUSE
It is late afternoon; pale light angles across the room. Dressed in cotton kimonos, my parents (MR. AND MRS. IZUMI) kneel on clean but worn tatami, facing a blazing hibachi. PAPA holds Chie's letter. MAMA, in accordance with Japanese marital form, sits a little farther back than my father. Both are stiff with unaccustomed formality. On the opposite side of the hibachi, I kneel before them, eyes downcast. I am pouting. I feel as if I am in some sort of trouble for reasons I can't understand.

PAPA

His voice and manner are stern.
You were right to bring us this letter.
He scrutinizes me, his hands shaking slightly.
She seeks to explain her actions. Do you understand what she means?

MAMA

Mama has been watching my father. She shakes her head; she murmurs almost inaudibly.
Poor pitiful woman.

ME

Not understanding but noticing my father's trembling hands, figuring there must be something terribly dangerous about the letter, I nod my head meekly.
Yes, Papa.
Then with a child's natural attraction to things that are morbid, I ask with some hopefulness.
Is she crazy, Papa? Will she kill me?

PAPA

Of course she won't kill you!

He looks and sounds annoyed.

But . . .

He leans forward, looking at me with great intensity.

As she says here, we all know the matter is closed. She herself
decided that we were to keep you. You must make no reply. In
this situation, contact could only bring pain.

He leans forward.

Do—you—understand?

He says the words with deliberate spacing.

ME

Yes, Papa.

*Though I really don't understand, my voice is compliant. I simulta-
neously speak and bow.*

PAPA

Good.

He looks at me with fondness.

PAPA

Let's never mention this matter again.

As we all stare at the letter, PAPA slowly lowers it into the flame.

OCTOBER 6, 1938

Early that evening, on that tenth-birthday week so long ago, I
crept to the rice paddy. Hiding behind the tall bowing grains,

balancing on the ridges of earth between the paddy's dark trenches of water, I took the candy out of my sleeve and touched it to my tongue.

It burned, a sudden searing like poison—like the imported peppermint it was but that I had never tasted. I hurled it into the mud.

OCTOBER 7, 1938

Of course it was a love letter. Though what kind—with no trace of "I know you are a good little girl" or any of the other sentences most adults would write to a child—I hardly can say. I remember it was confusing and scary, a confessional stream of words that tainted me with the shame of disloyalty before I could put it down.

At the time I thought it was a crazy letter; everyone in the village knew that Chie once had gone mad. Yet now, with Akira's poems hidden under a pickle vat in the corner of the kitchen, I know it was a love letter. And probably a compelling one at that. Burning the only letter I ever got from my mother? What could make my parents so cold?

Nothing but love fearing love.

OCTOBER 15, 1938

A Scene in Which I Undo (Partially) My Deceit

At a little distance we see the reception room of the Fuji mansion. It is an October afternoon. Hanae is expected home shortly. Through the shoji we see that the branches of the Japanese maple are bare. I sit at the table holding Akira's latest letter. This time it is quite thin.
I open it.

327

AKIRA speaks in a voice-over as I read. His voice is warm but formal. We understand that this is his usual letter voice.

AKIRA

Dearest Etsuko, enclosed please find the monthly allowance. I trust everyone is well?
   I rapidly finish reading the one-page note, then pick up the enclosure to Hanae.

AKIRA

Dearest Hanae, how are the autumn leaves this year? Here in Seattle it is rainy and cool. If you watch the mail, you will find I have mailed you a birthday surprise.

ME

   I chuckle to myself.
A sailor suit.

AKIRA

Please listen to your auntie and grandmother and treat them with obedience and respect.
   He pauses, his voice grows richer with sentiment.
With warmest regards, Father.
   Offstage a heavy door slides open. HANAE can suddenly be heard talking to the maid and clattering in the entry.
   I quickly take the packet of Akira's poems from beside me on the floor and slip them into Akira's new letter.

328

ME

Hanae!

My voice is slightly strained in its gaiety.

Come see, a birthday surprise! Your father sent the most wonderful letter!

OCTOBER 16, 1938

Hanae was thrilled by the poems. She started to read them right there. Then she looked up and blushed. "Is it all right? May I take them?"

I smiled and nodded. "Of course."

As she dashed away, clutching her treasures to her chest, I was happy. Although I experienced a pang.

I wished I still had Chie's letter.

And then another pang, this time of guilt. One that made me understand why Chie's letter had been burned.

You can't be *too* magnanimous; there's a chance that your child will desert you. Like my mama and papa, I'd calculated the risks.

I'd destroyed the letter where Akira begged to have Hanae sent home.

chapter twenty-eight

NOVEMBER 8, 1938

What do we ever know of our families? Like members of a so-lar system we move along our individual orbits. Sometimes close and astonishingly beautiful, like Mars glowing red beside the moon, at other times obscured for months by the clouds. Familiar and mysterious, necessary and useless. Trusted, even when not visible, to be there.

Yet each made of different matter. With different climates and needs. So that even with our children, whom we love enough to want to devour ("I'm going to gobble you up," I used to say to Hanae, and that was my wish and intention, to drag her into my orbit, to pull her under my planetary man-tle), we can do nothing beyond sending up lantern flashes and Morse code clicking.

Though often, through shyness or stupidity or the general haplessness of humans, we withdraw our signals at the most critical times.

Nevertheless—knowing full well our powerlessness to pre-vent our loved ones from straying into traffic, from having their hearts broken, from being taken away to war—we circle around. Flashing and clicking and stitching our sen'ninbari:

hoping our loved ones will glance toward the sky and find in our coded communications some warning and warming beacon.

My Decoding of Chie's (Contents Unknown) Letter

This is the way I see it. After my birth, when Chie rose from her long loony sleep, already it was too late.

I was gone. Given to a farming family whose own child had been stillborn.

"Etsuko is a happy baby, well loved," reported Most Honorable Mrs. Fuji. "I have kept close track."

She knelt in a pool of sunlight by the alcove, arranging eucalyptus and dahlia in the ikebana slanting style.

"Last week when I visited, Mrs. Izumi was showing me how well the little darling can talk."

Chie put down her tea.

"She can talk? How clever! What does she say?"

Now that her mind had cleared she was curious about me, her year-old child.

Chie's mother hesitated. An accomplished student of the Sensho Ikenobo School, she snipped at her arrangement. The longest branch, representing heaven, fell away in error.

"Oh, not much," she said, fiddling with an intractable dahlia. "Just one word, really. You know how babies are, always repeating nonsense syllables. I was just telling Kan, I doubt Etsuko has any real understanding of what she is saying."

Chie felt a subtle constriction in her chest, a small certainty. She took a deep breath.

"What does she say?" she insisted, smoothing and re-smoothing the folded silk napkin at her knees, wanting to hear it spoken, wanting to feel it hanging real in the air.

Her mother looked uneasy. She glanced at Kan for assistance.

Chie closed her eyes and waited.

Kan's voice came like the healing burn of antiseptic on an open wound.

"Mama," he replied.

However curious, Chie did not take me back. Bonds had formed. To break them would have been cruel. Besides, babies frightened her. My brother had died in her custody. I had driven her mad.

Chie knew ways to avoid a pregnancy. Times to yield and times to avoid. Four years passed. Her parents never pressed for an heir.

Then as a surprise, Naomi was conceived. With a mixture of anticipation and dread, Chie felt the first pangs of nausea, the cravings for pickled plum. Throughout the nine months she waited with tension, hands pressed against her high belly, checking constantly to make sure her baby still kicked.

When Naomi was born, Chie's family was overjoyed. Kan wept. Most Honorable Mr. and Mrs. Fuji forgot propriety and held each other in a long, close, public embrace.

Later, when the auspicious red beans in sticky white rice had been eaten and the servants had rewrapped the fancy platters and quietly stored them away, Kan went to the nursery.

He knelt by Chie's futon: rocking his sleeping Naomi, examining her papery nails.

"Sublime perfection," he cooed.

Naomi was tiny in his arms: pink and curled like a freshly steamed shrimp.

Candlelight from paper lanterns placed on the floor lapped at the hem of his robe.

"Beloved blessing," Kan whispered into Naomi's hair.

Chie studied the rapture in Kan's face and understood how much he missed his other babies.

She climbed out from under her covers.

For the first time she did what was common in other marriages. She knelt before her husband and pressed her forehead to the floor.

"I will not let this one go."

Chie kept her promise. She held tight. But perhaps her grip was too desperate. Somewhere between my brother's death and Naomi's birth, Chie had lost her suppleness. She carried her affections with too little playfulness. She was a stiff mother, a formal wife.

Other people had a knack for love; it grew and enriched their lives. For Chie, love had awakened something ominous. Something she felt she had to subdue.

Chie thought her love was immoderate, escalating from happiness to ecstasy, from ecstasy to insanity. She worked, always, to keep it in check.

We stayed apart. Until that disastrous tenth-birthday reunion, Chie and I never had met. Oh, she'd *seen* me. She'd searched me out, going to town, studying gaggles of schoolgirls as they hopscotched their way home from school. But that was our first meeting face-to-face.

The reunion hadn't been her idea.

"Just meet her," Chie's parents had coaxed. "We know how you long for her."

They lay shoveled up to their chins with hot orange mud, at the mineral spring resort of Beppu.

"*Long* for her?" Chie wriggled her toes, enjoying the warm, soothing oozing. "You're too romantic. Etsuko is a stranger to me. Besides, what good would it do? You've said yourselves that she's happy."

"She's our blood!" Chie's mother rose on one elbow, making a soft squishing sound. "Your blood. Why should she live in poverty when we could give her much more?"

Chie refused to look at her. She inhaled the sharp scents of sulfur and iron. "Poverty?" she said coolly. "I thought you said the Izumis are comfortable."

Most Honorable Mr. Fuji sat up. He leaned over, face flushed with heat and annoyance.

"Of course they're comfortable," he said with a glare. "Do you think we'd send our granddaughter into a miserable life?"

He shook his finger. Orange mud flew backward, joining his eyebrows like mortar.

"Don't pretend to be stupid. It doesn't become you. You know full well what our name could do for the child!"

At the reunion, when I cried and begged to go home, naturally Chie was disappointed. Of course she had harbored some hope.

She'd thought of me and Naomi—imagining a noisier house, filled with the quarrelsome music of sisters at play.

Yet when I looked at her as if she were a monster, Chie felt it was karma. Instinctively, I seemed to know what Chie always had feared. Once again, she would fail me.

NOVEMBER 11, 1938

Though my decoding is all speculation, for me it works as well as the truth.

I could ask Chie. Why did she write me the letter? What was

334

it she wanted me to know? It might be nice to learn the facts of the story, to hear warm sentiments coming forth from her lips. But perhaps there is little need.

I see Chie each night at the dinner table, as unknowable and constant as a planet. She has brought me into her house. Would her words tell me anything more?

And were I to ask, the chances are she would not be able to answer. If Hanae asked why I'd destroyed a section of Akira's letter, would I be able to explain a mother's primitive fears?

Perhaps in both Chie's and my cases, all one can say is it's impossible to face the terror of being torn from your child without some insensible cri de coeur.

chapter twenty-nine

FEBRUARY 15, 1939

Hanae Approaches Graduation

Whether Old Decorum likes it or not, Hanae will be valedictorian in this year's graduating class.

"You don't mind, do you?" she asks Kimiko as they crunch across the still-frozen school yard.

"Of course not, you've worked hard. Memorizing all those first-aid topics." Kimiko shifts the stiff leather book bag on her shoulders.

The act strikes Hanae as odd; she knows the bag isn't heavy. These days their bags carry little besides lunch and some pamphlets on first aid or home economics.

From the depths of Kimiko's book bag, Hanae hears the sound of a lone ink brush rolling unobstructed.

Hanae sighs. Emptiness *can* be chafing. "Bandaging and Baby-Sitting" is what she calls the curriculum.

"It's trivial, isn't it?" Hanae pouts. "I've reached ascendancy by knowing better than anyone else the least significant topics."

"First aid and child care are not insignificant," Kimiko recites. "They're about the continuation of life."

"And military drill?"

Kimiko blushes. "The way Sensei Matsunaga conducts drill, it too is about the continuation of life."

Hanae hears the title Sensei—Esteemed Educator—and studies Kimiko's blush. Does her friend have a crush on the lieutenant?

They wind through a narrow neighborhood.

It's a cheerful place. Small shops with wooden shutters lean into one another. Telephone wires carrying party lines tangle overhead, like all the inhabitants' lives.

Hanae sighs with nostalgia.

"This neighborhood reminds me of Seattle, of Japantown, not so much in its layout—like all of America, Japantown is spread out—but in intimacy."

Kimiko's mind is far away. "First aid, child care, even cooking," she suddenly says. "Nothing is insignificant if it's done with awareness and love!"

Hanae glances at Kimiko. She is sounding strange: didactic and loopy like me.

Hanae gives Kimiko a sly look.

"You've been going to Auntie's peace meetings, haven't you?"

On the other side of the street, three little boys with bamboo poles are pretending they are soldiers.

Kimiko stops and looks Hanae straight in the eye.

"Yes," she says.

The commitment in Kimiko's voice isn't something Hanae has heard in their conversations about novels and school.

"What do you do there?"

For the first time, Hanae finds herself curious about the peace group.

Kimiko looks pensive. "I don't know. Not enough."

They turn a corner.

"Look, there's a farewell committee," Kimiko notes.

A young man in uniform, maybe twenty years old, waits by the trolley stop. His parents and younger sister stand by his side. Bowing middle-school girls, lined up before him, are presenting comfort bags filled with cookies, notes of appreciation, and sen'ninbari.

Beaming over the entire proceeding is the local draft officer, who holds (in addition to his own exemption from military service) a large and wordy banner.

Kimiko reads the brush strokes.

"Congratulations on being called to service. Prayers for your triumphant return."

"That must be the family house." Hanae points down an alley to where a special rising-sun flag waves from a rooftop. "I like the way neighbors do that," she says. "Posting a flag for moral support until the soldier comes home."

Kimiko gives a short laugh. "Sensei Matsunaga's mother hated it. Waking every morning with this thing in the heavens."

She points at the trolley stop, at the tearful mother everyone is trying to ignore. "Tell me she doesn't think that little flag is a curse."

Hanae gives Kimiko a critical look.

"Since when do you know so much about Lieutenant Matsunaga's mother?"

The trolley arrives.

"Banzai, banzai," cheer members of the local National Defense Women's Association. In their white sashes and aprons, they look like a cross between diplomats and bakers.

338

Hanae watches the soldier as he starts to board.

His mother grabs his arm.

Gently, one by one, he peels her fingers away.

A Meeting at Mrs. Kawai's

Two weeks later I am sitting in Mrs. Kawai's salon, folding a pile of pamphlets in my lap, when someone knocks on the door.

"That must be Kimiko," says Mrs. Ito. "I'll let her in."

She leaves the room. From the entry I hear an excited exchange, Mrs. Ito's and Kimiko's laughter.

"Etsuko-san!" Mrs. Ito calls to me. "Kimiko has a surprise!"

They shuffle in giggling, concealing behind them some anonymous figure.

Finding this an indignity, the figure shakes itself free and steps forward.

"Hello, Auntie."

Hanae speaks formally, as if meeting me for the very first time.

A wave washes through my body, a simultaneous sinking and rising big as a tsunami. This is something I have been dreading ever since Kimiko joined the peace group: seeing my own young woman choosing her commitments and dangers.

As Hanae meets my eyes I have never been more frightened, and yet . . .

I have never been more proud.

"Welcome, Ha-chan."

My voice is soft. I say her baby name knowing this may be the last time.

"And these are Mrs. Kawai, Mr. Hashimoto," says Kimiko with animation.

Mr. Hashimoto bows and smiles.

"I'm not an original member. I met your aunt riding up the Mount Rokko tram on a day when my sole intention was hiking."

The smile broadens in his attractive, likeable face.

"Four hours later, we met again on the tram coming down and she turned me into a subversive!"

He chortles with delight at his humor.

"How do you do," Hanae says stiffly. She has no talent for conviviality.

More knocking comes from the entry. Mrs. Kawai goes to answer.

"Are the brochures ready?" asks a quiet voice.

Hanae startles at its sound.

As Mrs. Kawai's footsteps lead the way, a soft thumping noise follows.

"Hanae," I say as they enter the room, "I believe you know Masao Matsunaga."

Hanae endures the niceties. She drinks the tea, samples the snacks. It's the people that she studies.

Nothing escapes her: Mrs. Ito's theatricality, the kind way in which Mr. Hashimoto presses food upon others and wants to see them relax. She saves her deepest scrutiny, however, for Masao: measuring his smiles, his seriousness, his occasional lapses into absence.

"So tell me," she demands, stopping social chatter, "how did you become a war hero?"

Slowly, Masao reaches across his lap and places his teacup on a side table.

The room falls silent. A full sixty seconds pass.

"It was a time without reason," Masao finally says. His face is still. He studies his hands as they rest on his knees. "Men went to the homes of leaders they long had admired, removed their shoes, then shot them at point-blank distance." His voice grows harsher. "They pledged to free China—the civilization they most revered, the source of Japanese culture—then spent two months in Nanking killing any civilian who moved."

Masao means to shock. Leave this topic alone, he implies.

Hanae flinches but I know she will not back down.

Masao reaches for the crutches resting on the floor by his chair and stands. He swings himself to the window, parts the damask curtain, and stares blindly into the courtyard.

"And in this time of mind-numbing senselessness," he says with sarcasm, "I became a war hero."

Mr. Hashimoto looks concerned; in our cheerful, tactful group Masao has been doing so well. Mr. Hashimoto glances around, grabs a sesame cake, and rises halfway from his chair. He is about to take the cake to Masao when, seated next to him, Kimiko Takahashi places a restraining hand on his arm.

Mr. Hashimoto sits back down.

"What did you do?" says Hanae.

Masao turns from the window.

"I used an army vehicle in an unauthorized manner. I drove through the looted city of Nanking, collecting raped and mutilated women."

He looks straight at Hanae, issuing a challenge.

Mrs. Ito and Mrs. Kawai exchange an anxious glance.

Finally Masao continues.

"I meant to drive the women to their homes but they screamed and cried out for their babies. So I drove them around and around, searching for their children."

He shakes his head in awe, lost now in his story.

"All of Nanking was burning. The air stank of charcoal. Random gunfire sounded."

"And?"

"The longer I drove, the more I realized the women no longer had babies."

No one speaks.

Although Mrs. Ito first invited Masao to brief us on Nanking, for almost a year we've been careful not to ask him too much. He's always seemed too brittle, the topic too intimate and raw.

"Eventually I was stopped."

A detached wonderment creeps into his voice.

"In a way I was glad. I had no idea how to help these women. I found them water; I dressed their superficial wounds. But I knew we couldn't drive forever and that eventually I'd have to dump them, alone, in front of some smoldering rubble they used to think of as home."

Masao pauses.

I've heard his tone of wonder before. Once in Seattle, three men were crushed by falling logs. A fourth escaped. As he was hurried, mangled but still alive, into the hotel where I worked, I heard him describing what had happened, again and again, to anyone who would listen.

Masao hunches over his crutches.

"Yet when I was ordered to surrender the vehicle, I refused. In the argument that followed, a bullet ricocheted. Darkness crept from the top of my shiny black boot, ruining the crease on my freshly pressed pants."

He gives a small shrug.

"I was arrested and taken away."

"And the women?" Kimiko's voice is gentle yet firm.

Masao looks at us almost with eagerness, as if grateful to share his shame.

His voice is a hoarse whisper. "I have no idea what became of the women."

We sit together in bereavement, almost as if at a wake.

After a moment Kimiko stands. She walks briskly to the serving table, efficiently pours hot tea into a fresh cup, and takes it to Masao. Like a nurse who is dealing with frostbite, she presses his long fingers around the fragile cup, then backs away.

On his own Masao balances on his crutches, holding his cup. After a while he takes it in a gulp.

"Then what?" Hanae's voice is matter-of-fact, as if the information she seeks is nothing out of the ordinary.

"What?" Masao asks as if awakening from a daze.

"You were arrested and then what?"

Masao's smile is sardonic.

"By this time," he says, "my insubordination no longer mattered. Back in Tokyo, the War Ministry had heard about the atrocities. The men in charge were quietly recalled."

He laughs a low, wrenching cry like childbirth: full of pain and release.

"Since my superiors' orders were now considered illegal, since I'd been engaged in utterly ineffective but supposedly humanitarian acts, since my foot had grown gangrenous and had to be amputated, since I was clearly useless to the war effort—I was straight from officers' training school, contemptibly soft; probably I would be murdered by my own men within a week of my first assignment—I was quickly given an honorable discharge."

chapter thirty

MARCH 29, 1939

Hanae and Her Sensei

"You *were* a war hero," Hanae privately tells Masao, later, after she's been attending the weekly peace meetings for a while. "You stole a truck so those women could survive."

"No," he says. "The women were an afterthought, something to keep my mind off the terror. I stole a truck on hysterical impulse."

He pauses in the folding of a brochure.

"I thought I was committed to social justice but my commitment was all to self-image."

He looks at her.

"There's a world of difference between intention and action."

"Stealing that truck was action."

"But was it noble?"

"Of course." Hanae pauses a moment to recall "Moral Actions: A Hierarchical and Logical Means of Assessment," a chapter in one of the textbooks given to her by Miss Langley.

"'Stealing isn't noble on its own,'" she recites, "'but if the purpose of the theft is to save a life—such as stealing medicine for a sick child—then the importance of the act supersedes the violation of the social contract of a citizen not to steal.'"

She looks for her teacher's reaction. She is proud of her logical *and* moral mind.

He gives her a little smile.

"You sound like me when I was your age."

Hanae beams. She is heroic! She gives him the thumbs-up sign.

"What's that?"

"Thumbs-up, a way to share praise with a teammate."

She grins, pleased to be educating her sensei. Thumbs-up is one of the few cultural lessons she's found useful in all our outings to American movies.

Sensei Matsunaga shakes his head gently.

"I intended more warning than praise."

"But you *were* a hero!"

"I was pompous and lucky."

Hanae frowns. The lucky part is all right, but she doesn't like the suggestion that she's pompous.

"I enlisted believing I could ride into battle and leave my mark for social justice," he explains. "I never considered it was much more likely the battle would leave its mark on me."

"You mean that you might have been killed?"

"No, I'd considered that. Death was part of my heroic fantasy. I dreamed that my life might be fleeting, but like the cherry blossoms as they fall, my individual sacrifice added to those of my brethren would transform the world with blinding beauty."

Unconsciously he rolls the brochure he is supposed to be folding, into a telescope. He taps it against one palm.

"Just about all the enlisted felt that way, though their reasons for joining were more honest than mine. They didn't go to be the creator of some utopia. They went because they loved their families and wanted them to be proud."

"How could the battle leave its mark, besides killing you?" Hanae demands. "Do you mean losing your foot?"

"Oh no." Masao's voice is dismissive. "That was nothing."

Hanae thinks aloud. "So what could war do to you that's worse than being maimed?"

She is enjoying herself. Her teacher has posed an intellectual riddle and she is concentrating on its solution.

"It isn't being killed . . . ," she mutters to herself.

Masao interrupts with sudden harshness. "War turns you into a killer."

The comment stops her. It is something Hanae has never considered.

"But it didn't! You didn't kill anyone; you tried to help them. It was those other men who went crazy. You were noble."

"I was lucky."

Masao's voice is brusque. He puts his furled brochure on his forefinger and begins spinning it round and round.

"I'd just received my commission. Along with my fellow new officers, I was sent to China for a few days of in-the-field leadership training before we were assigned our men."

He shudders slightly.

"Our men. The first thing we noticed as we got off the boat was the eyes of the men we'd be leading. They glittered. We were afraid to look at them. We'd never seen such eyes on a human."

The brochure wobbles on Masao's finger, spinning like a prayer wheel.

"The officers' training camp was a sheltered site, far from the ravages of war. Our exercises were all intellectual—studying topographical maps of greater Nanking, discussing which tactics we would have used to ensure the city's surrender. I performed exceedingly well.

"On the second-to-last day of training, our instructor—a lieutenant commissioned only slightly less recently than I—held up his hands as if announcing a special surprise.

"'Tomorrow there will be a final ceremony of qualification,' he announced, 'after which we'll tour Nanking. This way, you'll be able to see if the tactics you devised come close to the actual thing.'"

Masao crushes the peace brochure in his fist.

"The next day the air smelled of grass and boot polish as we paraded before our commanders. Seats had been arranged for them beside a crudely dug pit. We lined the opposite side.

"'Now we shall see whether these men have the courage to become platoon leaders,' announced our instructor, bowing to our superior officers. 'I will demonstrate subduing the enemy. Lieutenant Kase, you will act next, so take note.'"

Masao pauses.

"Lieutenant Kase was first in the line, I was third-to-last. I strained to see so that when my turn came to demonstrate what I assumed to be a martial arts maneuver, I would perform honorably."

He shakes his head in befuddlement.

"A skinny, unresisting man in rags was brought forth to play the role of prisoner. He was placed by the edge of the pit and our instructor pushed his head down in a bow."

Lieutenant Matsunaga, for he seems more lieutenant than civilian now, drops his peace brochure.

347

"It struck me as odd. I was expecting a demonstration of skill and bravery, yet the enemy was already subdued."

Hanae feels a premonition and starts to cover her ears. "I don't think I want to know . . ."

She begins to rise from her chair.

But Lieutenant Matsunaga is ahead of her. He jumps up, crutches spread, blocking her flight.

"AHHHH!" he cries.

In a flash he unsheathes an imaginary sword and swings it in a deadly arc.

"NO!" Hanae falls into her seat, covering her face.

"THWACK!" screams the lieutenant. "THUMP!"

A cry rips from Hanae's chest. She shudders without any control.

Beside her, Masao wipes his imaginary blade.

"There, there," he says with absentminded gentleness. He seats himself and lightly pats her back.

Hanae's face is wet with tears. Her shoulders continue to shake.

After a while Masao speaks.

"I didn't steal a truck to save women," he says quietly. "I didn't even steal it to save my soul. I ran across the field toward the truck because it was close and I knew I was going to vomit. Something so awful, and my only instinct was not to soil myself in public."

They sit in silence.

"You want courage?" says Masao. "Don't look at me. When you look at me, know what you see. Luck. Luck and gangrene are what saved me. From the self-hatred, the horror, the loss of all hope that I saw in the veteran troops' eyes."

chapter thirty-one

MAY 3, 1939

My husband and I once took a June trip to Tokyo. It was iris-viewing time and we visited Meiji Park's famed iris gardens. At every vista that was particularly fine (an unparalleled one occurring at each bend in the path), we encountered a dozen amateur artists. There they were, jammed together, framing the view through their fingers, tipping their heads to refresh their perspectives, laboring over their palettes to produce tones of the truest hue.

Creating canvases that looked all the same.

It's not just a Japanese phenomenon. Think of the world—all those moonlit seascapes, those ink paintings of peonies, those representations of mother and child. All those overused images, born through so much effort to so little admiration.

Think of the artists! Knowing full well that they'll never re-capture Monet's garden, out in droves on any occasion, lugging their easels, eager for another go at it.

Do you laugh, or cry, or applaud?

There's a reason why I tell this story. To me these Sunday painters represent myo—the strangeness of beauty—an idea that transcendence can be found in what's common and small. Rather than wishing for singularity and celebrity and genius (and growing all gloomy in its absence), these painters recognize the ordinariness of their talents and remain undaunted.

It's the blessings in life, not in self, that they mean to express.

And therein lies the transcendence. For as people pursue their plain, decent goals, as they whittle their crude flutes, paint their flat landscapes, make unexceptional love to their spouses—in their numbers across cultures and time, in their sheer tenacity as in the face of a random universe they perform their small acts of awareness and appreciation—there is a mysterious, strange beauty.

Quite a lot has happened since I last worked on this manuscript, more than I could write at the time. And now that I've finally gotten around to fitting it into my story, I find myself at a startling juncture.

I have reached the end of my I-story.

Years ago when I first began writing, I wondered how one concludes an I-story. Would I be compelled to keep on, chronicling minutiae, until I reached the end of my life? Sometimes I longed to be writing a travel memoir, my suspicion being that this particular problem (ending) provides the motivation behind that very popular form.

What other tale affords such a convenient closing, the ability to say, "Then, I went home"?

Yet I've found life provides its own punctuation: generates paragraph, chapter, beginning, and end. And I think I've learned why we write our I-stories.

From the mundane flows an odd kind of music.

Although "music" may be too strong a word. What emerges is a random note here, a ragged phrase there, some fragmented hints of coherence. They're intoxicating even in incompleteness. The bare undertones of a tune.

The Telltale Squid

The day before Hanae's graduation, Chie found me swearing in the kitchen.

"Fools!" I picked up one after another whole raw squid and hurled them across the room. "Take that, take that, take that!"

"Etsuko!"

I turned, panting and staring.

I resumed my hurling tirade.

"TAKE THAT! TAKE THAT!"

"Have you gone mad?"

Forgetting her arthritis, Chie jumped from the high threshold down to the kitchen's rough floor. She tried to wrestle a squid from my grasp.

"Stop!" she demanded.

I felt the squid's slippery flesh between her and my hands. I held on. I whirled around, like a wolf protecting a piece of flesh from an attacking competitor, and clutched my prize to my chest.

"Etsuko! Talk to me!"

Chie wiped her hands on her silvery silk kimono and lunged for my wrist.

I whirled again, raising my arms, holding the squid above my head.

"Stupid, stupid, stupid!" I shrieked.

We stumbled around the kitchen. Though I wore kitchen

shoes on the packed-earth floor, Chie did not. Her split-toed tabi, the purest of white to symbolize a cultivated person's remove from all sordid aspects of life, grew unspeakably dirty.

Chie sank her nails into my skin.

"ETSUKO!"

I lowered my arms. I relinquished the squid, passing it into her palm, closing her fingers around it. Like an overly sincere American shaking hands, I squeezed both of my hands around her squid-holding hand.

"There you go," I said mildly.

Chie jerked away. She glanced at the squid in her hand, then flung it to the floor.

I bent to retrieve it. "Shouldn't waste good food," I said calmly. "Especially after you worked so hard to save it."

Chie warily watched me; she struggled to collect her breath.

"What was that about?" she finally demanded.

"Squid."

"I know it was about squid, but why?"

I sighed. I walked to the sink and put the squid in the basin. I moved to the icebox and poured two cups full of cold barley tea.

"Have you noticed that for the past few weeks, the only fish I've been serving is squid?"

Chie heard my voice turn strangely singsong.

"Squid, squid, squid."

Chie suddenly shivered. Maybe I *had* gone mad.

"So the menu is somewhat monotonous. It's not that bad; you've fixed it in various ways. And it's not like we *must* eat seafood. Why not make one of your other specialties? Your Spam sushi?" Chie heard herself cajoling, saying ridiculous things. She got angry.

"WHAT'S WRONG WITH YOU?"

"For weeks there's been nothing but squid at the fish market." I paused. "Do you know what that means?"

"No," Chie sighed. "You tell me."

"At first I had no idea. But after a few weeks I formed a suspicion. Today I went down to the harbor—where the fishing fleet docks—and I talked around."

I let out a long shuddering sigh.

"Squid are the only things in the market because they're the only things being caught. They're the only things being caught because they're shallow coastal fish and the only boats going out are shallow coastal boats."

My voice was flat.

Chie stared at me with incomprehension.

"Only shallow coastal boats are going out because deep-sea boats are being requisitioned by the navy. They're being refitted as gunboats."

I looked at Chie with a tight smile. "So, what do the squid mean?"

Chie shook her head in confusion. "That the navy wants more boats?"

"Not just that!"

I laughed, high and slightly hysterical.

"Japan is preparing to fight on the Pacific. There's going to be global war!"

Losses in Translation

"It won't make any difference," said Chie. "Hanae is a girl, she won't be recruited. A wider war won't make any difference."

"Of course it will. We can't keep her here. She has to go back to her father."

"We're a small village," Chie continued. "There are no strategic sites in Kobe. Oh well, there's the harbor. But we could move her, take her farther into the countryside. She really won't face any danger."

Chie's face was wooden. She looked at me without seeing.

"This is conjecture," she concluded. "You're making a crisis out of a little scarcity at the fishmonger's. Maybe it's just some sort of red tide."

She pushed blindly at the hair that had escaped from the hairpins of her bun.

I stared at that messy bun. When had Chie's hair turned all silver?

"Why did you fight me?" I asked, suddenly curious.

"What?" Chie looked blank, like a tired old woman.

"Why did you jump down and fight me for the squid? I'm younger and stronger than you. Why didn't you just call the servants?"

"It was an emergency. You weren't the same. I thought, I don't know, maybe you were having a stroke like your father." Chie sighed. "If your child is choking, you act automatically. You don't wait to call on the servants."

From my hands came the scent of the squid. A clean salty scent, like tears.

"I'm sorry I scared you." I made my voice gentle. "But Japan is preparing to risk everything. You understand why Hanae must go."

"Ahhh!" cried Chie, her voice like tearing silk.

I looked away.

Outside, the branches of a weeping willow swayed and tangled, making shadows on the wall like a woman who was washing her hair.

"Seventeen." I shook my head with disbelief. "Once, when Hanae was newborn, I placed her on the bed next to me. I wanted to watch the rise and fall of the soft spot in her skull; it moved me in such a primitive way. I nuzzled closer and closer, until like some mother animal, I found myself licking her head."

Chie laughed, a small, soft sob.

"You've raised her well," she said.

"I'm not Naomi—"

"No, you're not," Chie interrupted. "But you require no apologies."

We leaned against the charcoal-fired rice hibachi, sipping our tea.

"What will I do without her?" I said. "I'm nothing without that child."

Chie straightened. She looked at me critically.

"Stop that," she said.

"Stop what?"

"That retreat from life, that self-pitying lament. You do both Hanae and yourself a disservice."

She pulled at her kimono, tucked at her hair, regathering and repairing. "You can't huddle around a child," she scolded. "Ignoring her dreams, limiting her orbit."

More and more she was sounding like her old admonishing self.

"Find your own purpose if you want to love wisely. Don't expect that to come from another."

She looked at me sharply.

"I made that mistake," she declared with vehemence. "I suffocated my baby. I pressed the breath out of him with the weight of my attention, sure as if I'd used a millet-filled pillow."

"No!" I protested. "Those unexplained infant deaths just happen."

But Chie didn't want to listen.

"And then," she whispered, looking at me searchingly, "because I didn't want to make the same mistake twice, do you know what I did?"

She didn't wait for my answer.

"I threw you away!"

Her eyes were distant and desperate, like Masao's when he spoke of Nanking.

"Kan balanced me. With his help I raised Naomi, but as soon as he was gone I drove her away. She died in a foreign land."

She made a strange, low sound of longing, like a cat that is deep in heat. "What a thing love has turned out to be! Nothing but loss after loss."

"Not loss, *gain!*"

My voice carried an authority I'd only recently grown accustomed to hearing.

Chie looked at me.

I took a breath. "You didn't discard me, you gave me two families. You didn't drive Naomi away, you raised her to choose her own life."

Chie made a small wave of dismissal.

"Naomi is dead," she said flatly. "What does it matter?"

"So she's dead," I cried. "So Hanae's leaving. No one is ours forever!"

I paused, somewhat startled. I realized I was persuading myself.

I let out my breath. "Don't be so harsh with yourself," I said gently. "In the face of the universe, what can we do?"

Chie's neck was rigid with attention. Her eyes flickered.

She began moving through the kitchen, slowly at first, then with gathering animation. She picked up squid, rinsed them off, packed them neatly in ice.

I watched with astonishment. Chie had never been in a kitchen before, yet she was a natural at reestablishing order.

"So Hanae must leave," she muttered as she worked. "We must translate this loss into gain . . ."

I went to the sink to help her.

Chie looked up. She had seized upon something.

"Hanae is smart," Chie said. "I'm told, in America, a smart girl has many choices for college."

"She's a citizen," I added, "and in America women can vote."

Chie gave a brisk nod—almost deep enough to be considered a bow—to Hanae's golden future.

I held my tongue. I knew another side of America: the racial slurs, the restrictive laws. Hanae's life would not be so easy.

"What about you?" Chie asked, suddenly anxious. "Will you go with her?"

"No. She has no need for a nursemaid."

I looked directly at Chie.

"And as you've said, I can't rely on her for my meaning."

Chie nodded, pleased. "You have your peace group. Work hard, persevere. You can change the world if you try."

"Probably not," I sighed with sad resignation. "But the group demands that I know my heart, that I take a stand." I gave a small smile. "Perhaps I am changing myself."

Unbidden, a memory rose. It was Mr. Hashimoto. Kind and courtly, he'd always paid me special attention. And though I sensed that he found me attractive, he'd been respectful of my friendly indifference. Then, just one week earlier, as we worked together fixing the mimeo machine, I suddenly noticed his hands. The tendons, the muscles, the sinews. They tensed and stretched just under his skin: silent with knowledge and power. They fascinated me, this particular man's hands, like a distillation of life itself. Acute and aware, I stood by his side. I felt the heat rising from his body.

Back in the kitchen, I flushed.

I stole a quick glance at Chie.

She was studying me. Her nose was pink as she looked away.

"You are not a disappointment," she said roughly. "You are just like your father."

I hesitated a moment, then touched her face.

"Chie," I said, "I am like you."

chapter thirty-two

Hanae's Graduation: A Selected Look Back
Through My Journal

March 3, 1939

Throughout Japan, graduation ceremonies are held the last day of school, the hour after lunch, following a similar format. Families gather, diplomas are distributed, "Auld Lang Syne" is sung with great feeling.

The only part Hanae looks forward to is the end, where the valedictorian, on behalf of the graduating class, says a word of thanks.

March 7, 1939

A pipe bursts, ruining the auditorium. Graduation must be replanned.

March 8, 1939

Hanae's headmaster announced that graduation would be transferred, intact, from indoors to out. His broadcast was barely audible over the sound of hammering as—in the rear of the school—a stage was being built in the field-and-track oval.

March 12, 1939

Bleachers and folding seats have been assigned, but graduation plans are not moving smoothly. Since the site of the ceremony was moved, rumors are flying that *anything* can be changed.

Kimiko loves the uproar.

"Moving graduation was like popping the first stay in an overly constraining corset," I heard her whisper to Hanae. "The government should take note; too many restrictions make anarchy appealing!"

March 15, 1939

Today, Hanae reported that a delegation of about fifteen mothers accosted the headmaster at the gathering for morning assembly.

"Our proposal is to weave flowers through the links of the sports field fence," they stated.

All 483 students, busy with their whispering and fidgeting, stopped in their tracks and stared.

"That hardly seems appropriate," the headmaster responded. "This is *graduation*, not some garden wedding."

The mothers smiled with nervous politeness. But they made no sign of withdrawing.

"And flowers are so *unseemly*," continued the headmaster, "in this moment of wartime endeavor."

Mrs. Shimizu, the mayor's wife, stepped forward. Her daughter Sachiko is ranked third in the graduating class. "All this austerity is hard on community morale," cooed Mrs. Shimizu. "What we need is some public rejoicing."

The headmaster looked unconvinced.

"Oh, come on!" Mrs. Shimizu gave the headmaster a shove that, while playful, firmly established her higher rank.

"Honorable Headmaster," teased Honorable Mayor's Wife, "don't be so perpetually dour!"

March 23, 1939

With seven days left before graduation, the Mothers' Graduation Association, now forty-seven strong, arrived at Hanae's school. Their request was that an American tradition be adopted: the singling out and acknowledging of honor graduates.

Having once lost face before all of his charges to a group of dotty middle-aged women, the headmaster hunkered down. He sent his response by newsletter.

To recognize individual merit with more than a marginal note in the printed program simply encourages hubris.

Hanae was disappointed, but once again Sachiko Shimizu's high academic ranking saved the day, for it was her father—Mayor Shimizu—who intervened.

"Papa called the headmaster to our house and I eavesdropped," whispered Sachiko as she sloshed streams of rinse water heedlessly down the face of the rubber baby she and Hanae were bathing in home economics. "He put the pressure on."

"And?"

"Papa will award individual certificates to the graduating top five!"

Hanae clapped her hands.

"What's more," continued Sachiko, her stage whisper

growing progressively louder, "the time of graduation is being moved. From afternoon to evening."

She assumed an imposing bearing and quoted her father: "So as to ensure maximum community participation."

Hanae placed a towel on a table in preparation for the doll's drying and diapering. "The headmaster just *accepted* all this?"

Sachiko smiled. "At first he resisted, but by the end he was holding forth on how Western liberalism—endorsing informality and change—is the backbone of Japanese school policy."

"Sachiko Shimizu," cried the home economics teacher. "Where is your form? Stop swinging that doll by her foot!"

Commencement

On graduation night the air is electric. As if at a sporting event, the audience roars when the students enter the field.

"This is what a Spanish bullfight must be like," mutters Kimiko as she and Hanae step-drag their way between the bleachers and head out across the track. "Hysterical and funereal."

The night is warm. The scent of hothouse flowers, emanating from the fully matted fence, is oppressive. Like a long line of pallbearers, 120 girls stiffly move, two by two, toward destiny.

In front of the platform they separate. Kimiko seats herself with the other graduates. Hanae takes her place with the honorees on stage.

The headmaster comes to the podium.

"Ladies and gentlemen, comrades in this glorious national

endeavor. Graduates, handmaidens to the brave boys who struggle to liberate Asia . . ."

The plan is this. The crowd will bow and pay tribute to the emperor; the class will parade across the stage, receiving diplomas. Finally, the mayor will present, in order of ascendancy, certificates to the graduating top five.

"Applause," Headmaster Kido proclaims with confidence, "will be withheld until all diplomas have been awarded."

But of course it doesn't happen that way.

From the start, the crowd can't contain its excitement. For every single girl—ordinary, alphabetically listed girls whom Hanae feels bear no particular distinction—family members cheer loud and long.

"Atta girl, Junko!"

"We want Reiko. We want Reiko."

Their raucous behavior is highly irregular.

"What's going on?" Hanae whispers to salutatorian Midori Setsu, who is seated by her side.

Midori shrugs. "Too many celebration toasts during family dinners?"

Impatient for his daughter's glory, Mayor Shimizu glances again and again at his watch.

The sky bruises from blue to dark purple.

The audience begins to mutter. "Generator, generator."

Ever conservation conscious, Headmaster Kido tightens his lips and continues his dispensing of diplomas.

Darkness falls.

Hanae tips back her head; she begins picking out constellations.

"Generator! Generator!"

The crowd threatens to grow mutinous.

The mayor frowns and minor officials scurry to the edge of the stage.

For a full five minutes they impress Hanae with their conspicuous surreptitiousness: scrambling in crablike crouches, carrying notes back and forth along the platform. Finally with a deafening WHIR the generator switches on.

Floodlights blind everyone on stage.

As roll call trickles down to the final five, families grow restless. They rush the graduates, flashbulbs exploding, offering congratulations.

It's clear they are ready to leave.

The mayor looks distressed.

"Parents, decorum!" demands the headmaster.

The crowd ignores him completely.

"Cumulative grade point number five," screams Mayor Shimizu in alarm, "Nakamura, Kazuko!"

Kazuko stumbles forward as noisemakers bleat and the audience streams from the field.

Then as the mayor begins to panic—calling, "Number four!" but forgetting the student's name—Headmaster Kido has an idea.

He steps to the mayor's microphone and softly begins chanting.

"Showa, Showa, Showa."

The mayor steps back in fury. Hanae sees the clench of his hands. The headmaster is intruding into what was to be his glorious moment and adding even more distraction to an uncontrollable scene.

But the crowd turns in its flight.

"Showa, Showa," the headmaster repeats.

The crowd quiets.

"Showa, Showa," whispers the headmaster.

And the crowd catches on.

"Showa, Showa," they call, standing scattered across the field.

"Showa! Showa!"

Over and over, louder and louder, they say the name of the imperial reign.

The mayor is happy.

"Cumulative grade point number three," he shouts in triumph. "My daughter, Shimizu, Sachiko!"

"SHOWA!" responds the crowd. Some people begin to cheer.

"Thank you for the honor that I receive," murmurs Sachiko into the microphone. Her eyes remain modestly averted.

"Cumulative grade point number two . . ."

The countdown continues. For Hanae, the tension is like New Year's Eve.

"SHOWA. SHOWA."

Hanae begins to perspire.

"Cumulative grade point number one. *Minasama*, everyone please, let's give a warm salute to SHINODA, HANAE!"

"HURRAH!"

The whole field erupts, reverberating with sustained cheering.

"HURRAH! HURRAH!"

It's more than she's ever dreamed.

Hanae floats across the stage. She takes the microphone.

SCREEEE.

Hanae squints, searching for Chie and me, but she can't see beyond the floodlights.

A sudden breeze ripples her knife pleats. She takes a gulp of the sweet night air.

"SHOWA! SHOWA!"

Hanae wets her lips. She glances to the side of the stage, at the headmaster and faculty.

Sensei Matsunaga looks her straight in the eyes.

Then—with a quick smile—he sends her the thumbs-up sign.

Hanae bends toward the microphone.

"On behalf of the graduating class, thank you."

The mayor beams.

The headmaster's assistant prepares to drop the phonograph needle on the first notes of "Auld Lang Syne."

Hanae is all set to conclude with a few more pleasantries when something inside her takes over.

"Showa," she says. "Showa is a beautiful word. Its meaning is 'Clarity and Peace.'"

The audience quiets.

"In life we must choose a course of action, we must commit ourselves to a goal."

Hanae hears her voice echo into the darkness with sentences she never had planned.

"That's how tonight's graduates have come to this place in time."

"Hurrah, graduates!" shouts a parent.

"Yet triumph can blind. We can stay a course, not because it's just or good, but because we're grateful it has brought us glory."

The mayor's smile fades.

"Now we are engaged in a broadening war that we say is to benefit Asia."

From the corner of her eye, Hanae sees the headmaster rise

and start for the lectern. She sees Sensei Matsunaga trip him with his crutches.

She quickens her pace. "What I ask tonight is that each of us, in our personal and national decisions, consider our motives for acting."

"Silence her!" someone shouts.

Hanae moves toward the steps.

"SILENCE! SILENCE!" chants the crowd.

I jump from my seat. "Don't listen to them, Hanae!"

Hanae's head jerks toward my voice.

"SILENCE! SILENCE! SILENCE!" The crowd threatens to turn into a mob.

Hanae looks scared. Trying to get off the stage, she stumbles.

"BE PROUD, HANAE!"

As she feels Kimiko catching her, Hanae hears Chie shouting so violently that the crowd stops chanting, afraid that her vocal cords will tear.

Through a glare of floodlights, a jumble of individual voices, Hanae hears Chie shouting the words of Abraham Lincoln—quoting from the Western masterpieces Hanae never thought Chie had read.

"TO REMAIN SILENT WHEN THEY SHOULD SPEAK MAKES COWARDS OUT OF MEN!"

chapter thirty-three

MAY 12, 1939

The Strangeness of Beauty

"How did you handle the headmaster?" I asked Chie. "Hanae is a minor, but I heard him threatening to have you jailed."

It was early morning, the day after graduation. We were climbing an ancient path winding through a mountain forest of giant ferns and glistening spiderwebs, of cryptomeria and cedar.

Chie shrugged. "I'm nearly seventy years old. No one would seriously consider jailing an old woman whose crime is quoting Abraham Lincoln."

Pale sun slanted through branches, making patterns on the forest floor. With each step, the soft pine-needled ground released a sweet loamy scent.

We approached a series of forty or more rocky stairs rising along the twisting pathway. Small pagoda-roofed stone lanterns flanked each step like an honor guard of benevolent mushrooms.

Ahead of us, Hanae turned.

"Look, Auntie," she called. "Flowers!"

Together we paused.

On the edge of the cliff, purple blossoms emerged from a shrinking bed of snow.

I looked beyond them. Far below floated gray tiled roofs, and from their midst the diamond shape of a child's red kite circled upward like a prayer.

Hanae offered Chie her arm.

"Thank you for Mama's wedding mirror," she said, her dark head bent toward Chie's silver as they started the climb. "Auntie told me the story."

After our flight from the graduation grounds, Hanae and I had talked until well after two. Until our throats were dry and our emotions were stilled and even the house's old timbers had ceased to creak and had settled themselves for the night.

"But you've got to come!" she'd cried when I told her about America. "Who'll take care of Papa and me?"

I looked at Hanae—sitting on her futon, hugging her knees tucked up inside her nightgown—and felt a sad, subdued tenderness. I understood that I could not keep her, yet took no pleasure in her going away.

I touched a strand of her hair.

"Your papa and you."

"What if we've changed? He wrote those poems to some perfect little girl; what if he doesn't like me?"

"You will have changed; we change every moment. But you both still will love each other."

Hanae looked uneasy. She spoke to her toes.

"Maybe after a little while, you could visit?"

"Yes."

"And Obaa-san?"

"We'll certainly try."

She seemed reassured; she started to plan, imagining her future. Maybe she could go to college, maybe she could visit New York, maybe she could learn housekeeping and be a big help to her father. Did I have any recipes I could give her?

A faint smile brushed my lips. Recipes—I thought as I listened—as if life were an exact chemical science.

I'd been just as naive: a young woman who'd wanted to find her true self, her own special future. Thinking life was something that waited, like a pretty pet rabbit, to be captured and tamed.

I shook my head with rue. I hadn't really changed. Even though I'd learned life is random and heartless, I still longed to locate—to name and know—what it is that can make it good.

"Oh, Auntie!"

Hanae stopped short in her list making. She cried out with sudden anguish.

"My speech tonight . . ."

"It was brave and true."

"But it wasn't! It was just words, the kind of things I've heard from Mrs. Ito and the others. Don't you see? It wasn't me. That speech wasn't really mine!"

It could have been a scream—the small catch in her voice—it tore at me so. I saw self-doubt ravage her features like an explosive tossed at her dreams.

I hurled myself at her, grabbing her tight. She shivered in my arms; I knew that she was crying.

"It was you!" I hissed, wanting her to know with a ferocity ripped right out of my soul. "You sent those words into the air! Your genuine impulse!"

In my passion, I barely felt her soft skin, her soapy scent. The air between us had all been consumed.

And maybe that was my answer, my own genuine impulse.

Forcing me to suddenly want what she wanted—her adult-hood, her belief in herself—much more savagely than I wanted to keep her.

I may never know what makes life good, but surely that impulse is part. That sudden surge from deep within, forcing us—despite logic, ambivalence, fear—to say yes at the go-between's table, to print peace pamphlets when we come back from war, to send our beloved off with handwritten recipes (as my mama had done for me, as I surely would do for Hanae), to take some stumbling step forward.

I pulled away, just far enough for her to see clearly.

"Oh yes!" I said laughing and crying. "You made that wonderful moment! Now go to America, take your next step. You'll be all right, Ha-chan. You're ready."

That next morning, the path we were climbing led to a small graveyard in the midst of a forest clearing.

We entered. Birds rose, our eyes following them up to the high evergreen canopy.

"Oh," breathed Hanae.

Using a bamboo dipper, Chie rinsed her hands in a stone basin. She approached a wooden altar.

Plump grains of rice lay in offering on a dew-drenched lotus leaf.

Chie placed her palms together and bowed.

Clap. Clap. Clap.

Slowly a sense of spirits emerged. Most Honorable Mr. and Mrs. Fuji were smiling. Kan carried a chubby baby.

"I've brought Etsuko and Hanae," Chie said.

My grandfather was pleased. So that he could get a better look, he put on the eyeglasses that Chie had hung, years ago, on his gravestone.

Together we walked on the needled carpet, among the congregation of beautiful stones—each hand-selected and carried to this remote site—which served as grave markers.

We found the Fuji name.

Wordlessly, Chie removed some tangerines from a knotted silk square.

She placed a fresh red bib on my brother's gravestone and apportioned the offerings.

"I've brought tangerines for us as well," I told Hanae.

I spread a blanket and we lounged on the ground, living and dead enjoying a family picnic.

"Do you know?" said Hanae, after a while. "I think my mama is here."

Chie nestled her back more comfortably against Kan's gravestone.

She began to compose a poem.

> Family reunion!
> Kites spin skyward with diamond hope!

She paused, searching for her next lines.
I finished for her.

> Near the graveyard, snow flowers bloom.
> Morning rises from shadow.

bibliography

Condon, John. *With Respect to the Japanese: A Guide for Americans.* Yarmouth, Maine: Intercultural Press, 1984.

Cook, Haruko Taya, and Theodore F. Cook. *Japan at War: An Oral History.* New York: New Press, 1992.

De Mente, Boye Lafayette. *The Japanese Have a Word for It: The Complete Guide to Japanese Thought and Culture.* Chicago: Passport Books, 1997.

————. *Japan's Secret Weapon: The Kata Factor.* Phoenix: Phoenix Books, 1990.

Gibney, Frank, ed. *Sensō: The Japanese Remember the Pacific War: Letters to the Editor of the Asahi Shimbun.* Armonk, New York: M. E. Sharpe, 1995.

Hall, John W. *Japan: From Prehistory to Modern Times.* New York: Dell Publishing Company, 1970.

Macdonald, Fiona, David Antram, and John James. *Inside Story: A Samurai Castle.* Ed. Jenny Millington. New York: Peter Bedrick Books, 1995.

Macintyre, Michael. *The Shogun Inheritance: Japan and the Legacy of the Samurai.* London: William Collins & Sons, 1981.

Morris-Suzuki, Tessa. *Showa: An Inside History of Hirohito's Japan.* New York: Schocken Books, 1984.

Powers, Richard G., and Hidetoshi Kato. *Handbook of Japanese Popular Culture.* New York: Greenwood Press, 1989.

Saga, Junichi. *Memories of Silk and Straw: A Self-Portrait of Small Town Japan*. New York: Kodansha International, 1987.

Seidensticker, Edward. *Low City, High City: Tokyo from Edo to the Earthquake*. New York: Alfred A. Knopf, 1983.

————. *Tokyo Rising: The City Since the Great Earthquake*. New York: Alfred A. Knopf, 1990.

Storry, Richard. *A History of Modern Japan*. Baltimore: Penguin Books, 1960.

Sugimoto, Etsu Inagaki. *A Daughter of the Samurai*. Rutland: C. E. Tuttle, 1966.

Takami, David. *Executive Order 9066*. Seattle: Wing Luke Asian Museum, 1992.

Toland, John. *The Rising Sun: The Decline and Fall of the Japanese Empire 1936–1945*. New York: Random House, 1970.

Ueda, Atsushi, ed. *The Electric Geisha: Exploring Japan's Popular Culture*. Trans. Miriam Eguchi. New York: Kodansha International, 1994.

acknowledgments

For Mark Twain/Marx Brook anecdotes and aluminum-pie-plate and wire-coat-hanger prototypes of scientific wonder, for his enduring inspiration and warmth, I am forever grateful to the late Bernard Vonnegut—a modest, funny man—gentle genius, seeder of clouds and dreams.

Michi Minatoya Vonnegut inspired the image of Etsuko as a hot air balloon, tethered to the ground yet buoyantly bearing others aloft.

Marysue Rucci, my editor, believed in this book, provided suggestions that strengthened it immeasurably, and did so with grace and tact. I thank Sally Wofford-Girand, my literary agent, for her consistent generosity with her enthusiasm and acumen.

Hiroaki and Aimee Minatoya provided encouragement, responded to my many questions about the era, and helped me to understand traditions. Robert Shields offered child care, computer assistance, and other forms of steadfast support. In addition, I am grateful to the Seattle Arts Commission and the King County Arts Commission for their Individual Artist Grants.

Although this is a work of fiction, the sources listed in the bibliography provided invaluable depth and detail. Offering intimate first-person accounts, penetrating historical analyses, and illuminating cultural explanations, these works informed, moved, disturbed, and delighted me. I am very grateful to their authors.

With deep respect I thank the families of the late Koki Iwamoto, Shyogo Iwamoto, and Fumiko Ikeda for life lessons. At times, more than the heart could bear.

THE STRANGENESS OF BEAUTY

Lydia Minatoya

READING GROUP GUIDE

DISCUSSION QUESTIONS

1. The narrator of *The Strangeness of Beauty* announces at the book's opening that she is writing an "I-story." What is the significance of the I-story in Japanese culture? How is autobiographical writing especially important for immigrant cultures in the United States? What are some other outlets for the "confessional angst" that the narrator says drives the writer of an I-story? Why do you think the author has chosen to write a novelization of an I-story?

2. Kobe is an old port city with a history of art and international culture. Seattle is an upstart city in a young country. We tend to associate old cities with provincialism and young cities with dynamism. Yet is this always the case? Compare the cultural life of Kobe in the early part of the twentieth century to that of Seattle.

3. Hanae is born an American but is viewed as a Japanese alien by American culture. When she travels to Japan, she is seen as too American. Think about the complex relationship that children of immigrants have with America and with the original culture of their parents.

4. Consider the idea of kata, or form. Etsuko identifies the Japanese importance of form, and explains that the Japanese have a proper way of performing each action, a proper mode of behavior for each situation, even a proper language for each kind of literature and each social interaction. She considers kata to be the most alienating aspect of Japanese culture to Americans. Consider what might be particularly "American" attributes; how might some of these characteristics clash with kata? Another way of thinking of kata is as ritual. Think of rituals you practice; could these be considered katas? Would you like to incorporate some elements of kata in your life?

5. The author has said that one of her intentions was to blur the boundaries between ideas of "us" and "them." How successful do you feel she was? In what ways did you identify with these characters? Were you able to identify with parts of characters you initially may have found unappealing? With characters who seemed different from you? Was there a point when you began thinking of Hanae (or even Etsuko) as American or Japanese American rather than as Japanese?

6. *The Strangeness of Beauty* is, in many ways, a self-reflective book. As the narrator constantly steps outside the narrative to comment on her writing or the book, we become aware that the characters we are reading about are being actively created and changed as we read. How do these constantly shifting characters affect the way we read this book? What is the reader's relationship to the narrator? To the author?

7. Etsuko wonders if being a woman "hinders" her writ-

ing. She says she can't create traditional "heroes" engaged in large epic acts. Do you think this is true? Consider the role of gender in literature—the speaker's gender as well as the author's gender. Are there certain kinds of writing best limited to one gender? What about certain subjects?

8. When main characters provide a perspective from outside mainstream American culture, they often do two things for the reader. They may provide views of the outside culture (its values, customs, systems of thought) that are fresh, interesting, and illuminating and that may show it as less confusing, mysterious, or alien than we had thought. They may also provide a fresh perspective on American culture, showing how values, customs, and systems of thought that we may have assumed were universal can be seen by outsiders as confusing, confounding, and humorously idiosyncratic to American culture. Can you find instances in this book where you enjoyed learning something about another culture and where you enjoyed learning something about your own?

9. Etsuko's cooking may be seen only as comic relief. It may also be seen as a way for the author to comment on the ideas of creativity, the determination to create one's own world, and the courage to risk public failure. What other behaviors does Etsuko exhibit, what actions does she take, what people does she admire, that support the idea that her cooking is more than a joke?

10. Think of the women's political group. What tactics did they use to find information and distribute it?

How did the "female-ness" of the group help them?

11. Masao compares Etsuko's peace pamphlets to parents chanting prayers over their babies, or the women who sew "bulletproof" belts for their enlisted sons. Is this a fair comparison, or a cynical one? In what ways are pamphlets, prayers, and rituals expressions of hope even as they acknowledge larger, more powerful forces?

12. The Japanese word for "the strangeness of beauty" is myo. How does Etsuko come to understand the role of myo in life? What is the relationship of myo to Chie's comparison of a baseball game and a tea ceremony?

13. *The Strangeness of Beauty* may be seen as two interwoven tales: one a story of character, family, and culture; the other a meditation on how art—literary, visual, culinary, of professionals and amateurs, of kite makers and kimono weavers and housewives—informs and enriches our lives. At what points do these two tales intertwine and how do they culminate in the concept of myo?

MORE BOOKS WITH READING GROUP GUIDES INCLUDED FROM W. W. NORTON

Jack Driscoll, *Lucky Man, Lucky Woman*

Paula Fox, *The Widow's Children*

Hannah Hinchman, *A Trail Through Leaves**

Linda Hogan, *Power*

Patrick O'Brian, *The Yellow Admiral**

Jean Rhys, *Wide Sargasso Sea*

Josh Russell, *Yellow Jack*

Kerri Sakamoto, *The Electrical Field*

May Sarton, *Journal of a Solitude**

Ted Solotaroff, *Truth Comes in Blows*

Jean Christopher Spaugh, *Something Blue*

Mark Strand and Eavan Boland, *The Making of a Poem*

Barry Unsworth, *Morality Play*

Barry Unsworth, *Losing Nelson*

*Available on the Norton Web site:
www.wwnorton.com